DAMAGED MIND

DOCTOR VALERIE

ISBN: 978-1-7169-5956-1 (sc)
ISBN: 978-1-7169-4262-4 (hc)
ISBN: 978-1-7169-5955-4 (e)

Library of Congress Control Number: 2020908177

Lulu Publishing Services rev. date: 05/01/2020

INTRODUCTION

The story of a patient, and her doctor. This book is not to everyone's taste, well let me just say, it's not the easiest thing to write let alone read, even though I am a doctor, and has a doctor, I do find some things totally incomprehensible. But if girls who are abused, are to be heard someone needs to make, the world open its eyes, ears, and listen, to see the destruction, the damage of just one abused, sweet mind, that could go from a young adult, to killer. so don't say you haven't been warned.

But to be totally honest, I don't think any publisher will print it. But if they do…. you have been warned…..and as they say print it and be dammed, as the story of my patient, Aveling will haunt me forever, but after all the patients I have seen, and told, if they write it down, whatever that abuse was, that happened to them, they would recover more quickly, now it's my turn, to hopefully heal myself.

CONTENTS

CHAPTER 1   WAITING FOR AVELING.....................................1

CHAPTER 2   JUST LISTERN… 7

CHAPTER 3   I AM TELLING ON YOU.....................................17

CHAPTER 4   ANOTHER.BABY. 25

CHAPTER 5   THE DOLLY. 31

CHAPTER 6   A LOST SISTER… 37

CHAPTER 7   PLEASE SHUT UP… 43

CHAPTER 8   ANOTHER APOINTMENT….............................51

CHAPTER 9   SILENT TV… 57

CHAPTER 10   TOILET BREAKS… 61

CHAPTER 11   BANK HOLIDAYS… 65

CHAPTER 12   THE REVENGE….. 69

CHAPTER 13   MONSTERS AMONG US….............................. 73

CHAPTER 14   THE PHONE. BOX… 77

CHAPTER 15   RUN AWAY… 83

CHAPTER 16   FIRE WORKS… 89

CHAPTER 17   BETTIES DOWNFALL… 95

CHAPTER 18   THE NEW TEACHER… 103

CHAPTER 19   G.G.. 107

CHAPTER 20   THE REFLECTIONS… 111

CHAPTER 21   THE LIE…...119

CHAPTER 22   SO NIEVE…... 129

CHAPTER 23   SLAP.SLAP.SLAP.BED BUGS … 133

CHAPTER 24   JUST FRED…...141

CHAPTER 25   PENNIES HOUSE…..147

CHAPTER 26   WOLVES… 155

CHAPTER 27   THE RENT MAN, AND SECRET NOTES 161

CHAPTER 28   MUMS POCKET MONEY …...........................165

CHAPTER 29   RESPECTABILITY…THE PSYCHIATRIST…..169

CHAPTER 30   PUNISHMENT… 175

CHAPTER 31   SHE WAS THE CAPTAINS DAUGHTER….....183

CHAPTER 32   RAPE IS RAPE…...195

CHAPTER 33   THE LIE..199

CHAPTER 34   WHATS A FAVOR FOR A FRIEND …............. 207

CHAPTER 35   SUNDAY SCHOOL… 215

CHAPTER 36   DADS HOME…..219

CHAPTER 37   KIMS TIME….. 225

CHAPTER 38   ESCAPE….. 233

CHAPTER 39   BARKING DOGS….. 239

CHAPTER 40   YOUNG GIRLS... 245

CHAPTER 41   LOSE KNIFES… 251

CHAPTER 42   BACK TO THE DORM…................................255

CHAPTER 43   THREE MEALS A DAY… 259

CHAPTER 44   GETTING HELP…... 265

CHAPTER 45   SILENT TEARS. 269

CHAPTER 46   TRUST IN ME ….. 273

CHAPTER 47   REMEMBEING THE DAISY… 283

CHAPTER 1

WAITING FOR AVELING.

The surgery.

Just another day in the practice, It had been raining hard outside, but not too long to go, before the end of my shift, just one more hour, all that day there had been a never ending stream, of patients all shift, with an end-lessness, of all the usual complaints, coughs, sneezers, and everything in between, now I know being a doctor it was all part of the job, but when I had finished my training, I was hoping to go into another field of medicine, but at that time my life took me on a whole new road after getting married, my husband who was also a doctor, wanted to set up his own practice so here I am. as I sat waiting for my last patient of the day, I confess I had been day dreaming, just watching the rain through the window, looking forward to getting home to just relax, but nothing could have prepared me for what I agreed to take on.

I had been asked to see a young girl for the prison services, they hadn't supplied much information, only that at some time in her resent past she had suffered a trauma, causing memory loss, they also requested a medical, that to me did seem a little strange, as I knew they had their own doctor at the prison. As I looked up at the clock, they were running late typical, as I had promised my husband, I would try to get things finished up early. Then came a thunderous banging on the door, it almost scared me out of my skin. then without my reply in they walked, two huge police officers.

They were both hanging onto my new patient, they frog marched her into the room. as she finally broke free they barricaded the door, I was, I

1

admit a little taken back by this 'she's all yours doctor, do you have any windows in this room doc, because she has a bad habit of running off." "No, well no opening windows, as they are bared since we had a break in last winter", well then doc she's all yours for the next hour.

We will be just be outside the door, if you need any help with her". 'I knew her name was Aveling, from the request form the prison services sent with their instructions. but they hadn't sent any more details, there wasn't even a surname, or date of birth on the file.

As I looked over, I saw her eyes were down, her chin firmly in her chest, arms crossed, cloths tatty, shoes if that's what you could call them shoes, as they had been stripped of the shoe laces, and looked a good two sizers too big for her, the shoes, were barely hanging on. The paperwork said she was maybe about, eighteen/nineteen, but to me she looked more like maybe, well younger, but how could they not know her age. it wasn't what I had been expecting, when I agreed to see her.

Social servicers had told me she had been seen by another psychiatrists who couldn't get through to her, so now it was my turn. But looking at her I didn't know where to begin, so as I introduced myself, by just my first name, Valerie, hoping it would put her at ease, asking her to sit, she promptly sat down on the floor, crossed legs, chin still down, O! My god, what had I agreed to. The girl seemed almost Feral, it's the nineteen sixties for goodness sake, it's not the Victorian era, and how anyone can let her get so bedraggled. Her hair looked uncombed, her denim blue prison dress, appeared to have been covered in biro marks.

I chatted away but got no response. Just silence with my best attempts nothing, after the hour was up there was a knock at the door, before I got the chance to say enter, in came the two officers, 'time to go' bodily picking her up of the ground, she didn't get the chance to lower her legs to the ground.

her feet seemed to be still just hanging in space, it was then I saw for the first time, the look on her face, I had never seen such pain displayed that way before, for me being a doctor I dealt with more bodily pain than mental, but I knew then, that painful look would haunt my life till the day I die, but I also knew it was my duty to get her to confide in me, to talk about the abuse that had ended up with her being detained in prison.as

I have always believed, it is the mind that heals the body, but I could see this was going to be a challenge.

Now the arrangements that had been made, they were that, she would visit the surgery once a week, for a one hour session till a decision was made what to do with her, after my assessment she would be placed as I was told in the best treatment center, for her needs.

The following week the same thing, after they arrived I tried to get more information, anything that could help. but whenever I asked the officers for any information, all I got was blank faces, 'sorry doc they haven't told us much, just keep a firm grip on her, as we told you last week doctor, she as a problem of running off,' I asked if they had a surname for her, but they shrugged their shoulders, That visit wasn't much better than the first, but at least I managed to get her sitting in the chair,

The conversation was just as the week before all one sided, as I asked her for her surname, her age but nothing, I was running out of ideas. I knew from the look on her face that this was going to be a very long hour.

It wasn't till I mentioned that I had some pens, and paper, if she would prefer to write anything down. Now that was when she made the first eye contact, not much but it was a start, there was I small room off the surgery, where I kept a small office, and storage area.

she agreed to come with me, I was hoping if her story was so bad, maybe Aveling, like many of my other abused patience's, she would write it down, but when I returned to her, she had spent all of her time making repeated patterns of daisy's, it was then I realized that the biro marks on her denim dress were also daisy's, they had faded due to washing, but they were clearly daisy s, and it was clear from the drawings she had a natural talent for art.

not exactly what I was expecting, as most off my patient s I had counseled, often made crude drawing of what they had been through, or they would write me a short story, but not Aveling, just swirls of daisies over and over again. I started to think maybe she didn't know how to read or write, but I complemented on her drawings.

I was just thinking to myself, I just wished she would say something anything. she looked up, and gave me just a little smile, not much but I felt at last, I could get her to open up to me in time, but they do say be careful of what you wish for, After two visits still not much conversation, just repeated drawings of daisies.

but on the next visit I had to leave her, drawing in the side office, when I was called out of the surgery for an emergency, I explained to the officers to leave her be, has she wasn't doing any harm just drawing, but to be honest, one of them seemed more interested in the crossword puzzle in the paper, and the other officer, was chatting up the receptionist.

I hadn't realized the emergency would take so long, by the time I returned, they had left.

I began to write up my notes, when I heard a noise coming from the side office, so I went to investigate, It was then I realized it was my tape recorder, I rewound the tape, and began to listen. The voice spoke softly, I had always suspected as all too many of my disturbed patients that somewhere in that young girls mind there was bottled up, the nightmare of abuse.

As I sat listening Aveling spoke softly, her accent reminded me of my time at Oxford university, but as we were in Sheffield, Yorkshire I was expecting a completely different voice. it was barely a whisper, 'can I trust you, you mustn't ever tell on me, or they will lock me up forever and I, I cannot be caged anymore." 'Then the tape stopped, I was I confess, It was intriguing, but it would be another week till we would meet again. So the following week When Aveling arrived always at the same time, she sat as always with her arms crossed, chin down.

I informed her that anything she said to me would be totally confidential, and if she wanted to write it down, no one but me would see it. it would be just for therapy, I assured her there was nothing I hadn't heard before, so she could say anything that was bothering her. As it was my belief, just by writing it down, or talking about it that it would help most of my patients, so if this was the only way to get her to open up, so be it, and I felt the most important thing for now was trust.

But once again I was met with a wall of silence, it wasn't till I asked her if she wanted to sketch, or write in the other office, she looked up at me, and at that moment I swear, I saw her true face as she looked straight at me, her eye s were as green as emeralds, but they were strangely cold, as if the very sole inside her was fighting with its self just to survive.

Now I know that sounds a little dramatic, but those were the thoughts going throw my mind at that time. But I felt at last, maybe I could get somewhere. I confess I needed to put in some sort of report, to the social prison services, but there hadn't been much so far to report, each week I would keep it simple,<Aveling is making slow progress but she is starting to respond a little. >

When Aveling arrived that week, she was still accompanied by the same two officers, but she seemed a little less aggressive, in her mood, but I knew then it wasn't me she wanted to talk with. She said a quick hello, as she shuffling towards the other office, she then passed me, and Aveling gave me a wry smile, then disappeared, into the back office, sat down, then I heard that noise click, as she pressed record on the tape recorder.

CHAPTER 2

JUST LISTERN...

it would be a sound that over the following months, I would become so familiar with, at first I could hear nothing, it wasn't till she pushed the door till there was just a small gap, I could hear her whispering, but not what she was saying, I knew if I was going to get inside her mind, this was going to be my only chance.

so leaving her to complete the hour, then as always, she was escorted away by the same two officers, to me this did seem a little extreme, how can such a little thing be so feared, or cause anyone any problems. she seemed so little, so withdrawn, with a soft look of helplessness, falling over her face, it just seemed so full of sorrow, no I think a better word for it, would be angelic.

she reminded me of an angel, so yes I guess the word I would be looking for is angelic. but as my husband also tells me even, the devil was an angel, so he had warned me not to turn my back on her, has he himself did, with an earlier young boy patient, when he had received a very nasty head wound.

After Aveling and the officers left, that day, I went into the back office not knowing then, just how damaged this child was. Or what I would find on the tape. Now as she was still under the age of twenty one, she was still classified as a child by law in the nineteen sixties, I knew they were trying to get the age of consent changed to eighteen but until then the courts had to treat her like a child. I had to confess some girls, did seem to grow physically and mentally faster than others.

When I was given the tape recorder as a gift, I had never expected to be using it for treatments, but now, As I turned on the machine rewinding it back to the start, I sat back in my chair to hear, well where I would begin, to even put this information into my notes. She started slowly explaining that she had come from a large family of ten children, in the fifties large families were the norm, being a doctor I had over the years seen many abused children, I didn't believe anything would shock me, I was so very, very wrong, so I would like to warn you again, if you are reading this, to pay attention to my introduction, as some of you could be very disturbed by the following recordings.

Her story had started, has I had asked her, to begin with her earliest memory,

CLICK...TAPE...ON

Aveling then went on, It was the start of the summer holidays she explained, she had been five or six years old, it had been normal for her mother, who always seemed pregnant to farm out some of the youngest children, to aunties or grandparents, so whenever Avelings mum had to go into hospital, or go to doctors' appointments, as her mother was all too often left alone to raise the children alone, as Avelings father was in the royal navy, he never seemed to be their when needed.

Aveling had been the forth born, so she was often sent to stay with relatives, as she was consider too young to help with a lot of the chores, the earliest she could remember was when she believed she was about five or six.. when she was sent to stay with her mother's sister Rose, Aveling had been put on the bus by her sister Pam, it was a good walk to the bus stop from home, then about a fifteen minuet ride from that stop, to auntie Roses bus stop, where Avelings aunt would be to collect her.

Rose was her mother's elder sister, and after meeting Aveling at the bus stop that day, they still had a long walk home to aunties house, now Aveling hadn't ever stayed with auntie Rose before, and only ever met her at grandads house, but she had never met uncle Ben. so everything seemed so new and exciting, but auntie Rose made the walk from the bus stop to the house fun, as they played a game called, I spy with my little eye, and that carried on till they reached the old terrace house were Aveling would stay, the house was over three stories, Aveling would be sleeping in the attic bedroom, she was thrilled because from the widow, you could see the steam trains arriving at the station.

Has Aveling up to then, had never even seen a train, it was all so exciting. now auntie Rose had only one child, he had just had his thirteenth birthday, now the rest of the day, as all good aunties did, she spoiled Aveling, she had bought a new summer green dress, covered with white daisies, to Aveling a new dress, was something she could never remember receiving before, so to Aveling this was a huge gift, as up to then she could only remember having her two older sisters cloths when they had grown out of them.

has she swirled dancing, spinning around in the dress, she said it looked like the daisies were dancing in the wind, most of that day seemed normal, and Aveling didn't feel uneasy, but the next day after breakfast, auntie Rose had to leave to go to work.

Her cousin had gone out to play with his mates early, and there was no way he wanted a young kid following him around, let alone a little girl, auntie gave Aveling a kiss, 'will be home around teatime, when I get home, after tea, we will go to the park, and later I will take you back to the bus stop, your mums arranged for your sister Pam, to be there to pick you up at the cinema bus stop, till then uncle Ben will look after you ".

Aveling was to say confused, not just by what auntie was saying, but she found it strange that auntie Rose, had kissed her on the forehead just before leaving, it simply was not normal in her home, to show any affection but saying, 'see you later' auntie left for work.

Aveling looked over her shoulder at her uncle Ben, he was still reading his morning newspaper, she watched through the window as auntie Rose disappeared down the road.

It had started to rain, as she ran her tiny finger over a rain drop running down the window pane, chasing it to the bottom. That is when she felt a hand on her shoulder, 'how would you like to play a game called find a sixpence, so you can buy some sweeties', back in the fifties a sixpence was a lot of money, Aveling had no idea what was to come, as she turned round uncle Ben started to explain. If she helped him to do some cleaning he would pull a magic sixpence from her ear.

He started by telling Aveling, "as auntie didn't have much time to clean the house, as she worked full time wouldn't it be nice if we cleaned the house for her. And did the laundry" Now Uncle Ben was a huge man who smelled very unpleasant.

'As Aveling felt his grip getting stronger, she tried to pull away from him but he was gripping her so tightly it began to feel painfull.it wasn't till Aveling yelped, did her uncle let go, at that point Aveling just assumed, he didn't know his own strength, he had decided the first place to be cleaned was the kitchen, when they entered the kitchen, it was then, Aveling noticed a huge pile of dirty cloths mounted up on the floor, now even with all her brothers, and sisters Aveling s mother would never allow the washing to pile up. but this heap of cloths smelled of, well as Aveling explained the smell reminded her of soiled baby nappies, so they must have been there for quite a while, the smell was almost over powering.

Now back in the fifties not many families had washing machines, so everything had to be cleaned by firstly sorting out the colors.

The old house was over a hundred years old, and the kitchen had that old smell of musty damp ness, that once in your nostrils it was difficult to get out, now built into the old kitchen was an old copper boiler, and the heap of washing close by, it seemed to have a life of its own. It was then Aveling saw a mouse scurry from the bottom of the pile. it made Aveling jump, but she had seen so many mice before it didn't bother her, just about everyone's home seemed to have its own residential family of mice back in the fifties.

Now as she was sorting the cloths into different colors.it was then she got a whiff of another odor from the cloths, they smelled, of the musty old smell in the kitchen, and dirty nappies. But there was another smell that was clearly indescribable, till she saw feces on a pair of under pants that must have belonged to Uncle Ben, she held them as far away from her nose as possible then dropped them into the copper.

Now back in the fifties, the only way to get hot water in the kitchen, was to boil the kettle on the fire in the other room, and by placing pans on the gas stove, looking at all that washing they were going to need as much hot water as possible. then carry it carefully to the boiler, now as Aveling started to fill the boiler with some cold water first, as her grandad once explained if you put in the cold water first, then the boiling water, it would prevent any of the woolens from shrinking, it was then her uncle yelled at her, no hot water you silly girl, he ordered her to fetch the kettle from the fire, now this was something her mother never aloud, telling Aveling she was to young, to handle the kettle, so as she stood there looking a little hesitant, her uncles nature changed as he snapped at her again to do as she was told.

Now Aveling pointed out at that time she had always been small for her age, but she wanted to help so she collected the boing water, now as she was on the third run she tripped, spilling just a small amount of water, but that is when her uncle snapped yelling at her, he raised his hand it came down hard across her face, as he was calling her stupid clumsy. She decided she needed to get out of the house till he calmed down, she saw the anger in his face, as she tried to get out, of the room, she raced to the front door but it was locked, the only remaining exit was the back door that meant getting past him, she looked over in his direction, only to find he was just a few steps away, and his eyes still full of anger, trying to dash past, he grabbed her by the back of her cardigan, swinging her around slapping her again, it was then she bit him hard on his arm, she looked around the room, the only other door in the room led to the cellar, again she wriggled free dashing to the cellar door, pushing the door shut behind her, to stop him following, but he was far too strong, as he forced the door open she fell backwards, falling down the stairs to the damp concrete cellar floor, the air was strong with the smell of coal dust, and damp mold, trying hard to get back to her feet looking round for another escape, there was very little light it was then, he grabbed her yet again, Aveling tried so hard to wriggle free but he was to strong, as she struggled with him her cardigan was pulled off, spinning her around hard against the cellar steps.

It was then she had noticed he had left the cellar door open, and that is where she could see a small stream of light. beaming down the steps, he held her firmly, by pushing his knee down hard across her chest, she couldn't move, it was then by the light from the cellar door, she saw him reaching up to a dark dirty old tool chest on the shelf above the steps, pulling out a pair of rusty old pliers,

He then forced her mouth open with his hand, 'I'll show you, you little bitch, you won't be biting me again", trying desperately to get away, but he was just too heavy, he then forced her mouth open pushing in the pliers, he then began to pull out her teeth, one by one, the pain was unbearable as she gasped for breath, he seemed to be getting angrier by the second, but he was now, yelling words Aveling had only ever heard when adults were shouting at each other, Aveling went on to explain, tears were filling up in her eyes, she could barely see.

When he had finished pulling out all of the top front teeth, Aveling felt like, she was choking on all the dust, and blood. 'Now you little bitch, when I tell you to do something you will do it.'

Aveling could feel vomit, rising in her throat, she could taste the blood, she paused, her eyes had been so full of tears she found it hard to focus, it was then uncle Ben stood up, and began to clean himself up, it was then she screamed at him, 'I am going home, and telling my mummy on you,'

He then on hearing those words, (I am telling on you,) he flew into a rage, and began beating down on her again, slapping anywhere that, he could to make contact, as she was franticly trying to riddle free, believing at that moment he was going to kill her. Just when it seemed like he wasn't going to stop, he started to cough, possible from all the coal dust, it was then, when he paused, as he again started to tidy himself up brushing the coal dust from his trousers.

So it was then she saw her opportunity to break free, dashing first up the cellar stairs then trying the front door again, in sheer desperation, it was then she remembered it was still locked, looking round noticing the front window was open.

It was only open by just about a foot or so, it was a sash window, Aveling knew she wouldn't be able to lift it higher, but she knew being so small it was the only way out, so as fast as she could, pushing on the window as for as possible, she then squeezed out, falling to the ground with a bang, but when Aveling was finally free, hiding in the garden, Aveling could hear Him calling her name.

His voice had changed from the foul words she had heard in the cellar, his voice was now gentle, calm, but, Aveling had no intention of giving her hiding place away, not for all the sixpences in the world. it was then Aveling put her own hand over her mouth, she had been so afraid, so the shear thought of her letting out any noise, drawing him to her hiding place, was just to unbearable, so she scrunched herself up in to the smallest of shapes, staying as close to the base of the bush as possible.

She heard him calling her name again, 'it's ok, I've got your sixpence lets go to the shops, and buy some sweeties', but as she explained how she, had stayed so very still has he walked just inches away from her hiding place in the bush. when he was clearly out of sight, she crawled out, not wanting to waste any time, she dashed down the back ally, that ran behind a row of old terrace houses, that was the quickest way to the main road, but even being so young she knew if she could just reach the main road.

All she needed to do was head up the long main road towards the cinema bus top, remembering that is where her sister would be to collect her, later that day. But being so young Aveling had no sense of time, or distance, she had only just been learning at school how to read the time on a clock.

As she was walking she lifted, her pretty new cotton daisy dress to her face to wipe away the tears, looking down at her new dress all she could see was blood, Aveling didn't have any money for bus fare home, so she just started to walk, she had no idea how long the walk would be, but keeping her head down not to make eye contact with anyone, her only thoughts were to get back home to her mum.

it was still raining so the streets were eerily empty. but she carried on walking, her feet were sore, each step began to cause a blister on the back off her ankle, but she knew she wouldn't feel safe till she reached her sister Pam, now Aveling knew the long walk home would finally take her back to her mum, But she hadn't realized just how long it would take.

When she had arrived at the cinema bus stop, Aveling was soaking wet through, her hair, and body still smelled of that disgusting, monster, Aveling saw the clock on the school tower it was almost six pm, just about the same time the bus would have been due, she must have been walking for hours, it was then she saw her big sister Pam hanging around with some of her friends.it seemed to be the place a lot of teenagers would hang around, because there was a row of shops, and a movie house. Feeling a sense of safety she dashed over to Pam, to tell her all about what Uncle Ben, the monster did to her that day,

The response wasn't what Aveling was expecting, as they began to walk home she continued to explain, all the details of what she had been forced to do that day, it wasn't easy, some of the details, and words used that day of what had happened, Aveling just didn't understand.

as they approached home, Pam suddenly swung Aveling around holding her by the upper arm so tightly, she started to shake her hard, 'you can't tell mum,' feeling confused, Aveling insisted she was telling her mum, 'yes

I am telling mum, 'it was then Pam raised her hand up high it came down smack, Aveling felt her ear, and cheek feel like they were on fire.

'No you are not telling,' it hadn't been the response Aveling had been expecting, walking the rest of the way home in silence,

On arriving home Aveling explained, that Pam was the eldest at the time she must have been around twelve. She rushed Aveling round the back of the house where they met Rennie, the next eldest sister, Aveling explained she thought Rennie must have been about ten, 'what the hell as happened to you," but before Aveling could say a word Pam filled Rennie in with all the disgusting details.

They then rushed Aveling in through the back door to the kitchen sink, Pam was giving out the orders to Rennie, to get a clean dress from the closet, she grabbed Aveling by the neck, and began cleaning her up, over the sink with a dish cloth and carbolic soap, there was always carbolic soap in the old sink,.

By the time her mum finally arrived in the kitchen, there wasn't much to see.by then, most of the dried blood had been washed away. And before Aveling could say a word to her mother, Pam span a tail about how Aveling had fallen on the way home, tripping and smashing her teeth. as she was soaked by the rain, Pam said Aveling needed a change of clothes.

'Oh! You poor thing, let me make you a nice rusk, 'mum always had baby rusks in the house for the babies, and when anybody was ill mum would pour boiling water onto a rusk to soften it, then some milk and sprinkled it with sugar. It was seen as a treat 'now be a good girl eat up then its bed time.' Aveling family didn't have a phone in the house. so it was a neighbor who received a phone call.

after tea Aveling's mother had received a message form auntie Rose, it was the neighbor who dashed round with a message, from auntie Rose inquiring if Aveling was back home safely, I guess finding Aveling missing when she had returned from work, she had been worried, so her mum returned a message the same way, that Aveling was safely home, now messages were always kept to the minimum, due to the cost of using the phone.

Just before Aveling started to go up the stairs to bed, she went into the living room to collect a fire stone, to keep warm, it was then she saw her sister Pam rolling up her pretty new dress with the daisies on, and throwing it into the fire, as Aveling stood there, watching till it had burned down into the coals she felt her eyes filling with yet more tears.

Aveling shared a bedroom with her two sisters it was a little time later her two sisters joined her. Aveling pretended to be asleep. as she listened to her sisters she didn't understand all of the conversation, when her sisters started to talk about things of a sexual, and brutal nature, Avelings mind by then was running in overdrive, she wanted to ask them what, some of the words meant, but she knew that would end in another slap, it wasn't 'until Pam said 'we need to keep her quiet, or mum won't let us go back to aunties, if that happens we won't get any more magic sixpences,'

CLICK…TAPE OFF…

As I sat listening to that tape I found it heartbreaking, how could her own sisters not speak up for her, then the tape ended.it would be another week till Aveling s next visit to the surgery, but what I had sensed in that first tape, it was like Aveling had not just told me the facts of that day, but it was like her voice sounded just like that a five year old, it was to say a little strange.

CHAPTER 3

I AM TELLING ON YOU...

On arriving at the surgery the next visit started much the same as the previous, week, 'look Aveling we need to talk about what you said last week on the tape, 'Aveling just sat there in silence, it was clear she wasn't going to say a thing about the previous weeks tape,'

'ok maybe you would prefer to talk via the tape recorder again," Aveling then stood up slowly moving towards the back office, doctor Valerie was expecting to hear a continuation of the visit to aunties house, in more detail, but when she played back the second tape later, but that's not somewhere Aveling wanted to revisit, or to say much more about.

So it looked like if, Doctor Valerie wanted to hear all of Aveling stories, the only way to get Aveling talking again was the tape recorder. so be it. Not the best way, to communicate with the girl, but for now the only way.

Aveling continued walking through to the back office, again pushing the door behind her, till there was just a little gap.

CLICK...TAPE ON...

'I don't know what you want to hear doctor, 'I don't know what happened with Uncle Ben, I guess,

He must have told aunty Rose that I had just ran off, it was after that day, I would often find hiding places, even at home I looked around the house, and garden for hiding places, escape routes, just in case I needed them.

'Just talking about what has happened to me, it's all history, nothing

17

anyone can do now to change things, no one ever believes me anyway, and I am getting sick of repeating my self.it was then Aveling raised her voice, her tone was that of a very angry bitter person, as if she was grinding her teeth, she went on to say 'but if these visits are, what it takes to get the bloody police, and social servicers of my back. I just pray to god, someone, or anyone will get me out, of that god dam prison".

I had never heard Aveling raise her voice before or swear, and it was like I was dealing with two totally different little girls. Aveling took a long pause, then it was so strange to hear again, the softer voice. Then she continued,

It was a year later, just before my seventh birthday, the house had always been full of people. dad was one of eleven children, and mum one of four,…. so the house was always full at weekends' and holidays, one of dads adult brothers, uncle Terry had come to live with us, he was there to help mum with the bills, when dad was away working.

he hadn't been with us long when he started to bring home his latest girlfriend Alice, she was, when she stayed over, was supposed to share our bedroom, uncle Terry had moved into the boys room with my younger brothers mum still, as we say would top and tail them, but if you don't understand doctor.

let me explain, it just meant with the smaller children mum would put some, with feet laying towards the headboard, and the others feet to the bottom of the bed, they would all be sharing one big double bed, it wasn't till I was about six, that I was transferred to the other bedroom with two of my sisters, but it was rare, for it to be just the three of us as, we would often have cousins, or other female relatives over to stay most weekends, or one of uncle Terries girlfriends to stay over, sometimes they would move in, until uncle Terry got fed up with them.

It often seemed like we would just get to know one, when they were kicked out, so yes doctor everyone seemed to be packed in like sardines in a tin, with only three bedrooms, that's just the way we lived, but I can say I had dreamt, that one day I would have a whole, room all to myself, yet even now as I am locked up, I still have to share my cell, But there was something about uncle's latest girlfriend, Alice, I took an instant dislike to, she seemed to be, at first trying too hard for us all to like her. But whenever the house was empty, Alice liked to drink gin, but it was then she had an evil streak, her whole personality changed.

Now Uncle Terry had the single Bed in the boys room, to be honest there wasn't much more room for any more beds, or come to think about it, in that room that was all there was, the single bed for uncle plus the double for the rest of the boys, so in the evening, after uncle had his evening meal, he and Alice would retire, to the boys room before the boys went to bed, then shortly after Alice would join us in the girls room to sleep, I would often have to share my bunk with her, but she smelled so strongly of cigarettes and gin, I just couldn't sleep next to her, every time she breathed out it was like trying to sleep with a, well I just cant find the words Doctor Valerie, so let's just say auntie Alice smelled like a dirty ash tray.

So I would creep out of the room late, after everyone was asleep, I would take my blanket, creeping quietly down stairs were I would just curl up on the sofa. Now in the boys room, the clean boys cloths were just put in piles neatly on the floor, one pile for each of them, yes they sometimes got mixed up, so I always knew when they were wake, and getting dressed because of all the arguing, on who was supposed to wear what that day.

when the cloths were dirty they were just dropped on the landing in a piles, it was also the dumping ground for all us girls cloths also, mum would have the washing machine on almost every day, The youngest two boys were still babies. And still slept in mums room, we always said mums room, due to the fact dad was often as we were told, working away, he was at that time, in the royal navy, but it wasn't until just a few months ago, I found out that dad hadn't been always working away, but he had spent some time in prison for theft. But that's not what you want to hear right now is it doctor, so let me take you back to the week before my seventh birthday.

mum had to go into town taking my two older sisters, she would also take the two smallest, as one of them was still breast feeding with her, it also meant she would have the large pram to help carry the shopping, so we knew mum wouldn't be back home till the six o'clock bus, it was always the late buss from town on a Saturday, because mum liked to wait for some of the traders to close up, so as always at the end of the day, they would sell fruit and veg cheap.

I always loved it when mum came home with the oranges, as I loved them best of all, and squeegee bananas, wc called them squeegee, because they were the lose ones that often got crushed, but if they were to brown to eat mum would make banana custard, it was yummy.

now because Alice didn't work, mum had asked Alice to baby sit, on that day. but no sooner mum had left, the younger boys just took the advantage to bolt out of the back door, and over a hedge at the bottom of the garden, into the common field to kick a football around.

Now Aveling went on to explain, she had been digging in the garden pulling out weeds for her mum, it wasn't a large garden but she was the only one in the family, who would do anything out there, regardless of how young she was, she went on to explain that she always did love the daisy's best, because she had learned how to make daisy chains, with her finger nails, and wear them in her hair.

Well doctor, when I returned into the house. the new, so called girl-friend, Alice was sitting in the living room with a man I had never seen before.

as she stood up she introduced him, 'this is my brother Sam. just look at you, your covered in dirt, now I will get the bath, and you need to get cleaned up before your mother gets home', now doctor the bath back in the fifties, was an old tin bath hanging up in the kitchen off the pantry wall, it took agers to fill so we only had a bath on a Sunday night before bed, so we would be clean for school on a Monday.

Mum still washed the babies in the sink. I remembered that big old sink it never seemed empty, if it wasn't, nappies washing, or pots soaking, it was were mum put wet clothes from the old washing machine, while she pulled out the old mangle, so we could get as much water out as possible, before putting them on the line to dry, now I know it sounds a little silly doctor, but I liked helping mum turn the mangle handle.it just seemed so satisfying turning it. But that was the only sink in the house, so it was used for just about everything.so the washing had to be done, and dusted, as fast as possible to clear the sink for the next job.

But I had been too big for the sink bath for a long time, so we would use the tin bath that would be placed in the middle of the living room in front of fire on a Sunday evening.

So Aveling had protested 'Alice I am not that dirty, and its only Saturday, I don't need a bath,' 'do as your told or you will get the back of my hand,' 'no ' 'don't you dare say no to me young lady, 'it was then Alice raised her hand to slap Aveling, but before she could make contact, her so called brother, grabbed her arm, Sam then said, "don't hit her, it could leave a mark," it was then she noticed Alice s brother Sam, leaving the room, when he returned he was holding a camera.

as the camera was clicking away, Alice kept telling Aveling, 'wouldn't you like to be in the t v adverts, like that pretty little girl, who is always on the soap wrappers, Alice kept telling her she was so pretty, 'as she started to stroked her body,

Then when the clicking stopped, the room fell silent, it was then Aveling realized she needed to get free, as she saw Sam had put the camera down, as he walked over, with a look of evil in his eyes, she had after all seen that look before at uncle bens house.

Aveling then went on to explain, just how uncomfortable she felt, Alice then put her hand over my mouth to keep me quite, it was then I wriggled free, as I had tried to push pass Alice to leave the room. Sam blocked the door way it was then, Sam picked me up, and throw me down onto the sofa, and the sheer force of the throw took the wind out of my lungs.

I didn't know what their intentions were, but I felt the hairs prickling up on the back of my neck, my new adult teeth were still only just growing back, but they were sharp, I screamed as loud as I could, and then I bit Alice', as she tried to force her hand back over my mouth, trying to gag me again, to stop me from screaming, but the bite drew blood, she raised her hand slapping me hard across the face. at that second I knew I had to get away, but with the two of them now holding me down. I didn't stand a chance of breaking free.

At that time I believed Sam was going to punish me, as my uncle Ben had done, by pulling out my teeth for being a naughty girl, because I had bit Alice, so I was fighting with all my strength, But he didn't seem interested with punishing me that way, I truly had no idea back then doctor, what they wanted of me. As Alice was attempting to keep me quiet, I was fighting with both of them, but I stayed adamant I didn't need a bath till Sunday.

Sam was growing inpatient he seemed to be getting angry with Alice shouting at her to keep me still, I didn't stand a chance, of getting away it was then, there was a knock on the back door, bang, bang, I had never heard the door banged on like that, it was then Sam moved so fast, swiftly grabbing his camera he fled throw the front door.

Alice then smacked me again hard across the face, she then went to open the back door as it was still repeatedly being banged on.

I could hear voices it was the old lady who lived next door, the council houses were connected, and she had heard my screams, 'what's going on in there it sound like your killing someone, 'she must have pushed passed Alice, Mrs. Burgers was now in the living room I rushed up to her, as I tried to hide behind her, Alice told her, she just wanted to give me a bath before my mum came home, as I had gotten so dirty digging in the back garden. 'No she's lying Mrs. Burgers,' she had a man in hear.

Before I could say another word, Alice had lurched forward, grabbing me firmly by my arm. 'she tells such stories, she always causing trouble, now if you don't mind I have got to get the tea ready before her mother gets home,.' Mrs. Burgers, took a good look around the room, just as Alice was attempting to shuffle her out of the living room door, returning to the kitchen Mrs. Burgers was asking questions but I could not hear them from the living room very clearly, it was then I heard the back door slamming.

when Alice returned to the living room, it was then when I said those words, ('I am telling on you,')it is when she heard those words, Alice grew so angry, she lit a cigarette, I was sitting on the chair beside the fire place, trying to get my top lip from bleeding, Alice must have split it when she had smacked me, I was so cold, I was still trembling from trying to get free of Alice s grip, she made me feel so afraid, but in my mind I didn't understand why.

it was then, she sat on me pinning me down, 'you little bitch you cost me a week's money, 'I had no idea what she was talking about back then, but I do now, has she pinned me down she started to push her lit cigarette into the back of my hand, she had a smile on her face that was so sinister, Alice was now chuckling gleefully to herself, as she continued to burn me.

The pain was searing, and intense, but she didn't stop even when I started to scream again. But with the other hand she forced it firmly over my mouth again, as she ripped open the back of my dress, with her other hand, it had been buttoned down the back, so as the buttons burst open, she just kept pushing the end of the cigarette into my flesh, over and over again, it would be the smell of burning flesh.

I could never ever forget, as the smell was firmly stuck in my nostrils, but it had also left me with a fear of cigarettes, so whenever I saw someone lighting one, I would just for a second freeze, recalling that same nasty smell of skin burning, even now doctor Valerie after all these years I can still smell that burning flesh, I knew it was irrational, but that fear never left me.

When she finally got up, 'now young lady when my brother comes round next week, you will do exactly what I tell you to do, or you will get worse than a few little burns, 'as I sat sobbing, and shaking, Alice simply got up went to the kitchen, then I heard the cooker gas as she put the kettle on.

When she returned back to the living room.it was like she was a different person, her voice was softer she smiled at me, 'oh! You poor little thing, your dress is torn let me get you another, while I stitch the buttons back, on this one, after all you don't want to up set your mum now she's pregnant again, she could lose the baby if you upset her, and that would be all your fault, now wouldn't it".

It was after that day, if ever I saw Alice I would refer to her as a monster.

…CLICK…tape off

CHAPTER 4

ANOTHER.BABY.

It was time, for Aveling to leave the surgery, has always on the dot there was a knock at the door, as she left, Aveling looked straight at me, I could see she had been crying, now it wasn't unusual for children to have more than one abuser, but after hearing what she had left on the tape that day. I was lost for words, but it was my job to write up notes, but my god where I would begin. I thought the first recording of aunties Roses house, was a nightmare, but at least she surly wouldn't have to go back their again.

But now, not only was Aveling being tortured in her own home, but her torture was caused by people who had been asked to look after her, people living under the same roof, but I was so full of anger just thinking about it, not only had she been tortured by men, but this to me felt so much worse, because it was a woman, now I know it shouldn't matter who was guilty of her treatment, but for some reason for me this just seemed so unbelievable, how could any women do this to such a small child.

How on earth was I going to treat this poor girl? at that moment I realized Aveling had so much more to say, about her abusers, but on her next visit I was never too sure, what mood she would be in, or were she would start,

When Aveling arrived the following week, it was like everything seemed normal as she said her hello, Aveling paused just a little, then walked on past me to the back office, just leaving a little gap in the door as always, then once again there was that noise.

…CLICK…tape on

Do you know doctor you were right, what had I got to lose just talking to the tape, telling the truth. it's up to what you want to believe, I really couldn't care any more. at least these trips get me out for the day. It's a break from that prison cell.

Now when I was seven, when I arrived home from school, there was another baby in the house, now yes it did confuse me, because we already had a thirteen month baby, mum was just showing her next baby bump,

I don't remember seeing a doctor or nurse at the house, and if mum was having a home birth these people would call regularly, in the last few months before mums due date, the nurse would often be there drinking tea with mum when I got home from school. But this time as if like magic there was a new baby, well I say new, but he must have been about four or five months old, I looked around the house, mum was in the kitchen, so as the baby was crying I picked him up, saying, 'and who are you my little friend,' he had stopped crying as soon as I picked him up for a cuddle.

He looked directly at me with the biggest brown eyes, still wet from the tears, I gently rocked him in my arms, it was then he started to smile, I felt an instant bond with him. Has his little fingers wrapped around mine.

It was then mum came into the room. 'Well Aveling he must like you, so why don't you give him his bottle,' 'who is he mum, were did he come from, 'mum paused, 'but before she could say a thing, dad had appeared from the back yard. 'Stop asking so many questions girl,' by then I was sitting on the sofa, mum passed the fresh bottle, so I sat their feeding him. Shortly after dad left.

Dad never seemed to stay anywhere very long. if there was a baby crying for attention he would respond with, 'got to go things to do. 'looking back I never did see him ever pick up a crying child, as far back as I can remember, but the thing that got him moving the quickest, was the smell of a soiled nappy, I could never remember being picked up by my father, the boys I did see sitting on his lap when they reached about three or four, I can never remember him giving me, or any of us for that matter any affection, there was never a goodnight kiss, no bed time stories. He was as he put it, too busy, and mum was always busy with the youngest babies.

So after I settled the new baby boy into the push pram, I again asked mum, 'who is he what's his name, as I looked across at mum, I could see she had been crying but as always trying to conceal the fact. She smiled, 'he s called Greg, and he's your new baby brother,' 'but where did he come from mum,' 'never mind just you rock him to sleep so I can start the tea.'

Mum started to make sandwiches for all of us, two of my younger brothers always had a problem with Greg's name, and as Greg always seemed to be hungry, I nicked named him GG, for greedy guts, and that's what we all called him, if anybody asked who he was, we were told to tell them, he was our new baby brother, I guess with so many babies around no one ever questioned it.

sorry doctor Valerie, at that time there wasn't any more to say, because I just didn't know who he was, or where he had come from, but GG took a shine to me, he would crawl around after me, as he grew his nick name for me was Ling ling, and with so many of us, even I got Davy, and Danny names mixed up, all the time, but it was Greg who seemed to have bonded with me.

as he grew he was always standing at the window, watching, waiting for me to come home for school, and once home he became my little shadow, now I know I was only seven, but I knew babies didn't arrive like magic, so something wasn't right. But it was impossible for me not to love him like a brother, he had such a lovely nature. But later when I knew the truth, I was heartbroken. But for now that's all I have to say about Greg.

Now after being slapped so many times across the face and ear, it had started to affect my school work, if the teacher s had their backs to me when they wrote on the blackboard, then turned to face me I had missed half the instructions' my grades were dropping I was lucky if I got an E.or F s, I once asked another girl, if she could repeat what the instructions from the teacher were, but I got caught talking, so when the teacher saw me, hurdling throw the air came the wooden blackboard duster, that teacher rarely missed.

so by the time I got home I was displaying a huge lump on my head, now I did like school, but everyone just thought because my grades were low, I must be a little stupid, or as my older brother Luke put it, I was to him a retard, thinking about it all now doctor, I guess that's another reason why I didn't want to write anything down. I guess due to all the slapping and missed lessons, my spelling was atrocious, I didn't want you to think I was a retard to. Now because the only teacher who spent all her time facing us was the music teacher that was the subject were I excelled?

My teacher, Mrs. Green decided, when it was time to learn to play an instrument, we were handed out old plastic recorders, now doctor I am not sure, if you have ever heard a beginner practicing playing on the recorded, well the noise wasn't the best. but we were allowed to take the recorders home to practice.it was on one of those days, mum sent me out of the house to play in the back garden, as the younger baby was sleeping in the living room, well that's what mum said, but to be truthful it wasn't sounding good to my ears, so I knew mum didn't want to hear me, as I attempted to play London's burning over and over again. so mum had asked me to go and play in the garden.

so as I sat on the garden wall practicing, my brother Luke was sitting on the house step, now the garden wasn't much bigger than postage stamp, Luke my eldest brother at about that time, must have been around, twelve, thirteen, he was as he put it, trying to read his comic, so he did not want to be disturbed, I told him mum told me to practice in the back yard.

So every time I started to play, he would throw stones at me. but when that didn't stop me, he came over to where I was sitting, he snatched the recorder out of my hands, now at that time I was wearing an Alice band in my hair, it was made of plastic with a two rows of teeth stretching from one side to the other, to keep my hair firmly in place. Luke then raised the recorder smashing it down on to my head, it hurt, but as he had done so, the recorder had broken into two.

now when we were given the instruments, we all made the teacher a promise, to take good care of them. now I know doctor I was outside so I didn't wake the baby, but I was so angry with Luke, I started to scream at him, he by then was fighting with me, and I like to think regardless how much bigger than me he was, I was still getting in a punch or two, mum came out of the house, to see what all the shouting was about. when she saw the recorder, she knew it was Luke, she assured me not to get to upset she would glue it for me, but I knew it would never sound the same. now I also knew I would have to explain the damage to my teacher that was something I was not looking forward to.

It was then mum gasped, 'what's wrong mum, 'it was then she explained my head was bleeding, the teeth from the Alice band had gone deep into my scalp due to the strength that Luke had used to break the recorder, now the blood had begun to run down my forehead to my eyes, it was only then I had started to feel the pain.

mum ordered Luke to his room, but just as he turned around, he then told mum to go to hell, now no one spoke to mum like that, it was so bad, both mum and I gasped together, as she took me into the sink to check on the damage to my scalp, mum told him she would deal with him later, now the wound was taking some time to stop bleeding.

Luke had followed us into the kitchen, so mum told him when dad got home next, she was going to tell him, about Luke's bad behavior that it was unacceptable, Luke then turned to mum and said, if she opened her fucking gob, that he would tell dad, mum had another man in the house, mums face drained of all the color, dad was well known for his temper, if dad thought for a second that mum had, had another man in the house, she would get the third degree, now the baby had started crying so mum went into the living room. as mum sat beside the fire, I joined her still holding a rag, I was using to stop the blood from running down my face.

It wasn't long before Luke joined us, he had got a bottle of cider from the pantry, now mum never bought fizzy pop or cider, so she had never been sure where the cider had come from, he sat in the other arm chair like the lord of the manor,

It was then he said, 'that when dad was away he was the man of the house, and what he said goes, 'now I could see how upset mum still was, now mum was only about five feet two, but so skinny, with pretty blue eyes and blond curly hair. But Luke was growing fast and towered above mum.

I told mum not to worry Luke wasn't going to tell dad a thing, he just scowled at me as I continued, 'don't worry mum because if he says any- thing to dad, he will leave me no choice, it was then I took a deep breath because as they say squealing on Luke, always ended with me getting a smacking from Luke later.

but he should never have threatened mum, so I said Luke would leave me no option, but to tell the new corner shop owners, how their pretty little daughter Betty, has been stealing cider, out of the back door of the store, it was then Luke stood up as he did so I saw the empty cider bottle heading straight at my head.

My reactions must have been Sharpe that day, because I caught it before it hit any thing.so he stormed off, slamming all the doors behind him deliberately to wake the baby.

I knew Luke had been seeing Betty, because she was telling everyone that he was her boyfriend at school, now Luke, my monster of a brother would have new girlfriends every other week, sometimes more than one, especially if they could help him steel, the fact that Betties parent owned a shop, well to Luke that seemed like she was the perfect choice for a girlfriend, he could talk her into getting anything for him, but for Betty this was her first love.

But mum now knowing Luke s dirty little secret, it was only then mum seemed to get her smile back. She warned me to keep away from him for a while till he calmed down. I do remember thinking at that time, poor Betty she had no idea what Luke was really like, as her family had only just moved into the estate. But my sympathy didn't last long, when I found out more about sweet little Betty.

…CLICK…tape off

CHAPTER 5

THE DOLLY.

On the next visit Aveling seemed in a hurry to get past me, and into the other office, but again she just left a little gap between us. Then there was that sound again it was becoming a sound, that my ears seemed to directly tune into, although I never heard a word, of what she was saying, and yes I did try to listen through the door, but after a while I believed if she ever saw me, she would retreat back into her own world, but that was the last thing I wanted.

CLICK…Tape …on…

Now her voice as always speaking so softly. I would have to wait till the hour was over if I wanted to listen to her words.

She began to explain her mothers, mother was so very ill, and, each day on her way home from school, she would call in to see her grandma, and Aveling would ask her grandad if he needed anything.

his answer was always the same, he just needed Aveling to watch grandma for just a little while, so he could pop to the shops and get some shopping, Aveling went on to explain, how she would offer to do the shopping for him, but he told her he needed to also pick up some tobacco, and the shop keeper wouldn't sell It to her because she was so young, but Aveling knew the real truth, grandad just needed to get out for a little while, sometimes he would arrive back with that distinctive smell of beer.

grandma was always sitting in the fireside chair, she couldn't speak, as I learned later she had something called Parkinson's disease, so I would just read her books to her, grandma would smile so I believed that grandma was always listening to me, she went on to explain that her two. older sisters were too busy to visit or so they said, her older brother Luke, would go home directly from school so he could dash over the back hedgers onto the common field to play football. Aveling went onto explain.

It was late that summer when I arrived at grandads, the curtains were closed, I felt uneasy as I tried to enter the house, but mum was there she stopped me at the door, "be a good girl and go play in the garden, and I will come and talk to you later." Doing as I was told I heard a car engine, so going round to the front of the house I saw it pulling up in front of grandads house, then two men got out, I had never seen a car like that before, but then again I hadn't seen many cars.

The two men walked straight up and into grandad's house, then shorty after they came out carrying something big. Mum then saw me peering around the corner, and quickly sent me back to the rear garden.

Later that evening mum came into the garden, time to go home,' but mummy I haven't seen grandma, 'it's ok mummy will explain when we get home, that evenings walk home seemed so much longer than normal as mum never said a word.

I knew then something was wrong, mum had been so quiet. At home mum called us all into the living room and explained grandma had died. She then told the boys they could go and play, but she asked my two sisters, and me to stay behind.

Grandad wanted you to have something to remind you of your grandma,

First she pulled out of her shopping bag a small box, handing it over to my eldest sister Pam, inside was a gold and ruby ring that had been grandmas engagement ring, then for Rennie a gold pendant, that grandma had worn on her wedding day, as they tried them on, mum lifted a very tatty dark cardboard box from her bag, 'this Aveling is for you, 'I was thinking why such a big box for me. But when I opened it up, I found the best gift ever.

Inside was a doll with eyes that moved, when she stood up her eyes were a lovely shade of blue, just like mums, and when I laid her down her eyes closed. I had never seen a doll before only in picture books, it was the best gift ever. Over the next few weeks I asked mum for any leftover scraps of fabric, I had learned to sow just as soon as I could thread the needles, so by hand I stitching the scraps together, I made new cloths for my dolly, and the old cardboard box, I turned into a bed, with a pillow and blankets. I called her Nora after my grandma.

Over the following days things carried on as normal, but often in bed I would cry myself to sleep thinking of grandma, as I cuddled my new dolly After that I seldom saw grandad. mum said he needed time to come to terms with what had happened, but it seemed so strange not stopping at grandad s house on the way home from school, as I always had that year, but just when things seemed to be settling down after the loss of grandma,

Dad decided to pay a surprise visit, it had seemed strange, as he hadn't been able to make it home for grandmas funeral, but on seeing him I knew I had to keep well out of his way, now I know doctor it sounds crazy, but he, and I seemed to have what you would call today a clash of personality's.

I did try honest doctor, to be a good girl, but I knew sometime before he left again, I would get a beating for something or another, out of all of us children, you could almost be guaranteed, if anything went wrong in the house it was my fault, I remembered on one occasion money had gone missing from my oldest sister moneybox, now I didn't know why or how, but for some reason the evidence pointed at me.

now yes I did think I knew who took the money, as they had been out spending, but there was no point in telling on him, as it was one of those things you just didn't do, I naively always believed if you did something wrong, you needed to stand up for your mistakes, and admit when you had been wrong, or did anything naughty.

so yes I did expect Luke to own up, but even as dad beat me, Luke just stood there, and said nothing, now I hadn't seen Luke take the money so I had no proof, but he just stood there with that annoying grin on his face, I knew it would be hopeless telling dad, it was after all, Luke his first born son who could do no wrong, as in the past, Luke always riddled out of just about anything, or he would go on to blame one of my younger brothers, if I was out of the house. then that would mean the little ones getting a beating, even if they had done nothing wrong.

but that is something if I could, I would try to prevent, not knowing the full truth, I would just tell dad it was me, so it meant off with the belt, and I knew all too well what was coming next. Now doctor don't get me wrong, I did sometimes mess up, but if I for example broke a dish, I would confessed to it, now mum would say not to worry, but if dad was home, that was a smacking a fence, for being so clumsily but the thought of dad punishing my little brothers was just too much to bare. Over the years I think dad lost patients with me.

Now looking back one of the things I remembered all too well, was being out on an errand for mum, but when I got back home all hell was breaking out. But I wasn't too sure why, but dad was taking his belt of to my sister Rennie, now it was a rare thing to be happening, I first went into the kitchen to find mum, asking why was dad beating Rennie, she told me not to interfere. But as always there was no way any one was going to beat my sister Rennie.

she out of all of the girls was the gentlest, it wasn't in her nature to be bad, so without knowing all the facts I barged into the living room, just as he was lifting his belt to beat her, I grabbed the belt, screaming at him to let her go, well I made such a fuss every time he lifted the belt to beat her I grabbed it, finally pulling it out of his hand.

Rennie was screaming in pain from the few blows she had received, but she shouted at me, 'no no don't he will beat you to, 'but it was too late, as he turned his attention to me, after he had exhausted himself with me, yelling at my mum, 'that, that girl isn't normal,' as I would not cry, not one tear did he get from me, no matter how hard he rained down blow after blow, so totally frustrated he stormed out.

We knew at that point he would go to his mother's house, or so he would always tell mum later, that's where he had been, but I believed I knew where he was going, but it wasn't his mother's house.

Rennie was still sobbing on the floor, 'why, she said why you would do that for me, 'because I don't know and don't care what you did, he has no excuse for beating you like that. 'She just through her arms around me with the biggest of hugs, for me that was a huge thank you. I never did find out what she had done, but I guess it doesn't matter anymore.

Now my eldest brother Luke was always a bully, he tormented and picked. on my younger brothers relentlessly. It was on such an occasion, something inside me snapped, so when I saw him smacking the youngest, I pushed Luke hard, he lost his balance falling backwards, as my little brothers laughed, Luke was fuming, 'you little bitch, I will get you back for that, 'the next day on arriving home from school after tea, Luke knocked on the living room window, to get my attention,

He was pointing to the washing line, just below the line was a concrete row of paving slabs that made a pathway down the garden, but hanging on the line wasn't washing that day it was my dolly. I dashed outside, just as the fireworks he had pushed into her head exploded, the doll fell from the line crashing directly onto the concrete slabs, smashing into so many pieces.

I screamed, mum came running out of the house to see what all the noise was about, when she saw the doll, she knew what had happened, Luke was stood there laughing, mum never smacked any of us, but if we were naughty she would send us to our bed rooms, Luke didn't show his face till the next day.

I was heartbroken, mum said she would try to fix my doll but the bits seemed just too small.so after many attempts she had to fix her, mum conceded it was hopeless. That weekend I asked mum were do dollies go when they died.

I know now doctor Valerie, it was a stupid question, but I was only seven at the time doctor, mum explained that she would go to heaven and be with grandma, Nora.

So I decided to bury her, in the prettiest cloths, and her bed, I still had the lid so now her bed, was dolly Nora's coffin.

It was just starting to drizzle with rain, but I dug a hole at the bottom of the garden, as I was about to place the box in that contained my dolly. When Luke came hurdling over the hedge from the field. Were he always went to play football, when he saw what I was doing, he jumped on the box saying, 'just making sure she's dead you don't want to bury her if she's still alive now do you, there seemed to be no end to his cruelty.

I placed her gently into the ground, I said a prayer, the old lady, Mrs. Burgers from next door had seen what Luke had done, through her kitchen window, she came out to see me, my face was covered in tears, as she placed her arm gently around me, 'now don't you cry little one, god will teach him a lesson he wouldn't forget, someday.

…CLICK…tape off

CHAPTER 6

A LOST SISTER...

Now my appointments were running a little late, I had been told Aveling was waiting in the surgery, now, I Know just how bad this sounds writing it down, but I couldn't get the last patient out of the surgery quickly enough, so Aveling could come in for her treatment, but what am I saying treatment, the girl had barely spoken a word directly to me, and how could things get any stranger than a patient who only made contact with me via a tape recorder, but I had started to do something I thought I would never do with a patient, I felt as if like magic, there was a bond growing between us. I just needed to protect her, as if she was my own daughter, they say when two people meet sometimes it's like they have known each other, for a life time. I desperately tried to be rational, I had just drifted off into my own little world, trying hard to understand my feelings, I knew we had nothing in common, it's not like she was a small child that needed to be saved from the worlds darkness, Aveling was already a woman, but some days she just seemed so young in her mannerisms, I was suddenly shuck back to reality by that knock on the door, there was no mistaking Toms' knock, I guess being a police officer he was accustomed to getting the attention of the home owner with that knock of his.

Has Aveling entered the room, it looked like she had already been crying, she just walked straight passed me, and into the back office, not even stopping to say good afternoon, again the door was pushed so only a small gap was left, as it always was.

…CLICK…tape on …

I had come to know that sound, it meant she had begun but again so softly was her voice I couldn't overhear a word.

Well doctor I am her again, and I just feel so exhausted just knowing I have to be hear. When I first started coming, I thought it was a load of rubbish. then after the first few times, I did feel a little better later for a short while. But now on the nights before I arrive, it keeps playing over and over in my head, all the bad things we have discussed, so getting to sleep is becoming a real problem, so by the time I get here I am exhausted.

But let me tell you something about my big sister, It was a few years later, after my so called new auntie had burned me. my older sister Pam kept disappearing, uncle Bens, brother Joe would pick her up at the end of the road on his motor bike, and take her to aunties house on Saturday after auntie left for work.so she could play the magic sixpence game, or so she said, but that's not all she was doing for money uncle would give his son money for the football match, so he never returned till late in the afternoon,

Now I had been playing on the landing with some pens and paper, when Pam returned, looking back she must have just turned eighteen, but with so many of us I always found it difficult to remember all my siblings names, so trying to remember how old, and when their birthdays were, was something that wasn't important to me. now Pam was all excited. Pam and Rennie were talking in the hallway the doors to the living room and kitchen were closed, now the hallway was just the width of the stairs so ever word spoken, could easily be heard on the landing.

Pam held out her hand to show Rennie how much money she had, 'how did you get so much money,' 'it was easy all I had to do is pretend I was a palm reader, and tell a few of uncle bens friend s stories, it's easy Rennie you just get a few facts from uncle Ben, then make the rest up., it's fascinating Rennie, just how many of them believe ever word I tell them.

I have never had that much money before, and then uncle Ben said he would give me a shilling, if I did the same again next week.

Now Pam went on to explain, uncles started to get pound signs in his eyes, as he would charge two shillings, for people to enter, and Pam would get payed at the end of the readings, Pam did the same for his brother at his house, easy money, and he's going to pick me up again next week so I can do the same again, but you must promise me Rennie not to tell anyone, because I had to promised uncle I wouldn't tell a living sole,'

now I had heard every word from the landing, but said nothing because I knew if they saw me, I would have been beaten for sure, if what I had overheard was true, It just in my mind seemed so disgusting, making up stories, after all mum had said to us often enough, we must not mess with such strange things, like magic, and palm reading mum warned us it could lead to some very dark placers, it wouldn't be till I was much older did I find out the real reasons, for mum s warnings, but all would become so much clearer as I got older.

I didn't think what I was hearing on the landing that day, was the whole truth, I was just thinking, if it was just another one of Pam s tall stories, shame on her, but then again where had Pam got so much money from, Pam did like to tell I good story, but then again who would make up such untruthful stories, those people listening, believing her ever word, they would often change their whole life's, because of her stories.

The follow weekend again Pam came home all happy, Rennie asked what had happened. but Pam said she would tell her later in bed, so later that night when we were all in bed, I tried to be asleep, but they were chattering away about the events of that day has always, Pam told Rennie she had got a whole pound in money, she told Rennie they had to go to uncles Bens, brothers house, he said it would be safer there.

Joe did live with a woman, but Pam didn't think he had married her, as she was rarely there, but I guessed she must have been out at work on the days Pam visited. so it was then uncle Ben asked Pam if she would like to ern more money, so he told her, to get such a lot of all she had to do, is tell one of the men due that day, that his wife had been cheating on him, now there was no truth to the story, but Uncle Ben wanted to cause problems for the punters family,

So he promised her he would give her a ten shilling note, and afterwards he would explain later, So Pam agreed, and it's worth it for all that money, she boasted to Rennie, but when Rennie asked, her to explain why he had wanted her to tell such lies. Pam just shrugged her shoulders and said it didn't matter why to her, just as long as she got payed. after all mum had told us, not to tell lies, never to do harm by telling stories. Mum would have been so ashamed if she knew.

The next week the same thing again, Pam returned with so much money, and in bed she couldn't wait to tell Rennie all about it. It was then uncle asked her if she wanted to earn more money, "yes she answered what do you want me to do for it", "I need you to tell someone, not to go to London, or do any traveling by rail this week as you have seen danger ahead of him".

Pam told Rennie it did seem a bit strange but just as long as they pay her, what harm could it do, so she was willing to tell the punters anything uncle told her to tell them.

When Pam arrived the following week the man she had told not to travel, said she had saved his life. He said such lovely things to her, he made her feel so very cleaver, and special.

Pam went on to explain, the train he would have been traveling on, had been derailed just outside the city, now I did start to question myself after hearing a story like that, did she really have such power, but no, I may still have been young, but if god had given her any ability to do such things, trust me doctor she would have been only too happy to have used a gift like that for her own advantage. so She could have caused so much trouble, for just as many people she took a dislike to, Pam had no morals, so a gift like that from god to someone like her, is something I believed god would never have done.

Now doctor, yes I knew no one in my family had any time for religion, I had even heard Rennie having a discussions with Pam, she didn't say much, only that she didn't believe in god, but it wouldn't hurt just in case, but for me I felt so differently, I always had believed, I promised late grandma I would say my prayers every night, something I had to do before my sisters came up to bed, because they would love to tease me, so yes I believed god had a path for all of us.so I was determined to be a good girl. so looking back now how the hell did I end up hear.

but it wasn't till much later, I found out that uncle Bens brother worked at the local newspaper in the printing department, and he had arranged for a mock newspaper to be printed up with the headlines reading all about the train derailment, it was only when I discovered that, did things finally start to make since, how else would Pam have been able to fool the punter into believing her, but when something like that happened, her servicers had become in such great demand as the rumors were spread, by word of mouth, like lightening around the estate, the men were now queuing up for her so called predictions.

now over the coming weeks Pam came home with such bizarre stories, I think she truly believed she was a psychic, but it was when she told Rennie, uncle had asked her to tell one of the men he would die, if he didn't agree to put an offering up to the tree gods, by folding a ten pound note into four folds then place it into a marked tree in the woods, has it had become, by then common knowledge, about the man who hadn't traveled, and who was saved by Pams warning, the punters started to believe everything she told them however bazaar, uncle told her for every ten pounds they found in the tree. she would get one third, she told Rennie it had been the easiest way of making money she had ever used, now as you know doctor ten pounds to some men was a huge part of their full wagers, but they still fell for the con.

As Pam was over eighteen, I didn't think it was just palm reading she was offering, it was then when she started to tell Rennie all about the extras she had, been getting such large amounts of money for. But as she began to give all the sordid details that night, I just did not want to listen to them. So when she began to use those vile words, I had heard before, yes doctor, I know I was still supposed to be too young to understand, but trust me doctor when I had to share my bedroom with the two of them, there hadn't been anything they didn't discuss in detail.

Now it was impossible in such a small room, not to hear.so as Pam went on to explain in great details how she had been naked in bed servicing two men together, what Pam hadn't noticed was there was another man that day taking photos of everything, it wasn't till some weeks later, when she was shown the photos, did she have a huge argument with uncle, for allowing the photographer to take such disgusting photos, it was then she found out it had been uncle Ben himself who had arranged it, let's face it, she must by then have known he was capable of anything, and the photos to him, were just another way of getting even more money, out of the men by blackmailing them.

now on hearing that, I was growing more and more angry how could she consent to doing that, but again uncle had offered her a percentage, so she hadn't stayed angry with him for long, but as she was telling Rennie, Pam had no remorse, but when she started to laugh as she told Rennie about one man's wife, who had stormed round to our home, shouting at mum for allowing Pam to do such disgusting things, I hadn't been there that day but I do remember coming home from school to find mum crying,

It was then I said "I had heard enough."

"Will you two please shut up, or I am telling mum all about what you did with uncle ben and his brother, and I am not just talking about the blackmailing, I mean everything, and boy oh boy, did I have some nasty stories to tell, I knew then that Pam had been to see the doctor, called doctor Hanger, and I did know why, he was the doctor who performed illegal abortions, "it was then Pam came over to my bunk bed, she pulled me off with one pull, as she held me tightly around my neck. "If you say one word to mum I will bloody kill you." She then pushed me so hard, as I stumbled backwards my head hit the metal iron frame of the bunk.

now I knew whenever I watched cartoons, you would often see little stars around the characters heads, if they got struck with a bat, but I can tell you now doctor, that is exactly what I saw, little stars and black dots, I hastily got back into my bunk, it had stopped nothing they just carried on talking about all the gross things she did at uncles house.

on my bunk I lifted my hands to my head, I had such a large bump on my head it really hurt, but I knew if I went into mums room for help, or down stairs, it would mean explaining why I had the bump, in the first place, now that would have meant getting another beating from Pam. So I curled myself up into a ball holding my hands to my ears, but nothing stopped them as they continued chatting. Well into the early morning. The following day Doctor I made up my mind I was going to tell mum what was happening, I just didn't know when I would get the chance, as mum was always so busy with the little ones. But thinking about it, what could mum do Pam was old enough, so apart from upsetting mum it would achieve, nothing.

CLICK…Tape off …

CHAPTER 7

PLEASE SHUT UP...

I wanted to believe what Aveling was saying wasn't true, I can remember back to when I must have been about the same age as Aveling, I remember I was still being read fairy tales, my favorite was snow white, but for Aveling, all she was hearing were stories, no girl of that age should even be thinking about, taking advantage of men, lying just to con them out of money, actions like that have consequences, as Aveling herself told me it hadn't been long till her school friends, who found out about her sister, started to call Aveling a witch. I looked up at the clock it was almost that time for her to arrive,

I had no idea where she would begin, but I confess some of her stories were so hard to listen to, telling people they would die if they didn't do as asked, I knew only too well what damage the mind could do, if manipulated in the wrong direction, but I knew I couldn't stop now, I had to help this girl, well I was no longer sure what I was trying to do, on one hand I was supposed to be trying to help her, to remember who she was, and how she had ended up in prison, but on the other hand after hearing some of her stories, I understood why she needed, if anything she needed to forget.

It was then I remembered back to one day, I had been called out to a man in his mid-fifties, he told me I couldn't help him, as he would be dead before the sun set that very day, at that time I hadn't been a doctor for very long, so I examined him he seemed as fit as a fiddle, so I told him he was fine, later that night I received a message from his mother to inform me he had dyed, to this day I still don't know why, nothing showed up on his autopsy, so I knew the power of the mind was something not to be messed with.

Later that afternoon As Aveling entered my surgery, as always I smiled as I said hello, she replied with a quick hello, then she just walked on into the other office.

CLICK… Tape on…

Well, doctor there was nothing to stop them as they continued, I thought about going down stairs, pretending to go to the toilet but I knew mum could still be up nursing the baby I didn't want to worry her with anything, so I decided against it, so I just curled up in my bunk trying my best to shut out there conversations, by covering my ears with my hands again,. Now doctor I did think twice about telling you about Pam.

I didn't even know if I could bring myself to say such things on this machine, but you did say I had to be honest, and talk about anything that caused me well you know doc, things I would not, or could not, tell anyone face to face, so I do apologize to you doctor, so if I am over stretching the mark, and you would prefer me to, leave things of a sinister and abusive nature out, please tell me now doctor, because things are only going to get harder, and harder to listen to, because as Pam got older her choice of profession, reading a man's palm would often lead to much worse. As I don't want you to feel uncomfortable, because I know how I felt, as I was trapped in that bedroom with the two of them, telling some off the most disgusting stories.

I had remembered doctor Valerie, one day at our local library I started to read a book called little women, but after just few chapters, I had understood it was set in a time when evil things happened, but the book just didn't seem to care about those things, with its family of giggling girls, the perfect sisters, it was as far from the reality, of my life, it just seemed so genital, well I am sure you know what I mean doctor, now I wasn't sure if it was because I had grown up to quickly, or if it was the author who had not fully seen the world in all its filth, and evil vile monsters that now parade around in my head. But maybe if I had read it all, it would have at some point taken a more lifelike turn.

But it wasn't my cup of tea as they say, so I would choose books, with less dainty stories, and more modern stories, I liked the murder mysteries, but just saying that on this tape just now made me snigger, as I thought to myself it's not just reading those stories anymore, but I was now living one of my own.

So then Pam just continued, "Anyway where were we Rennie, before that little bitch interrupted me." "Oh I remember I was telling you to never settle for a life like mums, if you want money, there's more than one way to get stupid men to just give it to you.

"so uncle told me he would give me more money the next time I turned up but he then said, the more men I sucked in, the more money I can make, and it doesn't bother me, if the men are so gullible that's their fault not mine, he says he will collect the money then he will make sure I am well looked after. So I am going back next week. 'But I have told him in no uncertainty she was not going to do any women, they just didn't want to pay as much as the men", and were not so keen to believe her farfetched stories, she seemed so proud of what she was doing, to me it seemed so disgusting, well I am not too sure doctor, but I think there is a name for men that take advantage of young girls getting then to do such things, it's just not normal, but no one would listen to me.

Pam had been doing it all summer, just disappearing, and sometimes in the middle of the week. uncles friend made up a story that his girl-friends, sister had a new baby, and they needed Pam for babysitting, so they often picked her up mid-week, but I knew what Pam was doing, it was some months later when she arrived home she wasn't happy.

Rennie asked her what had happened, but again she said she would tell her later, and as always when they thought I was a sleep, Pam told Rennie that one of the men had pushed her hard against the table because she told him his father was not his real father.

The following week she disappeared as always, but when she came back it was a day later, it was clear she had been very unhappy, Pam was so upset, Rennie again asked what had happened, later that night in bed, as always she started to tell Rennie all about it, Pam s face was black around the eyes, her lip was split, when she arrived home that day she managed to stay out of mums sight, but there was no mistaking someone had beaten her,

Pam told Rennie it had been uncle's idea, if she let some of the men do things to her, you know what I mean don't you doctor, things I am not allowed to talk about, but I think Pam had turned eighteen that summer, and didn't care what she did any more, but I knew my sister, there was no way any man could get her to do anything she didn't want to do.so she must somehow have allowed it to happen, I had heard stories about how some men liked to beat up on women, and how some women encouraged it to happen, it's just mad doctor, it doesn't make any sense in my mind at all, so at first I didn't want to believe it. But she was now coming home with such a lot of money she was hiding it all over the bed room so I knew it wasn't just palm reading any more.

She would go on spending sprees, buying new things, even hiding new cloths, under her bed so there was a strange atmosphere in the bed room. Pam told us we needed to keep the bedroom so clean, that mum would have no need to enter it. So when I say us Doctor, Pam and Rennie looked directly at me, so I knew who would be doing all the cleaning.

Now Pam was a very, well there is no kind way of saying this, but ever since she started getting so much money that summer, she had such a sweet tooth, she would buy large amounts of chocolate, and sweets and it started to show, so by the time she reached her eighteenth birthday her clothing size was a ladies size extra-large, and even when her cloths always looked tight, she insisted they would fit, sometimes forcing them on, she was definitely getting fatter, by the month

Now the night she stayed out all night the first time, she sent a message home by ringing mums friend who let mum know, Pam was helping out babysitting,

She was after all supposed to be babysitting. But Pam was telling Rennie that, that night seemed a bit of a blur, When Pam asked Uncle Ben about what had happened the night before, uncle said she had been drinking his whisky in the orange juice, "I told him I remembered, some very strange things happening to me, "uncle Ben said it was rubbish," he told me I had just had too much to drink, but I told uncle Ben, I remembered doctor Hanger being in the room, and my legs being pulled up, then I remembered sitting up because I could feel so much pain, between my legs and I swear Rennie, I thought I saw a tiny baby on the bed",

Pam went on to tell Rennie, "That she didn't know what to think.im just confused, I haven't told mum anything, best not to", So at last maybe Pam had finally had seen some sense.

Then a few weeks later uncles brother called, and asked mum if Pam could babysit that weekend, I saw Pam s face I thought she was going to say no, but instead she said she would only baby sit again if they gave her a lot more money, and again on her return she could not wait to tell Rennie all about it.

But things had changed, uncle had told her now she was eighteen they would have to be extra careful, because the gossip was getting around, and some of the punters wife's had been spreading rumors about, "well you know doctor nasty rumors. "It had all got out of hand when Pam had agreed to make a movie, uncle had told her the money was unbelievable, but when I say movies doctor, these were not the kind of movies, that were on the television, but well, if what Pam told Rennie that summer, they were movies involving, multiple men,

But nothing was going to stop Pam from getting all that money, they had promised her so much, she found it impossible to turn down, now it was then I heard her trying to get Rennie to join her. Again Pam explained to Rennie she could earn so much money, uncle said he would pay her extra, as she was still a virgin, she could earn so much if she agreed to do a movie with Pam, the money they earned would be enough to set them up for life, well doctor I don't want to say, this but if Pam was earning so much money, why did she never give mum any to help with the bills, or she could have helped mum, to buy the boys some new winter boots, but she to the best of my knowledge never gave mum a penny.

But has I lay hiding under my blanket, as they discussed it, Rennie said she just couldn't ever do such a horrible thing, but Pam had no problems trying to persuade her with so much money, she could buy anything she wanted, now I didn't know for sure, what Rennie was doing, but she too started to, simply disappear mid-week then turn up with huge amounts of money, but she at least gave mum some money, she said she had a part time job at the local supermarket, and who was I to say anything different,

It was a little while later, I found what the movies were really being made for, yes they were being sold to some very vile, and evil men, but the real reason was, to blackmail, some of the punters who had been coaxed into appearing in them, I believed some of the men must have known, and others trapped into it, so now I knew what all the palm reading had lead up to, it was just an evil way to blackmail people.so doctor tell me why did some people get away with such evil things,

But it was about that time uncle had stopped asking mum to send any of us over to play the sixpence game. But now he had Pam doing whatever he asked her. Things had changed. That summer I didn't know how to feel, my emotions were all over the place, I wanted to tell mum everything, because I didn't want to share a bedroom with Pam any more, but with no space in the house to move to, I was stuck,

Now the two of them seemed to tell each other everything, but what Pam didn't know is that Rennie had a new boyfriend, I knew this because I had caught them kissing in the back seat of his car, she asked me not to tell Pam, so I promised that I wouldn't. after all a promise was a promise, well to me any way, everybody I ever told a secret to always told others, so I quickly learned tell no one a secret, as for me, my promisers were my bond my word. I guess that was something I had picked up watching all the old movies. as they say silence is golden.

I was disgusted with what I heard Pam telling Rennie, but she went on babysitting most of the year sometimes mid-week and most holidays she would stay over at that house, later that year I overheard her, telling Rennie that, she had some of the punters eating out of her hands, again that is when. they had offered her so much money to do an unforgivable thing.

But with all that money at stake she didn't want to say no, I wasn't sure I fully understood what I had heard next, because I was half asleep that night, but from the little I did hear, it sent a cold shudder down my spine, she said that one man wanted another man dead, and she was to help to arrange it, now I did think at first, I needed to tell the police, but what could I tell them, only that I had overheard some gossip, I also thought my sisters could be setting me up again, to get me into trouble, by making up stories, after all it was common knowledge on the estate, I was a quite the story teller.

Or did she mean she had to convince anther punter to kill, with her special psychic powers, I just didn't know anything for sure. I still had so much to learn back then doctor? But I don't like thinking about these things anymore, because if they knew I hadn't been asleep that night, but listening to the two of them talking then maybe they, would cause me to have a little accident, now you may think they wouldn't dare, but believe me doctor Pam had no morals, and I wouldn't put anything passed her, so back then my best chance of survival was to keep quite.

it wasn't until I first heard Pam talking to Rennie, about palm reading, that I learned, just how evil the world can be, But I confess I should have not been listening, but it was difficult when all I had to hide under was my blanket, not long after that happened, mum noticed Pam was putting a lot of weight on, mum said she knew Pam had been buying a lot of chocolate with her baby sitting money, but mum decided she was going to take Pam to the doctors to have a checkup the following Monday. When she returned from the doctors it wasn't just the chocolate making Pam fat again.

...CLICK...tape off

CHAPTER 8

ANOTHER APOINTMENT...

'Well doc here we go again…shall I go through."

After Aveling had passed through to the other office, I started to think things over, what Aveling was telling me, the stories just seemed to be getting so hard to listen to, was this all real, or just a teenage girls vivid imagination, it was about then I decided I would transfer the tapes into a written file, just in case any of the tapes got wiped or lost. But I knew I had to convert them, in her words, even when I hadn't fully under stood what she had meant, but I needed to stay as close to Avelings words as possible.

But again it was as I typed up the notes, reading them back to myself, on one hand she sounded like a younger child, then in a split second she sounded like the most experienced woman,

I had in the past had a patient with a split personality, but Aveling seemed to cross not just form one person to another, it was as if she could transport herself from being an adult to a young child in just a few words.

…CLICK..tape on …

Well doctor, telling you about Pam I was getting ahead of myself. as I think it is probably best to keep things if I can in the order they happened, so let me again take you back to when I was younger. back to when aunty Alice was still living with us, I made sure if auntie Alice was in the house when all the others were out playing, and uncle Terry was at work, and mum was off somewhere, Before entering the house, I would always look in through the window, to make sure the coast was clear. I say auntie because that's what we were told to call her, so many of uncles Terry s women were all called auntie. I knew they were not relations but collectively, just given the title auntie.

Over the summer if I hadn't done as she ordered, she would often burn me, Always on my back or the top of my legs, were no one saw the burn marks, she would order me about like her own private slave, fetch in the coal, clean my shoes, make me some tea, when I told my sisters all about getting burned their advice was, oh just keep out of her way. But I never did see her so called brother again. But whenever I threatened to tell my mum on her, Alice would threaten to suffocate my little brother G.G, it's only now I am telling you doctor, and I realize it was her way of controlling me.

But on one sunny summer's day I was playing out, I knew she was in the house but I was just keeping out of her way. She spotted me through the window, I knew she had been drinking gin all day, she came into the garden, 'get inside you,' it was just starting to drizzle but I preferred it outside in the garden than in the house with her,' 'no", 'what have I told you about saying no to me, 'she grabbed me by my ear lobe pulling me inside, now trust me doctor when someone as your earlobe like that, all you could do is get dragged along with it.

It was then there was a knocking on the front door, she opened it up to a huge man dressed all in black leathers, he was holding a motor bike helmet.

She pulled me in front of him, still keeping a firm hold on my earlobe, 'well I told you she was a pretty little thing didn't I, he was looking at me if I was some sort of, well it's difficult to describe, but I felt very scared, has I looked up he seemed to be the biggest man I had ever seen. He then handed over what seemed to be a lot of money, Auntie Alice quickly pushed it down the front of her dress. It was then he said they needed to keep me quite till the pickup arrived, at that point doctor I had no idea what they were talking about,

But I had worked out if they were waiting for someone to arrive I still stood a chance to get away, by now aunty, and her friend had dragged me kicking and screaming into the front room, the man told auntie to keep me quiet, I knew Alice wouldn't be too keen on getting her hand across my mouth because of what happened last time, she knew my bite only too well, as the last time it had left a mark that took months to heal properly.

It was then Alice said, "oh just let her scream no one will hear her", I confess that comment made me worry, what did she mean no one would hear me, it was then Alice said she knew the old lady next door was out, it was pension day, so Mrs. Burgers had gone shopping.by then I was sitting in the armchair with my arms tightly crossed, Alice then leaned in placing a hand on each side of the chair, leaning into me till our faces were just inches apart. "well now let's see you get out of this one," she had that same look on her face as when she would burn me, she then walked over to the window were her visitor was looking through the window.

As I was looking around the room there was no hiding places then I came up with a crazy idea, the chairs around the table had been given to mum by her father, they were solid wood and so very very heavy, I thought if I could climb under, then wrap my limbs around them tightly, if they wanted to take me out of this room, they would have to take the chair to.it was then Alice looked over in my direction, laughing, she turned to her visitor saying to be careful of what he said even if it was just a whisper, as she explained to him I could read lips,

It was then I saw a white van pulling up outside, it was then the visitor turned to me, he too was laughing at the site of me wrapped around the chair, "well well we have a little monkey, "it was then as he lifted the chair Alice was prying, and trying to untangle my limbs from the underside of the chair. as the chair was so heavy I just couldn't keep ahold of it, so as it dropped to the floor with a bang, he held me in midair by my pony tail I was just hanging in space.

It was then he asked Alice, if she had the trunk ready, she replied, "yes ",as she pointed out the old chest in the corner of the room, she had arrived with when she first came to stay with us, but I just couldn't break free, my mind was in over drive, I felt like my mind was like the hamster on a spinning wheel, thinking of so many scenario's, I was thinking is this just her way of scaring me, because of what had happened with her brother, but no that couldn't be right, now I knew uncle had won some money on a big card game, maybe she knew uncle was getting fed up with her, and she had decided if she was going to get kicked out she wouldn't make it easy for him, she was always drunk by the time he came home from work, and I had heard him saying to mum she would have to go.

On hearing that comment, I couldn't have been happier, the walls in the house were all so paper thin, it was difficult not to hear things I shouldn't, and she did know uncle had always spoiled me, so maybe I was being kidnapped for ransom, so she could get her hands on uncles winnings or worse, my mind kept spinning maybe they were going to kill me, all I wanted to do is get away, but in my young mind I just couldn't understand what the hell was happening to me, as he stopped smacking me one minute then demanding I get into the chest the next minute. But there was no way I was getting into that chest voluntarily, as he tried to lower me into the chest again he was pushing me hard, but with no success.

whenever he tried to lower me in, I would place a foot on the top of the open chest, with one foot on each side, refusing to bend., I had been crying, I knew is grip was causing bruising, but I was not going to make whatever they were up to easy, well doctor Valerie when I say I had been crying it was more like sobbing, but I was not going to stop fighting, but all I could do was keep wriggling as that was all I could do, as his grip on me was so strong.

when he began hitting me yet again, shouting at me if I didn't stop fighting, things would only get worse, yes the pain was getting bad from all the slapping and pushing, but I believed at that moment in time, if they got me inside that chest, I would never see my mum again, I cannot tell you why I felt that way doctor I just did. Because I thought I knew what was coming next, so there was no way I intended to stop fighting, his hands were so big, but then when he started to push me again he was pushing me so hard, too hard, I felt he was going to break my bones.

he then decided if I wouldn't go in feet first, keeping a firm grip on me, then he lifted me vertical upside down, by my ankles, like a rag doll, he was holding me so tight by the ankles it must have humored him because he then started to swing me from side to side like pendulum.it was then Alice shouted at him to stop messing about, they had to get me out of the house before mum returned.

It was then I heard the door opening again. And I thought others from the van were coming in to help, All I just wanted to do was dye, by then my mind was so full of fear, I was only young but the other thoughts that had crossed my mind was maybe, they were going to sell me to the, well I don't have to say it doctor do I, because you know what I mean don't you

Doctor. It was impossible to think straight. I tried with all my strength to pull away, but by then I knew there was no escape.

It was then I heard a growling noise, like dogs, loud growling,

It was then my two younger brothers Davy and Danny, came snarling charging, jumping on him, each grabbing an arm each, they started to bite, he stood up again I fell to the floor with a thud, crawling over towards the arm chair, once in the chair I pulled a blanket mum kept for the babies pram of the back of the chair, I pulled it tightly around myself wrapping myself like a caterpillar inside a cocoon I don't know why but it gave me comfort.

it was then I looked over, the biker was shaking my two brothers like rag dolls, as they clung to his arms, but they didn't let go so easily, they were punching, and biting, even though there feet were not touching the ground, till finally he shuck them off, till he was free.

He shouted for Alice, she didn't Answer as I looked around the room I guess she must have panicked when she saw my brothers, and left the room. he bounded toward the front door then slammed it with a bang my younger brothers just wrapped them self's around me, reassuring me I was safe, and the bad man had gone.

But where was Alice, finally when I had stopped sobbing, I asked one of them to go and see, where she had gone. when he returned, 'she's In our bedroom, and it looks like she's passed out drunk again, on the bed. time passed, the boys didn't leave my side, till we heard the front door opening, and uncle Terries voice, 'were is everybody, 'it was then the elder of my brothers Davy went running to greet him, I could hear him tell uncle to come quick that I had been attacked by a bad man.

Within seconds uncle was by my side, 'now young lady what's been going on hear then, 'I tried to speak but when I opened my mouth, I just couldn't speak, the words just wouldn't come. it was then the boys told how they had found me, they explained the big man had been hurting me, but he had ran off, "after we beat him up, said Davy," Proudly.

'where' is auntie Alice ',she's in our room,'he sent one of the boys to fetch her but when he came back, he said, 'she's fast asleep in our room, I tried to shake her awake but she s snoring very loud," Uncle took me gently by my hands and said, "let's get you cleaned up little lady", he slowly coaxed me from the chair, it was then he saw the burn marks on my back,

I guess during all the fighting my dress had been ripped,'who did this to you,' I didn't think he would believe me, I tried to answer him, but my voice still failed me.

"Let's get you a clean dress, young lady". He was so gentle and kind. Then you can tell me all about it, it was then one of the boys asked if he could go to the phone box, and get a police man. uncle replied, "not yet he needed to get to the bottom of what had happened".it took some time before I could tell him all about my burn marks, then only when I was confident he would listen to me, I wasn't thinking straight, I thought it was me that I had done something wrong at first, by not telling him about what aunty Alice had done to me in the past, and I was about to be punished for keeping quiet, so for me It was a very confusing time, but once uncle Terry had started me talking about everything that had happened, I told him the whole story.

…CLICK…tape off

CHAPTER 9

SILENT TV...

CLICK...tape on

well here I am again doc, now I know you will want to hear what happened next, with auntie Alice, and normally I would not go back, but I think you should know the whole story. when uncle Terry had come to live with us, he had rented a T.V, it was always a treat when it was switched on, after tea, when mum had returned home that day, she made us all some sandwiches for tea.

We all settled down to watch T.V, as if nothing had happened, no one was saying anything. After tea uncle had disappeared I hadn't noticed him leave, but when he returned, he was holding fizzy pop, and crisps for all of us, now I had never had crisps before, and I had never tasted fizzy pop. Mum never had money for such luxuries.

We thanked him, and shortly after it was time for bed, it wasn't the norm for uncle to see us up to bed but he followed us upstairs, he first saw me to my room, he told me to say nothing, he would take care of everything, and he had already talked to my two brothers. But he reassured me that this could upset mum, so it was better for everyone to let him take care of it, so I just nodded in agreement I didn't know what else I could do.

Now as my brother's bed room still held Alice, Uncle Terry went in and told the boys to go to bed, he then came into my room with Alice, "its ok Alice won't hurt you ever again, and it's only for tonight she will be leaving tomorrow". Later that evening when everybody had gone to bed, I could not sleep, all I could hear were the snoring noises from my older sisters, but the loudest snoring came from Aunty Alice, she was out cold from all the Gin I knew when she woke up, she would deny everything.

so I slipped out of the room, and down stairs. quietly I turned on the TV, but not the sound, sitting closely to the ending embers of the fire, I would watch the old black, and white movies, till they finished just before midnight, then I would sit there till the little black dot on the screen finished by fading slowly away.

this would be over the next few years something I did often, sneaking down to watch T.V., It hadn't been something I had given much thought to, but over the months if people were facing me I could read their lips, sometimes the words would sometimes appear across the screen in little boxes if the movies were very old. And after all the years with so many smacks across my face from a combination of so called aunties, and my older sibling.

It had started to affect my hearing quite badly, so much so the school had me attending a special clinic for hearing, I had so many ear infections, so my ears were often covered in thick dressing, mum was getting worried I was losing my hearing, she had told my older siblings if she caught any of them slapping me across the face, there would be trouble, but they never listened and, if I didn't do as they ordered, I had often received so many slaps, always across the face.

but for me it was the norm, if the older siblings were asked to get coal in for the fire, Pam would tell Rennie to fetch it in, then Rennie would tell Luke, they would pass down the order till it reached me, so to me it was my choice, to obey the order, or inflict the same orders down to my younger sibling, who I knew would struggle, so I just did what I was asked to, fetch in the coal, I polished shoe s, for me it was just normal, it was the life I was living, it wasn't such a big deal, but I did laugh one day when G.G. tried to help me, he couldn't lift the bucket off the ground he was just too small, so I would let him use the small fireplace shovel to help me fill the buckets.

The next day at school I kept myself to myself, but after lunch a teacher asked me if I was ok I simply said I had tummy ache. so he told me to get off home early. Has I walked home, I couldn't get what had happened to me the day before out of my mind, why did uncle stop Davy from getting the police, nothing seemed to make any sense, the streets seemed quiet as the other children were all still in school, just as I was nearing home I thought, I saw uncle Terry in the distance but he was too far, to catch up to, I just assumed he had popped home from work for dinner.

It was then the weather took a turn for the worse, has the havens opened up, and the rain poured down, with the sky getting blacker and blacker. On reaching the house not knowing who was in there I decided to go around the back, this meant I would pass through the back garden of Mrs. Burgers as I looked up Mrs. Burgers was in the garden hastily collecting in some washing.

She smiled and inquired if I was ok, 'yes thank you,' I didn't know what else to say, has she disappeared into her kitchen, I dragged up my young brother go-cart to the window to stand on, so I could see who was inside. The living it room, it was empty, now I know Uncle Terry said Aunty Alice would be gone, but I needed to check to be sure, so quietly as possible sneaking in through the back door, hoping and praying she was gone.

The rain was still coming down so fast I didn't have much choice. I was soaked through and needed to change my cloths, but she was there, auntie Alice was in a funny position half kneeling forward slumped over the oven in the kitchen.

I thought she must have passed out drunk again.so I crept slowly passed her, so as not to wake her, on reaching the living room, not knowing when Alice would wake up, I decided to hide behind the sofa. Till mum got home.

Now the sofa was touching the wall with just a small gap at the bottom, I had often hidden in there when playing hide and seek with my little brothers so I believed, if Alice did come in to the living room she wouldn't spot me. Looking up at the clock it would be another hour before mum would arrive.

I hadn't been there long when I started to feel very tiered, so I rested my head on my hands, I hadn't slept very well the night before, because my mind kept going over, and over what had happened to me. Had I somehow caused it, by not telling on Aunty Alice the first time she hurt Me., but I quickly feel asleep.

I was only woken up, when I heard my name being called over and over again, as I looked up I could see flashing lights coming in throw the window, from outside, and someone was calling my name over and over again.

It was then someone pulled the sofa from the wall, he shouted to the others all wearing the same uniform, it was a fireman, he swooped me up in his arms, and rushed outside with me, it was then I saw police cars, the fireman took me into the back of an ambulance, they placed a mask over my face but I hadn't a clue why, it was then I heard uncle Terries voice calling my name, he dashed into the back of the ambulance grabbing me close to his chest, demanding answers from the nurse is she ok. I tried to remove the mask, to tell him I was fine but then everything went black.

I woke up in the hospital, I didn't know why, but there I was, and there I stayed for the next few days, no one came to see me, I knew it would take two bus rides for mum to get there, the bus fares were not cheap so I understood, and as always dad was away yet again, but the doctors told mum everything was ok, by getting a message to her via the police. The following week they sent me home in the ambulance.

uncle was there to pick me up straight out of the ambulance, 'it's ok, I'm ok' uncle Terry, 'the younger brothers were there to make a fuss over me, I asked uncle Terry what had happened, no one had told me why they had taken me to hospital, he explained auntie Alice must have been drunk again, she had fallen in the kitchen, banged her head knocking one of the cooker knobs off, causing the house to fill with gas, I hesitated before asking 'is the monster dead,'He then put his finger slowly to his mouth making a small smile,

'She is never going to hurt you again shhhh.

…CLICK…tape off.

CHAPTER 10

TOILET BREAKS...

The weather outside was dreadful as I waited for Aveling to arrive at the surgery, it was getting late, I knew when she arrived I must get her to speak to me directly, I need to convince her we must get some of the abusers arrested.

When they finally arrived, she was smiling, and laughing with the two officers, she had decided to nick name them Tom and Jerry, I didn't know why but when I asked she just giggled.

'come in Aveling sit down, we need to talk, she remained standing looking closely at me with that look of defiance, I raised my voice, just a little, please Aveling we need to talk face to face.'

She started to move towards the back room but I insisted, 'no Aveling sit down here, 'it was then again I saw a different girl looking back at me.

'We made our deal already have you forgotten so soon doctor,'

'If so let me remind you, nothing on paper, nothing to sign, you gave me your word, doctors patients confidentiality. You tell no one, 'she addressed me in that voice I had only heard once before.

Oh and by the way doctor it's a long way from hear back to my prison cell, so I would be grateful if you could request the officers, to make a toilet stop on route thank you.

Once again Aveling stepped towards the back office, just as I was about to open my mouth again she gave me that look, and for once I felt a little afraid, maybe finally I was seeing the real Aveling, and she was to be handled carefully, very carefully, just as my husband had warned me, I must never turn my back to her.

With the door again just a little ajar, I waited listening for the click but nothing. The time dragged on, then coming back into my office exactly on the hour, she then reminded me to request a toilet stop for her on the return journey,

After Aveling had left I felt maybe, I had taken on more than I could handle, now my husband was also a doctor at the practice, so I felt it was time for me to seek his advice, and help at first he was reluctant, but when I asked him to just listen to the first tape.

He agreed, I had asked him to hear it alone, he thought that a little strange, but to be honest I didn't want to hear again how her uncle had pulled out her first teeth with rusty pliers.it gave me such conflicting feelings I wanted to cry, I wanted to cause that man, just has much pain he caused Aveling, the poor girl had to call that monster of a man, uncle.

I know being a doctor how I should feel, but if only I could get through to Aveling to make a statement to the police. I knew Aveling s last tape was hard for me to hear, but I had asked her to say it, as she remembered it, when talking into the tape recorder. But I wasn't expecting to hear, well I guess I just hadn't expected anything like that, what kind of a monster would do something so horrid.

It had been a while has I waited for my husband to exit his office, when he did come out I swear there were tears in his eyes, he looked at me then asked, if he could hear the second tape, I handed it over by the end of the evening it was getting late, but by then he had heard them all.

'ho my god, 'he said, I knew he had done some work with people that had some real mental problems, and nightmare stories to hear, but this was like nothing he had ever handled, after a lengthy discussion, he advised me to just let Aveling continue in her own time via the tape, I agreed. I didn't think If any of those things had happened to me, how could I have written the stories down on paper, for strangers to read, for the first time in my life, I realized that my life, compared to Aveling must have been a very privileged one. has a child I can remember my parents saying that your childhood was supposed to be the best time of your life.

now as Aveling was still only a teenager she was still a miner, and my husband, advised me to bring in someone from the social services to hear the tapes, it did feel a little like I would be betraying her wishers, but it had to be done.as both my husband, and I believed it would be the best thing to do, so Aveling could, at least get placed somewhere she could get the best treatment, and help for her problems. I remembered thinking to myself if anything like that had ever happened to me, who would I have told, would they have believed me, and I was beginning to feel totally out of my depth.

I requested a female social worker to visit, so we could get Aveling all the help she needed. On hearing the tapes the worker who had been assigned to Aveling case, was so shocked, when I played the tapes for her, all she had known about Aveling case, was in her file, but the file had so many redacted blanks, it seemed like we were deliberately being kept in the dark.

But it was only then when the woman said she had another file, that I hadn't seen, but there were still so many blanks. I guess the prison service had their reasons, so all we knew from that file, was that Aveling could be violent, she had stabbed someone, and caused another man to have hospital treatment, that was the first time I had heard, Aveling could be so dangerous, I did think that information is something they should have shared with me from the start, but I remembered back to when my husband had said, I should never turn my back on her,. but this was making my job so much harder. So the social worker couldn't give us much more information, but she did agree this was not going to be an easy case

My husband had completed his surgery so he had joined us in my office. Between the three of us we decide if we were to get to the bottom of this girls demons, we would have to let her continue in her own time, but regardless of what Aveling had told us, she had attacked at least two men, so she would need to be handled very carefully.

And if that means using the tape recorder so be it. We must get to the bottom of all this girls nightmares so we can finally help her. but things were so messed up. I had tried to convince her to let me call the police, to make formal statements to get the abusers, arrested. But it was then she reminded me, what she had told us, was for her, so many years ago, her so called Aunty Alice the monster was dead,

She never knew the real names of the two men who attacked her,

As for uncle Ben she was told by her sisters they would make her life miserable if she said anything, Aveling then went on to say it was for her history, regardless that we were only just hearing the stories for the first time, Aveling also told me, that she hadn't even scraped the top off her stories, it was then I knew we had to let this poor girl, do this in her own time, and as always by the tape, on having heard what I had. I now know how hard it was for her to tell anyone face to face.

Each story just seemed to get more painful, but I was still struggling, in making my reports to the social services, now if I was worried what and how to write, the stories, down, I had heard on the tapes, how on earth did anyone expect a young girl who had lived through them.to put pen to paper, I did now understand why she would only communicate via the tapes.

But the more I felt about what she had suffered, and why she had been sent to me, at that point I thought I had heard the worst of the stories, but Aveling had only just begun, each story seemed more and more horrid, even as a doctor I never believed so many monsters lived amongst us, well I have started to call the abusers monsters, as that is the word Aveling refers to them has. I was also feeling a little ashamed of myself, for forcing this girl to remember the nightmares, she had tried so desperately to forget.

CHAPTER 11

BANK HOLIDAYS...

There had been a bank holiday, Aveling hadn't been seen for a week so when she finely turned up, she said hello it was like I had gone back to the beginning, as when she entered the office her chin was down, and as I tried to make eye contact she looked away, like she had done the first day I met her, she then went directly into the back office, it was a good few minutes before I heard that distinctive click.at first I thought she most have found out from someone that I had betrayed her secrets, but no it was me, I was just feeling paranoid, but there was just something on that day that made me feel uneasy.

As she began her voice was quiet and soft, I tried to get on with making out prescriptions and writing up my notes, as I always did when she was in the back office, but for some reason that day it was more difficult than normal.

Click...TAPE...ON...

Well doctor hear I am yet again, I have started hating coming here, and relieving my past, it's the past for a reason, and should be left there. But I know if I am to get the hell out, of that god forsaken prison cell, I am sharing with a real schizoid then hear I am.

Well doc it was the start of the summer, and we had just broken up from school, my school uniform has been cleaned and put away. The only thing left was my black pumps all the other footwear had simply fell apart

65

due to the fact, they had started as my eldest sisters, Pam s then Rennie, before I had to wear them, so they were now just to worn out to wear.

So mum had thrown them away. Now I would be eleven that summer but I deiced I didn't want to be a girl anymore, and mum was struggling finding me something to ware, 'it's ok mum I can ware Luke s old trousers he's finished with them,'as the younger sibling were all too small for them.

But they would fit me, if I tied them up around the waste with some string, mum smiled at me,' ok young lady if that's ok with you, 'Luke was my eldest brother, and one of the most horrid boys anyone could ever meet, but I think I have told you that before doc but anyway, often when we arrived home from school for tea, we would have had free school dinners because mum couldn't afford to pay for them. I at that time didn't give it much attention, but thinking about it now.

what did dad do with all his money because, I knew for sure he wasn't giving much to mum, has we had always been counting the pennies, I also remember poor mum asking her dad for money, so I knew things were difficult for her. Mum never smoked, never drank, so every penny she had went to feed us kids.

on returning home for tea, we would each be given two slices of bread with jam or just marge, for tea at weekends when mum had gone to the market, if she went late in the day when the stalls were all closing down, mum would get cheap bananas and fruit, and sometimes when she could afford it, she would get a box of broken biscuits but that was always a special treat, I loved it when mum got the bananas we would mush them up for our sandwiches and that was always a treat at the weekends.

But when I was younger I never had a big appetite and my two younger brothers and GG, were always famished, so after mum gave us our sandwiches cut into four quarters I would give them each one of my quarters, then at bed time we would get a drink plus a few broken biscuits, then a drink of tea in the morning, and our next food would be the free school dinner,

It was on a Saturday when mum had just returned from the market she made our sandwiches Luke always got three slices of bread as he was older. I had been playing outside with my two younger brother's Davy and Danny, they had been born just nine months apart in the same year, everyone believed they were twins. but to me they would always be little supermen,

Mum called us in for tea,'wash your hands or there will be no treats after,'there was only one sink in the house in the kitchen so we had to take turns, that day the only soap was a chunk of green slimy thing mum washed everything with. after washing we went into the front room to sit at the table, mum had always insisted we may not have a lot of food, or money, but we would always have good manners, as I was washed up first.

I picked up my sandwich and went through to the living room, to the table Luke was smirking but I didn't know why, until I picked up my sandwich and took a bite, it was then I tasted dirt, looking at my bread it was crawling with live worms, Spitting it out as quickly as I could Luke just stood there laughing,

I dashed into the kitchen just as my two younger brothers had finished washing up. I grabbed the bar of soap, and began washing my mouth out with it, still spitting and gagging to be sick. Mum asked what the hell was going on, it was then Luke came into the kitchen telling mum, that I was just being a baby, and worms wouldn't poison me. but mum didn't share his sense of humor. mum very rarely got angry, but on that occasion she sent him to the bedroom, that meant he wouldn't be allowed back down till morning, this meant he would miss his favorite tv show the man from uncle.

After that I lost my appetite, and would only pick at my food eating very little, but only then after I had examined it fully. Luke was just evil, a monster, he would get fireworks, and tie them to the cats tails just to see how they would react when he lit them, his sick mind had no end to it, and telling you hear and now doctor the things I saw him do, not just to animals, but he would play the most awful tricks on our younger brothers.

It would take me forever, to explain to you, they say children who behave like him, are born that way. But all my other brothers would never dream of doing the evil, and vile things Luke does. so I guess it's true what they say. Luke was born that way, but I had no intentions of letting him get away with hurting my little brothers.

But Luke would have his revenge for missing his favorite T.V show, and he told me in no uncertainty, that he would have is revenge, and I wouldn't see it coming. Now that brother of mine was getting worse with his nastiness, but I knew I needed to be very careful, whenever he was around.

He seemed to have collected over the years, a group of other boys around him, who seemed to think he was some sort of roll model, he had them well trained, so if he wanted anything, he would go to the local stores, then it was his job to distract the store owners, while one of the younger boys, would steel for him, they always targeted cigarettes, at first I think they were steeling them to order to sell. But it wasn't long before Luke started to smoke himself, every time he lit one, I could still smell burning flesh, was I ever going to get that smell out of my nostrils. He seemed to think smoking made him look all grown up, and smarter than the rest of us. But to me he would always be my nightmare of a brother, a monster who needed to be caged, after all isn't that what you do with monsters.

…CLICK…tape off…

CHAPTER 12

THE REVENGE...

Now on Aveling s next visit to the surgery, has always never knowing where she would start, I was surprised she picked up where she had left off.

Talking about her brother Luke, I knew if anyone, who would behave like that to his own sister, probably needed to be having counseling more than Aveling, this wasn't going to be the last time Aveling would be referring to his hatefulness, but I now did understand why she felt the way she did about Luke.

CLICK…tape on…

She explained that summer she had decided to dress as a boy, it was the early sixties and she wanted her mum to let her have her hair cut short, but her mother wouldn't hear of it, so Aveling asked her grandfather for his old flat cap, and he was only too happy to let her have it.

So all summer long she hid her hair beneath it. 'Now I know what you are thinking right now doc, because everybody who knew me told me, that I looked ridicules but. At the start of that summer my bust was hardly noticeable, and in the trousers my hair hidden, it was amazing how many people I did fool. Now during the summer Luke, and his friends would play cricket on the common field, at the rear of our home.

they often needed extra players. I asked to play but they, in no uncertainty said I couldn't play because I was a girl, so I would sit and watch.it was well into the summer when they were joined by a new boy Jack, then one day when the ball came across the field it landed at my feet, I picked it

69

up returning it directly at the stumps knocking off the bails, the new boy called me over,' can you do that again,' he asked me, but this time let's see if you can throw the ball over hand, and at those wickets at the other end.

I asked if he wanted to put a player in to try to stop me from knocking off the bails, ok was his reply, so I ran up bowled directly at the wicket, it shot straight passed the batter downing the stumps,' 'ok Luke why didn't you tell us your kid brother could play like this, 'if you could have seen Luke's face doctor he was fuming, 'don't be stupid that's not one of my brothers it's my crazy sister.'

"Look Luke we are short of players, so if she can down the bails again, with the next two balls she is on the team," he then called the rest of the players on the field that day, for a team chat, I knew they would be playing another team the following week, and desperate for a baller, so Luke was out voted, and I was on the team, as long as I could keep my hair hidden, has the other team would never allow a female on the pitch.

But all too soon the summer was coming to an end. Mum started to get out my school cloths but nothing fitted, during the summer I had to cut out the toes in my pumps because they were too tight, so mum looked through the old cloths in the cupboard, but nothing fitted, so she would have to take me down town to get some cloths, but when she tried to get a dress out for me to where into town, everything was too short.

Never mind we can look for a dress in town also, you can't dress in those trousers and cap, forever they do seem to have got very shabby over the summer, they are more than ready for the rag bag, So it was a trip down town, to buy some new cloths, now when I say new, I meant new to me, we never bought new cloths, but mum knew of a shop that sold good secondhand clothes.

when we arrived mum rummaged through the piles till she found something to fit me, they had a back room to try things on, but after I removed my old trousers and cap the assistant smiled at me,' well young lady you sure fooled me '.it wasn't till I removed my top my mum gasped oh dear young lady you are going to need a bra to, I looked down to see what she meant. Now I know, this sounds crazy doctor, but I hadn't realized how big my breast had grown that summer it was, then the assistant pulled out a measuring tape.

My my young lady you are a thirty six inch bust, with such a little waist, mum returned to the piles of cloths. But it wasn't long till I had my new dress, and school skirt, and blouse, mum even found some shoes, and they had very little ware I was so happy with my new things, but still in a little shock about my bust I knew some day they would grow but never that quickly, I had only just had my twelfth birthday that summer.

I didn't like the thought of having something my school mates seemed obsessed with, I knew at some time when school restarted, it wouldn't take long before the girls would want to compare tits, to me this seemed crazy, after all we are given what god gives us, but if I am honest I would have preferred not to have any tits at all, And as for wearing a bra it just seemed so strange, the elastic cut into my skin, It just didn't fit right, but I think the worse was the hook in back, I just couldn't seem to get them hooked up correctly.

it was about then, I heard on the news about a group of women had decided to burn their bras, well it was the swinging sixties, it seemed to me the right idea, mum was watching the same news report, so when she looked directly at me she said, 'now don't you get any crazy ideas Aveling those bras, may have only been second hand, but they cost me too much money just for you to burn. Mum was right that had been exactly what I had been thinking, oh how I wish I had been born a boy.

It was there on that day Aveling paused, the tape continued to run but Aveling had nothing more to say. Then the tape ran out

...CLICK...tape off

CHAPTER 13

MONSTERS AMONG US...

Now Aveling had been arriving with two officers, but on the next occasion there was only one, Tom was running late, apparently Aveling was being a perfect prisoner, and hadn't tried to run away in months. but by the time they had arrived at the surgery, Aveling just as soon as she realized there was just one officer that day, has he was driving, she decided to jump out when they reached the traffic lights, but Aveling hadn't got far when a member of the public caught her. Tom was livid with her, if he had lost her, he wouldn't have stood a chance in hell of getting his promotion.

Officer Tom told me the whole story, but asked me not to put it into her notes as he felt so embraced. But I could see on his face just how angry he was with Aveling, so after she passed me, I asked her to wait, in my main office, before going into the back office, I then had just a small chat with Tom, I couldn't say much because of being Avelings doctor, my hands were tied, but I did explain her life had been a true nightmare.

so I asked him to be, just a little more forgiving, he responded with a grunt, Tom did say he would not allow Aveling to get away with that again, so he was going to insist the next visit he would have his partner with him, he also said if she caused any more problems for him, he would use the handcuffs on her, now I knew that would be a very bad idea, it could cause her to refuse any more treatments, causing her to shut down completely.

As Aveling entered with a distant look on her face, that day I had no assumptions as to where she would pick up, or even start the next tape, but before she tried to pass me into the second office I wanted to ask her, why she had tried to escape. "honestly doctor don't you know, I thought you of all people would understand what it is like for me to be held in a cell locked up, I just wanted to be free to sleep under the stars, and wonder the world in my dreams, freedom is all I think about.

but trust me doctor, when I say I need to be released, because I am after all innocent I could never do what they are acquiescing me of, don't you know I only ever do gods work, that was the first time Aveling would mention doing god's work, "I hadn't understood her fully that day but I do now. It was then she continued into the back office, but after she sat down again there was that distinctive sound. Click.

…CLICK…tape on.

now doc on that last weekend of that summer, I had always known what an evil, son of a bitch my brother was, but that weekend he went over the line, now I know doc I shouldn't swear, mum always pulled me up at the weakest of swear words, telling me I will never be a lady if you use those kind of words, now I know I was naive, but my poor mum.

I didn't know back then that she was only fifteen when she got pregnant by my farther, and her mother having been so ill for such a long time, my poor mum, she had no knowledge of sex, it simply wasn't talked about back then in the forties, and the only discussion I had with her about sex, was about a group of women, who hanged about on the street corner I asked her why the group of ladies, and girls that had collected at the end of the street, always shooed me on, when I got close to them.so finding herself pregnant at fifteen my grandparents insisted mum got married. So her explanation of the ladies at the street corner, started like this,'

'now Aveling you know when a lady is a lady, because you will never hear her swearing, and you will never see a lady standing on a street corner, and you must promise me you will keep well away from them. ' "I promise mum", and that was that.so if I wanted to know anything about sex, the older girls at school were only too keen to explain, but believe me doctor there explanations, were to my ears so bazar. I never wanted to ask my older sisters, as their actions to me were not that of ladies.so I believed when I need to know the truth, it would come has I grew older, but only then, when god wanted me to know, has I had always believed he had my Destiney firmly in his hands,

Now that last weekend of the summer holidays, the boys were playing cricket, and I was invited against my brother's wishers, to join them, we won easily, once again dad had been working away. It was Saturday mum was down town and wouldn't be back till the six a clock bus.

After the game, Luke invited some of the boys to come home to our house for a drink, there was the new boy Jack, he must have been about sixteen, Luke was in the same class with Luke and the other boys at school,

Now when mum, and I got home, the day she had bought my new cloths, Luke had been in the living room listening, when mum was discussing with my two older sisters the problem about my need for a bra.

When we arrived at the house Luke and the other boys were whispering, the older of the boys then gave my two younger brothers some money to go to the shop, and get some sweeties.at first I thought how kind,

But just as soon as the younger boys left, Luke lunged at me pulling my tee-shirt up over my head. 'well boys what did I tell you one pair of big boobs,' I was desperate to pull my shirt back down, but before I could Luke asked his friends, 'anybody want a photo, I was still wrestling with Luke to get control of my top, Luke then throw me to the floor, kneeling down behind me pinning me to the floor with his knees on my shoulders, now I knew Luke did not like me joining the cricket team so any chance he could he would make life difficult for me. now I had always been a fighter but mum had made me promise, if anyone started a fight I needed to just walk away.

just because they wanted to fight it didn't mean you had to, but this time Luke was going to wish, he had left me well alone, I was getting to that age where I wasn't a little girl anymore I was a young woman, but Luke just had a way to make my blood boil, and this time he was going too far, so it was time for him to find out, just because I was, as dad always said, a member of the weaker sex, girls don't fight because they don't know how to.

So now my blood was boiling with everything that had happened to me in the past often without finding out why, I had taken it upon myself to learn, and unbeknown to Luke I had been taking lessons from a friend, who knew some very good defense moves, but also how to attack, now if I am being honest doctor, I didn't like fighting but on this occasion I had to make an exception, so the first thing was how to get back to my feet, that simple action must have shocked Luke because the look on his face was a picture.

But this time he had gone too far so once back on my feet I wasted no time, as I hailed down on him so fast blow after blow, it was he who was now laying on the ground, as he was begging me to stop, but it was his friend Jack who started to pull me off, because looking back doctor that was the first time I lost complete control of my actions, and but for Jack, I can say I just didn't know how to stop, now I had heard someone on tv calling it the blue mist when someone losers control of the situation,

It was then my two little brothers returned from the shop, but as they were about to enter the living room. Luke screamed at them to get out.

I thought it was all over until out of the corner of my eye as I was leaving the room, I saw Luke had picked up the cricket bat I raised my arms to deflect the blow turning my back on him, but he kept raining down the blows. Now using the bat took the beating to a whole new level, all I could do was try to deflect the bat, as the blows were coming fast and furious.

It was then the older boy Jack told him to stop.

But Luke just struck me harder. it seemed like he was making a point that nobody told him what to do. he only stopped when I had fallen to the floor, and that is when the older boy Jack, took the bat of him telling him yelling enough is enough, I was then finding it difficult to get back to my feet, I had no idea of the damaged Luke had caused, but he didn't give a dam, he was just in his words getting his own back, for me telling on him about the stealing, he had only stopped, when he didn't have any more strength left, to beat me anymore.

He said if I told anyone, about me flooring him, I would be sorry, he then went on to say, that when the boys come back next week, they would teach me a lesson I wouldn't forget. "It was then Jack looked at me with pity in his face, I don't know what he was expecting from me, as I gave him a cold stare, Jack then out stretched his hand to help me to stand, it was refused as I pushed myself to my feet by crawling over to the wall, then with my back to the wall shimmering up to get back to my feet. Keeping as much space between me and them, after they both left the house, I had made my decision, this was something they were not going to get away with, and using the bat left me thinking he must have broken a bone or more.

…CLICK…tape off

CHAPTER 14

THE PHONE. BOX...

The more I listened to Aveling tapes I was finding it harder to believe what I was hearing, why didn't she tell someone. when she arrived at the surgery later that day, it was the same routine, but when I started to play the next tape after she had left, it was like she had read my thoughts.

...CLICK...tape on

Well doc you may be wondering why I didn't tell someone, but you would be wrong, when Luke and his friends had finished, I had, had enough,

It was very difficult to walk, just about every bone in my body felt broken, but step by step I made my way down the road, to the phone box it was over a mile away from the house, but step by step, I kept walking. I knew the neighbor had a phone, but I just could not use it, as it would mean she would hear my conversation.

looking back now, I was in two minds, it would have meant I could have saved myself a miles walk in pain, but then with Mrs. Brown listening to every word of that conversation to the police station, it would have been a huge mistake, as she was well known for being the estates biggest gossip. Has many of the other families also used her phone for emergencies.so if anyone said anything gossip worthy, then it would travel around the estate like lightning.

After my first attacks, I didn't know how to get help then, only being five or six, seven. But I was older now, and I knew the police would listen.

at the phone box I knew I didn't need any money, I picked up the phone and rang, nine, nine, nine, it was a lady who answered, so it seemed easy to talk to her, she told me to stay where I was, and she would send a police car to pick me up, the local police station wasn't too far, there were only a few officers stationed there, so the car arrived very quickly.

They returned with me to the police station to make a statement, they wanted to see my bruisers, it was getting harder to breath each time I took a breath it was agony. I asked if the lady I had spoken with on the phone, could be there, so some one went to get her. Her kindness helped me through, when she saw my back they rang for a doctor to come at once to see me, after he had examined me.

He couldn't believe I had been able to walk at all, let alone so far to the phone box, but after he had finished, he believed there were no broken bones, he told them it could be fractured ribs, so he had wanted me to go to the hospital. For x-rays to be sure, but he also seemed more interested in the marks left by the cigarette burns, so when he asked me, I told him the truth, it had been one of my uncles girlfriend but sadly she was dead now, I don't know why I use that word sadly, if I am honest I couldn't have been happier that she was dead, he did give me a strange look.

but the marks were old so he didn't press the issue, I also knew if they insisted I went to the hospital, they wouldn't do any think more than give me a few pain killers for the bruising as for broken or cracked ribs back in the early sixties as you know doctor, the hospital wouldn't do anything. But issue pain killers, if the ribs were broken or very badly damaged they maybe, they would operate to put them back into place, so I knew if I went to the hospital they would want to keep me in for a while,

So I explained I needed to get home, and tell mum what was going on, if I had only known then, what was still to come that night, it was by now after six o'clock, and I knew mum would be home worrying. After a long time talking among them self's, they decided to take me home, but only with the understanding, if I started to feel more pain, or found it too hard to breath, they emphasized to me, to call for an ambulance.

That drive seemed so long, and, each time we hit a bump in the road I felt myself holding back a scream from the pain, by putting my hand tightly over my mouth, just as I had done under the bush in uncle Bens garden. When we arrived at the house, I was helped from the car and down the path, it was then I saw him,

dad was home on leave from the navy, standing there in the door way, still in his uniform he had just been promoted to captain he always dressed so smartly, he behaved like I gentleman, with his clean shaven face, his whole body oozed authority, he would never allow any body to talk down to him, but if you could have seen him doctor, he would wear the best of everything shoes, watchers, he acted like he was the most important person, in the land. With every word he said, it was like receiving a direct order, no one would never dare answer him back.

When he spoke with people, he spoke with that posh accent, I only ever heard on T.V... Now we all knew not to speak, as his favorite saying was children should be seen, but never heard, and disobeying, meant getting a beating with the belt, he had the ability to adapt into any group of people he met, he was the most charming chameleon, in the room, but I knew the other man, inside that uniform and it wasn't a nice man.

He reached out his hand, I thought it was for me, but no it was to shake the hands of the two police officers, I learned over the years this was his way, of making people feel comfortable in his presence, he then invited the two officer into the living room I tried to go with them so I could explain.

But dad pushed me towards the kitchen, saying mum needed some help. I couldn't hear what was being said, but mum hadn't needed my help, she seemed confused when I told her dad said she needed me, it was mum who then asked me to explain what was happening, now I was older, but there was no way I could say out aloud the things I told the lady on the phone, and the police officers at the station, what had happened to me that day it was just so disgusting, I wouldn't even know where to start, my mum to me just seemed such a lady, and in my eyes she always would be.

where would I start, no there was no way I could explain that horrible day to mum, we had never even had any real conversations about anything much., it was to the best of my knowledge even though mum had baby after baby, just taking about sex to me, or if my sisters started a conversation about sex, mum would make an excuse to leave the room, she just would not talk about it, the whole subject seemed to give her a tied tongue.

I told her not to worry dad would sort it all out, has that is what I believed at that moment in time, he would do, then it would be up to him to explain why the police were there, but I was amazed over the years just how little dad did tell mum, she was again being deliberate kept out of the loop. So I just hung around outside the door waiting for the police to call me into the living room.

So I could tell dad what had happened, in my own words. The house was so small, too small for all of us, but as it belonged to the council it was the best they could do, so I shouldn't complain at least we had a roof over our heads, downstairs there were just two rooms the kitchen that included a small pantry, then one livening room, The toilet was outside with the coal shed.so if I hung around at the bottom of the stairs that separated the two rooms, if voicers were raised maybe I could over hear some of the conversation. as I waited, and waited I sat down on the stairs, it seemed the bruising was getting worse, just the effort of sitting was agony.

Then I heard the living room door opening, dad was showing the two officers out as they left, I heard him say. Thank you for coming, typical teenager's stories, but don't worry I will take care of it from hear. Luke emerged from the room with a grin on his face, has he passed me he said, "he told them we had been play fighting on the landing and that I had fallen down the stairs, "I couldn't believe it, when my farther called me in, his tone had changed from that polite posh voice he had just used with the police, his posh voice, he put on with strangers,

Now is voice was raised, it seemed so unreal, has he lifted his hand it came down so fast, he slapped my face so hard, my feet left the floor, as I crumpled to the floor he shouted at me, 'how dare you bring the police to our door, you stupid girl, now get out of my sight, and stay out till I leave. He wouldn't even let me say a word.

Now I had in the past asked mum why dad spoke with such a posh ascent, she explained to me that when he had been very young, grandma who also had a house, full of children had been approached by her sister who had no children, of her own. So she had asked grandma if my dad could go and live with her and her husband, now grandmas sister had been married to a very wealthy business man, it would mean dad would then go to live in a small village down south, at that time his name had been put down for one of England's greatest schools, so when he was old enough he would attend a school, called Eaton.

At that time doctor I hadn't understood why Eaton was so special but I do now, he at that time joined a group called m.e.n.s.a. were he would help set the questions, that would be used to evaluate a person's intelligence, but just after dad had finished his education, he left his aunties house, and went to live in London.

it was then he fell in with some bad people, and it was then he had been arrested, after he had received a prison record, grandmas sister said she washed her hands of him, so after he had been released from jail, it was then when he returned back to live with grandma, that is when he met mum. Now mum wouldn't tell me, what he had been arrested for but I knew it was bad, when I learned he had been sent to the same prison as the Kray twins, who I had read about in the newspapers.

Now I hadn't been told when dad would be leaving to return to his ship, but the next morning mum got me up early, I had no idea what dad had told mum, but she seemed angry with me to, I tried to explain to her, I hadn't started the fight, but she said dad had told her about the horrible stories, I told the police, so when I got down stairs mum gave me some bus fare, and told me to go and stay with one of dads sisters.

…CLICK…tape off…

CHAPTER 15

RUN AWAY...

'Well here I am again doctor, you must be getting fed up with me by now,

And I guess maybe you don't even listen to all my tapes' 'Aveling again walked over to the other office, before I could even answer her. then there it was again that sound. Aveling had been coming to me long enough, so I thought it's time to try again to get her to sit down with me face to face, to analyze some of what she was saying.as she had already gone through to the back office. That day, to start the tape recorder.

I felt it best on that occasion to leave her, but maybe before she leaves, I could just ask her how she would feel, next time to chat face to face, but I was under no illusion when it came to Aveling, it would very much depend on what mood she would be in, but I knew I had got to keep trying, if I was going to get her the real help she needed. Now by then it was becoming harder for me to fill in my reports, so I was still keeping it to just the minimum.

...CLICK...tape on

Well When I was given my bus fare to go to aunties, I decided I wasn't going to go, I should have been starting a new year at school, and I didn't want to miss it. so that morning I had already put on my school uniform when I got up, so I was going to go, I knew I would still get my free milk, and dinner, all I needed was somewhere to stay at night. And thinking about my so called aunties there wasn't one of them I could trust.

Now I know it sounds strange, but trust me when I tell you we didn't have a phone, but none of the other members of the family had phones, so we were for one reason or another sent to relatives without warning, they knew if we said dad told us to go, they just had to accepted it, often just throwing a blanket over a chair or sofa, to sleep on, and let us stay.

looking back now I guess they must have been just as afraid of dad as the rest of the family.so they would never have dreamed of saying no. but I knew for sure one of dads sisters was a prostitute, because she would have a different man staying with her, every time I went, but it was something not open to discussion with me, but after one visit when I had been sent to stay with her, I had to sleep on the sofa in the living room.

,she did have four children of her own, but every one of them had a different father, now on my last visit when I was sent to stay, due to mum being back in hospital again to give birth to yet another baby, one of aunties so called gentlemen callers got up early I was awoken sharply by someone running his hand over my body, I screamed, when aunty came running into the room, he was still pawing at me, when she saw this she picked up a poker hanging beside the fire, it all happened in a flash as she lifted the poker whacking him over the head with such force.

he fell to the ground with such a loud thud, at that time aunty lived just a few doors away, she bent down to feel if he was still breathing, it was then she yelled at me to fetch my dad, and uncle Terry, I did as asked, but when I tried to return with them to the house, I was ordered to stay with mum, trying to remember back, I think I was still only in the junior school, so I didn't fully understand what was happening, but their I go again doctor, straying from why I was sent hear.

So there I was in school as I should be, but I spent most of my day trying to work out where would I sleep. at the back of our home beyond the common field was a derelict farm, but no, that wouldn't do, as my brothers all new of it, as we had played in the old barn, during the summer holidays, it was when I had to change from the math's class, to another, for English, I did remember, thinking maybe it hadn't been a good idea to go to school that day, but there was so few options open to me.

I was feeling so stiff form all the bruising, so I found it so difficult to walk, when one of the teachers saw how I was walking, she called me over,'what's with the funny walk Aveling ',not wanting to explain to her, I simply told her I fell down the stairs at home, and bruised my back,. We'll have you seen the doctor, yes miss it's just bruising. After all wasn't that the explanation Luke had told everybody, and they all believed him, I knew no one was interested, in my side of the story so why bother.

But all the time in my head, trying to work out where the hell was I going to stay that night, now it was a good five miles or more to my dad's parents' home, but I knew there, it should be, maybe safe, depending on who was at home, but I decided against it, as I wouldn't get back in time for school the next day. The walk was just too far, with my body so bruised, but it was looking like my only option.

But deep in my mind I kept playing over and over again what had happened, why the police hadn't taken Luke to the station to make a statement. it was almost tea time, and then I was stuck with nowhere to go. But to hanker down at the school.

now there was a school caretaker, an old man who I believed was a little shell shocked from the army, after the war, he would say hello to everyone, then just return to his office. so he didn't always check all the rooms or toilets each evening after school, now I had hidden there once before, it had been cold, but not as cold as my bedroom.

It was also a little scary, but better than the streets. I at least would have a toilet, I would also be able to wash. the gym had matting for me to sleep on, if I got hungry the canteen often had left overs in the fridge, come the think about it, it seemed to me to be the only option left, so there I was hiding in the girls toilets till the care taker finished his rounds.

But during the night when it got so dark outside, with so little moon light from the window, I swear I could hear children running up and down the corridors, it was like all the children's sprits from bygone days, were still there relieving their child hood memories, if I listened very careful, I believed I could hear them singing, and see them dancing. I knew it was just my imagination, but back then doctor they did seem so real.

But when I was younger I remember grandad telling me, that if I was ever alone, and afraid, just remember grandma was always there to look after me. So as I had ran out of choices, I decided that is where I would stay that night, I would need to be careful not to switch on any lights, and the last thing I needed was for the care taker to find me. He did seem like such a nice old man, but as I have found out from experience, age as nothing to do with the way men look at me. Then tomorrow I would try to think of somewhere else, but if the school was my only option I believe I could get away with it, for at least till the weekend.

But during my hiding at the school, I had been giving it a lot of thought about Luke and his mate Jack there was no way I would not have my revenge. Now I know doctor what you are thinking because it says in the bible, turn the other cheek, I really have tried to be a good girl, but if I was going to be bad, it would be Jack, and Luke who would find out just how bad I could be. Now doctor you may be thinking why I had such hate for Jack, well he could have taken the bat from Luke much earlier than he did, he knew Luke was out of control.

Now I kept thinking about my dad's reaction, it was then I remembered, the year before he had given me a beating, for something I just did not understand, well let me start at the beginning doctor, at school there had been a new boy starting that term, but nothing unusual with that. But he was black, the only black boy I had ever seen.

he was younger than me, now at home time I found him upset, crying, he had a slip of paper with his new address on, but he was so disorientated he didn't seem to know which way to go. I think he had been teased at school by the other children, and he couldn't remember how to get home, I knew where he lived because I had seen the van pulling up with furniture, that morning on my way to school, I had remembered because I stood just for a few seconds when I saw it was a black family moving in. now I know it sounds strange just saying that, but I had never seen black people before. so I was just curious.

now there house was just around the corner from where we lived, so I told the young lad 'don't worry its ok, I know where you live you can walk home with me,'.he held my hand so tightly as we walked home, he didn't say a lot but, when I asked him if he had been bullied, he just nodded his head, I told him if anyone started to tease, or bully him tomorrow, to come and find me at lunch time. I promised him I would stop the bullies, as he looked up at me he looked so sad, he seemed so tiny I think he was only just stating the first year at the school. but moving home at the same time it all seemed so daunting for him.

he was so sweet, when we reached his house, he gave me a little kiss on the cheek to say thank you, now my brother had seen this, and before I reached the front door of our house, dad was standing in the doorway, calling me over, 'I see I need to teach you a lesson Aveling,' 'but dad I haven't done anything, 'don't you lie to me, Luke saw you kissing a black boy, 'by then he had pulled me in the house, by my hair, he had his belt in his hand, and I knew what was coming.

Beatings for me happened all too often, I had learned over the years, if I fixed my eyes on the lamp post light outside the window till the beating passed, I felt for some unexplainable reason the pain wasn't so bad. I know now I was unknowingly self-hypnotizing myself. But by fixating on the light, I could hold in my tears.

now over the years when dad, and he boys watched the wrestling on television they would rumble around the floor, copying the moves they saw on screen if they got hurt, dad would give them a clip around the ear saying, 'don't you dare cry, only girls cry, well most girls would, but not me.

I was never allowed to join in, even if I wanted to, but I still thought it important to learn to fight, so after being bullied most of my younger life, I had learned how to deal with it, and if that meant someone was going to get a black eye, then it wasn't going to be me.so although I wasn't allowed to join in fighting with my brothers, I did learn a lot just observing, but it was then I felt I needed to know more about how to defend myself, looking back it was a good decision.

And I had learned early to never let dad see me cry, always believing if I didn't cry, so I could in mind, if not in body be stronger than him.it was something I knew infuriated him, so when I was getting a beating he just struck me harder, he would snap at mum, telling her I wasn't normal, I could never understand why my dad hated black people, and yes doctor that is not the words he used to describe people of a different race.

I remembered on one occasion, there was a knock on the door, I answered, it was the post man, but it was a telegram from the navy for dad, the post man stated, he could only hand it to my dad, so off I went to find him, he was stripping a motor bike engine apart, he was covered in oil, and wasn't pleased to be disturbed, I explained the post man wouldn't hand the telegram to me, due to its importance.

When dad arrived at the front door he saw the postman wasn't English, or so dad said, he then went on to rant and rave at the poor man, the poor postman just stood there with the telegram in his hand, attempting to get dad to accept it. Dad was shouting some very unpleasant names, he then insisted the poor postman, had to return the telegram back to the depot.

Dad insisted, he would only accept it from an English white postman he then slammed the door in the poor postman's face. But on returning to the kitchen, calling me some very unpleasant names shouting what the hell was I doing opening the door to a black man, was I so stupid?

Later that day the telegram came back with a white postman. Later that week when dad left to return to his ship, I tried to have a discussion with my mum about why dad behaved like that, she told me she hadn't got a clue, but we must respect his wishers and avoid all colored people.it was then for the first time, I saw a look on mums face, what I saw confirmed to me, that it wasn't just myself afraid of dad. I had never seen dad ever hit mum, but then again he didn't have to, with the look on mums face it said it all.

CLICK..tape off

CHAPTER 16

FIRE WORKS...

CLICK...tape on

Now Luke was getting into all sorts of trouble, as he got older he had been caught shop lifting, in town he had wanted an expensive radio, but I remembered mum being so ashamed, that night when the police returned him home, mum never would punish us, but always say, she was telling dad everything, when he gets home, mum told Luke he would be in serious trouble this time, now if I am honest at that moment I took some delight in thinking Luke was about to get what he had deserved for so long. after all bringing police to our front door meant big trouble, or so I thought.

But after dad got back home at the end of his tour, this was one punishment I wanted to see.

now I know doctor just how bad that sounds, but all the same, if you knew everything Luke did do, you would be so shocked, now it was late when dad did return that evening, Luke had only just got home himself, I had been listening on the landing for raised voicers, at first I heard mum tell dad what had happened, then dad told mum to go to bed, and he would take care of this, as mum climbed the stairs, she saw me on the landing, she told me to go back to bed, yes I did turn to go back into the bedroom, but only until mum disappeared into her bedroom, then I waited on the landing, for the fireworks to begin,

But nothing not even a raised voice, a little while later I heard the door open, it was then I heard dad saying to Luke, 'now remember boy next time don't get caught, 'It seemed so unreal.

But now Luke had just turned eighteen, he when dad was away Luke ruled the house, it's so hard some days because the way he treated mum infuriated me, Luke had still been seeing Betty on and off, but instead of steeling cider, it was now vodka, now at school the rumors were rife among the girls, what Luke was getting up to, but nothing he did surprised me, but then I heard something.so vile.

It was low even by Luke's standards, but thinking about it Luke didn't have any decency, or standards, he was just another sole less monster. The girls at school were gossiping about a girl, Luke had taken to the old barn, she must have been in the same year as Luke, but the girls s at the private school were never put into the same classers as the boys. I didn't know the girl but she was very pretty, but Luke was by then old enough to take reasonability for his action, he was by then attending the private university, just across the road from the public school. I was still attending,

Now I had asked mum, why dad was willing to pay, for Luke to attend such a school, but when I asked if I could go also, I was told no, and never to ask again, mum just explained that dad believed girls would only end up getting married, then have children, so it was a waste of money sending them for further education.

but I still at that point in my life could not understand where the money was coming from for Luke to attend a school like that, I did find out many years later, that dad had some very persuasive ways of getting what he wanted. and if what I found out was true, how he was blackmailing the head, and then when I look back at how Pam got men to do her bidding, I guess she was one apple who hadn't fallen far from the tree.

Sorry doctor I diversified, so let's get back to Luke after he took a girl I now know as Gemma to the old farmer's barn, where he and Betty hung out. Now it was Betty who had stolen the vodka that night, it was Betty who asked the girl, Gemma, if she had wanted to hang around after uni, with her, and Luke, Betty told Gemma there would be some other class-mates joining them, but the only other boy there that teatime was Jack.

So Betty as always had been lying. but I don't think Gemma had any idea what Betty had in mind, but it was my brother Luke who I believed was behind such an awful thing to do to any girl, it made my blood boil just thinking about it,

when they all met up in the barn Luke started giving Gemma vodka and orange juice, because apparently you couldn't taste the alcohol, in orange juice, after Gemma was quite drunk it was then, when Luke with the help of Jack raped her, now this was only gossip at the school, because the girl had got pregnant.

so I decided I needed to know the truth, so I waited till after school at the gates of the private school, where I met up with Gemma, I wanted to get her side of the story, because girls could be very cruel when it came to spreading rumors, has I knew only to my cost over the years, I had been accused, of sleeping with just about every boy in the school. According to the gossip girls, but trust Me doc their wasn't a word of truth to that gossip, but the more I protested the more the rumors took flight, so I learned very early on to just how to handle them.

It was called a fist, they soon backed off me, and the gossip stopped. I had often heard dad say to the boys, if you are going to fight always punch first, and make sure it counts, but if the gossip about Gemma was a pack of lies, I needed to help her stop it, the other girls knew not to mess with me, now normally I think of myself as a good girl, but if there was the one thing that made me so angry, it was boys/men forcing themselves on others.

So I believed if I heard the facts, the truth, directly from Gemma, I believed I would know for sure, if she was lying by the look on her face, but I was still hoping it was all lies, but knowing Luke I wouldn't put it passed him.

Now she at that time hadn't told her parents, because she was too ashamed, but what she told me shocked me, after she had missed her period, she told Luke she thought she must be pregnant.

he told her not to worry he could take care of it, by then she thought he meant he would own up and tell her parents, explaining it was his fault, but that was never Luke's style, he even went on to demand who else she had been fucking with, he said he hadn't believed he and Jack were the only two. Who had been the first to fuck her, because no one gets pregnant the first time, I had no idea where Luke got is information from,

Now I know doctor I am in a lots of ways still naive, but poor Gemma hadn't got a clue. now Luke had told dad, not about the rape, only about he had got a girl pregnant.so dad knew of a whore house were the girls would often have unwanted pregnancy taken care of, by Doctor Hanger.

Now Luke talked Gemma into meeting him again in the barn, so they could talk about what had happened, now she had no recollection in detail of the rape, because she had just been too drunk to stop them, so she believed she was in some way just as responsible for the situation as Luke, and Jack were.

But when she arrived at the barn that night, Gemma was having second thought about getting rid of the baby, Gemma thought she was only meeting up to talk thing over, but Luke had already made all the arrangements, Luke and Jack were determined, they needed to get her drinking, because they had already payed for the abortion to happen that very night, with or without her consent, so again they offered her a drink, she declined but he had then insisted, he convinced the poor girl if she wanted to talk about anything, she needed to have a drink with them first.

But shortly after she had, had a few drinks, she just didn't want any more, and Gemma had decided that she wanted to keep the baby after all, so as Gemma was getting up to leave they grabbed her, and as Betty and Jack held the poor girl down Luke forced her mouth open and started to poor the vodka directly down her throat, after she had in Luke s opinion had, had enough they pulled her to her feet, with both of them now holding her up, she could barely walk.

it was then he told her, they should go because someone was waiting for them at a friend's house, Luke told her he knew someone there, who was going to take care of the problem, now Gemma could barely string two words together, she told me with tears in her eyes, she had no idea what was happening, she believed they had forced the vodka down her throat so they could rape her again. Now I believed he was trying to get her to drunk. Not to help the poor girl.

But it was, so when he took her to the whore house, she wouldn't remember how to get there again.

it was only then when they arrived at the whore house, Gemma was offered a drink of milk by one of the girls, Gemma believed it was only milk, so it was alright to drink, thinking it would help her to sober up, but shortly after she had finished the milk she seemed more drunk than, when she had drank the vodka, has Gemma tried to stand, so she could leave, but her legs buckled, Gemma explained to me,

It was then a man entered the room, he carried her upstairs were she saw what looked like some sort of table with straps on. Gemma told me she tried to get up again, but was just to week to even stand, it was then they strapped her down, lifting her legs up high, strapping her tightly into some high stirrups, it was then a man started to push something inside her, even though she begged them to stop they didn't. Gemma also told me that Luke had insisted he wanted to watch, to me that seemed so sick, but when it came to that brother of mine nothing shocked me anymore.

She felt such pain but they didn't stop for what seemed like agers,

Afterwards she just wanted to sleep, but they got her standing on her feet, someone just kept shaking her till she could walk a few steps by herself, then it was Luke who walked her to the end of the road where she lived, he then pushed her in the small of her back, in the direction of her home, telling her to go home, but he told her what to say, by the time she arrived home, she was bleeding badly but she was still too ashamed to tell her parents what had happened that day, so she explained to her mum she was just having a bad period.so she went directly to bed.

now it was Betty who was telling everyone at school, that Gemma was a whore because she had, had an abortion, so the first thing I did was show Gemma some understanding, Explaining everything that happened to her was not her fault,

I told her, no I promised her, Betty would not say another bad word about her, so for the next few weeks, I told her if we were out of school to stay close to me, as I believed if the other girls saw her with me, they would think twice about spreading rumors, as it was by then common knowledge I was someone who was not to be messed with, it wasn't a reputation I had wanted but after a number of fights, I didn't have many friends, and if I am being honest doc, I preferred it that way. I found out very early never to trust anyone.

But trust me doctor it wasn't in my nature to go looking for fights they just happened, so I just believed it was my duty to stand up to the bullies in this world, so I assured Gemma, no I promised her, after a short while everyone would lose interest in the gossip, and move on, now doctor. I just wanted above all else to be a good girl, so one day I could be a true lady. After all I had promised mum. Now I was still a little naive when it came to so many things, but I had learned even if I knew nothing about a subject, it was often more than most of the girls my age, so I would as they say bluff my way out of most problems, to avoid fighting but you know what it's like doc, things just happen.

CLICK…Tape off,

CHAPTER 17

BETTIES DOWNFALL...

"Good morning doctor, is it ok for me to go through," "yes Aveling, but just before you do, I have been requested to supply a medical exam report for the social services, it will only take a minuet," "oh I don't think so doctor, if it is, one thing I cannot stand is people pawing my body, and if I remember didn't you already have this conversation with me, well my answer hasn't changed there will be no exam."

"Aveling we just need to check you are ok," "so doctor what kind of test do you need me to take, well Aveling we could start with a simple blood sample," "and what exactly will that tell you" "well we can check for any disease s like anemia, or any sexual transmitted disease s," "look doctor I am not ill, and I assure you, I do not have any sexual disease so you can forget about it, so shall we get back to why I am hear."

"Now I don't know how many pregnant teenage girls you have seen doctor, but I can only imagine it's a lot, but I can only hope none were due to rapes, but in the world we live in I guess that would be impossible, I have come to the conclusion all men are animals. oh how I hate my brother, now yes doctor I know how wrong it is just saying it, but I have hated him for so long, the things he does are so repugnant, I cannot even begin to list them all, but has Mrs. Burgers once told me god will judge him one day.

But at that time, if I am being honest, I still believed his down fall would one day be by my hands. But first Berry. So doctor if you want me to continue, shall I go through. "Yes Aveling but you will have to have a medical someday," "maybe but not today" Aveling then continued to the back office.it was then I was thinking, is that why she is hear, was it her brother who she had stabbed.

CLICK...tape on...

So doctor it was then time for me to keep my promise to Gemma, I had known all about Betty s steeling, for a long time ever since her parents moved onto the estate, Betty would steel for Luke, so my first stop was to the corner shop on my way home, now I had no idea how I was going to do this, so it was just going to as they say, be one step at a time, I did feel very unconfutable, but I knew I needed to choose my words very carefully but it had been the only way I knew of how to stop Luke from getting his hands on any more vodka.

Now just how Mr. and Mrs. Clark were going to respond to the information about Betty steeling, I had no idea, but Betty needed to be punished. So I paused just outside the shop, looking in the window to see who was in there I didn't want to say anything in front of other customers, but as I was looking in the window, I saw betty with her coat hanging over her arm, stealing yet another bottle of vodka.

I could only guess what poor girl they were going to destroy that night, up to then I hadn't been too sure of what I would say to her parents, but I felt somebody had to stop them getting the alcohol.so they couldn't do to another girl, what they did to poor Gemma. So perfect timing as Betty walked toward the door with her loot, I barged directly into her, causing her to drop the bottle, it smashed with such a bang as it dropped on the floor.

as I apologized, for bumping into her, her mother had seen it all, now Betty was smart so at first, she said it had been me steeling the bottle, but I looked directly at Mrs. Clark raising my hands as I did so, showing I had nowhere to hide such a thing, and any way I had only just arrived at the shop, and the vodka was kept behind the counter.

It was then Mrs. Clark called for her husband, he took one look at the mess on the floor, telling Betty to get the mop and bucket, so it was now or never, to speak my mind so I did, I told Mr. Clark that Betty was joining up with Luke, to drink the Vodka in the old farmers barn, but it wasn't only vodka, Betty was also steeling, cider, cigarettes, sweets just about anything Luke asked for.

.but the steeling wasn't the worse of it, so I described what Gemma had told me but I used a different name, I didn't what them to know Gemma s real name, only that she had been drinking what she believed was orange juice, but Luke had spiked the drink with vodka, till the poor girl didn't know what was happening, it was then, Betty helped Luke to remove the girls cloths, it was then Betties job to help hold the poor girl down, then Luke and Jack had raped her. I confess doctor I did feel very unconfutable even saying those words out aloud, it made me feel so sick inside, but it had to be done.

Mrs. Clarks was fuming, she was shouting at me, for making up such disgusting lies about her perfect daughter. But it was then I told Mr. Clark he should take Betty to see the doctor, as I knew Betty, and Luke were also having sex together, now I knew Betty was old enough, but her parent were very religious, so if anybody needed a medical for sexual diseases it was Betty doctor not me, it was then the shit has they say hit the fan.

It was then Betty flew at me without stretched finger nails, screaming she was going to fucking kill me, if she could have got close enough, she could have caused real damage with those talons, but I had handled worse, so I raised my hands to protect myself, by that time Mr. Clark, grabbed Betty by the hair, has she screamed at him to let her go.

Mr. Clark asked me to leave the shop as I did so he locked the door behind me, but I could still hear raised voicers coming loud and fast, I did think at that moment, maybe I shouldn't have been so crude when I gave them the details of Gemma's rape, but I knew Gemma would never tell her parents or the police, so I had at first tried to convince myself, it was none of my business.

but then if I had kept quiet, it wouldn't have been too long before Luke repeated his actions with another innocent girl, and that I believed would have been my fault for keeping quiet, by the time I had walked the rest of the way home, the police car was already there, they wanted to see Luke, dad was also there, so once I was inside I was summoned to the living room, in the room were to two same officers who had visited after my attack, as all eyes were on me, dad demanded some answers.

Now I didn't want to bring Gemma s name into this, but I told the police all the facts as I knew them.

That It was Betty who was telling everybody at university what she, and Luke had done, boasting about how they were stealing from the store.,that Betty and Luke were also having sex, the police told us they had already spoken to Betty, I remember thinking to myself that was quick, I believed I would have been back home before any police turned up, but I did think the first person to arrive would be Betties dad as he had been furious.

I knew I was only walking slowly, I had paused for a chat with one of the local tramps /or Fred as I called him, but clearly I hadn't realized how long it had taken me to walk home.

Now Betty, who denies everything, about having sex, but had admitted to stealing, I didn't see how she could riddle out of that one. has it was her own mother who saw her trying to steal a bottle of vodka, now Luke said he hadn't known she had been stealing, he also denied having sex, so it was me who was getting into trouble for spreading rumors.

It was then dad said to the two officers, "it was so typical, that I had always caused trouble, telling stories about Luke", Now I was Thinking, this was the same thing, that happening last time, police were at our house, that as soon as the police left, I was going to get yet another beating, for bringing the police back to the door,

so it was then, I asked the officer, I now know to be officer Sam, if he had a pencil, and paper, I needed to wright something down, he took out his note pad and pencil, then righting just a short message, I returned it to the officer after I had finished, the officer opened it, read it, but then he quickly closed it again, dad insisted he showed him the note. but the officer told the second officer they were leaving, and without saying another word PC Sam, and his partner both left.

Now Luke was still sitting on the sofa, with that cheesy smile, he always had when he got away with things. by now dad was demanding, to know what I had written in the officers note pad, I needed a quick answer, so I lied, but dad bought it, now I can say in all honestly that was the first lie I ever told dad, so believe me when I say, I couldn't believe I was getting away with it.

just as I was leaving the room mum asked me to help her in the kitchen, I think that was mums way of getting me out of that room, before dad had another one of his anger bursts, mum knew only too well what dad was like if any one crossed him, or caused the police to return to the house for any reason.

now don't panic doctor, I will let you know later what I had put in the note pad, but for now it's just my little secret. but it had saved me from yet another beating, but trying to think things over in my head, it had been dad who told Luke were to get doctor Hanger. the man who had taken care of so many abortions, so thinking about it, I believed nether of them wanted to say too much in front of the police just in case someone slipped up, and said anything about the whore house, now mum was too close to the living room, so if she overheard any such conversations it could have coursed more problems.

Now I know doctor, you don't have to ask me what Doctor Hanger did, but as I understand it, he uses the wire coat hanger to fashion, a hook like tool, that he users to push inside, the girls then he aborts the fetus, and if I am honest doctor I don't really want to know, all the gory details, and I pray to god it never happens to me. But it didn't take a genius to work out that was how he acquired his name, as Doctor Hanger. But after all the years he had been doing the terminations, I didn't think anyone wanted to know his real name.

But I do intend to fight with every breath in my body, always to try to prevent any man raping me, and trust me doctor if any man did, he would need to watch over his shoulder for the rest of his life, because one way or another I would kill him. . now I know what my sisters think of me, because when I told them if any man did rape me, after I settled the score, I would kill myself, Pam just laughed, saying the best place for me was a convent, and Rennie told me not to be so stupid, its only sex, but to me it seemed, well I just cannot find the words to say, but to me it is something I will not change my mind on, rape is not just sex it's so very wrong. when a woman says no, no means no.

but why did Luke always get away with everything, he always seemed to have, the quickest answers the perfect lies, he was yet again getting away with everything, as they say on that occasion I had to accept defeat. But Luke wanted his revenge, after all he had just lost his nice little supply of alcohol.

It was a few nights later, after dad had returned to his ship. I was fast asleep when I felt like, The very air in my lungs were suffocating me, I started to grasp for breath something was over my face, I couldn't breathe it was then I felt the pillow across my face, I pushed with all my strength, I had even raised my legs to push the pillow off along with whomever was holding it.

now I think I told you before doctor, that I shared a bunk bed with my sister Rennie, well it was a very old bunk bed, so the steel springs from the top bunk would be vicious, if you sat up to quickly, your head would meet the springs, always ripping out clumps of hair, as I knew to my cost on many occasion, but I must have gathered just enough strength to push my attacker up, on doing so he caught his hair in the springs, so you see doctor, it was him who yelped, waking my sister Rennie on the top bunk, has I gasped for breath, Rennie hung her head over the bunk side, demanding to know what the hell was going on.

Now it was then, Luke dashed from the room, causing the door to bang as he did so, this now woke my older sister Pam, and she was demanding to know what the hell was going on, I told both sisters Luke had just tried to kill me.

It was then my older sister told me to stop being such a drama queen and go back to sleep, but sleep was the last thing on my mind.

As I hadn't been left with any marks on me who would believe me. I at that point in my life, I knew my older brother wanted me dead, and he was only too willing to do it himself, I knew that night he would bide his time but I was convinced he would try again.

It was then I knew I could no longer sleep, laying down, so it was then if I was in the bunk, I would wrap my blanket around myself pushing the pillow between the mattress and the wall, tight into one corner, it was a very hard way to sleep, but I always, from then on, I went to bed as late as possible.

always curling myself up into a tight ball in the corner of the bunk, resting my head on my knees, often trying to keep awake as long as I could, just staring out of the window waiting for dawn, after that night the things that were swimming around in my head, were not those of a young girl, who wanted to be a dancer or singer, no more playing with childish dreams, it was as though my days of being a young girl were over, instead the thoughts in my head, were no longer, telling me I was mums good little girl,

The thoughts in my head were, how can I just survive day by day, it was like I was, back then doctor living in a prison in my mind, not knowing when the next attack would happen, I spent my thoughts trying to convince myself that revenge is wrong, as the bible teachers us, but it was no good, my thoughts were consumed with, just how was I going to teach Luke and Jack a lesson, hopefully staying alive long enough to do so.

the only book I owned was an old bible, that the old lady Mrs. Bridger's from next door had given me, on the day she had seen Luke jumping on my dolly, now I had tried to read it, even though I didn't understand, all the old language, but it had the most beautiful imagers in color it was so comforting to me, so whenever I could. I would just open it up and close my eyes, picking were I should start, randomly, by sticking an imaginary pin down on the page, in the hope, god himself would steer me to the right passage. So I could then do the right thing.

now I used to keep my bible under my bed in the hopes, that Luke would not find it, has he would get so much pleasure in destroying anything I owned, I can remember owning a small metal crochet hook, that my father's mother had given me, so I could continue with my patchwork blankets, it had so little value but to me it felt priceless, but Luke snatched it from me one day, has I was working, he then bent it backwards, and forwards till it snapped in two.

but I didn't let him win because I had learned from mum, if I cut a small branch of wood from the bush in the back garden, I could push the broken end of the old needle into the wood to make a new handle that worked, it was never has easy to use has the metal one, but mum always said life is never intended to be easy, but if we looked at a problem, then looked more closely we would find a solution. I did feel at that time, the only thing I had received from my mums, mum was my doll, that Luke had also destroyed, then the only gift I had ever received from dads mum was the hook, that Luke had also destroyed, now if it was his intention to destroy my mind and spirit, or push me into another fight with him, it would take a stronger man than him to break me, but for now all I had to do is keep breathing.

now I had been sleeping curled up for a while, when I gave my sister

Rennie, quite a shock On one occasion she needed to use the toilet, as she slid of the top bunk, In the hopes of not wakening me, she looked at me, only to be met with a blank stare, now Rennie thought I was dead, she screamed for mum, who came dashing in when she saw, me, now doctor, I can only tell you what I was told later by Rennie, that they tried to shake me but, I didn't respond, mum felt for a pulse, telling my sisters I was fine, so they could relax, it took some time for them to wake me up.

I think they all didn't have a clue why my eyes were wide open, but I was fast asleep, but according to Rennie, it was something that freaked her out, but she told me that she would always look when she got out of bed, only to be faced with me asleep with my eyes wide open.

I just believed I must have been too scared to sleep, that my eyes just didn't want to close, strange I know, I didn't believe I knew anyone who could, in fact I questioned if it was even possible, to have slept with your eyes wide open.

...CLICK...tape off.

CHAPTER 18

THE NEW TEACHER...

Well doctor I am back again, but were should I start, 'Aveling you know it's wrong to think about revenge, but what your brother did to you should have reported to the police,' 'well doc don't worry about that, let's face it I told my two sisters what had happened that night, but they hadn't believed me, so why would the police, they already believe I am the estates story teller.

but believe me when I say I have already given them there punishment, 'maybe one day I will tell you all about it, so is it alright for me to go through now,' 'ok Aveling but remember you can come out of the back office at any time, an just talk to me face to face, I am always here for you." 'as I walked into the back office I was thinking to myself, if doctor Valerie knew how I had taken my revenge, she would never let me return here ever again, but for now that my secret.

CLICK...Tape on ...

Now back at school we had a new teacher she was to teach us German, she asked us all to call her Miss Heidi, because she told us her surname was to complicate to pronounce. Now during that first lessen she just kept staring at me, to a point I was starting to feel very unconfutable, I was thinking maybe she knows about my hearing problems.

so she was making an effort to face me when she spoke, now at the end of class miss Heidi called me over, she told me I had surprised her with the German I knew, it was only a little. but often when dad returned from his trips he would try to teach the boys German, and as always girls didn't need teaching anything, because all we were good for was domestication, in fact I had heard on many an occasion, dad telling the boys to keep women pregnant, and chained to the kitchen sink. Because that's all they were good for.

But I knew trying to teach the boys German was a waste of time, they had no interest in the subject.

But if I was in the room it was difficult not to listen, so I picked up a little, but if I am honest the boys were not paying attention. They just did not want to learn a new language.

Now miss Heidi asked if I had ever lived abroad, but I had hardly left Yorkshire let alone the country, it was then she removed some photos from her bag, she told me it was her niece back home, she looked so much like me it was uncanny, then she showed me some photos of her sister with her husband, I stood back in amazement, her husband looked just like my dad, it wasn't till the last photo, I knew without a doubt, this man in the photo, was my father it was only a head and shoulder shot, but he was wearing his navel cap,

Without thinking I said, "that's my dad", Miss Heidi looked shocked, but I think she must have suspected something before she showed me the snaps,

She asked me a few more questions, my head was spinning, how he could be Miss Heidi s brothering law, and also my dad. But she then dismissed it, and put the photos away saying it must have just be a coincidence,

But at the week end when I returned from getting mum some shopping, there was a strange car outside the house, at first I thought dad was home, so I crept round the back of the house to put the shopping away, as quietly as possible, but it wasn't dads voice coming from the living room it was a woman's, as I walked into the living room I saw it was miss Heidi,

Now back in the fifties, sixties doctor, teachers only came to see your parents if you had been very bad at school, it was then I noticed mum had been crying, but when she saw me she hastily wiped her tears, quickly putting her hanky away into her piney pocket. I asked, "What's wrong mum," it was then Miss Heidi told me that her brother in law, and my dad were the same person, 'but how mum, how it can be.' my mum believed with the information miss Heidi had given her there was no doubt, after seeing those photos. mum then asked miss Heidi to leave so she could talk to me, 'now Aveling I don't want you to tell the others ok,' 'ok mum but,' 'no buts Aveling this is for your farther, and me to sort out when he comes home,' but I knew Miss Heidi would tell her sister the truth before dad came home, and I believed somewhere in that conversation my name would come up, so when he finally turned up, it would be me again who would get punished. But why oh? Why, in the whole world did Miss Heidi end up at my school, teaching my class?

It was very late on a Saturday night when dad finally arrived, we were already in bed, but the house had exploded with raised voicers, mum never normally raised her voice, but by now my sisters were awake, and my sister Pam was demanding to know, what the hell is going on, by the time we left the bedroom the boys were all on the landing huddled behind the banister just looking bewilder it was Pam who went down stairs first.

it wasn't long before she was shouting at the top of her voice, yelling for dad to get the fuck out, now mum never swore, but Pam well that was a different matter, I can honestly say I learned words I had never known before that night, but as my name was mentioned, I thought here we go again now I am in for it. then the front door went bang, it had been so loud, it caused the windows to rattle, then the house fell silent, Pam stayed down stairs, as Rennie and I got the boys to go back to bed.

When Pam did return as per norm I got a slapping, just for talking to miss Heidi, then another slapping for not telling Pam all about it, but there was no way I would break a promise to my mum, so it was nothing more than I had expected from Pam.

It was weeks before things seemed to get back to normal. but if I am honest I was hoping dad never would return, but just, then there he was again. One day when I arrived home from school. Mum told me later that evening he had promised, to sever all connections with Miss Heidi s sister, as they had not been legally marred, there was no reason for a divorce, so mum said she was giving dad another chance, dad had also convinced mum miss Heidi s sisters children were not his. now I had seen those photos and trust me doctor, I knew who their father was.

It took me all my strength not to tell mum about Pennies house, but I bit my lip so hard I drew blood. but I would never do anything to hurt mum. Now I will explain all about Pennies house later doctor but for now, let me tell you about my mum.

She had her hands full just looking after all of us day after day, she would wake up so early, make a fire, by the, time we rose mum had the washing machine loaded, plus another line of cloths outside drying, she always seemed so tired, there was never any spare time for her, so I did what I could, but all the time believing if only she had married someone, anyone but dad, but that is some think I needed to accept, after all she had decided to give him another chance then so be it. But I knew then if I ever married, and my husband betrayed me like dad had betrayed mum, well I had better not say what I would do to him on tape doc,

I always believed mum knew dad had affairs, but this was something so different to cope with.as I had learned dad, and his German wife had, had five children together, but it was years later when I found out why dad had spent so many years going back and forth between families. All the German children seemed to be just a few months between our births and therein. some of the photo s I had seen, they seemed so much alike my own sisters and brothers it all seemed so uncanny."

CLICK..tape off.

CHAPTER 19

G.G...

CLICK...tape on...

now my little brother G. G was just about to start school, so mum asked me to take him so he didn't feel so over whelmed, then see him safely home at tea time, he seemed to have grown up so quickly, full of mischief, he was just the most gentlest of boys but he was so much bigger than, the average boys of the same age, now after waiting for so long at the gate, where he was supposed to leave school by, but he didn't show, so I went in and found his teacher.

She explained Greg, had been picked up earlier that day by his mum, I knew mum had asked me to wait for him, I started to panic I ran all the way home, barging in the front door to find mum, screaming for mum, were is G.G. mum the teacher said he had been picked up by you..

Before mum could answer, I had just got a strange feeling as I dashed from room to room looking for him, mum, mum where he is. He was nowhere to be found, ok mum where is he, she looked up from washing some cloths in the sink, she just didn't seem to be worried, but by now I was in a blind panic, it was then dad arrived home.

'What's all the shouting for,' 'where's G.G.I demanded to know, and without an emotion in his voice he said, 'he's gone back to his mother.'

I started to argue, and demand to know where he had gone, now some of my other siblings were there in the room, and they knew no one ever raised their voice at dad.

in fact it was dad who would say.no he demanded, children should be seen but never heard, so as they stood there with confused looks on their faces, I relentlessly screamed at dad, 'where is he, where's G.G.,' but for once dad looked at mum, she gave him such a look, he didn't even return a word he just left the room.

But I didn't give up I demanded mum told me where G.G. was. Mum dried her hands, calmly took me by my hand leading me into the front room, 'he gone back to stay with his own mum. 'I felt tears building in my eyes. 'but mum he's my brother, mum had a look of despair on her face, as she then turned around and started to return to her chores, I grabbed her by her dress, 'and were exactly does his mum live 'there was no way I was giving up, but, she turned to face me, her eyes were filling up with tears, but she said nothing, 'just let it go Aveling, 'as I looked through the kitchen window dad was there in the garden messing with the engine on that bloody old bike of his.

'Well if you don't know, or won't say then he will.' 'No Aveling no, 'but it was too late I charged into the front garden. I snatched the spanner from dads hand he was, to say at the leased, he was caught off guard, as I did so I yelled at him if he didn't tell me, where G.G. was I would ring the police and tell them he had murdered G.G. now just as I expected he raised his hand swiping me clean of my feet with the sheer force, but this time I was not giving up, so I throw the spanner directly at his head, it missed by just inchers, but trust me doctor when I say, how I wanted to hurt that man just as much as he had hurt my mum,

But I had no intentions of letting him get away with just giving GG back to his birth mother, still at the top of my voice screaming you've killed him you've killed him, being on a small council estate, people had started to twitch there curtains, some had even come out of their homes to see what all the commotion was about, by now dad had his hands around my neck, my feet had left the floor as he started to shake me by my neck, mum who had seen everything through the kitchen window, mum came out. She demanded he drop me.

Now I had never seen mum like that, she had always been so placid, but she was by now directly in his face, as she was trying to prize his hands from around my neck, I was barely conscious as he dropped me. He looked around, it was then he had noticed a group of people gathering.

He stormed of inside the house, mum flowered him, as I was still just lying on the ground, where he had dropped me, but as soon as I gathered my censers I got to my feet, a small crowd of people who were there, not one of them would walk through the gate to help me, one younger woman went to open the gate but was pulled back by her father, 'no he said to her, that's the captains daughter,'

Now I knew dad could kill me with his bare hands, but I didn't care all he had to do is take me to G.G.

Back in the house mum told him to take me see to G.G. to put an end to it. She said she couldn't cope with me calling the police again, the shame would be unbearably, he relented ordering me to get in the bloody car, from the start of the journey till we pulled up outside a house we must have been driving a good twenty miles. Without speaking a single word.

As we pulled up there was G, G. looking through the window, I believed and still do he was looking for me, just as he did when he was just a toddler,

Dad stayed in the car I dashed out barged into the front door without even knocking, were G.G. came running over to me, he had clearly been crying his little heart out, its ok baby I've got you, we hugged for so long then as I looked around the house, it was a squalor, another baby still in dirty nappies was crying in the corner of the room. Now I know we lived in an old council house, but mum kept it clean she always made sure her house work was done daily.

It was then I saw her, she was no more than a few years older than me, she picked up the crying baby, she must have seen dad's car outside. I demanded to know what the hell was going on, she explained dad was Greg's farther but her family were Catholics, and it was impossible to have an abortion, at that time, she herself had only been a teenager, so she had been sent away to have the baby.

But when she returned she couldn't cope with Greg, so she was going to put him up for adoption, but when dad found out, he said no child of his would ever be adopted. I found that strange, it was then I started to learn all about dads extra families, as I got older the numbers just kept growing, so he had taken G.G. to mum, and that is when he had turned up into my life. The lovely new little brother who I would grow to love so much.

But now it was time to say good bye, I tried to stay calm for G.G. but I had one last question for his real mother why then, did she want him back now, she explained that she couldn't get any money from the social services for just one baby, but if she had two they would pay her family allowances and her rent.

I felt my guts clinch, how could she be so bloody callous, I asked her if I could come back and see G.G.,but she told me she was in the process of moving, but she promised when they were settled she would send me her new address, but as of that day to this nothing, I never received any letter s, but I honestly believe if any had turned up mum would have burned them, and I never have seen G.G. again, looking back it was then I promised myself I would never let any man take me, and use me like dad had used those girls. I don't think I will ever know how many young girls' lives he destroyed, but whenever I think of G.G.my heart just breaks.

after dad left to return to his duties well if I am honest doctor, he s supposed to be a sea captain, but how can he have so many women, and children everywhere, how did he find time between his duties, it did however make sense, that when he was home, he had never had time for any of his kids, he never stayed anywhere long enough, but it would be his next visit home, that I remember with all the details, on his arrival I had overheard him telling mum and some of the boys he had finished with the royal navy, so he would be home to stay.

I didn't understand why he had left the navy, but mum seemed to be happy about it, I just knew I had to be out more often, and I learned how to keep well away from him. I had Sunday school, then I asked the girl guides if I could join them but they asked for a fee, and money to buy my uniform, so that was out of the question.

so I told mum I was taking extra studies at school, it was a little white lie, I would spend the time at the library reading, some of the books were amazing with full color pictures of ladies in costumes from the Elizabethan times, but the library closed at six, I can remember one librarian asking me, if I would like to take some books home with me, I so wanted to say yes, but I knew if I was late in returning them there would be a fine to pay, but at the back of my mind I believed if Luke got his hands on them, he would burn them debility, to cause as much trouble for me as he could, so taking them home was out of the question.

CLICK…tape off

CHAPTER 20

THE REFLECTIONS...

Good afternoon doctor, can I go straight throw, Aveling didn't always seem so chirpy in fact I cannot remember her ever really smiling, sometimes she would give a little smile always looking down, as she did so, it was as if she was embarrassed, just to have a happy moment. So I nodded as she passed by. But I was thinking it was more than time, for her to sit down with me to have a little chat, but every time I tried she just ignored me, it was starting to infuriate me inside, but I knew deep down the stories she left on the tape, even now would take some explaining to any one, so knowing what I did, I felt the only way forward was to continue to use the tapes. When I think back to my own childhood, I remembered people would say, that childhood was the best time of a person's life, so the damage people had already caused Aveling, seemed so bitterly cold, so who was I to judge her, it was my job to help her,

CLICK…tape on…

Now doctor what I am about to tell you, you will simply not believe, but I do assure you Doctor Valerie it's all true. But I need to go back a few year to when I must have been evenish,

Now it was during school time, that mum had received a letter from the clinic, they needed me to attended for my annual hearing test, now the clinic was in the center of town, so it was arranged the younger children would be left with yet, another one of uncle Terries new girlfriends, with the other children at school, it had been decided that dad would drive mum, and me to the clinic, then after he had wanted to go over, and visit grandma, it never succeeded to amaze me what a different person my father was when we were out in public.

His very persona changed his voice was the most noticeable, it sounded like he was the lord of the manner, at the clinic things did not go to well for me, my hearing had been reduced by as much as fifty percent, so it had been decided that I would need hearing aids, and special help at school. but the thing I remembered most about that morning, was dad telling mum, not to worry I was still pretty enough to find a husband.

After the clinic it was time to go to dads mums, grandma's house, for me this seemed Like a good break from the school bullies, and believe me doctor, when your cloths are shabby, and you come from a poor family bulling was just something I had learned to live with.so there we were outside grandma's house she hadn't been expecting us that day, as we had no way to contact her, I guess it's what you would call a surprise visit.

so after we pulled up dad told me to go play in the garden, as they had something important to talk with grandma about.so I couldn't wait I dashed down the garden to grandads old shed.it was full of some very strange things, items from the war, I wasn't supposed to play with them, but the old shed just seemed full of secrets, it over the years had been a very good hiding place for me. But that day it had more secrets than I was expecting.

As I began to push the old wooden door open, I first heard a loud scream coming from the house it was grandma's voice, 'Aveling come her right now, 'before I could turn around, to return to the house, there I was face to face with myself, it was like I was looking into a mirror so yes doctor you can be confused but not has confused as me, or the girl I was now stood face to face with.

She looked as shocked as I was, I think we both said at the same time, 'who are you, 'we didn't just look alike we almost sounded alike, but for her posher accent, she sounded more like dad, I had barely absorbed her image in my mind, it was then we were joined by dad along with grandma then mum, they instantly pulled us apart, mum was frozen to the spot, I was hurriedly taken back to the car by my father, only to be pushed inside, and told to stay there, it was then I saw dad locking the car doors. now it seemed to be to me they were gone for such a long time before they returned. I had a million questions racing through my mind. The journey home was painful every time I tried to speak, to ask what the hell was going on, demanding to know who she was.

Dad told me to be quiet, but mum just sobbed into her hanky. After we arrived back home mum was so clearly distort, she disappeared into her bedroom, and didn't come out again till the next day, but no one was saying a thing. The next day I had been told to put my school uniform on, and take the younger ones to school, but after I dressed I sat on the sofa, and refused to move until somebody told me what the hell was happening. My dad told mum to explain, as he knew me well enough by now, that when I get so worked up, it was better to tell me. What I needed to know.

He then said he would drive the boys to school. Now the sheer thought of the boys being driven to school delighted them, so they charged to the car with full speed,

After they had all left the house, mum sat down on the sofa, beside me, it was then I would hear the craziest story I would ever hear in my entire life. She promised me that before that day, she had no knowledge of what dad had done, so she too was still in a state of shock.

She started by explaining, still teary eyed, that when she had been pregnant with me she had contracted T.B. mum had recovered but it had left her very week.so it had been a difficult pregnancy, but unbeknown to her dad also had got another teenager girl pregnant, now the family of that girl, was a very well to do family,

.

but they had kicked the girl out of their home, when they discovered she was pregnant by a married man, so with nowhere to go, dad took his new mistress, Amy to his mums house, now as I said earlier, grandma lived over five miles away, so mum with all us children only got to see grandma when dad was home to take us to see her, so dad felt safe mum would never find out about his latest mistress, and that had been the plan.

So Amy would live with grandma, and mum would never know, I think back, it did now make sense why Uncle Terry lived with us because grandma needed his room for her new guest Amy, dad had been grammars first born, and after grandad had died. my dad just seemed to take care of everybody, and everything, now regardless of how many times I asked mum the young girls name she wouldn't say, or didn't know but I found that too hard to believe.

Now what happened was the girl/woman, I now know to be Amy, had gone into labor, and was rushed to the hospital, grandma had sent a message to the girl's parents, and another to dad,

Now dad at that time was still in the navy on shore, so he needed to drive home from Portsmouth where he had been recalled, something to do with his navy job,. looking back I think mum said it was about that time, when she was pregnant with me, that he had just received his captain's stripes. From the navy.

Now has it happened mum also started in labor earlier than expected, it had been at that time, believed to have been something to do with her illness, so she was taken to the same hospital, and of all things, mum was put on the same ward, as Amy, dads mistress. Back then when a baby was born they had the surname put on a little band around the ankle, if there were more than one baby with the same surname it was common practice, just to put a first name if the mother had given the new baby one.

Now unmarried girls would need to put the fathers name on the record, has that was the law back in the fifties, but something not many of the new mums would do, but it was amazing how many new babies were just given the name Smith, Now on that day both mum and Amy, were to each give birth, dads mistress Amy, gave birth to her first baby, a girl, now at the same time mum gave birth to twins both girls, now back in the early fifties as you know doctor, the hospitals were very different to what they are now, everything was run on each ward by a very strict matron. the wards would normally be full of some very young girls, and often more than fourteen patients to a ward well that's what mum told me.

Now on that day, it had been quiet late for mum to have given birth, but as she was wheeled in from the birthing ward to the main ward, they had put her bed, of all placers directly opposite, dad mistress Amy. But it was late in the evening, it had taken dad hours to drive up the country.

so when he arrived he was still wearing his uniform, and back in the early fifties not that long since after the war, everybody would respect the uniform of a sea captain. so when he arrived it was dark, and most of the lights had been switch off on the ward, but dad talked his way passed the matron. he always could wrap any woman around his little finger, now he believed he was there to see his girlfriend Amy s baby, he had no clue that mum was also there, that night.

now having a baby out of wedlock was shameful so most young girls would say they were married, so his mistress Amy was also booked in with my father's surname, now when my farther arrived at the bedside on his right the name tag on the bottom of the baby s cot was correct, it was in fact my mother's bed but mum was fast asleep, he went to first, and purely by chance, seeing the name tag, he had picked up the baby. Amy was also asleep. After all it was quiet late, and they had just given birth.

Now it was when he was holding one of mums twins, he saw grandma standing at the end of the ward, she had escorted Amy to the hospital in the ambulance that day, she had been waiting for dad, but must have just missed him arriving, but when she saw him lifting a baby up from what she believed was another woman's crib, she waved to him, after catching his attention he walked over to her, standing at the bottom of Amy's bed, grandma pointed out he had picked up the wrong baby, it was then grandma passed him Amy's baby.

Now dad told mum he had just been driving over three hundred miles and was to say he had just been tired and confused,. but has he walked over to take the baby grandma was holding, he had placed one of the twins into Amy s baby's cot.

Then as he was holding Amy s baby, mum woke up she thought she had heard dads voice, talking with grandma, so still holding Amy's baby he turned to sit with mum, I guess the shock of seeing mum there on the same ward, would have caused any man to panic, while his mistress bed was only feet away.

After a short time grandma had gone to wait down stairs to give them some private time, I think grandma had been a little shocked to finding mum their also. And when the matron returned to the ward shortly after she took the baby, from dad saying it was time to go, as mum needed some sleep, when he left the hospital catching up with grandma to take her home.

It wasn't till the morning things kept going round, and around in his head,

But when he arrived at the hospital the next day, he was informed that one of mum's twins had died. And mum had been moved to a much quieter ward.

But he kept going over and over again in his head, but he wasn't sure if the right baby had been placed into the correct cradle, but what did it matter really in his mind, all three babies were his. Mum had her hands full with just one new baby, as she still wasn't very well after the T.B. and he had learned from grandma, that earlier the previous day when Amy's parent arrived to see their new granddaughter, they had been smitten.

they insisted, due to grandma's age, it would be better for Amy to return home with them, it was as dad said, for the best. they were well to do with money, to give the baby the very best start in life.

So there we were due to his mistake. when I had come face to face with the girl in the shed, she was my twin, I could not see mum allowing dad to get away with this. But apparently they had discussed things before leaving grandma's house, that when Amy returned to collect her daughter, it would be up to grandma to convince her that because we were both dads' daughters we just looked very much alike.

I knew mum, and dad had been up most of the night deciding, on what they would say to me, they maybe could convince Amy, and her daughter there was a strong likeness, as we did have the same father, but over the years mum had often mentioned to me that I had been a twin, but sadly my sister hadn't made it, so now I demanded answers.

After dad went to drive the boys to school it was up to mum to explain things to me, I hadn't realized my voice had been so loud, so when dad returned I just, told him I was not going to let him get away with this. It was too important, it took mum some time to calm me down.

'Now Aveling your father and I had decided, that your twin sister, is better off with Amy, it would break her heart now, to be told her baby had died the same day she was born, Amy s parents were giving the girl a good life,'

I grew angrier by the minuet, it seemed to me at that time mum was just being to understanding, and then I yelled at mum never before would I have dreamed of raising my voice to my mum, but all this was too much.

'Mum first he gives you G.G.to raise, another woman's baby, then after six years G.G. Was dragged away from the only home he had ever known, to live with someone not much older than me, who he didn't know just because she wanted money from the social services, but now you are letting him get away with giving away my sister, my twin sister. Well if you won't do anything mum I will. So I will be phoning social services on him, I will call the police.it was then I heard the front door closing, he was back.

'it was then he grabbed me firmly in his hands by my shoulders, he held me tightly, demanding I had to understand, this was for the sake of everybody, just as I felt his grip loosened, he went on to say the police wouldn't listen to me, as I had wasted there time before, telling them stories about Luke, he then said no one would believe such a story, on hearing him dismissing me as though my feeling just didn't count it was then, that I started kicking him to make him let me go, I started to call him a bastered, he was the son of a bastered, now in our family the word bastered was a very bad swear word, but as he raised his hand to smack me, mum in an instant flew at him,

This was something I had never seen before, mums nature was always so gentle, it was totally unexpected for mum to act in that way, but very appreciated by me. Then she demanded he left to go to see if grandma had managed to persuade Amy. That it was just an eerie likeness due to us having the same father.

I couldn't blame mum, after all none of this mess was hers, she hadn't known but as I spoke with her later, I said things had started to make sense, she asked me what I had meant, 'come on mum be honest, dad always seemed to have one rule for me, but another for the rest of my siblings, he had always treated me differently,'

mum said she had always thought it was because, I had been born a girl as at that time mum had two girls but only one boy, I just laughed quietly to my self-knowing what I did, dad had more kids than Genghis khan, but thinking back I guess he never did know for sure who's baby I was, it hadn't been till he saw my twin that day he realized what he had done, mum asked me to be a little more understanding, as they had all been so young at that time, what did it really matter.

Oh mother it mattered more than you know, but I guess mum was just doing her best in an unforgiveable situation, but in my mind I believed dad had brain washed her, into believing my twin was being raised with so many opportunities, so everything was for the best.

I had wanted to shout at mum for letting him get off so easily, but the

117

more I thought about it, I just felt so sorry for her, she had been raised into a world, who thought all women were just there to serve their husbands. I had heard dad saying to some of his friends, if they want their marriage's to last, the best way, was to keep the wife's bare foot, pregnant, and chained to the kitchen sink. But I did start to ask myself just how much grandma must have known, but she had told no one over the years.

Over the years whenever I ask were Amy and her daughter lived, mum said dad wouldn't tell her, so I had no chance of ever finding her without getting that information, but one way or another when I grew up, I will find my twin, and G, G. I had always believed lives could get complicated, but dad was right, who the hell would believe me, this story was all too much. Now remember I did tell you at the beginning of this tape, you would find this has hard as I did trying to understand why. Oh why me.

CLICK…tape off…

CHAPTER 21
THE LIE...

Well doctor I would love to get your opinion on that last tape, but I still find it so painful talking about G.G., but knowing out there I have a twin I would be robbed of ever knowing, infuriates me. "Now Aveling if what you are saying is the truth", "well now doctor don't tell me, I can guess you don't believe me, well there you go, no one ever does believe me, so forget it doctor, I sometimes ask myself what bloody good am I doing here, but trust me doc if it wasn't for getting out of that bloody prison for the day I wouldn't be here, and let's face it doc all you really want to know is why I stabbed that evil bastard",

Well that was the first time Aveling had ever mentioned why she was in prison, but the anger in her voice was so sharp, and determined to get me to believe her, but she was right who the hell could believe such a story, I guess thinking about it, it is so strange who was I to call her a liar, being a doctor I had heard some strange things but this was one story, I knew no one would believe, even as I am now putting it down in my notes, trying to convince myself, it had to be true, who could make up such a story, but these notes are just for myself, I only started to put them down on paper just in case the tapes got destroyed.

But these notes just keep growing on one hand I just want Aveling to bring everything to an end and tell me why she had been sent to me, but in my heart I know she had to get there in her own time.

CLICk...Tape on

Now I did have a reputation for running away, whenever Luke had friends over to stay, they would have to sleep in an old army tent in the back garden, or when another one of the men, who Dad worked with was staying over, we were all just told, the stranger was there to help dad

But I truly didn't have any idea why, or who most of those men were, I knew dad had spent time in prison, but has he had been arrested in London, that is where he had served his time. so I believed some of the men must have been crooks, I just felt so uncomfortable, I had on one occasion over heard them talking about the Kray twins, now I did know a little about the Kray twins because of the news on T.V. and the newspapers, uncle Terry brought home.

Now I had in that summer created a new den under a bush in the fields at the back of the house, close enough to get food if I was hungry, and close to the toilet if needed. I didn't exactly think of it as running away, to me it just felt like my safe place.

now it was on one those days I had crept back for food, mum had caught me, she told me to stay put, because the police, were out, again looking for me.so she had to ring them to tell them I was back, but if I am honest doctor by that time, I had gone missing so often I don't think now I was older, they took looking for me as a priority.

I recalled even telling the last offices that found me, they were wasting their time, they didn't half give me a lecture about all the dangers out there, if only they knew about all the dangers inside the house, but what am I saying I told them about what Luke, and his so called friends did to me, the police doctor himself had seen the burns on my body, but nobody was listening, dad said I was the story teller, so no one believed a word I said, so what's the point.

But mum had made me promise her, to keep things that happened in our family to ourselves, I always thought she was afraid if any of the stories got back to the social services, they would take us all into care, I think the thought of that would destroy mum, she lived for us kids.

But the worst was if mum had to tell dad, I was missing again and the police had been to the house again, so I believed after I had been doing it for a while mum just didn't tell the police, she knew I would be back when I got hungry.

but I felt safer out there, in the den with its cardboard floor, and plastic bags woven together to create a roof to keep the rain out, I just knew, I felt safer out there, than my own bed, I think mum knew why I did it, so when the weather was good, she would tell me to be careful, but mum just grew to accepted it, has I had done it all too often, I must have been so young when I did it the first time, but I don't remember just how young, as it was something I just did, I knew she didn't like me doing it. But it was her dad, grandad, who said I must have been born with a wondering star in my pocket, so I liked sleeping below the stars.

but inside the den you would be amazed doctor, just how comfy it was I had woven some of the twigs from the hedge row to reinforce the walls to keep the wind out, I hated the wind, because when it was blowing to strongly, I could never hear anyone approaching, but on most occasions, people would walk passed oblivious that any one was hiding in the bush.

I remembered on one chilly morning as the sun slowly crept into the blue of the most perfect dawn, as I looked up skywards I realized I wasn't alone, when I felt something, it was soft under my hand, I froze to the spot not wanting to look down not knowing what the hell I had my hand on, but when I had plucked up enough courage I slowly lifted my head, to my amazement it was a fox,

He was just curled up by my side, as I stirred just a little, he lifted his head, then on seeing me awake, he calmly stood up and walked away, it truly was a very serial moment. I know I should have been a little afraid but that was not how I felt, I simply felt protected, safe.

Now I know doctor some people in our community, never go to church, so whenever I say anything to do with the bible, they tell me to go and preach elsewhere, but not in such a pleasant manor, no one else in my family ever went to the Sunday school, held at the church each Sunday but that morning when the fox just calmly walked away I felt, the fox had been a gift from god to keep me safe. Now I had seen in an old black and white movie, if you need sanctuary, if you went to church you would be kept safe, not true doctor, I had tried that in the past, even stating I wanted sanctuary, but they still returned me back home, so I saw my little den, as my very own little sanctuary, were god himself would keep me from harm.

Now dad hadn't been home for a while, we never knew when he was going to turn up or why, I was just great full knowing anything I did would not result in a beating, while he was away. uncle Terry never hit any of us, mum would tell us off, when we were out of order, but she never hit us, mum didn't drink, like many of uncle Terries girlfriend, who would spend more time drinking than looking for work, they seemed content just to live off uncle, but after my so called aunty Alice, I would just keep well away from all of them if they stayed over, but none of them ever seemed to last that long.

But on one occasion when dad arrived home with yet another one of his gentlemen friends, mum had never met before, but dad introduced him as a work college John, now at that time, dad was working on the oil rigs in the sea off the coast of Africa, well that what I heard him telling mum, so he hadn't been home for a while. John had a strange accent, that wasn't to me, with my hearing problems, easy to understand, I did try, whenever he spoke to me, but he started to make me feel uncomfortable with all his questions.

He would be so keen on looking at my eyes, he was one of those men who just made my flesh crawl.

it was dad who then said to John, 'I told you she was smart, pretty, but those eyes of hers are amazing don't you think,' it all felt a little strange for dad to be talking about me in that way. normally when he was home, I was the last person he wanted to see was me. but on this occasion he kept calling me into the living room where he asked questions, I believed no father should have, been asking, he asked me if I had ever had a boyfriend, had I ever been messing around with young boys, now I told him I had never messed around with boys, and I never would, it was then I noticed John smiling broadly,

All these question were not like dad, things really started to feel weird when John was having a conversation with dad about what I was wearing, that it was total unsuitable, but they would stop on route and buy me some new cloths in London.

So when I could, I just avoided him. now it was mum, who later that day told me to go hide, and stay hidden in the field den, till she sent for me. If I am being honest I was starting to feel something was wrong but I just couldn't think what.

Now mum had never asked me to do that before, so I knew it was too important well at least to mum, so I did has I was told. But as the day wore on it was getting dark outside, so I wondered if it would be safe to return home, I hung on for as long as I could, but I needed the toilet, my stomach was grumbling so I knew I had to get some think to eat, I thought with all the other things mum had to do, maybe she had forgotten me.

Just as I was about to leave the den, one of my younger brothers turned up with a sandwich for me, 'what's going on, 'he didn't know everything, but what he told me was, everyone had been sent out to find me, but mum had taken him to one side, given him the sandwich to take to me, she had told him were to find me, but mum had told him not to tell the others were I was. but it is what he had overheard, I was more interested in, he had overheard dad, reassuring John, not to worry they would find me in time for the flight.

I just couldn't understand what was happening, now during every one looking for me, it had been one of the neighbors, who had been alarmed by all the shouting outside, as everyone was looking for me calling my name, it was then one of my young brothers, who hadn't got a clue what was happening, told the neighbor I was missing.

so it was the neighbor who had called the police, it was the following day they found me by using the dogs. I was taken to the local station, they must have asked me a hundred times, why I had run away from home. but I had no answers for them, they never listened anyway, I couldn't tell them, I was just following my mum orders, but until I could find out from mum what was going on, I knew it was better to keep my mouth shut, so until I saw my mum I was saying nothing. I was just hoping I had been gone long enough, for mum to sort out what the hell was going on.

Now at the station, after the interrogation with so many questions, my head was buzzing, I had no idea what was going on. They put me in a cell but left the door open, they told me someone had gone to get my parents, at hearing that I did panic a little because if dad turned up, it wouldn't be long till he got me home, so I was preparing myself for yet another beating.

So until they arrived. I was to stay inside a vacant cell the door was left wide open, I just believed has it was such a little station there was nowhere else to put me, my mind was full of questions, but it was then two new officers were standing just outside the cell door, I don't think they had seen me in there, as I was sitting at the end of a steel bunk.

They were talking about wasting all day looking for a girl, I think they had been drafted in from another station, to help look for me, because I knew most of the local police officers, but they were talking about being pulled of another job, I couldn't help, but over hear them saying that someone had just returned from the mortuary were the latest body had been taken. now I hope they hadn't seen me sitting there, because what they were saying was to me, just about the worse story I had overheard,

they were taking about the body in the mortuary, it was the latest victim, believed to be so similar to one of the moors murders, the police now believed they had a copycat killer out there, as one officer explained to the other, the body had been discovered in an outside toilet naked it appeared, someone had thrown a bucket of urine over the child, that had already been tortured, now some of the more graphic details forgive me doctor, but I would rather not talk about them, shortly after my mum arrived to pick me up,

The two police officers that had been talking, and comparing the moors murders with the new killings, were the same two officers, that drove us home, as they did so I got another lecture about how dangerous it was to run away, but because they had another murder out there who hadn't been caught, but mum, and I just sat in silence till we got home.

Once inside the house, mum put her arms around me with the biggest hug, It was then I wanted some answers, mum told me dad had already left to return to Africa, at hearing that, I at least could relax or so I thought till I heard the whole story, it was uncle Terry who had warned mum to get me out of there.

Now I was confused, but it was uncle Terry who had picked John and dad up from the airport, he had overheard a conversation, Dad Had an agreement with John, to get me over to Africa, it was later that day, mum was told by dad it would be good for me, he had arranged for me to be a live in baby sitter for a very wealthy family.

Mum told him no, but dad had insisted, he had already got a new set of papers for me, he tried to explain to mum, that if I was out of the country, then they would never have to worry about me finding my twin. So he was taking me with them to Africa, weather she liked it or not.

but mum was worried, she hadn't believed for one minuet that dad was taken me for babysitting duties, so when dad and his new friend left, to visit someone else, mum wasn't sure who, but mum had decided if she could find, and hide the papers, they couldn't take me anywhere, but not being able to find the paper work, mum decided it would be best for me to hide in the den.

Now Uncle Terry had been out at work, he had pulled a double shift that day, if work offered double shifts, Uncle Terry always grabbed them with both arms, I knew he had expensive tastes when it came to the ladies, but he also gave mum, housekeeping and when he pulled a double shift.

He would not only give mum extra money but he also give all of us a few coins for sweeties, I remember once being told what a lovely dad I had because a neighbor, new to the estate who saw us playing tag with uncle Terry on the street, so he assumed uncle Terry was our father, I sometimes wished he had been.

So Uncle Terry hadn't heard about all the commotion of the police being called in.

But when he had returned home, mum and I were just pulling up in the police car. Once we were inside it was left to Uncle Terry, who had started to explain the whole truth, when he had returned from the airport that first day after picking them up. he hadn't told mum the whole story, he just didn't want to scare her, he hadn't realized they were making there move so soon, he believed dad would have asked him to take them back to the airport to save money, but he hadn't bargained on John, booking an earlier flight, has he was told to move up the extraction.

But now, Uncle Terry started to tell me the whole story, but only after mum had left the room to feed the baby. Now according to Uncle Terry, dad was hanging around with some very rich people, he had been working in Africa but not on the rigs, but he was flying the helicopters from rigs to land, at that time I didn't even know he could fly a helicopter, he always did have has they say, the gift of the gab. so if he wanted a job he always got it, with or without the necessary papers, he just had such a convincing back up story, everyone who ever met him, would say what a gentleman, now I knew dad was as cunning as a fox, so if he could, he would get himself invited to anywhere if it meant he could profit by it.

Now he had met John at a very exclusive dinner party, dad had only been invited because he was due to fly someone home after the party. Now at that party, there were some of the most beautiful women in the world, "you know Aveling the kind of women, men like me only ever see on the covers of magazines.

but they were there to entertain the men who could afford them, but they knew what they were doing", 'uncle Terry do you mean like the women at the end of the road, who mum calls ladies of the night, but Luke calls prostitute's" uncle continued, 'not really these ladies were called escorts or companions, but thinking about it Aveling yes your right they were prostitutes, now it was at one of those parties your dad met John, he was the, go to man, to a very rich diamond dealer.

Now I can only tell you what your dad told me, so I am never too sure when it comes to your dad Aveling, has you understand, he often likes to tell stories, so I take everything he tells me with a pinch of salt, but that particular party was for the diamond dealers sons twenty first birthday, the son, was studying in England but had returned home just for the party, now his father had told the boy when he leaves university, and returns to live in south Africa, one of the first things he needed to do is get a wife.

The boy called Edward, told his father he would only marry, when, and if he found the right girl, now looking around the room that day there were so many beautiful women, his father said, "well son you have plenty to choose from", after Edward looked around the room, Edward smiled, "no thanks dad, I am looking for someone special," it was then his father asked Edward to describe what he wanted, now at that point most of the people in the room had started to listen into the conversation, because they thought if they could find the right girl for the diamond dealer son, they would be reward handsomely.

Now that's when Edward went on to say the perfect girl for him had to have, fair skin, now in south Africa that ruled out over fifty percent of the females, the boy then went on to say she had to be a virgin, that back in the sixties, that was not going to be easy, after all the sixties did have a reputation, for sex, drugs, and rock and roll, as they would say.

But then the diamond dealer said, 'is that all son,' it wasn't anything money couldn't buy for him, it was then the boy said "no, she would have to have green eyes". That is when, some of the people listening said, it would be easier to walk on the beach, and pick up a ten carat diamond than finding a green eyed girl who could meet all the necessary requirements.

It was then your father told John about you. after he had spoken to the diamond dealer, it had been arranged for your father to bring John to England so he could see you for himself, the girl with the green eyes. After he had seen you with his own eyes, he reported back to his employer, that you had everything they wanted, so it was then the wheels had been put in motion for your papers to be arranged.

Uncle Terry went on to tell me, how everything had been arranged when, your mum and I decided to hide you, it was only after the police had been called, did John say on that visit they would have to leave, and return later to pick you up, when all the commotion had died down, because they above all else could not be involved with the English police.

Now Aveling trust me when I say, the amount of money your dad was being offered, would make your eyes water, so I know your dad well enough, to know he will be back, because finding a green eyed girl is rare, but finding one who is also a virgin, well I would say that is almost impossible.so I will keep you informed when I get my next phone call, asking me to pick your dad up from the airport.

Now Aveling I am only telling you this, because of the amount of money that is being offered for you, when the word gets back to Africa that you are the girl with green eyes, and meet all the necessary requests. then just about any of the men who know, the details of where you are, and the price you will bring, they will come looking for you, with or without your dad, so you need to keep your wits about you, I also have got you this, but don't tell your mother, uncle Terry then pulled out from under his jumper, a six inch bowie knife in a leather case.

now doctor, up to that moment I just thought well, I am not too sure what I thought, my life was always full of strange things, it just all sounded bazaar to say the least, I had never consider my eyes to be, well to me they had only been one problem before, at school when some of the other girls, had started calling me the girl with the frog eyes, that is when my nick name at school became frogit.

it didn't last too long, after I had given the ring leader a black eye, now yes I had gotten detention for fighting, but sometimes you just need to stand up for yourself. but I am not a bad girl, but the school had sent a

127

letter of notice, stating my bad behaver, warning I could be excluded from school if it happened again, my mum just told me, she said, when I told her about the details, I must had been provoked, and that I was still her good girl.

But I decided after all the problems I had been having with men and boys, I did feel strangely comforted by having the knife, so it was then I started to take it everywhere with me, I knew I had to be careful so I would often tie it onto an old belt so I could conceal it under my skirt.

Now doctor this must sound a little strange to hide a knife in my skirt, but uncle Terry had warned me, if someone comes after me, it could be anywhere, any time, so snatching me from outside the home, could even prove an easy option for them.

Now I thought I knew after, what my farther had done in the past, he could not be trusted, but this was low even by his standards. but I knew he wanted me out of the way, as I had always been a thorn in his side. but that really was extreme, selling me for money, when I think back to what he's done, nothing surprised me what that man was capable of.

…CLICK…tape off…

CHAPTER 22

SO NIEVE...

'Well doctor her I am again,'

Now Availing's stories did seem to be getting of track, I was never too sure if they were lies, but she just seemed so convincing on the tapes, so I decided to have a little chat to her about the real reasons we were there.

We needed to get to the bottom of why she stabbed someone, but when I insisted, she told me in her mind it was justified,

'Self-defense doctor self-defense, but if you want the whole truth, and as they say in court, the whole truth, and nothing but the truth. then you need to let me keep making the tapes because I sure as hell, I am not going to sit down looking, and watching someone pull faces when they get disgusted with what I am saying, I find some people even pull a face for just saying a swear word, so yes doctor this is the best way.'

Aveling then again went on through to the other office.

CLICK...tape on...

now Pam must have been in her early twenties, she was writing to a new pen pal, he was a solicitor working in London or so she said, but he seemed when I met him, I thought maybe a solicitors assistant, but he just looked too young to be a solicitor, but it wasn't till she met up with him again, did she began dating him seriously, when he started to visit, always turning up at our house, on the weekends. With dad always as per normal, mum agreed to let him stay. but when he did he would share Pam s double bed. At that time my sister Rennie was sleeping on the top bunk, myself on the lower,

It felt wrong and uncomfortable for him to share our room, but Pam said I was behaving like a baby, and anyway what did I have that he hadn't seen before, Pam had only been dating him for a short time, when he invited her to join him in London.

Pam left to stay with him, but just a few weeks later she returned home with someone else, he was yet another new boyfriend, but he must have been a good twenty year older than her. Shortly after he had been to stay for a few days, mum suspected he was a married man, and pointed it out to Pam, who said she didn't care. But mum did,

till then Pam had been getting away with ever thing, but to mum when Pam started dating a married man, mum knew what it felt like to be the wife, of a cheating man, so she told Pam he could not stay again, but after just another few weeks he was dumped,

It was then Pam found out she was pregnant by him, but again Pam hadn't noticed till this time it was too late for the coat hanger man, so she told mum she was keeping the baby, now Pam must have been about seven months pregnant when she started to bring home yet another boyfriend.

He did live local but he was such a creep, but again mum would let him stay over, he had a nasty habit of staring at me, if it was my bed time, he would make some excuse to follow me up to the bedroom, sitting on the double bed, waiting for me to start getting changed into my nighty, he would make creepy hand actions with his hands, he asked me on so many times, questions that were just so inappropriate, but I tried hard to ignore him.

But after everyone was in bed, the lights had all been switched off, but there was still a light coming in from the landing light, plus a little from the street lamp across the road, from outside the bedroom window, now whenever I rolled over in the bunk, I would find myself face to face with him, staring at me, through the bars of the double beds headboard, on seeing me he again would start with the rude hand gestures.

Now I had started sleeping curled up in a tight ball again, wrapping my blanket, tightly around my whole body, each and every night, I just felt so afraid to go to sleep, I told mum but she said, it wouldn't be for long as Pam had been looking for a house of her own.

Now on one occasion we had all been in the bedroom it was getting late so I had been stalling getting changed, hoping he would have to go out of the room for something, so I could quickly get my nighty on, But no such luck I tried to wrap my blanket around as I often had to do. Just to get changed,

now Pam would just laugh, she thought it was funny, Pam would say I was just putting of the inevitable, keeping my body to myself, I was just being selfish, I had remembered just after my last birthday, when Pam told me it was time I got a man's cock inside me, claiming I would enjoy it, she had tried in the past to get me to go with her whenever she had dates with local boys, Pam would just laugh when I told her I was staying a virgin till I got married.

but some months she was relentless with her request for me to go with her, she keep repeating herself, that once I had, had a man's cock inside me, I would feel like a real woman, Pam would say if I picked a good one, he would spoil me with gifts and presents.

It was on one of those times she was pushing me to have sex, that Pam told me her boyfriend had someone to take me on, and show me the ropes, it was then when her boyfriend had been listening to the conversation, he offered his services but not until after Pam had left the room, he just made me feel sick, come to think about it so did she, it was bad enough late at night they would have sex In the bed just feet away from me, it was impossible to get to sleep.

so I would just wrap myself in the corner of the bunk, with my head on my knees, till the room went quiet, then came the snoring, I would then listen to the house, no feel, if the house had finally gone too sleep, then I would creep down stairs, if anybody asked, I would just say I needed the toilet. But the truth was, with the house all to myself I would watch T.V always remembering to turn the sound off, till the days viewing stopped.

I can remember it was early in the sixties the local council, were going around the estate installing bathrooms, they were installing them just of the kitchen, the toilet would still be outside, but just having another sink, inside was a dream. Not having to use the old sink were mum would have nappy s soaking, or it would be full of dirty pots. The thought of not having to sit in the middle of the living room, to get a bath felt like a dream.

so a new room where we could wash, but my dream soon turned to despair, has we were still only aloud to have a bath on a Sunday night due to it being necessary to light the fire, and with the cost of coal, this would mean when the bath was full of hot water, mum would put the younger boys in first, so she could get them off to bed, after their baths, so I would just have to take my turn, this would mean the water was not as hot as I wanted, mum also would not allow a lock on the door in case any of the boys got locked in by mistake.

Now I could guarantee, if I was in the bath on a Sunday night, Pam s boyfriend would decide he needed a shave before they went out, so he would just walk into the room has I was bathing, I lost track on how many times, I screamed at mum to get him out, it was every weekend, but all I got told was he needed to shave, but has he stood their shaving he would be watching me through the mirror, he was just another one of the men, who made my flesh feel like it was being pawed over by their grubby hands. All I had in the bath was a face cloth, but it covered so little, Pam just said to stop making such a fuss, why would any man be interested in me, I was such a cold fish the best place for me was a convent, it was a comment she seemed to spit out whenever I objected to any of her boyfriends,

So I decided I needed a new routine, It was then I would wait till they had gone out, this meant the water in the bath was too cold, by the time I got the room to myself, I can remember Pam s boyfriend whispering to me, obscenities he seemed to get a thrill out of all the shouting and commotion he caused, it was weeks till they were due to move out, but after his comments, I decided I would just fill the sink and give myself a flannel wash, until they left.

And that doctor would be my routine till they did move out, now I knew what he was saying was nonsense, but he just made my flesh crawl so badly, I think I could have been physically sick, now when I was in the bath, it was amazing that he would take thirty minutes or more just to shave, but now he couldn't get a cheap thrill, it took him barely ten minutes.

I did remember on one occasion when I was in bed, after he had sex with Pam, she had gone to sleep, I thought it was safe to roll over in my bunk, only to find him staring at me, it was then he whispered, did I enjoy that, I just ignored him, he then said he was looking at me all the time he had been having sex with Pam, and thinking of it being me under him, I told him then as I had done on so many occasions he was so sick. And he could go to hell, the sooner the better as far as I was concerned.

CLICK…tape off

132

CHAPTER 23

SLAP.SLAP.SLAP.
BED BUGS ...

'Hi doctor is it ok for me to go straight through,' 'ok Aveling,'

now I believed the poor doctor, hadn't really understood that day when they asked her to take me on, that after all these weeks, I was still seeing her, well I say seeing her, but what I had come to look forward to was a day out of my cell, but being allowed to simply make a recording of what had happened to me, was so much easier than trying, and looking at some ones face, as they looked at me with disbelieve on their faces, or in the past whenever I was trying to explain, they kept interrupting, so it would take forever just explaining the shortest stories.

.CLICK... Tape on...

It hadn't been long before mum was back in hospital having yet another baby, I was getting a bit too old to keep getting sent off to the relatives homes, but then again I didn't want to be in the same house as my brother Luke without mum, so mum suggested that I go and stay with my father's mother, grandma now although she lived over five miles away, I would as I got older, try to walk it there, in the hopes of seeing Amy and her daughter again, but it never happened.

Now most of dads brothers and sisters, had moved on with their lives, the only one left at home was my auntie Kim, I had always got on well with Kim she was older than me, and grandma spent most of her time collecting old wool jumpers from jumble sales for just a few pennies.

Grandma would have us unpick them, rolling up the wool. to make new balls, so we would spend hours crocheting them into blankets, grandma knew with so many children, and grandchildren, it was about then grandma also had her first great grandchild, we were always cold at home, we each had one sheet on the mattress, one blanket each, and one pillow, I can remember spending so many nights as a child crying myself to sleep, because I had been so cold in the winters.

but you could always rely on the bed bugs to bite, even when it was so cold they were relentless scurrying over the walls, during the night you would often hear slap, slap, slap, that noise was my brothers, and sisters and yes me, killing them, we would whack them with a shoe, in my home you would never hear a dawn Corus of birds, but as we awoke in the morning, the first thing you would hear is slap, then again and again, the boys even tried to turn it into a game, to see who would get the most, but that wore off as time went by, mum had complained to the council, but they just kept promising they would get to us, as soon as possible.

no one ever wanted to talk about the problem openly it was just another one of those taboo topics like hair nits, we would all too often get sent home from school, by the nit nurse as she was called came to visit, but I knew from my friends at school most families were having the same problems, but some of the girls were made to feel so ashamed.

Now the frost in the winter wasn't just on the outside of the window. But would cover the inside of the windows, it was thick enough to write your name on the inside of the glass. Mum would use fire bricks that we would heat in the oven beside the old fire place that was the only heating in the house, so late at night when the fire went out, the whole house seemed to shudder with the coldness of winter.

mum would wrap the oven stone s into an old bit of towels or whatever, mum had, so we didn't get burned but once the brick had gone cold, that was that, we didn't have hot water bottles, mum would not allow them, she was always worried if they burst or the cork top came off, we would get scolded.. now doctor I remembered when I was very young, starting to make little crocheting squares, with the old wool, then stitching them all together, the first one I finished I gave to mum for the new baby. Mum was thrilled, I told her the next one would be for the other cot.

now mum over the months had knitted us mittens and hats from the same wool we had collected from the jumble sales, yes they were to be worn outside, but we would also sleep in them, anything to keep warm the cold was bad, but not as bad as needing the toilet, in the middle of night, now the only toilet was outside, we were only allowed to use the potty under the bed for urine, now the one in our room was meant to be just for us girls, but all too often the boys were too lazy to go outside, so they would sneak in to use the girls potty, if the one in their room was to full to use, looking back now doctor just thinking about it I can still smell that strong smell of stale urine.

The outside toilet in the winter would often be frozen over with ice, so we had an old small fire poker to break the ice before we could do our business. I can remember being told when I was old enough to use the poker, to be careful not to be too heavy handed, as that was the last thing we needed was a broken toilet, with so many of us that would have been a new nightmare to live with,. So just tap the ice gentle, but not to worry if the ice didn't break,

But that is the way it had always been, I can remember mum often in the mornings, boiling a kettle just so we could use the toilet. if we had used sanitary products we would wrap them into a sheet of old newspaper, then put them on the fire, the only way to clean ourselves was old newspapers that were torn in to squares, the squares would then be hung on a home-made hook hammered into the back of the toilet door, we were always told if we used the last square, it was important to replace the squares for the next user, we didn't subscribe to a morning newspaper, but uncle Terry would often pick up the evening paper on his way home from work.

It was amazing how many users we had for the old newspapers, mum would use a sheet to draw the fire in the mornings, it would also be used to light the fire with, Now on one of those early morning visits to the loo, it must have been around four o'clock in the morning, and bitterly cold. But the night before I thought I had heard noises, coming from the coal shed that was joined to the toilet, so I was trying to hold on till morning, but as they say needs must, but when I told mum about what I had heard, she said it must have been, an animal crawling in just to keep warm...

So the following night when I needed to go, I tried to convince myself mum was right it was just an animal keeping warm, it was bad enough going outside just for the toilet, but that night there was no moon, looking up skywards it looked almost like magic, as I saw the first flakes of winters snow, slowly gliding down to earth like paper doylies, now in my heart I wanted to stay there forever, it felt like god himself was putting on a show just for me, the only light was coming from the kitchen through the door, that I left open so the light could guide me to the toilet. But I didn't stop, and stare to long because the cold, was sending I shiver down my spine.

But again I heard a noise from the coal the shed, so after I had finished cleaning myself. I again heard a noise that was no way an animal, because to the best of my knowledge animals did not sneeze, so there I was, it was still so dark, bitterly cold, and I found myself, trapped inside the toilet, wearing just my nighty and a pair of nickers. Now if it was, has I was often told, just my imagination, then it's nothing to worry about.

On the other hand, if it was a man, and he heard me in the toilet. I knew I couldn't stay there, so I decided, after a long pause, I would make a dash for it. so I picked up the old poker just in case I needed it, I made a dash for the back door, but on dashing inside, still holding the poker, quickly locking the door behind me, thinking I was safe, but as I turned around their he was, he most have slipped into the kitchen as I was cleaning myself,

as we stood there just staring at each other, I wasn't sure which one of us was most afraid, he had a look about him, that didn't make me feel afraid, it was then I looked at his hands, he was holding some bread he had taken out of the cupboard, and don't ask me why doctor, because I could not answer why, but I said it, but I did, I calmly said,

'would you like a cup of tea with that,' at first he just looked so shocked, but I just moved over to the sink filled the kettle and put it on to boil, now, how anybody could survive out there in the middle of the winter, it didn't bare thinking about, I would often shiver in bed, let alone outside in a coal bunker,

I looked up at the clock it was almost four thirty am, I heard one of the babies crying upstairs, so I knew mum would be soon walking into the kitchen to make a bottle. But I carried on putting in the tea leafs to the tea pot, I asked our new visitor if he would please sit down, then he just, calmly sat down at the table, still eating the bread like he had not eaten, for so very long.

People often think when you are so very hungry, you would push the food in your mouth quickly. But I knew that wasn't true, whenever I had been so very very hungry, I took small little nibbles, so I could enjoy each, and every bite, so has I watched the tramp doing the same I understood. now in our home with so many of us, mugs and cups were scarce, the adults would all have their own mugs made from metal with their names scratched on the side, the younger boys had plastic cups and a few of us would have to drink from old washed out jam jars.so I poured out the tea into two jam jars.

It was then when mum joined us, but has I heard her footsteps getting closer, I did raise my voice a little to say, its ok mum it's only me. I didn't want to panic her, as she walked into the kitchen to see we had a visitor, she did seem to be taken back at what she saw, I quickly reassured her, "its ok mum its only Fred, he was cold outside so I offered him some tea."

Now mum carried on making the bottles, she, I admit seemed a little stumped as to what to say, I didn't really know our visitors name but he just seemed so cold and lost, but his eyes, you know doctor it's always in the eyes, they were so sad, and lost, his cloths looked like they hadn't left his back since the war, but that was nineteen forty five, but it was now the sixties,

after mum finished making the bottles, she asked me if I was ok, I just nodded then she returned upstairs as now we could hear both babies crying. now I think I know, what you are thinking doctor, but it was just so strange, when he finished his tea, he quietly got up to leave, but whilst he was drinking his tea, I noticed the soles of his boots were totally worn out, you could see his bare foot, inside the socks he had been wearing were also worn through, so I asked him if he would like me to fix them, he looked a little bewildered, so I showed him on the pantry floor were we kept a box with old leather strips and bits, we would buy at the jumble sales, it was always a treat if we found old leather handbags or anything made from leather.

Grandad, mums dad, had shown me how to break up handbags so they could be reused, to make new soles out of the scraps, first you just needed to put the shoe or boot onto the leather scraps, then draw around them, then cut out the shape, sometime in the summer if I didn't have any leather scraps I would use cut out cardboard. But that never lasted long, if it rained, but it was amazing how it kept your feet comfy when there was nothing else to use. Being one of ten children, shoes were always wearing through, so most needed new insoles.

but our new visitor was in luck, as only a few weeks earlier, I had managed to pick up an old doctors bag, and it was good thick leather, the corners were all busted out, and the frame of the bag was falling off, but I had only been interested in the leather parts, has he first passed me his first boot, I gently laid it onto the leather, but I knew I would have to double it up, if it was to make any difference to him.

The hardest part was cutting the leather it was much tougher, than the normal hand bags, so it took a little longer to do, but I knew he was depending on me. So has he waited I poured him another tea, he held that old jam jar so firmly, you would think it was someone's best china.

has I pushed the new innersole inside the boots, I remembered I had also collected some old jumpers from the last jumble sale the week before, they were still waiting for me to unpick them, I had started with the back and fronts first, but I knew I had two full sleeves. so I went to collect them from the hobbies basket on the pantry floor, I grabbed my darning needle, I think Fred at that moment thought I was going to attempt to darn his old socks, but trust me doctor there wasn't enough of them left to sew. so what I did was take a sleeve pull the cuff s gently together then sew them closed.

Then I removed his old socks, oh if only I could, find the words to explain the poor man's feet, so I gently pulled on the new sleeve socks.

Then I helped him to pull his boots back on. So if you could have seen that man's face doctor, anybody would think I had just handed him the crown jewels, now it was only ever a temporary solution, but the thought of him out there in that cold, I found unbearable to think about. Then I unlocked the back door then he left. I never expected to see him again but I was wrong. Just a few days later our paths crossed again.

He was sitting on a park bench, I walked over to him I had a packet of sweet mints in my pocket, I offered him one, and that was the start of a long friendship, strange, but a friendship just the same.

I found out his name wasn't really Fred, it was Vincent, I told him I liked Fred better, so he smiled, and from then on that's what I called him, I always did see the street people, who were homeless not as tramps, I believed, that was like calling them all villains. I knew some of them were villains but not all, I felt when you looked at someone's face closely, but especially the eyes, and it would help you to understand them.

So just for being homeless didn't mean you were bad, so I did have a bad habit of calling all tramps Fred. I remember a conversation with my mum, what I couldn't understand, Was I would often see a group of Fred's sitting in the library. during the days in the middle of the winter, now the library at the bus terminal was huge, with toilets, heat, but come six o clock they were all kicked out. Now I don't know about you doctor, but to me seeing the same men shivering on park benches, just trying to keep warm. Wasn't the obvious solution, well for me, it was let them remain in the library?

After all some of those men had served in the war, many of them were still wearing old navy duffle coats, I recognized due to the way they fastened with wooden toggles.

There were often articles in the newspapers in the winter, that people had been found frozen to death, I think back at how many times I had helped at jumble sales, and fund raising for the church's to repair roofs, so surly the church could let them in during the winter.so what a mad world we all live in. some of the tramps didn't even speak English, mum just explained that some of them, were men who had been interned during the war, or even prisoners of war,

but after the war, for one reason or another they decided they had nothing to go back to, it was then mum told me to be extra careful who I talked to, I did tell her Fred was English as we had many a conversation, but all the same mum warned me, Aveling trust no one

CLICK...TAPE OFF...

CHAPTER 24

JUST FRED...

CLICK...TAPE ON...

Now doctor I remembered on a visit to the library after school, I had chosen a book, I took it to a table sat down, and began to read, I remember looking at a picture, it was a painting by the artist Blake, and one of the worst pictures I had ever seen, the painting depicted a war scene, where horses were beheaded, and dead bodies ever where, it was then Fred came over to the table.

he saw I was troubled by the painting, so he asked me what the problem was, so I said it was the picture, he gently placed his hand on my arm, and said "do you know what to do when life gets so hard to look at Aveling," "no Fred what should I do, "he smiled down at me and simply said "what you do Aveling is turn the page," so as I turned the page, I began to think, it's so strange how different people looked at the world.

I remember another conversation I had with Fred, it was a strange conversation, as it was about money, something I had no real knowledge of, it was something I never thought I would need to hear a story about, because I thought at that time, I never would have enough money to worry about, whatever little I had back then, was by getting up early to deliver newspapers in the morning, it was never more than a few shillings, that would go on sweets on my way home from school,

I normally got paid at the weeks end, then dividing up the money so I could take home little paper bags of sweets one for each of my younger brothers, mum always taught us to share, I always remembered on the

141

Friday nights as I approached the house, there would be little faces all squeezed up at the window, just as soon as they spotted me the smiles were a true thank you, mum was right it did feel so good to share.

It was on one of those nights I stopped to talk to Fred, when I opened my school bag, and took out a sweet for him, he looked inside, asking me why I had divided the sweets into different bags, so I explained who they were for, it was then I asked him if he had any money, I only had very little left, but it would be enough for him, to buy a bag of chips at the chip shop, he smiled at me as I tried to give him the money, but he insisted he had more than enough. But it was then he began the story, he referred to a friend of his, who had been as rich as any child could be, but now had nothing, and he too was walking the streets.

Fred started by explaining it had all began in the First World War, when his friend was just a teenager, he had lived in a huge estate with staff, and had everything he could ever have wished for, but then in the First World War his friend's father had been killed.

so it was then the government came for something called death duties, till that moment I had never even heard of death duties, so Fred explained all about it, but his friends mother had to sell many of the antiques from the house that over the years, her late husband's family had collected over generations, some were even painting of old family members painted by important artist, but they were a part of the houses very sole. But they still had to be sold.

After the first war, the family were only just getting back to normal when the Second World War began, so the eldest son went to war, now has the estate was held by a very old will that stated, that the whole estate would be inherited by the first born son, when he too was killed. the family had to find even more money to pay the government more death duties, so the family still owned the big house, but most of the land had to be sold, it was then Fred made a slip of the tongue, as he said, "now I, no I mean, my friend the second born son, was still in the army at that time.

so it wasn't till he returned home after the war, he found how bad thing were. he did tell me Aveling, he was thinking about signing the house over to the national trust, at least they would repair it, and return it to its former glory."

Now I had overheard my dad having a conversation about a house owned by national trust, I remembered the conversation because dad and his so called friends were planning to rob it, before the national trust, could take an inventory. Now the trust were planning to sell of everything on that estate. So as I was telling Fred all about what I had heard, that the national trust didn't always repair old estates.

But they would sell them off to the highest bidders, after stripping them bare. Now when I explained that to Fred he seemed very disturbed. He believed the trust would keep everything together, "no Fred they would sell them using the excuse, that they needed the money, to keep only the best properties for them self's or as they say for the good of the public, but I don't know about you Fred, but I don't think I will ever get the opportunity to visit a stately home, so tell your friend not to sign over anything ",it seems to me his family have lost more than any family should lose, there prized possessions, the land, but most of all, other family members.

"Now Aveling when you own a big house like that it needs a lot of upkeep, you have the staff to pay, workers farming the land, and normally by farming the land, that would be where the money came from, to pay the bills so without the land, the house fell into a terrible state," "oh Fred that's awful but surly your friend could still sleep there." "well he's a very proud man, who feels that he has let the family down, so he feels to ashamed to return, he couldn't even pay the staff, who had worked for the family for years, so they hadn't been payed for a very long time".

I told Fred, to tell his friend to go home, that all the estates loyal staff know what his friend has been through, so I believed they would be more than helpful to rebuild whatever was left, so he was needed there to help make thing better, he shouldn't be walking the street, he has a responsibly, no a duty, that he should get a job even if it's only sweeping the roads, no matter how little he earned.

It was his duty to help the remaining staff, and their families to make things better for them, by doing anything he could to help, so your friend Fred, should stop wallowing in his own shame, and be brave he needs to go home, and help the others there that need him "Looking at it now Aveling it's only talking to you, and how you see thing so differently, things seem to make more sense."

Over the coming months if we had sausage at school, I would sneak one of my plate, bread if I was lucky, to be honest anything I could just so I would have something for Fred on my way home, now doctor I don't know what you know about the war, but Fred told me he had been injured. I asked him why he simply hadn't returned home.

Now he had told me earlier in our friendship that, his wife had passed away before the war, but during the war he had lost both his sons.so he had never gone back to his home, he believed his sister if still alive would still be there, but he said there were too many sad memories.

On one occasion when I was speaking to Fred I told him it was time for him to go home, the same as his friend should, but at that time I believed Fred and his friend, were the same person.

"Now Fred, I always believed that when people die, a little of them always stays behind," I even confided with him how I had on occasions sleep in the school, and how I would often hear the singing voicers of the children of years gone by, he smiled as I went on. That it is those sprits, and little memories in our minds, that help to heal us, just remember the happier days. and Fred you know what to do when life get difficult, and hard to look at, it was then I gently placed my hand on his arm and said, we turn the page, it was then he looked up at me and gave me the biggest smile. the following day when I came out of school he was gone, but he will never be forgotten.

As I have grown up we would be told stories, of how bad it was in the war, but how everyone pulled together, the camaraderie. Was good and ever one helped each other, so yes I understood all about hardship, but even when we reached the sixties, we were still being, as I called it brain washed, not so much by family, but the media, with all the gory details, even the movies were old repeated, war movies as they tried to, ram inside our heads all the horrific things of the of war. I did remember I would hate it when I crept down stairs to watch TV only to find it was yet another old war movie.

Well I guess they just didn't want us to forget what they had all done, it was after all, always for us, but I often wanted to shout, sometimes so I could tell them it wasn't just the forties, when things were bad, has a child I can remember things were still on rations, in fact I can remember mum telling me she always remembered in the mid-fifties they had only just then, removed the rationing on sweets. But some food goods were still hard to come by, now we were still all playing outside, in bombed out old houses, we would have to be so careful has we often found unexploded shells, the boys thought it was great, we were all told in school if we found one, we needed to call nine nine nine at once, and clear the area. But for the boys it was all just a big game, now I know doctor this has nothing to do has to why I am here, but I should like you to know, just how close you came to not having a patient at all.

It was on one of those sunny summer days, as we all rummaged over an old derelict house, the boys has always were playing soldiers, so I was looking out for useful things to be recycled, it was then out of nowhere I heard one of the boys shouting grenade, as I looked up something shot over my head, now I could not explain why, but I jumped for cover, then there was a loud explosion.as I laid there thinking that was real.

I felt slowly over my body for any blood, starting with my head, then has I first sat up felling down my arms, then body, and legs no blood, I could feel no pain, so I shakily stood up looking if I could see any of the boys, so I could give then a piece of my mind, but the site was empty, I guess the explosion had caused them all to panic, and run for cover, it was when I realized I couldn't hear anything, no traffic no bird song nothing, as I put my hand to my ears, it was then I felt the blood, I started to stagger home, I only just made it to the front garden gate, were I collapsed.

It was then a group of neighbor's had gathered around, I could see their lips moving, but couldn't hear a word, so once again I had to rely on lip reading, apparently the bang had been so loud many of them thought it was a bomb going off, or gas explosion. it was then one of the men picked me up and carried me into the house, mum bless her hadn't got a clue what to do, so it was one of the neighbors then told her they had sent for the doctor, another said he had called for an ambulance.

Now the doctor arrived first, he began checking me out, it was then he told mum, that one of my eardrums had burst, but in time some hearing would return, but I wasn't so sure, but when the ambulance arrived the doctor sent it away, explaining to mum to just keep an eye on me, and other than my damaged ears he couldn't find any other problems. now as I laid there thinking, dear god not my ears again, it was then the doctor put huge padded dressing over both ears I did think it was a rather silly thing to do, but after he had left. has I was trying to remove the dressing, mum stopped me, thankfully she explained the dressing were to stop any infections, but he had given mum a bottle of antibiotics.

It was a few days later, on my walk to school, the old derelict house was crawling with builders, and the whole site had been roped off, I never did find out what idiot had thrown that device, but if I ever get my hands on him!

It was after that explosion, if there was a loud noise outside, like a car backfiring or thunder, my poor mum would still dive under the table, dragging all of us with her.so yes doctor the forties were bad, but the fifties were no picnic, but their I go again doing the same thing, has the people harping on about The war, and how they did it all for us. Trust me doctor I could never forget the war, but I was trying really hard to not to dwell on it, wars are bad, but why or why did the world keep fighting,

Let's just say the past is the past and move on, oh doctor how I would love to forget things, and just move on.

CLICK…tape off

CHAPTER 25

PENNIES HOUSE...

It was getting late, as I looked up at the wall clock, Aveling and her chaperones were a good fifteen minutes late, just as I was thinking to myself they were not going to turn up, I heard Toms voice, "come on Aveling hurry up we are so late, you know the surgery closers at six," as they came through the door, I could clearly see Aveling blouse was stained with quite a large blood stain, Tom looking at my face, "sorry we are so late doctor, there was an incident at the prison, we had to pop Aveling up to the hospital to get a few stitches,

But she insisted we still came here, we told her it wasn't necessary but she insisted." "what's happened," "well doc I told you my cell mate is a schizoid well she snapped, and slashed me at dinner, but don't worry it's only my arm not so bad, just a lot of blood, but hopefully they will now move me into another cell, or pack her off to the insane department were ever that is, just as long I don't have to see her face again." Aveling then gave me a quick grin, as she passed me to go into the back room.

I didn't have all the facts from Tom, but there was something about that grin that made me think, maybe this was something Aveling caused herself, so she could be moved, so it will be interesting to see if she talks about it on the tape today.

CLICK...tape on....

Now doctor I wanted to go on to university when I finished school but when I asked dad he just laughed, "if I have told you once Aveling I have told you a hundred times boys go on to university but not someone like you, you just don't understand, the cost, and let's face it girl you don't have the, well Aveling you don't have the academic mind, so be a good girl and, stop pestering me and your mum," so when I left school I had to get a job, and of all placers the store where I worked, was just a stones through from the university gates.

Now we would often get the students in the store, most were just messing about, but it was then I met a girl called Penny as she lived close by the estate were I lived, we would often walk home together, she was one of those girls that was always immaculately turned out, I dread to think how much her uniform cost, but she seemed so natural and sweet, so different from the other girls I knew who hung around on the estate, she was telling me, her parents had moved into a new house and the toilet was inside, and upstairs, oh what a treat that must have been.

I guess she thought I hadn't believed her, when she told me about her new home, and that the toilet really was upstairs, but Penny then went on to explain, that there were another two toilets upstairs, so one day on our walk home, she asked me if I would like to see it for myself. Yes please, 'when we arrived at Penny house. it looked huge there was a long drive to a house that oh, to me seemed like a mansion, it was standing alone, nestled in trees.

Oh I thought how lucky she was. We needed to go around to the back of the house, inside her mother was cooking, and the smell was so amazing, Penny then took me upstairs.

The whole house was unbelievable, everything was new, Penny had her own closet full of cloths, she had a whole bedroom to herself, I asked her if she was an only child, Penny went on to tell me, she had two older sisters, and two older brother, they all had their own bedrooms, then there was a bed room for her mum and dad, they even had another two bedrooms for guest. I tried hard to think of anything we had in common, but I couldn't think of a thing, it wasn't until she told me, that she was taking art at university, I felt a little jealous, but when she found out that I loved art, she would often let me borrow her books to read.

Penny seemed down to earth so we quickly became friends, but has Penny was showing me around her bedroom there was another door, I asked her if that leaded to her sisters bedroom, 'no don't be silly that's my bathroom,' when she showed me inside, it all seemed like a dream, not only did she have her own bedroom but she had her own bathroom, it was then I noticed a strange pretty pink brush, beside the sink, so I asked her what it was for, Penny looked at me so strangely, 'it's a tooth brush, silly don't tell me Aveling you have never seen a tooth brush before, how do you clean your teeth.'

Well mum cuts a twig from the bush outside, then we bash the end on a rock to splay the end, then we have some grainy powder in a tin tub, we would dip in the stick- brush, then clean our teeth. Pennies face was a picture, but the more she showed me, the more I learned, her life was so different to the one I was living, as I walked home later that day, my emotions were so confused, but I thought how little we had, compared to Pennies family, but as I got to know all about her family, I would never have exchanged my life for hers, even if mine was a nightmare, compared to hers I had got it easy.

I remembered grandad once telling me, be careful what you wish for. And never take anything for granted. The more I grew, the more I became to understanding his little quotes of advice.

When I got back home that day, I was telling my little brother all about the house with a toilets inside the house, and I had seen it, he seemed so impress, as was I.

Now mum had overheard our conversation, she asked me to repeat were I had been, and what I had seen with my own eyes.

Mum then looked a little pale, 'promise me you will never go back inside that house again, 'why mum; 'I will tell you later when the little ones have gone to bed, so later that evening my two older sisters were out somewhere with their boyfriends, my older brother out with his mates. So it was just me and mum.

Mum began to explain that the house had already got a reputation, because in the evenings Pennies mother, and daughters would invite men into the home, for as my mother put it, for sexual favors.

I confess I was shocked they all seemed so nice, 'are you sure mum, 'yes dad told me, uncle Terry was a customer there, 'but mum, Penny is still a teenager, 'I know but you must promise me you mustn't go in that house again,' 'ok mum, 'I stayed friends with Penny, but our paths didn't cross every day, and when it did we would just walk home together, but

I would keep my promise to my mum, and I never did enter that house again. Penny would often ask me in for tea, but I always refused after all a promise to me was a promise.

It was a few months later I was out after tea, just hanging around with some friends I had a strict curfew, silly when I look back and think of, it I found more danger inside my home than outside, but on that evening I had been walking down the road when I saw the shape of a man I thought I knew.

He was walking with Penny, but it couldn't be, dad was still abroad working, it was at a time when dad had retired from the royal navy, and joined the merchant navy, and not due home for another week. So I dismiss it as coincidence that the man I saw just looked like my dad. When I returned home it was still on my mind, I just kept telling myself I had been mistaken, just as mum said 'ok kids bedtime, so we set of upstairs 'the front door opened, and who should walk in, none other than my dad.

the boys ran back down the stairs to greet him, he then looked directly at me still standing halfway up the stairs, 'didn't I just hear your mother tell you to go to bed, 'so I turned around and continued up to bed, since I had stood up to him about G.G. he barely spoke to me.

I could hear the boys laughing, it wasn't long before Pam, Rennie and Luke who didn't seem to have a curfew, were also laughing and greeting dad, it had been a while since he had been home.so they were making a fuss of him, later when Pam and Rennie came up to the bedroom all excited about dad giving them money to go to the pictures that weekend, in the morning the boys were still excited about the gifts dad had given them.

That night in bed I confess, I felt very left out, it was like I was living there but not a part of the family, it reminded me back to on one occasion we were all together as a family, it had been Easter Sunday, mum had us all dressed up to visit a relative, forgive me doctor I know you don't really care about these details, but as it is on my mind, and you did say anything that still bothered me. now as we were all walking together in the park, I think I must have been very young at that time, maybe six or seven, we were approached by a man who made a direct bee line for dad, as they chatted away like old friends, the boys ran off to play on the swings, so as dad chatted away, the conversation, turned to mum, it was then I overheard dad as he introduced mum, saying this was his wife.

He then went on to introduce his two eldest daughters, but when the man asked who I was, dad replied that I was just one of his sisters urchins, he had allowed to come along as we were going to the park. He then bent over and said, "Run along now go play on the swings ", I think when that happened. I remember feeling so angry, how could he be so heartless, but I believed he knew exactly what he was doing from the look in his eyes, I wanted to reply but I was lost, for anything to say,

looking back I was wearing my sisters old dress, it had been a morning mum couldn't find any shoes for me, so I put the only footwear I could find that would fit me, and that morning, it had been my bothers Luke's old wellies, mum had cut them down to ankle length, because they had been so high on my legs they had caused rubbing marks just below my knees,

it wasn't the first time I had worn them, but mum said she would get me some more shoes, to go back to school at the end of the Holliday, but with dad arriving home, and with so many of us, she simply hadn't had the time, when I had worn the wellies before it never bothered me it was just the norm, always mend and make do, as grandad would say. So I guess compared with the rest of my siblings, I did look a little tatty.it didn't help having huge dressings on my ears again.

So I believed dad must have been a little embarrassed, but I do remember the comment hurting. it made me feel totally like an outsider, a child who was simply not wanted or needed. I looked at mums face, I knew she wouldn't interrupt dad when he was speaking, but she looked directly back at me, I believe she knew how hurt I had felt but for the moment, she just smiled at me, I then just fell behind has they walked throw the park, I didn't feel much like playing, so I simply followed twenty paces behind them,

But there I go again doctor Valerie, going back to old memories, and I do try so hard not to revisit the past it always ends up with such bad thoughts. So let's get back to when Penny and I were walking home, we chatted mostly about Penny, but often about her family, but only after I told her, what I had been told by my mum, about what went on in her house, I was hoping she would tell me it was all a packet of lies. I thought at that moment, she would deny everything.

But no Penny seemed delighted that I knew, Penny was surprised how much I knew, but it did mean she was now only too happy, that she had a friend to chat to about, what went on inside the house, so as she mostly did all the talking I felt she just needed a friend she could trust to talk to, someone who wouldn't judge her, after all my family were hardly normal, so who was I to judge her family.

she would tell me all about her mum, and the house clients, now it was on one occasion She started to tell me a story, now at that time I thought she was just making it up, but no, why would she, after all Penny did prove to me her home had toilets inside upstairs, Penny went on to tell me, that there was a building at the rear of the property where there was a special room above the garage.

Now that room was only used for the special customers, but you know me doctor I had to ask, so Penny went on to tell me more, she went on to explain it was, were the clients who liked to be whipped, now that I did find hard to believe, but Penny went on to say, that it was also used, mostly by just the men.

to me it was hard to believe, why would anybody want to be tortured, Penny said they liked it, then she explained it wasn't just used to whip people, it was the only room that was aloud for men to have sex with other men, now that is something I had never given any thought to, I knew they were called homosexuals, but that was just about all I knew.

but I found this conversation just a little too farfetched, so she asked me if I wanted to see for myself, now I had promised mum I would never enter the house again, but convincing myself the garage didn't count, and I would only be looking at an empty room were the whipping took place, after all it was only three o'clock in the afternoon.

So we walked around the back of the house, as it was still early in the day I wasn't expecting to see any one there, so as we needed to climb the steps, then the first door opened up to a small room with a huge mirror, the door leading of that small room had a red light lit up above the access, because it was lit, Penny said we would have to wait till it went out before we could enter, to me this all seemed a little cloak and dagger, so I ask why, then Penny asked if I would like to see what was happening, inside the room, so I just shrugged my shoulders, not knowing then what I was going see, but it was totally unexplainable, but as you're the doctor I guess I didn't have to explain what I saw to you.

Penny pressed a button, and the whole mirror turned into a clear window showing everything, well doctor my mother had warned me, but I think this was one of the strangest things I had ever seen.

In the room were four men all naked, having sex with each other, I know doc, I still have problems thinking about it, my brain was just processing what I was seeing, when the door behind us opened up, two men entered. 'well, well, what do we have here then,' I felt my face burning with shame, but Penny just laughed, the men then asked if we would like to join them, it was then I fled, I never even stopped to see if Penny was running behind me,

The next day as we walking home, Penny asked if I had told anybody, oh my god I don't think I would know how to explain what I had seen, Penny then became very serious, well I got into trouble, I should never have shown you.

You see Aveling it's still illegal for men to have sex with other men. so swear to me you will tell no one, so from that day to this I never had.

CLICK...off

CHAPTER 26

WOLVES...

Hi doctor just a little note to tell you, I was surprised not to find you her today, I've just left Tom and Jerry in the waiting room, hope you are ok, the receptionist, showed me into your office, so I guess it's ok to start without you today, now where was I, ho yes now I remember, I would rather not remember, but that after all that is why I am here isn't it, not too sure I want to start without you, something just seems strange.

And these days I don't like strange, but I guess you had emergency call out, so ok,

CLICK...Tape on

now it was mums idea, on her last hospitals visit, for me to stay at grandma's house, now you have heard the story all about the wolf in grandma's bed, now I wish that was all that there was there that day, the day had been fun auntie Kay, and I had fun making woolies figures in the shape of animals, for mums new baby, but it wasn't till bed time when Kay, and I were getting ready for bed that I noticed, when Kay lifted her big baggie jumper over her head, to put her nighty on.

It was then I realized she was pregnant. now she was eighteen but she had been so strictly raised by grandma, being the last born, in the family, Kay was never let out alone, she was chaperoned everywhere, I always felt grandma kept her close, because of what had happened with dads mistress. Kay saw the look of shock on my face, 'who when,' were the words that just fell out of my mouth. She then went back to the door, after she had covered herself up with a very big nighty, to check the down stairs door was closed that led to the living room, so grandma couldn't hear us talking,

'I don't know who the father is,' 'what on earth do you mean, 'it was then she told me her story, her youngest brother, Adam had left to work the fairgrounds, he was older than Kay in his twenties, and he had been living on the road as they say, at the end of some summers he would turn up skint, and lived off grandma's pension, sometimes he would turn up with so much money, we knew he had been on the rob, he would steel just about anything that wasn't tied down. And he was no stranger to prison. It was when he was last home, Kim's older sister was having a bad time with a pregnancy and grandma went to stay with her for a while.

One evening her brother Adam came home late in the evening grandma wasn't even expecting him but their he was, when he discovered grandma wasn't there, and wouldn't be back till Sunday he arranged a card game with some of his mates.

They were playing cards in the living room, Kim had been watching them, they would give orders for Kim to get them beer from the fridge, it was getting late and the game had gone on till the early hours, then everyone seemed to have what they thought was the best hand, but when Adam ran out of money to bet with, they told him he would have to pack in his hand, or come up with the goods to stay in the game,

As he looked around the room there wasn't anything of value, it was then one of the player looked at Kim, it was then Kim went on to explain. "I felt a cold shudder down my back, but it was too late my brother Adam had said highest hand takes all I stood up with the intention to run, but it was too late the cards were down on the table, Adam had the lowest hand, the other three men, seemed to lose all interest in the cards, it was then they lunged at me,.

They started ripping of my cloths they then dragged me kicking and screaming upstairs, I was terrified", Kim having been the last born, and youngest in the family,

grandma had always kept a close eye on her, so she had never had a boyfriend, "Aveling I didn't know what they were going to do to me, once in the bedroom they finally ripped of my knickers, they all stood back, the man with the highest card hand said he was first, I remembered feeling sick, he was horrible, smelling of old tobacco and beer, he looked over, and as they were all just standing their staring at me.

he then turned to Adam and asked if I was still a virgin, Adam replied yes, it was then the men got more ajitated.it was then they started to argue, about who was going to be first, the oldest said he had the best hand, so it was only right he went first, then one of the others, offered to pay the other two ten quid each if they let him go first. He said he had never had a real virgin before, so they all agreed for ten quid each.

It Was then They grabbed me, I started to scream, and the old man told Adam to put his hand over my mouth, he had to shut me up, It was then one of the other men took of some of his cloths throwing a sock to Adam, he pushed it hard into my mouth. They then, all of them started holding me down till my arms and legs were pinned to the bed I couldn't move, then the man who had just payed the other two, climbed up on top of me, as the others, pulled my legs apart they were hurting me,

But it was nothing compared with what was to come, when the first man pushed his cook into me, he was so violent, it felt like he was ripping me inside, but it took him just seconds, then he climbed off

But when it was the turn of the older man, the smell of his body odor is a smell I will never get out of my nostrils, he was so disgusting then forcing his cook inside me, I was just praying he would stop, but he went on and on, till the last man told him to hurry up. He then climbed off saying he hadn't finished.

I desperately wanted to scream but couldn't, the others by now were growing inpatient, with him, so as he pulled away, the remaining man, just climbed on top of me, Aveling his cock looked huge he then fucked me so hard, my head kept bashing on the head board. When I thought it was all over, the youngest of the three, said he had never had a virgin before, but he said it had felt so good. it was then one of the others said".

'Stop Kim please, why or why have you never told grandma what they did to you, I am sure grandma would never let Adam back in this house again. Why didn't you call the police?'

'Please Aveling you are the only one I can trust please don't tell grandma, just let me finish telling you what those awful men did to me, then Aveling, I will explain why you cannot tell grandma, I am only telling you now because if I die giving birth, it's my last wish, I need you to tell your dad everything I am telling you now, Aveling he is the only one who will see Adam doesn't get away with it,'then Kim continued, with her story.

just when I believed the worse was over, it was the old man who said he hadn't finished with me, he wanted to be my first bum fuck, as he still hadn't had satisfaction, but has I could see him standing by the bed as he was referring to my bum hole his cock seemed to grow so big and hard.

I had no idea what he meant, but the men just got all worked up again, and before I even dried my eyes, the men had rolled me over, they then started to make a pile of cushions in the middle of the bed, they then bodily pulled me over them, it was then the youngest started to pull my bottom cheeks apart, he then kept pushing his fingers inside my bum, I was at that time being held down by my arms I just could not break free there just too many of them.

It was then The old man then started to push his fingers inside my bum hole as the younger man held my buttocks apart, it wasn't long till the dirty old man jumped on my back,

I could feel him trying to force himself into my bum hole, but my bum hole was so small, but it didn't stop him, he kept pushing, and pushing so hard Aveling it hurt so much, I could feel the skin tearing as he just kept pushing, I thought he was killing me, I started trying to scream again, but with the sock still in my mouth, the more I tried I just felt I was choking but they just didn't care, when again I thought it was all over, and he got off, it was then I felt another man climb on top of me, but I didn't understand because, the other two men were still holding me face down, and the only other man in the room was Adam.

when they started to get dressed, I started to scream again at my brother that,(I was going to tell your grandma,)they all then froze, turning back to Adam, they told him if he couldn't keep me quiet they would.

'it's ok she isn't going to say a thing, 'they then left but Adam stayed in the room, 'so you're going to tell on us are you, 'it was then he started to act really strangely he looked around the room, I was still trying to clean myself up there was blood in the bed and I thought I was going to dye, I had never seen that much blood before, I had only just started my periods, Adam, started to shout at me as I was still shaking, and looking at the blood ''you stupid little bitch that's normal, 'it was then he found what he was looking for, it was my diary. 'It was then Kim's eyes started to fill up, but you know me well enough by now doctor, I had to ask.

Ok Kim why would anything in your diary stop you from telling grandma,' 'it was about your grandad,' you see Aveling when he was very ill, grandma went to stay with your aunty for a few days, and she asked me to make sure grandad always took his pills on time each day, but on one day, I overlaid, I was in such a rush to get to work on time, I forgot, then in the evening when I saw them still on the table I panicked, because grandma always counted them out, so, that teatime I gave grandad two of everything.

he died later that night, and it's all my fault,' 'oh Kim you didn't kill grandad he was so ill, and just giving him a few extra tablets didn't kill him,' 'but I wrote it all down in my diary, Adam must have found it and he's been calling me the little killer,' But it was my fault grandad died, because I also forgot to give him his insulin, so I had written it all in my diary. Adam then told me if I told your grandma, what had happened that day after the card game,

he would give grandma the diary telling her, I had done it deliberately that I had poisoned grandad, I knew how much that would have hurt her, I know you don't believe me Aveling, but I know it was all my fault, grandad had died so I said nothing, about that night to any one, I have only told you now, but I need you to promise me you won't tell on me, unless things go wrong, promise Aveling, 'I had no choice but to promise as by then Kim was in such a worked up state.

shortly after what had happened. Adam left with the fairground travelers again. it wasn't until several months later, Kim was in the bath when something strange happened, she looked down at her stomach, it moved uncannily like something was trapped inside, she panicked and called for grandma. Kim thought she had a tape worm inside her.

Has Kim explained she overheard a conversion that grandma had, had with a friend, talking about tape worms. Grandma came rushing into the bath room, when she saw my stomach, she screamed. The following morning she took me to the doctors, who confirmed I was pregnant, she asked if I could have an abortion, but the doctor said it was too late. She kept demanding who the father was, but I didn't know,so in about four or five weeks when the baby comes grandma says I have got to give it up for adoption. I don't want to give the baby up but I don't have any choice."

CLICK...tape off

CHAPTER 27

THE RENT MAN, AND SECRET NOTES

'Morning doctor Valerie, 'didn't know if I would see you today, someone in the reception said they thought, you had been called out, again shall I continue," 'yes but remember this is about you not your relatives, 'well doc as they say fore warned, is fore armed,'

trust me, information can kill in the wrong hands", I knew doctor Valerie wouldn't understand what I was trying to tell her, but all would become clear later. I had been shocked by Kim's story but like her, who do you tell, and even when I did tell on the abusers, I still got a beating. now doctor I do want to say thank you for convincing, Tom and Jerry, To let me use the toilet on our the journey back to the cell".

Aveling again then walked into the other office

CLICK…tape on

Now whenever we stopped for the toilet the officer, would walk into the toilet to check it out, if anyone was in there he would make me wait,

Then once I had gone inside, he would stand at the door and not allow, anybody else in, now I knew that was his job, as I had run away so many times, but as far as I was concerned, i was simply surviving. Over the weeks Tom and Jerry, would take it in turns as to who would escort me into the toilet, over the past few months I had never been too sure who would accompany me inside, but once inside they would only take me to the first door, then inside the toilet I would have a choice of four cubical to pick from. If I am honest doctor, I just felt uncomfortable around all males. But I never did see a female police officer, but when it came to Tom and Jerry, they always behaved like gentlemen",

I by now had become very cynical, or so the prison warden would tell me only too often, but I knew inside the toilet just for a few minutes I was totally alone, and the first few weeks, I was never too sure if they would allow me to be alone.

Now doctor I don't want you to know, what I have been doing, but it will become clear later.

Now it wasn't until some months later, after Aveling told me where I could find them, I found some papers in an old envelope, with the added notes in, Aveling had been hiding them in the back office, I believed she knew it was risky, but she also knew if I was going to get the full story, these notes would be important

First note just a few of my thoughts, I cannot record right now doctor, but I hope you will find them useful.

once I was confident Tom and Jerry, wouldn't enter the inner toilets when I was inside, I got to work, I had managed over the weeks to get my hands on a coin, it was just one old penny but it was just the right size to fit into the screws heads on the bars at the windows, I swear that's why that toilet block was chosen to stop at, because it had bars at the windows, I started by loosening the screws luckily for me, that they had been fixed via the inside, so each week I got just a little further into unscrewing them, It wasn't going to be easy, I knew I had to pick my moment if I left it to late maybe the trips to the surgery would stop, so I needed to be sure not to act to late or too early. But act is what I intended to do.

End of note.

Now doctor Valarie, it's difficult for me to put things in chronological order, sometimes, my brain dwells too long on the bad in the world, I can remember mum always saying to me that, I was her good girl, mum had gotten pregnant with Pam when she was only fifteen, then married at sixteen, mum once told me, dad had been her only boyfriend, I knew he controlled her every move, and I believed he knew exactly what he was doing. He would come home at all times of the day and night, from were ever he claimed to be.

if mum had a male in the house she got the integration, who was he, how long had he been there, on one occasion dad had been away quite a while, and if I am honest, I was hoping he would never come back, I believed mum could do so much better than him. but dad turned up just as the rent man had been calling for the rent. now it was common knowledge on the estate, that some of the rent man's calls took longer than others, we all knew he wasn't collecting money but he took his payment with sex.

I had heard him chatting mum up so many times, I had also heard so many other men chatting up mum she was very pretty, with big blue eyes and natural blond wavy hair.

She wasn't from a rich family, but she always behaved like a lady. she would never even think about having an affair, it just wasn't in her nature, but on one of the rent man's visits, dad arrived home just as the rent man was propositioning mum, dad had arrived mid conversation. shortly after the rent men left, so did dad I knew what dad had been thinking, as they say it was in his nature, so I followed, being very carefully not to be seen. And sure enough once in the back lane dad grabbed him, fists started flying,

Dad told him if he spoke like that again to mum, he would break every bone in his body, now dad was over six foot and built like a boxer. But a part of me, was hoping the rent man would come out on top, and I wanted to be there to see it, I know just saying that makes me sound heartless. When the poor man got back to his feet, dad also warned him to keep away from other men's wife's to, I found that comment so hypocritical.

I should have known better dad always came out on top, but when I knew what I did about his extra woman. Well I say woman. But that's not exactly true, I knew everything about him, due to my friend Penny, on our walks home from work, she told me more details than any daughter needed to know.it was on one occasion she told me, dad had been at her house, when a fight broke out between her two brothers, it had been dad who pulled them apart, the fight had been about the older brother, who the younger one Michael was accusing, that he spent too much time in the garden, and not enough time helping out in the house.

I never did remember the name of the older brother, I am sure Penny would have told me, but for the life of me doc, I just cannot remember, it, I knew Pennies dad was still in prison, so it was then my dad who had got involved, at the request of Pennies mother, the fight had been, according to Penny a storm in a tea cup, it wasn't till months later Penny had explained that the younger boy had been arguing about the bodies at the bottom of the garden, but sorry doctor I just don't want to think about that right now.

So I will if I remember I will tell you later anyway I was never sure if Penny s stories were real or not. But as you know doctor, some stories, well they just seem to be so unbelievable,

but over the months knowing what I did about her family, she swore me to secrecy, but then it was like the flood barrier was down and looking back, I believed she needed someone she could trust to talk to.it had always been in my nature as they say, and I knew not many people would keep their mouths shut, but if I gave a promise, I kept it and if I gave my word then that was unbreakable, but some of the things she told me were just too sick. But I needed to take things Penny told me with a pinch of salt, now I know what it's like not to be believed.

But if I did repeated any of the stories to anyone, who did take them seriously then only to find out they were all lies then I would have been in so much trouble.

CLICK…tape off

CHAPTER 28

MUMS POCKET MONEY ...

Well doctor if I keep this up you will need to buy a new tape recorded, because I will have worn this one out, 'now Aveling why don't you tell me about what happened to you, why did you use a weapon, after all that's why you are hear,' 'well doctor I will get to that in my own good time, after all its you who once told me to start will my earliest memory.

So it's all relevant, I have cut out so many bad stories I just couldn't bring myself to talk about doctor.'

I paused as Aveling walked on by to the back office, what had she meant the bad stories, surly they couldn't get any worse, than what I had been listening to.

CLICK... tape on

Penny once told me, how my dad had wanted more than just one of them in bed together, then he wanted to bring in his friend, Penny described it more like a brothel, she took every opportunity every time dad had visited, she would give me all the gory details, and to be honest it just seemed so sordid. Penny once asked me to join her, when dad was away, she told me because I was still a virgin her mum could auction me, and we would make a lot of money.

Sorry Penny that's not for me, she seemed surprised. but you could make as much as a fifty pound note, again thank you but, no thank you, it was then she told me it had been her mother's idea, Penny went on to explain her mother had a sick way of getting her so called gentlemen callers, to pay her extra, and even if they didn't want sex, they would still call and pay a members fee, as her mother would call it, her extra pocket money,' but most of the men were only there for one thing, and that wasn't conversation.

What do you mean Penny', they would pay even if they didn't want sex. Penny took a deep breath, and began to explain, after a gentleman was a regular, they would get him on tape, so if he caused any problems, later mum would use the tapes to blackmail them, so they would call in on pay day, with money for mum, she told them it was a members fee, but honestly Aveling most just stayed for sex. But if they didn't turn up with the member's fee, mum would then bring the tapes into play.

But if some of them had a daughter it was Pennies, and her older sister's job, to convince the punters daughters, to join them in the house. They would first befriend them. But not telling them about what went on in the house. But Penny and her sisters were always careful to make sure the girls were over eighteen.

They would first ask them in to see how lovely the new home was, then later ask the girls to call in for tea, then over a few weeks when they became comfortable in the house, it was then she would be spoiled with sweets and even given new cloths, we didn't do it with all the callers, just the ones mum said would be, useful to us if we needed them.

They had to be careful because regardless of what the men payed for, some of mothers, and girls were from some very poor families, but they were very proud people, so often to make it work, they would be told, to tell their mothers, that they were old cloths Penny, and her sisters had grown out of, they would remove the tickets from the new cloths.

once the girls did that, Pennies mother, would get us to take the girls upstairs to play at trying on cloths, Penny explained, after they became used to the house, one of Pennies, brothers has close to the girls age as possible, he would turn on the charm, he would convince the girls to become their friends, then each visit the boy would ask for just I little more. maybe just a kiss, at first, then just innocent cuddles.

Then it would all be planned by Mrs. Willkie when she thought the girls were ready, the girls would be invited for tea, but when the you girl arrived, The family would all be out of the house, except the brother he would then tell the girls some obscure story that the family had all gone to visit, someone and wouldn't be back till very late.

Then he was to gently coax them upstairs to the bedroom, by that time he had to be sure he could talk the girls, Penny had recruited from university, into getting a little help from him to remove their cloths, but secretly behind a glass mirror was a video camera.

Everything they did would be recorded, his instructions were to get the girl to be as gross as possible, and as close to the mirror as possible, but no intercourse. Penny went on to explain, that some of the other gentlemen callers would be paying, just to be watching everything, from what Penny called the mirror room, it sounded just like the one above the garage, so I knew what she was talking about.

After that first time, when the girls had given blow jobs on tape, or worse it was easy to control her. Mrs. Willkie, used to say if the house was good enough for the fathers, then it was good enough for the daughters, after all sex is just sex. Now I know Penny knew that's not the way I saw it, Penny never told me how long it took the girls to become house girls, but I guess it didn't really matter just as long as they got them to do as ordered.

so most of the girls, by then had no choice, Mrs. Willkie would then offer the new girls for sale, as most of the girls were still so innocent, some were still virgins, they had no idea what was about to come, the price could be as much as double for a virgin, if they were very pretty the price would often shoot up, Mrs. Willke's instructions were clear, she would get her sons, to only allow the girls, if they were virgins to just give them a blow job on film, leaving her virginity intact, it was like printing money as Penny s older brother once said. This was all his mother's idea, Michael had said it did get him frustrated sometimes, but if he disobeyed his mother orders, there would be punishments.

The girls once on the tape would be threatened if she did not do as she was told, the tapes would be shown to their mothers. so come a Friday night the girls would be sold to the highest bidder. The tapes would then be Mrs. Willkie's extra insurance, if the men ever caused any major problems, and if the tape of the clients didn't work, then she would use the girls tape to keep, them in line by threatening to give the tapes to their mothers. But Penny quickly said her mum wouldn't really have done that,

now I wasn't too sure by what Penny meant, surly a tape of the father s visits would have been enough of a threat, but Penny went on to explain some of the men were hard, and some wouldn't give a dam about their reputations, or what their wife's found out. but their daughters reputation, then that was a whole different thing. But Penny said she didn't believe her mum had ever used any of the tapes, it was just for insurance if she needed it.

it was difficult some weeks, to ensure the fathers visits didn't interfere with their daughters, but Mrs. Willkie had it all worked out like an army exercise, has the last thing she needed was fathers and daughter meeting face to face at the house, Penny even went on to tell me some of the girls enjoyed it, because they could make money. I found it hard to believe, but then again the more I learned, I felt it was just me who had decided to abstain from sex.

On one occasion one of Penny's sisters Anna, had taken upstairs a new client, who had beaten her almost to death, now the punter was a well-known and very influential man in the community, he had gone to the house that evening for the first time, but when you are well known being discreet was vital, after he had been accepted by Mrs. Willkie, he had requested his preference was for virgins, so he was invited back for the Friday auction, but has he was already there that night, he wanted to sample the house goods.

so it was Pennies older sister Anna, well I say older, but she was only few years older than Penny, so I think at that time she must have been in her early twenties, who took him upstairs, that was when things got out of control, and he had started the sex violently, but by the time he had finished he had beaten Pennies sister so hard her mother had to call out the doctor, so Penny's mother decided he had to be punished, she knew she couldn't just cancel his new membership because of who he was, but punished he had to be.

CLICK…tape off…

CHAPTER 29

RESPECTABILITY...
THE PSYCHIATRIST...

Now I knew it wouldn't be too long before my visits would come to an end, so I needed, has they say to check the waters. 'Morning doc, well do you want me to still keep coming,"

Note, 2 start just my private thoughts

It wasn't really an answer I was the looking for, but the look on the doctor's face. I knew then I could get another possibly six or eight more visits, it seemed to be taking longer than I had expected with the screws at the toilets. But Doctor Valerie s face showed a little disappointment.it was the look, I was looking for.

It felt like she was looking forward to the next finished tape, so it was in my mind I could keep things going, till I could at least tell Doctor Valerie the story of Sally Scott.

End of note.

'oh and Aveling I don't want you to think I am not listening to all of those tapes, but after listening to the last tape, I do confess I do think however hard it is to talk about, well you know Aveling, someone being punished for anything is wrong, that's what we have the courts for " "its ok doc, yes some things are harder to talk about, and I am going to attempt, to tell you all about what happened next at Mrs. Willke's house but it just seemed so very cruel, and disgusting, I will probably struggle even explaining it on tape."

"Its ok doc let me speak to the tape it doesn't feel right just standing, hear in your office", Aveling then walked on by, and into the back office.

CLICK tape on...

"I am not too sure where to start describing something so disgusting, it was pure evil, so please forgive me doctor for what you are about to hear.

I was hoping to leave what happed to punters, that beat prostitutes, out of my mind. it is so confusing doctor, at Sunday school I was always told good things, and good girls will always grow up to be ladies, and I so want to be a lady when I grow up, but just these things in my mind, keep swilling around, and just talking about some of them is so hard. I remember trying to tell the prisons shrink,

sorry doctor I meant psychiatrist Doctor Milton, just anything about sex, it was like he was getting to close to my personal space, and has I began to describe what was going on, he got closer and closer, till it felt like he just wanted to hear a dirty story, I swear on one visit I saw him in a reflection from the mirror hanging above is desk, when he went to stand behind me, he was rubbing himself, you know doctor down there.

he once said to me, if I think of the brain has an egg, in an egg box, it wouldn't do anything but think, but if you took it out of the box, how much you would enjoy a fried egg or boiled egg. now having listened to that rubbish for about an hour, I really didn't think he was helping.

Now I don't know for sure, but I think he was trying to tell me to let go of my virginity, that way I would enjoy life better. But on my second visit, he over stepped the mark, first he offered me some help with the schizoid sharing my cell, he told me he could get me moved to a more private cell all to myself.

It was while he was running his hand up my leg getting closer and closer to somewhere, he had no right to be, it was then I knew for sure, all he wanted was me to be moved into a private cell, so he could visit whenever.

It was then I slapped him hard telling him, to go to hell along with a string of word, I would never repeat to you on tape.

But believe me doctor some of those words I never even knew, till I was locked up with some of the worst females, I ever had the miss fortune to meet, now don't get me wrong doc, some of the girls were, has I believed, there due to circumstances out of their control, just to give you one example one of one young girl, I only knew her by her nick name Sobby, she received that name in prison, due to the fact when she had first arrived, that is all she did all day was sob, she told me she was in prison for five years, because she had been stealing from one of the new supermarkets.

when I asked her what she had stolen, she told me bread butter and crisp, but because she had resisted arrest, she had pushed a female officer, who broke her wrist when she fell, so please don't tell me that's ok doc because it isn't, and don't even try to tell me she wasn't telling the truth, because I know she told me the truth.

because when I had been allowed one day, to help out with one of the guards doing some filing, she asked me to take a file back to the wardens office, I had opened it, and read it, the file belonged to Sobby, so that is why I believed her. So doctor do you think it was the correct sentence, because I don't. Now some of the other girls were there for simply being prostitutes, again is it fair, to lock up the girls, and not the men who were using them, again I don't think so.

When you consider the monster of a psychiatrist who was prowling the prisons, for any girls that just took his fancy, now doc he is one of those creepy men who had all the correct answers, for example, when I hadn't been there long, it was quite late when I overheard a new guard stopping him, and asking him, who he was going to see at that time of night, his answer was he had some medication, the girl needed to take, to help her sleep.

now I had overheard the guard offering to take them for him, but he insisted, no he bellowed out, "how dare she cross question me, it was his duty to administer the drugs", the following morning I discovered, the drugs, tablets were for Sobby, so I guess the guard thought she needed them.

Now the next day, I ask Sobby if she was ok. Did the sleeping tablets work, what Sobby told me next shocked me, but knowing as many monsters as I do I wasn't in any doubt. What she told me was true, she told me, the only pill he took her, was a contraceptive pill every night, then he would abuse her. Sobby, then told me what he had done to her, when she first arrived at the prison, she was scared, she was sent to him for therapy, were she made the mistake of telling him, she had a phobia of needles.

When Sobby had only been there a few weeks he came on to the prison wing looking for her, he had a female guard with him, when he found Sobby, he said he needed to give her an injection, to help her, now when Sobby saw the needle, she started to resist, and fight, it was then the guard called for help, when other guard arrived it was decided to put Sobby into a strait jacket for everyone's protection, she would then be transferred to the padded cell till she calmed down.

Now once in the cell, he gave Sobby an injection, he told the guard he would stay with her till he was sure she would go to sleep. Now it was getting very late, some of the guards were changing shifts, he had everything planed, and when he was alone, and he then gave Sobby another injection, and removed the straight jacket.

Then Sobby went on to explain to me, she could not move her limbs, everything seemed so heavy, she open her mouth to speak but her voice was silent, it was then he told her, "now he had her all to himself, she was all his, "after removing her knickers he raped her, after that night she was removed to the new wing, were he would, bring her the so called sleeping pills.

Then there were the girls who I felt needed to be locked up for life, like my cell mate the mad hatter, as by then that is what I called her, Sorry doc, I was letting my thoughts ramble on again, now where was I oh? I remember that monster of a man, a psychiatrist someone who should have been helping the girls. Now because he worked at the prison, every time he passed me in the corridors he would lean in, and each time offering me more and more.

on his last visit he told me he could get me moved, to a new wing that had all mod cons, it was then I had to bite my lip so hard because all I wanted to do is kill him, now I know, I shouldn't be thinking like that, but I had heard from some of the other girls, that were there for long sentences, he would get them moved, but as new girls came in, he soon got bored with the older ones, so he would then sent back to the old wing,

Now I know I should have told you about Doctor Milton agers ago, but would you have believed me, now it was only because the courts had insisted I must have counseling, before they could pass judgement. And I flatly refused to be seen by him.it was then the prison warden sent me to you? But I now knew doctor Milton was just trying to get me angry, so he could get me in a strait jacket, but you know me doc, well let's not go there, you will just get upset with me again, but I had always said I would kill myself if a man forced himself on me, but now the first thing I would do is protect the other girls. But trust me doctor you don't need to know how.

And doctor, remember what we say in this room, on those tapes it's not for sharing, and I believe if you say anything, and doctor Milton gets questioned he will only deny everything, then he would then unleash such anger out on me and the girls. I know the girls are all too afraid of him, so please doctor what you hear, on these tapes is strictly for your ears only.

CLICK…TAPE off

CHAPTER 30

PUNISHMENT...

On Aveling next visit, she seemed distant, I had watched over the months her mind was becoming more and more aggressive, but I couldn't blame her, I knew it was the environment she was being held in, I had wanted to tell the warden what Aveling had told me, but she had seen my face, then she reminded me everything she had just told me that visit, in that room on that tape, was strictly for my ears only.

CLICK...TAPE...ON

"well I'm sorry doctor Valerie, but I want you to know if anything happens to me you know who is responsible, but for now all I can do is continue with our tapes, but I am not too sure how much longer the warden will allow me to continue.

I guess that's why the tape just seems to work, just being able to stop it, when I need to think about some words, that I need to say, to explain fully, I still find some words offensive to my own ears, mum always told us not to use bad words, never to swear.

Poor mum if she only knew what I had seen, and was now having to say to anybody, let alone on to a tape recorder. But she never will know, and she will never know because I have left that life, so very far behind me. I loved her so much but with so many other children, I would like to believe she will never miss me. After all I had caused so many problems for her, and I think she sometimes looked at me but was thinking of my twin.

'Sorry about the long pause doc. it was thinking about mum. I don't want to talk about the prison anymore, it is just making me angry and that would play straight into that monsters hands.

So let's get back to what you really want to know, 'how to punish a man who could be so nice out in the community, and so evil to anyone, who he thought had crossed him. Well doctor Valerie, it's just so bad, but thinking about what Penny told me, I just feel so bad for that man's daughter. but Penny had to do has she was told. Or so she said, but I was beginning to doubt it, I didn't think anyone could make Penny do things she didn't want to.

After her brother had befriended the man's daughter, and no doctor I won't use the man his real name. Nor that of his daughter, but when Penny had first told me what they had done, she never used his name but more to the point what he did for a living.

But Pennies brothers name who did most of the befriending was called, Michael he was I think about nineteen, and I must admit quite hansom, but he reminded me of my own brother Luke, so there was just some think in his eyes, you know doctor that evil look. so I made sure to give him a wide birth, but the man who beat up Pennies sister Anna, and his daughter was just referred to as the mark, the man's daughter was a beautiful girl but to Michael it didn't matter a mark, was a mark.

Michael called all the girls, his new challengers. Now he talked his way into becoming this girl's boyfriend, after a short while he would take her upstairs, and everything was recorded. But this girl was special she was still quite small and very pretty. So Pennies mother who only saw money, decided because of her father's actions, has he had hurt her daughter, it was fair game for her to hurt his.

It seemed like Mrs. Willkie had no feeling for the poor girl at all, just the money she could make for the house, if all went well with her sons powers of seduction, getting the poor girl to do as he asked, all Mrs. Willkie had to do was step back, and give out the orders.

now after Michael convinced the poor girl, to give him a blow job, his mother had insisted on that occasion, that was all he was to do, because the men behind the mirror had only payed to watch a blow job, by now the girl had stayed over on rare occasions when the house was closed for special days, it was Penny who would ask the girl's mother if she could sleep over for a girly pajamas party, I guess the poor girl's mother hadn't been as well informed about what happens in that house has my mother.

but it wasn't Penny who would be spending the evening with her, it was Michaels job to kept taking her to his bedroom, to play at first innocent games, he would have her trying on new cloths she would be given expensive gifts, but he told her he liked blond girls best, he coaxed her into wearing a blond wig. when she was there at the house.

Then a little while later he asked her to wear a very pretty hand painted mask to roll play, he kept everything low key, and kept her happy. Now it seemed strange to ask some of the girls to wear the pretty masks, but over the years Mrs. Willkie Penny's mother found with some of the more shy girls, it seemed to help with their confidence.

When Michaels mother decided everything was ready to make a move she summoned all her most valued clients, stating she was going to have the prettiest little virgin ever, for the Friday nights auction, the virgins auctions were mostly on the last Friday of the month, but when she had as she called it a very special virgin, then she would change the day, she knew the girl's father wasn't going to be there that night, 'but he did have some very strange requests.

has he, one month would ask not just for a female, but also one of the young men to join him in a private room, it was an expensive evening but he wasn't the kind of man to worry about the price of anything, he always asked for the most expensive drinks, and Mrs. Willkie was only to please to give him what he asked for, but after he had beaten her daughter so badly, she did threaten him if he could not control his temper, no matter who he was she would ban him.

Mrs. Willkie didn't know then, but when she had told him, he could be bared

That it was him who would see to it that whenever Mr. Willkie was due to be released from prison, his parole was put on hold. but knowing Mr. Willkie was in prison, was just one of the reasons why he had chosen Mrs. Willkie's establishment in the first place, another reason was, he had been told about the Friday night auctions for virgins, also he could choose from not just girls but boys also, in the sixties it was still illegal, for men to get together in that way, so every precaution was taken, on those special nights.so security was everywhere.

Now normally the girls are placed in pretty dress s, and were walked into the living room to be displayed for the punters to drool over. now knowing the girl's father was not going to be there that night. But one of the other men who was known for being a brute of a man was, now he also worked with the new client, so Mrs. Willkie thought he was the perfect man to fit into her devilish plan, now when that man arrived he was escorted into the kitchen were Penny s mum was waiting for him. she offered him a large whisky, and told him the last auction of the night was special so he needed to hang on to his money.

There were two other girls that night to be auction,

But she only wanted him bidding on the last virgin, so she explained that the other two girls, may not be true virgins, now both the other girls that night had been working at the house for some months, and were still young, but definitely not virgins. When everyone had settled down in the living room, the boys kept refilling their glass, the auction wasn't going to start till late. But when the time came the other girls had their buyers, most men had dropped out when the prices kept going up and up.

but all the other punters knew that after the girl had been broken in has Penny put it, the other men were allowed to bid again, for second place then third excreta, but during the evening Penny's mum kept leaning in to her new nemesis, telling him the third girl was so, so special, but on virgin nights the men were not allowed long with each girl.

Now the auction for the special girl waiting upstairs, would be held last she was to be laid out naked, on a bed of rose petals, and she would be wearing a mask because the girl didn't want any of the men to recognize her. if he saw her in the street or town. it was then when one of the men asked if the girl was willing, why I don't know, but he also asked for extra time, Mrs. Willkie went on to explain the girl had agreed for a high fee, because she came from a very poor family and they needed the money, all lies, but that never bothered Mrs. Willkie but she needed to keep her identity private. But no one was allowed extra time on those special nights because of the numbering system, the rules were, enter the room, shag the girl, then out, so the next man could enter.

Now upstairs the special girl had been kept busy by Michael, he had been also giving her just small amount of alcohol all night, she wasn't drunk, but he had also given the poor girl drugs, I think Penny did tell me what it was called but I don't remember the name.

It was easy for Michael to get her clothes off, then he kept talking to her till he was sure, she was ready before putting on the mask. That night. She had trusted Michel, he was after all her boyfriend. Up till then he had never given her anything that would have caused her to worry.

She had always done as she was asked, he then laid her on the bed. He then stayed holding her gently, whispering into her ear, he then asked if he could have sex with her, Michael started to stroke her Brest then kissing her all over, regardless of her sometimes saying no don't, but she seemed to be responding like a woman wanting to be taken there and then. He wanted to be the first, so it was taking all his willpower, to keep his mind thinking of other things.

but he knew by then, she was more than ready, his mother had arranged a signal, with Penny waiting down stairs till the auction was completed, then Penny was to creep upstairs, quietly opening Michaels bedroom door, so there was full access the young girl who would be laying their naked, laid out on the rose petals, with Michael holding her head gently to stop her from ripping of the mask.

Within minutes, with the door wide open, Michael told the girl to open her legs as wide as she could for him, so when Mrs. Willkie's nemesis. seeing what he thought was his new little blond haired virgin, he had just payed so much for, he was so eager to take his prize, jumping on top of the girl, violently forcing his cock hard inside her, has for him, that's the way he liked it, the more violent the better, before the girl even knew what was happening trying to scream, trying to pull away, but the tape holding on the mask that night was too tight, it all happened in a moment, as Michael was still holding her head firmly so she couldn't rip off the mask.

just as soon as he had finished, he was hastily rushed out of the room, by Penny, but once back down the stairs, he was boasting it was his best fuck ever, the little virgin was so tight it had been amazing, to be the first, pushing so hard, so he could feel her ripping inside, he was bragging to the other men waiting. He claimed it was the best feeling ever, and encouraged the other men to take up their winning bids second, third, normally when the men had finished they would leave the house.

But this man had other ideas, he went looking for Mrs. Willkie, who was in the kitchen when she saw him just for a split second she thought he knew who the girl upstairs was, but no, it was then he went on to say, he thought the girl upstairs had been a bit too skinny for him, has he preferred them with a bit more to hold onto, so maybe next time, he explained, and went on to express he didn't like the numbering system, or the mask, as he liked to see them, when he forced his cock inside them. But Mrs. Willkie didn't give a dam what he preferred just as long as he payed for her servicers.

Penny went on to explain to me, for money her mother would promise them just about anything they asked for, it was then I raised my voice at Penny, how could she be involved with anything like that, it's to cruel, I mean doctor, rape is bad enough for any woman, but to rape them when they were drugged, and then they were being blackmailed, and threatened was immoral, that just made my so angry. But Penny was adamant it wasn't rape, because they had been payed for their servicers, it was no good doctor I just couldn't get through to Penny.

I told Penny that it was unforgivable, and she needed to stop it, now I remember hearing a word on the news, that I had to ask my mother what it meant, mum tried her best to explain, but it was Pam who explained what a bisexual was. I told Penny then I didn't want to hear any more of her stories, but I knew I would have to do something to stop what was going on in that house.

Penny just didn't know when to keep her mouth shut, so she continued explaining what they did next to those poor girls was, Penny seemed to think it was justified, as her father had hurt her sister Anna that gave them the right to hurt his daughter.

by now upstairs, the girl had managed to remove the tape, and mask, but Michael held his hand over her mouth, pinning her down tightly so she could not escape, the other guys all knew, new girls always screemed.so they just carried on, they didn't care that Michael was still in the room, after all they had all payed highly for the special one, as she had been named.

it was then, part of Michaels job to keep her there in that room till morning still giving her drinks till she pasted out, in the morning again it was Michaels job telling her she had agreed, and if she told anybody what had happened. he would tell her parents. He then kept telling her it was only him who had had sex with her, but she had been too drunk, to understand, that story had always worked with the new girls.

he then promised her, has she was now his real girlfriend, when she comes back the next weekend, he would show her he, was the only one, who had sex with her.by the time the girl left for home she was so confused she was feeling ashamed. She didn't know what had really happened, because of the mask, she had no idea that she had been also drugged. But by now Michael knew what was expected of him.

so when the girl returned to the house, the following week, she felt she had got to know the truth, and naively believed it was Michael who could tell her, but Michaels job was almost over, he had now complete control of the girl, but they didn't want her to see the rape tape of that night, but she was a pretty little thing that could earn good money for the house.

now that after all, is going to be good for businiess.so when Michael again coxed her up to his bedroom, he was so sweet, he had presents for her, he treated her so well, Michael could get the girl now to do just about anything he asked for, he told her if she let him fuck her again, He went on to explain that it was always difficult for girls the first time, so he had only given her the drink to help with the pain, but he hadn't realized she had drank so much. So he convinced her to let him fuck her again, so she could feel what it was like to have a man's cock inside without the alcohol.

At first she said no, but Michael was so good at his job, now he had to get a new tape, of them having sex for his mother's plan to work, with just the two of them having sex, because his mother said she needed it, to complete her plan. Michael never questioned his mother's motives he just did as he was asked.

So it wasn't long before he again had her clothes off, he then fucked her as close to the camera, as possible.

So the men who just liked to watch got a good show. After he had finished fucking her, and she finished redressing, it was then, Michael told her, he had something he wanted her to watch, it was then he put up a film screen in the bedroom, and showed her the earlier tape of when she had given him a blow job, it was then, he said he had just made another tape of what they had just done, it was also then, the game was in play, or as Michael put it the mark, marked. so she was to join the other girls later that very night, to be sold along with all the other girls for sex, if she refused then the tape of just the two of them fucking, would be given to her mother.

The Willke's knew her father wouldn't be there regularly, because he only wanted to attend the very special virgin auctions, on the last Friday s of the month. But now Mrs. Willkie knew what he was really after, it would mean on those special days the house would be closed to all other clients. Because of the laws.

The Willke's knew his daughter could only be used on certain days. It didn't matter how much the girl would earn for the house, just as long she kept the money coming in, this wasn't something she didn't want to do, but regardless of how much she begged, and sobbed to Michael. Not to make her do something so awful, the girl was so distorts, but she would be a good asset for the house, for the men who preferred skinny women

But Michael didn't give a dam about how she felt, money was money and she was just another little whore, as that is what he called them after they had been sold. the first time, after that, he lost all interest in them, the girls too afraid to tell anyone, they would get a few shillings for working at the house, they were also told if they didn't turn up, on request, the tapes would be given to their mums. I can only imagine how hard it was for some of those girls.

But the Willkie family didn't give a dam, money was money, and Mrs. Willkie had what she needed. revenge

CLICK…tape off

CHAPTER 31

SHE WAS THE CAPTAINS DAUGHTER...

When Aveling arrived the following week, the doctor had her head down writing something that seemed to have all her attention, 'Sorry about last week's tape doctor but sometimes it's difficult. when I started coming to see you, I thought I could keep some things like that, so tightly wrapped up in my mind, but I seemed to be all over the place, and I was never too sure when it came to Penny, she did tell such stories, so I find some of the stories very confusing, and I am not to sue if I am explaining them correctly, oh well now that's the way I have started I don't want to go to all the way back to the start, that would just confuse me more, so shall I continue were I left off,'.

"ok Aveling just let me know if you need me, 'Aveling felt a little confused that the doc hadn't even looked up at her, she felt maybe, what she had said on the last tape, had embarrassed the doctor so much she couldn't face her. Aveling knew what happened at the Willkie's house had happened so long ago, but she still thought Doctor Valerie would want to ask questions as to where the house was, but Aveling knew that house, was no longer there.

CLICK...TAPE...ON

I was confused doctor, some things were bugging me, did Penny after showing me into her home, all those months ago, is that what Penny had intended to do to me, I need to ask her, Penny seemed for the first time since I knew her, she dipped her head as if a little ashamed, she then went on to explain, "do you remember mum asking you for your full name," yes, 'well when she heard your name, she know you were the captains daughter, so mum knew all about you and your brother Luke."

"it was because you called the police, she knew you would not be an easy mark, but it was when she offered you a glass of orange juice, and you declined, now I know Aveling because you told me, that orange juice was your favorite," well I knew from my sister Pam s experience, and again by what happened to Betty there was no way I would accept any drink from anyone, and defiantly not orange juice from a strange woman.

so after my brother worm sandwich, if I hadn't made the food myself I didn't want it, has I said doctor fore warned, the better my chancers, Penny went on to say her mum would often offer the new girls drinks with drugs in. but regardless of all the little things, you were the captains daughter, and mum was so afraid of him,' so she thought better of it, regardless of her constant grumbling that you would have made the house good money.

'Why I don't understand. you have just told me, what your mother did to the V.I.Ps. daughter,' 'yes he would be, and will be a danger for us all at the house, but mum has the tape so, ok Aveling I will tell you who he is, he is the chief of police, so if mum finds out from any of the other police officers that use the house, if there are any raids planed, on the house mum will blackmail him with the tape, of him with one of the young men who work at the house.

Not only would he lose his job, but as they would say, they would throw the book at him. "I mean let's face it after he used the house not for just the women, but men. But the tape they had on is daughter wearing, the mask as Mrs. Willkie would say was to conceal who her nemesis was, as he was also a police officer, a sergeant with one of the curliest streaks Mrs. Willkie, knew all about his temper as she had used him before for jobs, and just referred to him as her nemesis, so she couldn't take the risk of the girl recognizing him.

After Michael had the recording, he would cut it to make it look like the worse tape ever, and that the officer had known all along, it was the chief of policers daughter, and it was him who has sold her to the following men with numbers. "But the tape had another use if the girl's father ever tried to bring down the house, he would use his best men, and that would include the sergeant, but now with the tapes in her hands she had extra insurance, because if necessary she would as I was told use the tape to show the chief, with the result of turning officer against officer.

Penny went on to explain, "But your dad Aveling. Well that's a whole different matter, he is a killer, and we all know to handle him, very carefully, very carefully, in fact mum has never warned us of any of the other punters, like that before,' 'stop their what do you mean a killer,' 'I don't know but mum says, he is the most feared man she as ever met. Now Aveling you know my dad's still in jail, but my dad's told mum all the details, now my dad's a very tough man.

But when he found out the captain had become a punter he warned mum, telling her all about him, 'but your dad Aveling was one of the men who used our servicers at the old house, but my dad didn't know at that time who he was. I think mum was shocked when she saw him hear the first time, but I think mum already new about your dads temper, it was then mum found out that he only lived a few streets away. With such a large family."

So doctor I don't know how to explain it, but I can confirm dads temper knows no limits, but a stone cold killer, I guess I didn't want to believe it, but deep down I knew it was more than possible, after all it was dad who held me by the throat till I almost blacked out, if it hadn't been for mum that day, who knows what would have happened.

Now on one evening as we walked home from work, I made a mistake in asking Penny, why I never saw her eldest brother, she told me it was his job, to do what Michael did with the girls, her older brother would do with the boys, she went on to explain because it was still illegal in this country, they had to be extra careful, so it was better if we didn't discuss it. after Penny said that, I agreed less said the better. after all I had already seen the special room above the garage.

Now when I had first met Penny her eldest sister was pregnant but I hadn't seen her out with the baby, so I asked Penny if the baby had been a boy or girl, 'what are you talking about Aveling,' 'you know your sisters baby,' 'Aveling there is no baby it was still born,

'I told her how sorry I was doctor Valerie, but what she said next, shocked me, she said they always used condoms in the house, but, her eldest sister, was the milk maid so whenever her milk dried up she would have to get pregnant again, but after this last baby.

Her sister said she wouldn't do it any more, now doctor you probably know more about this than me, but you know me, I had to know all the details, so I asked Penny to explain, and this is what she told me, they had some clients who would pay a premium, for a full night, with the house milk maid, so it was always important to have a sister who had a supply of breast milk.

Penny did say she hadn't done it yet, as her mother said she was still too young, and that may cause too many questions.

but she had found it funny when one night, as she was walking up to bed to sleep in the early hours, a man dressed as a baby, with giant nappy little baby booties, and a huge rock dummy, came running down the landing, with her sister in hot pursuit, saying, 'you naughty little baby, you come back her at once, then when she caught him, she sat on the top stair and smacked his bottom.

after he had been spanked, she took him back to the bedroom where he would suck her tits till she was empty, but the funny thing Aveling, was the next morning, when he came out of the bedroom he was dressed in a suit with expensive rain coat over his arm and wearing a bowler hat.

Now Aveling I didn't know how to say this but, I had to go back into my room, because I just couldn't stop laughing, I wasn't sure if it was the sight of him as a baby the night before, or the city gent, that made me laugh so much. Now mum is a big believer in condoms, but sometimes we have accident, but to be honest Aveling it's my other sister Anna who has had the most accidents.

Mum even said if she got pregnant, again my sister Anna would have to keep the baby, because the coat hanger man had just put his prices up. I found out from my sister, she was taking payments behind my mums back, so some of her client picked her because she didn't always insist on a condom, and for that they gave her, well you know Aveling a back hander.

Penny have you ever had sex without a condom, "no never", it was then Penny paused. I could see from her response, her tone of voice that Penny was lying, after all the other stories, I believed I knew when Penny was lying to me, sometimes I was hoping it was all lies, but when she said again "no never," so I told her it was alright, I wasn't going to tell anyone, it was then she told me, she had got the idea from her sister, if she had a private client she could make some extra cash, all for herself, so she asked me if I remembered the man who used to make snide remarks to us when we walked passed his house on the way to work, well yes of cause I did.

"well. One day when I was on my own he beckoned me over, it was then he asked me if I wanted to earn some extra pocket money, well I had never seen him in the whore house so I knew he wasn't a client, but I don't think he knew who I was, I believed he thought I was still a virgin, in fact he actually said to me, he had to have a clean girl, as he didn't want to give his wife any stds, the bloody cheek of the man.

but anyway Aveling we agreed a price, but it was all a bit strange, he only wanted me at eight thirty in the morning because, that was after his wife left for work, then he had to get to work for nine, the evenings would be out of the question, because his wife would be home then, so when I arrived at his house he told me, to have my knickers off, has he didn't have time to waste because his bus was always on time.

So I would arrive not wearing any pants he would be waiting just inside the front door wearing a shirt and tie very smart indeed, but he had his trousers around his ankles, so as soon as I arrived, he instructed me to lay on a hall bench, it was the most uncomfortable thing ever, but money is money Aveling, but I would never let him enter me without a condom, so as soon as his cook was full, but trust me when I say I had never seen I man, any man get a full cock so quickly, it was then, on with the condom, and down to business.

to be honest Aveling when I say quick he barely got started then finished, the first time he was so excited, he no sooner got is cock inside my fanny when he was done, I barely got to my feet, when he was fully dressed then we were out the front door, like lightening.it went on like that, every time till one day, when I arrived he asked me to bend over so he could enter my fanny from behind, but as he was paying it wasn't something I hadn't done before.

So I would bend over the hall bench, but just as normal it was quick,

After a few months mum asked me why I hadn't asked for any sanitary products, it was just something if I am honest I didn't think about, I told mum I hadn't had a period for almost three months, it was then mum, who insisted I needed a visit from the coat hanger man, but I told mum no, I couldn't be pregnant, because I had always used a condom, but mum insisted.

apparently the coat hanger man had a test he could use to see if I was pregnant, the test was positive, so the arrangements were made, and when he came round to do the abortion, mum had been angry, she just thought I had let a punter fuck me without the condom, but I knew I hadn't but the more I thought about it, I just didn't understand.

but what I do remember is that visit from the coat hanger man, it was my first time Aveling, it hurt so much I decided there and then, I would never let another man fuck me without the condom. the following week when I returned to university, stopping off at my private punters, everything was just the same, no knickers bend over the bench then it was all over, but that time has he was hastily pushing me through the front door, I felt something wet run down my leg,

Then it dawned on me, it was him taking me from behind, I hadn't seen him putting on a condom, it had to have been him, but then I remembered, I had just let him do it again, I grabbed him by the arm and demanded to know why, he just pushed me off," 'saying he wasn't paying for fucking condoms', "he then told me not to come back again.

That I hadn't even been a good fuck", but trust me Aveling he will get his punishment, I already have something in mind". Later that week Penny was only to please to tell me what she had done. Has always she seemed to get some excited pleasure in telling me all about it?

well doctor, Penny went on to explain as she puts it, men don't change their habits, so Penny had asked one of the other girls from the house to help, first of all she would start passing his house at the same time in the morning it wasn't long before he beckoned her over, so as they say game on.

Now she was to tell him she was still a virgin, with that he seemed only to keen, to want to get her knickers off, so it was arranged she would turn up the next morning, pants off and ready. now Penny had told his wife what her husband had been doing, but like all the wife's 'she hadn't believed her.

So Penny said she would prove it, so on that morning the new girl had told him, she would only do it in a bed. as this was going to be her first time it needed to be special.so he had agreed, he went on to tell her he had booked a whole day off work, so he would make it so special for her, so the front door would be unlocked so she could walk in, and go directly upstairs were she would find him waiting for her.

Now before the girl went upstairs she left the front door wide open. After the girl had removed all her cloths, she was also told if possible get him naked to, her signal was to look through the window.

so Penny, and the wife could see her, so Penny had told the girl to stall him because he was always so quick, so just as he was taking his new little virgin, Penny had timed it perfectly, so in they walked, the wife flew at him, so Penny could see his face first hand, it was then she, told the wife that he had made her pregnant, Penny didn't mention the abortion, she felt it was his time for pain, Penny then went on to say, her friend was a whore, who worked at the whore house, and she had just given him an s.t.d. that wasn't true, but the more pain she could cause him the better.

now Penny saw no wrong in anything she was doing, but I believed somewhere in the back of her mind, she must have been thinking about the pain he had caused her, to experience during the abortion, Penny told me when they were leaving, he was curled up on the floor, with the wife knocking six bells out of him. she told me it had felt so good, I told Penny it wasn't right, she looked at me, as if to say what the hell would you know.

'Penny why do you let your mum use you like she does, 'well it's always been that way for me, all this is normal, for as long as I can remember. Look Aveling look at where I live, I have everything I need and want, it was then she made me feel so, well you know what I mean doctor I was made to feel uncomfortable, that was something Penny was getting good at.

Penny went on to explain she had always opened her legs for anyone who will pay mums price, as I am still young, and mum gets more for me in one night, than both my older sisters put together, mum says I am her favorite, 'Penny can you remember the first time,' Penny smiled she seemed only too happy to tell me all about it.

I guess just to be able to talk to anybody about what her life was all about, but the more Penny told me the more anger I felt inside, I was thinking how I can help her. how can I get through to her, all those men, it just isn't right, then I thought I could tell the police, what was I saying, what was I thinking.

Penny had just explained her family had the chef of police in their pocket along with other officers. When I considered the prison, and the girls who were there for prostitution, it all made my blood boil. When I thought so many monsters roaming free, what did they care, they didn't give a dam about the girls, in prison, but in my head I had what I called my monster list, that someday I would be able to reduce one way or another.

Penny went on to explain, her earliest memory was when she had been eighteen she had asked her mother for a puppy, her mum told her if she wanted a puppy she had to ern it, all Penny had to do is let her mum auction her to the highest bidder, Penny didn't know back then that would also mean, all the other bidders who would have numbers.

Penny went on to explain because she was so innocent, when the word was out that Mrs. Willkie was having a special auction, her mum had a room of very special clients that night, you know Aveling men who had lots of money, mum said she would only use her best clients as it was my first time, they were all so keen to get the auction started, as we didn't have a nice house back then, mum held the auction in the living room, mum told me it would hurt a little, so she wanted me to drink some milk it tasted awful, but looking back Aveling I believe she must have put something in the drink.

so I could only drink a little of it, mum then explained I would fetch more money if I acted, you know Aveling act innocent, so she put plats in my hair, and told me to act all shy. When mum showed me to the men that night, I was taken into the room naked, mum held my hand at first, then she stood me in the middle of the room. I did feel a little strange but I think that was the drugs, some of the men closest to me leaned forward stroking me, they were all saying such nice things to me, it made me feel so pretty, but they kept going in and out of focus, it was so strange, so it must have been the drugs, but I trusted mum,

It felt strange but mum told them if they liked what they saw it was bidding time, has the bidding went on mum, and the punters seemed happy with me. I knew when mum put her hand up, it meant I had earned enough to buy a puppy, all I had to do then, is lay down and open my legs as far apart as possible. but if I am honest Aveling, the first man took me there and then in front of all the other men, I remember screaming so loud because it hurt so much, but it was then one of my older sisters put her hand over my mouth, to keep me quite, you see Aveling, the old house was an old terrace house, and the people living next door would consistently complaining to of all people the police.

but mum just pored some baby oil on the next man's cock, and told him to get on with it, but it still seemed like forever, but they had payed, and although I was trying to cry, and trying to scream no one seemed to care, I looked at mum I wanted her to stop them, you see Aveling back then I believed it would only be one man, the highest bidder, and only then after we went upstairs, but she didn't, stop them so one after another they kept going, it seemed like the longest day of my life, till mum said it was over.

'I remember being so mad with mum, I asked her why hadn't she stopped them, when I begged her to stop them, she said she hadn't seen anything like it herself, she could only describe it, as like a feeding frenzy. Then she showed me all the money. Then promised me we would go and pick up the puppy in the morning, I remember the morning after, I couldn't get out of bed it still hurt so much, and she never took me to get the puppy, she just kept saying the garden wasn't big enough, and I would get one when we moved.

When we moved house to come and live here, mum told us, all that screaming, and gentlemen callers in the old house had caused problems, because someone had reported us, to the council, and the police had been ordered to call round, it was an officer from the local police station who was a regular suggested we should move, he said they could keep things quiet, when the neighbor's phoned them, but the council that was a different thing all together, because they could evict us without warning. I had no idea how we could afford such a lovely house, but thinking about it back then Aveling.

mum must have been saving the money, from all of us working as gentlemen's friends, mum always referred to us that way, because she hated the title prostitutes, as that is what she had been called when she was a young woman working from the street corner, she told us how other women treated her so badly calling her names, it was then she decided just as soon as possible, she was going to get off the street now mum was smart, and only did work the street corners till she met dad.

They married shortly after meeting, mum always told us, that she had only married him because he had his own house, even though it was only a council house it was better than standing on the street corners. But I think mum was just kidding. Sometimes mum would boast about some clients, being the husbands of the women who called her names, so if she saw one of her clients wife's, during the daytime while shopping, mum would taunt them, by saying, how much she had enjoyed spending all the money there husbands had given her. this on occasions would end up with mum fighting in the streets, we lost count how often she had been arrested, but they never kept her long, after all she knew too much".

"so when we moved here, I was still angry with everything, and everybody because I didn't want to move, mum picked this house, because it's away from the road, and no one can hear screaming, but mum did the same again, telling all the new members that I was still a virgin, but I told mum I wouldn't let more than two men use me per night, when we first moved here, but mum had other ideas",

"But Penny why did you agree to do it", "oh Aveling you are so naïve, we had a father in prison a new mortgage to pay, bills to pay, and let's face it what kind of jobs would we get so much money for, just, look at you, sometimes when you leave work you often complain about how tired you are, you start at seven thirty in the morning, and for what, you get payed three pounds a week, and I knew because you told me you give your mother two pounds a week. I ern five pounds a night for the house and I receive five pounds a week from mum", " but Penny why do you go to such an expensive university, if your mums worried about the mortgage," "ok Aveling let me try to explain, I knew mum had no intentions on letting me have a dog, she couldn't risk it digging up my brother prize roses, so to keep me quiet, the only other thing I wanted was a qualification from university, so she arranged with one of the special punters who like boys, to pay for my fees.

but what mum doesn't know, is as soon as I am twenty one, I am out of here, and that house, you see It's not just art, and math's I have been studying, but jobs in London, so you see Aveling, I will pick a company with assets, and I private owner, then I shall get myself noticed and let's face it I don't think any man will rebuff me, I mean just look at me Aveling, I often get so many complements on my long legs, and being five foot seven, I did think about modeling, so I can always do that if necessary till the perfect job comes along". "I see so you have everything worked out",

"Till then I will let mum think that when I leave uni I will join the rest of them and work in the house, anyway I was telling you about the virgin nights so the men would line up to get their turn by the end of bidding, the men were only too keen to get their prize. Before that auction mum again gave me the talk, she told me again to act more innocent as the more I acted all innocent the more money I would fetch. but I made it clear on that night, I would only allow, no more than six men to shag me.

so on that night she dressed me up, it was a bit weird if you ask me Aveling, but she wanted to dress me up like a bride, she told the men I was still only eighteen, but that birthday past a long time ago, After I had been taken into the living room that night, I was taken back by how many men were there. I looked directly at mum, she just shrugged her shoulders, and I told her there were too many she just smiled, saying I could handle it, and she would have a special treat for me later.

It was my older sister Anna who would remove my cloths so slowly, then item by item, she would throw them to the men. Mum knew some off the men liked to keep souvenirs of the virgins they had taken.

By the time Anna had removed my knickers, the men were well agitated they were starting to get inpatient. Anna then gave my knickers to the first man as that was his trophy.

So once again it turned into another feeding frenzy, when I entered the room that night, I wasn't expecting quite so many men. There must have been eleven or twelve, the room was much larger than our old house, but until I entered the room that night, I hadn't given it a seconds thought that mum would allow so many, she knew how I felt. So one after another they just continued, the men were going mad.

she had barely got the money from the first punter, when there and then, naked he just pushed me down on some cushions, he was so rough, but just as soon as he got up the second was already to start, after just four or five I was feeling quite sore, I tried to push the next man off, telling mum I was too sore to do any more, but the punter just pushed me back down, and started to fuck me again, on seeing that," it was my sister Anna who dashed into another room to get some lotion just in time before the next man was about to enter me.

After that night I told mum I wouldn't do any more virgin nights, there were just too many men. It was then mum gave me almost anything I asked for, or I just wouldn't let any men shag me anymore. But it was about that time mum started her tape collection, so she could blackmail the new girls, I brought home. Mum told me if I didn't want to do the virgin nights any more, then I had to get some girls from uni, so she could still have her special auctions, so that is when it had all started, up to then it was just my brothers sisters, mum, and me".

It was then I got so cross with Penny. "how could you do it Penny, you know how much it hurt you, so why would you help her to take so much from such innocent girls," "oh Aveling wake up, I was only eighteen, when I had my first cock inside me, and when you have had one they all feel the same, any way I was doing the girls a favors, so I think if they are still virgins at eighteen they are more than ready.

let's face it some of the girls were great full for the money, and gifts mum gave then, most of the girls from university, Aveling you know some of them are so poor, on scholarships so they were only too happy to take all the gifts, and let's face it Aveling you are the only one I know who is so against sex, and if any family could do with some extra money it's yours. And I do honestly believe if you let us auction you, mum would get such a high price.

You would be in such demand at the house, you could be the highest paid girl there. You just don't understand Aveling when you get all that attention from the men, they would be eating out of your hand, they would buy you anything you asked for. look Aveling just think about it, I have already had a chat with my brother Michael, he says he would be so gentle breaking you in, so you would hardly feel a thing. "And he promised me, he wouldn't give you anything to drink unless you asked for it", I gave Penny such a look, she just didn't get it, that kind of life was not, and never will be for me, at any price.

CLICK...TAPE... OFF ...

CHAPTER 32

RAPE IS RAPE....

"Morning doctor shall I go through,"

"Yes Aveling but I may have to pop out for a few minutes, will you be ok by yourself, I won't be gone long, I just need to fetch so more notes from the reception," "its ok doc I am not planning on going anywhere", looking over my shoulder at Tom and Jerry, chance would be a fine thing.

CLICK...TAPE...ON

Now doctor, I wasn't too sure if I could believe everything Penny was saying to me, but then again it was her life, Penny went on to explain, just how crazy her life could be.

Penny said she had remembered one crazy experience, when she had arrived home from university still in her uni cloths, her mum was at the door to meet her, she told her, she had a special request, there was a man in the living room who had played over a lot of money, and his fantasy was to rape a girl, still in her uniform, all Penny had to do was play the part kicking, and screaming.

so after it was all over Aveling, he acted really strangely, "you do know what I mean don't you Aveling, "I didn't fully understand but I simply shrugged my shoulders, Penny went on to explain the man, behaved just like it was all real, that he truly had rape me, he was so sorry, and asked me what I would like to keep my mouth shut, well I decided it was about time I got something more out of the punters,

after all the money I had earned for the house, I at that time knew my

195

sisters were getting back handers. so now it was my turn I asked him for a new gold bracelet, I told him I had a love of jewelry, so if he ever wanted me again it would cost him. He didn't even flinch it was like money was not an issue to him.

Yes mum gave me everything I asked for within reason, but when I wanted money, all I would get is a few extra quid, she used to tell us all she needed the money to pay the mortgage, and it was much more expensive than the old council rent. so we would all have to take on extra clients to make up the difference. So I decided it was time to get my own trophies. So I told him how much, and when he needed me again I would go to his house. Now I knew mum would be angry, as she had always warned us it could be dangerous, to go to a punters home, I remembered back to the early morning man, but I didn't care just as long as I made my new client wear a condom after all why should mum, and my sisters have all the extras.

I told Penny it was so wrong what she was doing, by letting him act out a rape, she told me she was doing society a favor, if he was play acting out with her, then he wouldn't be doing it to any unwilling girls, as hard as I tried I just couldn't get through to her, I did try doctor. Her stories were getting more gross every time, now I know that was partly my fault, for after all I did give her my word, I would tell no one, so by then I felt Penny had me trapped, I thought at first Penny just needed a friend who she could confide in.

But now it was like I had become her very own personal psychiatrist, it's like at the end of each day she heads straight for me, so has we are both going in the same direction, it seemed childish for me to start ignoring her, because I know she does still needs help, so I must try and try again if I have to, so I can convince her she has been brain washed by her family, telling her what they all do is normal.

But with a life like mine I was beginning to doubt I knew what normal was any more, I told Penny her mum was right, about going to a man's own house, as she would have no one to call for, if she needed help, Penny told me not to be such a kill joy, and that I didn't know what I was talking about, she told me she knew how to handle any man if he got out of control, she went on to explain her mum had shown her, how to bring any man to his knees, all you have to do his grab him by his cock and balls, then squeeze hard.

Penny seemed to take pleasure telling me that she had used it on one man, who had tried to enter her in her arse hole, now that was one rule of the house, her mother only aloud, if they wanted to enter any of the girls working at the house in the rear, they had to pay extra money and the girls must consent to it, so Penny grabbed him by the cock and balls, till he fell to the floor begging her to stop.

Penny said it had made her feel good to be able to floor any man if he got out of control, I tried to warn her that maybe, that was just one punter, but other man could, just as she released them they would then take their revenge, Penny went on to remind me that her family were experts when it came to revenge.

Now I did remember my sister Pam telling me sex is all just a game, most of the men just want to shag you, and they will then, give you anything you ask them for, in the hopes you will let them shag you again, well doctor.

tell me is it just me who thinks like I do, that if I stay a virgin till I marry, surly that is what the bible teachers us, and my mum says is right, but thinking about it mum was only fifteen when she first had met dad,.

So what's your opinion doctor, do you agree with my sister who does it for, has she says fun, money, and favor, or with Penny, who does it for money or gold, or am I the one who is right, I do confess it's all getting so confusing in my head anyway, I must remember to ask you that question when I turn up next week, because I would love to get your opinion on the subject, I should also like to ask you, why do some girls say it's nothing to lose your virginity, and other girls say it is so painful, they would not want to ever experience that pain again. Now when I hear that knock on your office door, it's time for me to go again. I knew Tom and Jerry would want to get back as quickly as possible,

They were, I felt even getting impatient with me for asking for toilet stops, but that was one little luxury I was not giving up, it always seemed strange when we reached the prison gates, it was like here we go again, telling myself to act normal, well as normal as the rest of them, but some of the girls in there, they were far from normal. But I tried to do has I was told, and behave, but it was getting harder and harder.

DOCTOR VALERIE

CLICK...TAPE OFF…

Private little Note for later doc

Here I was again another long hour stuck in this back office pouring out all my bad memories, has the doctor told me, it was to do me good, but all I could think about, how many more turns of the screws it would take to escape. This is torture, just a few more visits should do it, and I must remember tell doctor Valerie were to find the notes. End of note.

CHAPTER 33

THE LIE.

CLICK …TAPE ON…

Now doctor Valerie I had been walking home with penny for some months and although, I could not understand her life, it seemed to me she just needed someone to talk to who wouldn't judge her, sometimes it was hard, but it was my belief if I tried, and hopefully convinced her to come to church with me, maybe I would stand a chance in helping her, to see what she was doing is wrong, I remembered telling her if she wanted money I could get her a part time job where I worked, it wouldn't pay much but it was honest work. We could ern our own money.

I remembered her response that day, "Work for three pounds a week, getting out of bed at god knows what hour, are you mad." Now what Penny didn't know was if, and when possible if I chatted to some of the new girls I met in the store, I would tell them, don't ever go into Penny Wilkes house. Because her brother would attack them.

I did my best to convince them to keep as far away from Penny as possible, I never gave to many details, I felt ashamed with myself for saying anything, because of my promise to Penny, but some things were just to important, I felt I needed to warn the new girls, the rest was up to them. But it wasn't long before one of the girls, betrayed me and told Penny, what I was saying about her family, but I didn't find out about that till sometime later, looking back I knew in my heart one of them would betray me sooner or later, so it was no big shock, but what happened next did take me a little by surprise. Just how far she was willing to go to get her revenge on me.

It was about that time doctor, her brother Michael would sometimes meet us as we walked home together, he was creepy, Michael would walk a few steps behind us often coming so close to me, he would whisper in my ear, he loved me, I was special he would say he knew I was still a virgin because Penny had told him, his comments would be relentless.

he told me he would never let his mother auction me, I was to special for that but, if I let him love me, oh how he would worship me, but just the thought of him touching me, over the following months just freaked me out, if he ever got to close, my body seemed to react with instinct, and pull away from him. But I believe now that it had been Penny who had set him on me, as part of her sick revenge.

now there had been a young man, I often walked home with if Penny wasn't with me, I knew he didn't like Penny, he knew Penny and I were friends so he never said anything directly to me, but I just knew, he was the same age as me, and so sweet, if he saw me walking home alone, he would join me, he would take my hand, it was so innocent.

But it was one of those nights Michael, had been following me, as he got closer he walked between us, pulling us apart, he then told the lad if he saw him touch me again he would break is fucking arms. It was the following night as I walked alone, their Michael was again, he was relentless. On that occasion he knew I was mad with him, but I thought his treatment, you know doctor that rough manner he had shown me the first time I had met him, somehow wasn't their anymore.

his manner just seemed to change, even his tone of voice had changed, since I had told him off for putting the fear of god into a young man who was just so kind to me.it was then, and only then he seemed to be more respectful, but then knowing, his family I was never sure when they were, being honest. He did remind me of dad, and just how easy it was for him to turn his, as I called it is posh, gentleman's voice, then in a click of his fingers he would be as verbally common as the hardest of men.

Now two strange things happened that night, the first was, as Michael and I were walking, who would walk up to us, it was none other than Jack, now I had wanted to get my revenge on Jack for what seemed like such a long time, has he approached us I swore he hadn't recognized me, I was no longer wearing my brother old trousers, and grandads flat cap.

But I was wearing my smart uniform for work, with my hair falling lose over my shoulders, as he approached he seemed to know Michael, as he then asked Michael if he could get one of his sisters to do him a favor. Then Jack looked directly at me, he then asked Michael if I was one of the new girls at the house, Jack had clearly forgotten all about me, now I wasn't sure, but it was then Michael lunged forward grabbing Jack by the throat, saying if he ever laid a hand me he would fucking kill him. I was his girl and not a house girl.

Now I just found this timing perfect, it was has he was still holding Jack by the neck, I told Michael all about the day when Jack had stood by when I was beaten by that monster of a brother of mine, and how I had been so badly beaten, the doctor believed I had broken bones.

I was watching Michaels face as he turned to me, Michael was still holding Jack by the throat, he looked over at me, and asked did I want him punished, my reply was yes please, it did feel weird, and I wasn't even sure why I had said please, so I told Michael I would like nothing better, but not in front of me, I looked over at Jack face, it was pure panic in that boys eyes. I knew what I was saying doctor, but I felt no regrets.

What Jack had put me through, and little Gemma. I also knew I would owe Michael a favor, Michael then pushed Jack to the floor, simply saying see you later. I didn't doubt for one minuet that Michael would take care of him for me, but it did feel like I had just made a deal with the devil.

It was that night, as we continue our walk home, Michael suddenly pulled me aside just as we were approaching a secluded hedge row, I had been ready for something like that for months, I quickly under my coat put my fingers around my knife on my waist band, I knew I had only just asked for a favor, and I knew one way or another I would need to pay for that.

but it's what he did next that was so strange, he suddenly dropped to one knee, and asked me to marry him, I was, to say, at the least, speechless, I had in no way in my mind given him any signs of any affection, what could he have been thinking, was this just another one of his tricks. Now I knew from Penny that Michael was a master at his trade in getting girls to do just about anything for him. But it was then He told me I had to say yes, it was the only way he could protect me from his family as they had plans for me.

I asked him why now, he explained, he said I was simply worth so much money to them, has his mother had, over heard my dad talking to another man all about, what I was worth to him if he could only get me out of the country to Africa, so Michael explained his mother intended to kidnap me, and hold me for ransom, through her contacts, the captain, would never know she was behind the kidnapping.

Michael told me they were just waiting for all the pieces to fall into place, Michaels dad was soon to be released from prison, they needed to find out when my dad was due home next, but thinking about that, it was Mrs. Willkie who my dad seemed to visit within hours of getting home, but when it came to dads visits, we never knew when he would just turn up, day or night, sometimes we would go to bed, then in the morning there he was.

Oh why oh why doctor, did everybody seem to want a bit of me, I was just trying to be a good girl.so I decided the best thing at that moment was to play along with Michael, by allowing him to believe I would be all his if he kept me safe, I would marry him but not till I was twenty one, and only then would I have sex with him. I knew it was so very wrong of me, but it was like I had no choice if I was to keep control of things, whatever those things would turn out to be.

well I had never seen anyone so excited he was over the moon, as he place a huge solitaire diamond ring on my finger that was something I wasn't ready for, I told him we had to keep it a secret, because I was still too young, so I would put the ring on a chain and ware it around my neck. He then told me about a rock star in America, who ran away with a girl, and got married no fuss, only, I told him I had no intentions of going to America, to get married so he would just have to wait.

It did make me worry why had he mentioned America, was it all just another one of his family's dirty tricks to convince me to get a passport, he then held me tightly, and he only agreed to wait if I promised to always have the diamond with me, we then continued the rest of the way home to my front door were he kissed me. but I didn't doubt for one moment what he was really capable of. The stories that Penny told me about her brother, I had no intention of allowing him to have sex with me. At any age.

It was getting late that summer, the nights were drawing in and it was getting colder. We were walking home from work, Penny seemed quiet,

So I asked her if anything was wrong, it was then she told me the nightmare she had been living, it had started that summer when she took on a private punter, his name was, Arthur he worked as a lecturer at the university she attended, she explained at first he had been so gentle, kind, and as he was a teacher, it seemed to make it somehow easer after all, if she didn't get good grades she knew who to see.

She went on to tell me, she had gone around to his house, directly from university, now Arthur lived in what Penny could only described as a huge old Victorian mansion, Penny told me if I thought she lived like a princess, I should go with her to see Arthurs home, it was beyond grand, now everything Penny said I took with a pinch of salt, some of her stories were just getting to strange to believe, as she continued to explain what had happened next that night. When she had arrived at the house, as always she went around to the back door,

But that night he wasn't alone, sitting in the kitchen at first, he offered her a drink, 'now my little bitch hope you don't mind but I have asked a few friends to join us, 'now she always got good gifts of gold jewelry from Arthur, but she told them, it would cost extra, 'it was then Arthur opened a velvet box inside was the most exquisite gold and diamond necklace.

'Well now my little bitch if you want this, you will have to ern it, he then removed it from the box, and placed it gently around her neck. 'Now their hadn't been much. She hadn't seen or done for her mother's punters so she had no objections, but she was worried that one of the men was black, now her mother had a policy at the house no black men, but the money was so good. But that necklace was unbelievable, she was then taken three floors upstairs. But she was taken into a bedroom she hadn't entered before.

it was dark but she could make out whips, chains, along with sex toys, in the middle of the room was some sort of pummel horse, she was told to remove her cloths, but leave the necklace on, everything seemed, a little strange but she kept stroking that necklace, telling herself that necklace was too good to give up.

it was then one of the strangers, took her by the hand and slipped on a cuff with chains, she then asked him if he had the condoms, he said yes, but she found out later they were not used, Penny was then attached, to another cuff chain, she was then dragged face down on the pummel horse, that was standing in the middle of the room.

The chains were clipped onto hooks on the floor, she admitted to me it was then she realized, as I had once warned her, she couldn't just shout for one of her brothers, if things got out of control, at that point she believed it was all just a game. Until they then cuffed her ankles to again fixing them onto the floor hooks.

it was then the lights went on, it was blinding, Arthur had so many lights lit, it was almost impossible to see anything, clearly at first it was then Penny saw they had so many cameras set up, so she thought to herself, that's what they were up to, she believed they were going to whip her before sex, and during filming

Now she had told me she didn't have many punters who liked sex from behind, but never in the arse hole, as she had insisted to her mother that was something she didn't want to do, because one of her sisters who allowed it, warned Penny how much it hurt. it was then one of the men, started to enter her, she screamed,' 'no not in there, you have got the wrong hole,'as he pushed harder,' 'well now my little bitch that's a surprise after all you do work in a whore house,'

the pain was worse than Penny had ever had, or could remember, she knew he eldest sister allowed men to use her arse hole, but they did pay extra, plus they had a special cream at the house to help the men to get in with out to much force., or that's what her sister had told her.

When Arthur was finished, he dismounted her then went over, to one of the others, he was whispering to the man working the camera. Penny went on describing all the nasty little details of that day, I felt so bad for her, she told me she hurt so much, and didn't realize it was going to get a lot worse, first the second man took his turn.it had hurt so much she had been crying.

But as she thought only one more left, but it was then, after the second man had finished fucking her arse hole, the second man also picked up a movie camera knowing what she did, that movies like that of such a shackled girl, were often sold, onto the black market, she did think if her mother ever saw them, how much trouble she would be in. it was then she heard the door open.

it was Arthur she could hear him asking the others if they were ready. it was then she realized it wasn't just the three of them that day, How could they, how could she have been so stupid, as she began to feel like the ordeal, was never going to stop, as more men took her from behind.

When she thought it was all over Arthur left the room, and the black man who had been working the camera stood in front of her,' 'now my little bitch you are going to keep that pretty little gob of yours shut, nodding her head was all she could do, but it still wasn't over, the guy then removed the leg cuffs and chains, he pushed the pummel from under her, as she fell to the floor in a heap, still chained to the floor by the hand cuffs,

after all he hadn't had his turn yet, she was now laying on her back, on the floor it was then she noticed his cock, "Aveling it was so dark but it was the size Aveling, I had never in my whole life, never seen a cock that size, I was terrified, he lifted my legs as high as my face, I thought there was no way it would fit in my fanny, then as he had to force it in, I felt like he was ripping me, then he just fucked me so hard, but the pain was unbearable Aveling when I finally tried to stand it was so difficult" by the time Penny had been released, and getting dressed, she felt so sick as she was about to leave, one of the men throw a condom at her, 'see told you I had some. 'but let's face it girlie we didn't need them for arse holes now do we, it was then Penny realized the man who had done most of the filming, the black man hadn't used one, so the thought of having to go back to the coat hanger man, had made her very sole panic, Penny just remembered how much it had hurt, but if as her mother had threatened, now she was older if she got pregnant again, she would have to keep the baby full time, as it was her turn, to be the wet nurse, as her sisters were so sick of being pregnant. So if the baby went to full term if it was born black, the thoughts were too much to bare.

It was then Arthur came close up behind her, whispering in her ear, as he removed the necklace from her neck, saying you didn't really believe I was going to let you leave hear with this now did you.

he then pushed a ten shilling note into her pocket, now my little bitch, we will see you next week now wont we, because I have a very special treat for you, Penny knew from her sister Anna that some men had some very strange ideas when it came to sex,

She was told if she didn't show up, they would show the tapes they had just made to her mother, now Penny knew how much trouble she would be in for allowing it all to happen, but not as much trouble she would be in, for allowing a black man to fuck her in her fanny, without a condom, if her mother ever got that information Penny would have been kicked out of the house.

So now it was Penny getting blackmailed.

CLICK...TAPE OFF...

CHAPTER 34

WHATS A FAVOR FOR A FRIEND ...

CLICK...TAPE...ON

Well doctor, I was so shocked by her story how could anyone be so sick, Penny told me when she arrived home, her mother had lined up the first punter for the night, but she told her mother she must have eaten something that had made her sick. And she needed some space. But that night after she told me her story as we walked home, my heart and soul just cried for her, how could they treat any girl like that, I know how naïve I was doctor, but I was learning all to quickly just how evil men could be.

Penny then went on to tell me she hadn't been able to service any of the men that came calling, she explained to me she was worried if the black man had given her any diseases, as her mother always said never have sex with black men, as they all have, or have had to many diseases, so she had just asked her mother for some time, her mother only agreed, if Penny wanted to take a break, she needed to find another virgin for the Friday night auction, or its back to work for me, and I just can't face it,'you do understand don't you Aveling,' 'oh my god of cause I understand,'.

'but it's like this Aveling you're the only virgin left I know, so you will do this for me won't you, 'I drew back from her, I was so shocked, she knew how I felt,' 'no Penny no way,' 'but Aveling I can't live with myself, I just want to kill myself, you have got to help me,' 'the only way I will help is, you must run away I will help you to hide,'.

207

It was then her hands came up, and she begged me. please Aveling please, you have got to do this for me.my reply was a firm no. then she took me completely by surprise.

Her hands opened, and with the flat of her hands she pushed me hard backwards causing me to fall awkwardly, I knew then that was going to leave a very nasty bruise, so there I was sitting on the floor I guess the look on my face would have been a picture, I remembered the ground feeling wet, as It had rained earlier that day, and the ground felt so cold.' then from nowhere her brother Michael appeared, it was what he said next that completely floored me. "You did tell her the story mum told you to tell her,' 'yes everything, but the heatless bitch still wouldn't help me,' 'I told you she wouldn't fall for it,'

he went on to ask for money, from Penny as she had lost the bet, It left me thinking my god all that story, and I had fell for it, I truly felt so bad for her. How gullible was I, how stupid was I, it was then Penny said I had no idea how much money I could get for something that, I would only end up just giving away one day, she then said, her mother wanted me to know, she could get as much as a thousand pounds for me, oh ! Penny just shut up, you just don't get it do you, I am not for sale at any price". Now back in the early sixties that was so much money you could buy a house with it, and still have money left over.

Penny then walked away, as I was left asking Michael, 'what the hell was all that about, you told me your mother had given up on me for the auctions,' 'its ok Aveling I was just having a bit of fun, with Penny, I did tell her you would never consent to it ' 'no Michael that was not fun ",I was so angry with him, so I told him if he ever did anything like that again I would never marry him, I told him he could no longer walk me home, he needed to give me some space.

Honestly doctor how could they be so sick, that was the last time I ever spoke with Penny, I wasn't sure but looking back I think that was her kind of punishment, for me having told the new girls at university all about Pennies house,

But the following week, Michael always seemed to be shadowing my every step, if he passed me it was always so close, he would whisper to me, I love you, and one day you will marry me. The only man who will ever have you is me you are mine,' 'Michael I told you to give me some space,' but he wouldn't listen, if he ever saw me anywhere on the estate, he would rush over, nothing I ever said would stop him. I tried hard to come up with something anything to say to him, to get him to stop, following me about, but he said he had to.

He explained that although his mother had called off the kidnapping, he said he hadn't believed her, so therefore just to keep me safe he would be there at every moment, to protect me, he told me the kind of men his mother knew wouldn't take no for an answer he told me, he believed she was only waiting for his dad to get out of prison in a few weeks.

Now over the last few months, my shape had started to change, my breast was getting to tight for my bra, my hips no matter how hard I tried, they just would not fit into my old jeans. So I had no choice but to wear the dress s my sisters had grown out of.my Mother had acquired some more bras for me as she explained, I was even bigger than my sisters. So their old bras wouldn't fit me, that night I took a long hard look in the mirror, but it didn't seem to be me looking back, I felt that I had grown up so much that summer. I had come such a long way from, grandad's old flat cap, and old trousers tied up with string, that I wore as a child,

Michael was as always a pain. Even when I thought I had given him the slip, he always found me, mum found me hiding one day behind the wall at the corner shop, 'I thought that was you, Aveling, what on earth are you doing down there, aren't you a bit to old now, to be playing hide and seek' 'oh it's the boy from around the corner he's being a pest, as always,' 'do you mean the Willke boy yes mum,' 'he's everywhere I go, I have told him over and over again, to leave me alone, but he just won't." I did think quietly to myself some of it, was my own fault for allowing him to believe I would be his one day. 'Well don't worry your dads coming home this week end. he will have a talk with the boy's father."

So he won't bother you again after that," I was confused I had been lead to believe by Michael that his dad wouldn't be released for a few more weeks, "mum are you sure Mr. Willke is home, because I was told he would still be in prison for a little while longer," "well it was something your dad said Aveling, he was arranging something over the weekend, I don't know what it's all about, you know your dad Aveling if he is up to anything, I am always the last person to find out,"

Now I knew dad never worked with a crew these days, after having been arrested and questioned, about someone who had simply vanished from the face of the earth, now dad had, at that time been released, living in such a small house the sound travelled, so I had overheard a conversation I shouldn't have, as he was telling mum not to worry, but I believed dad could talk himself out of anything, and everything, that would put him back inside prison, so since then dad always worked alone.

"But mum don't tell dad, he will just tell me, I have to fight my own battles. Now I am older' 'oh you silly girl that what dads are for, and now you are older, boys like that are only after one thing,' 'I know mum, I know, but trust me he isn't getting any think from me,' 'yes I know Aveling, your my good girl,' there was something about the way she said that, it was like she must have known what my sisters had been up to, but mum never would talk about sex, or whatever my sisters were getting up to, well not with me. Mum finished her shopping and we continued home together.

Now the following night there was Michael standing at the store exit that was used just for the staff, yet again, I just gave him one of my angry stares as I left work.

Has I began to walk without saying a word to him, he paused just for moment or two, he then just walked about twenty steps behind me, he never tried to close the gap, to tell me all about his love for me, I just felt something was wrong as we neared the same hedge were he had first proposed, something was bothering me, I turned slowly, to see him, he had a look on his face I had never seen before, at first I hesitated, was this just another one of that foul families dirty tricks.

He stopped walking when I did, has I stood there for what seemed like a long time, we were just starring at each other, so ok I beckoned him over, as he closed the gap I never took my eyes of him, why oh, why doctor was he the one who kept pulling on my soul, and heart strings as if there had been an unbreakable invisible bond, because I knew all about how he treated all those young girls, who had trusted him there was no way he was ever getting that close to me.

when we were face to face, I could see he had taken a beating, his face was covered in bruising, he asked if he could talk to me, I smiled, "well nothing I have ever said has ever stopped you, so why ask now," "its important Aveling, ok let's go to the end of the road we can sit on the bench."

When we reached the bench, he asked me if I still had the ring, I slowly lifted it up from under my blouse, with it still attached to my neck he lifted it up, I asked him if he wanted it back, he seemed shocked I would even say such a thing, "no Aveling I, I, just didn't realize when I gave it to you, that you would have it on a piece of string," "well sorry Michael, it's not like I have a gold chain, is this what you wanted to talk to me about,"

"No Aveling it's just that I didn't think you had any feelings for me, but you know Aveling that wouldn't matter to me, I would still love you with all my heart, I so need to see you every day, to see if you are ok. I know exactly what you think of me, and my family, but I have told mum no more, I wouldn't do any of the things that would cause you to be ashamed of me anymore, I know you are so young, and that love to you or feelings can be confusing."

"Look Michael I know it's the only life you know, but why, oh why after you were old enough to know it was wrong, would you keep doing it," "Aveling I need you to know, I have never thought it was wrong till I met you, when I was young, mum told all of us, we needed money to pay the bills, my dad was often in prison. What my family did was just a means to an end. I hated it, I believed my sisters had it a lot worse than me, so what did I have to complain about, but I can tell you in all honestly, the night I heard my sister Penny getting, as mum said broken it, those screams I heard, well Aveling I found them soul breaking, I tried to stop it but I was locked in upstairs, I told mum Penny was to young she had only just had her birthday,"

"Now Aveling I was hoping never to tell you any of this but, I feel like I must tell you the truth, mum did have some rules in the house, the girls were always to use condom, and no talking to anyone, about what we did in the old house to anyone, I was amazed when I found out you knew all about us from Penny.

Now I was only a very young man, when mum had a client called the sailor man, he had been coming to the old house as long as I could remember, they were both in the front bedroom, now Aveling because Penny as told you all about the special room above the garage, I knew you would understand what I am about to tell you, because of what you have seen, and now know, all about homosexuality, and so if that's what my brother prefers that's up to him, but that was never going to be for me, I liked girls too much.

211

"Now Aveling the old house, was a cold damp smelly place, but It didn't have a garage so my brother worked out of one of the bedrooms on the same landing as my bedroom, the old house was a bit of a rabbit run inside so sometimes punters would get lost, on the landing and instead of turning right for my older sisters rooms and the bedroom of my older brother, they would come into mine by mistake so I got used to locking the door.

but on one of those days when I forgot to lock the door, a stranger entered my room by mistake, I yelled at him to get out, he said he didn't like my tone of voice, and before I knew it, he punched me in the face, I could feel the blood running down my face, then when he punched me again I heard a cracking noise so I knew then he had broken my nose, it was then I screamed so loud, that mum came running from her bedroom.

When she entered my bed room on seeing all the blood, she flew at him, yelling calling him, well I think you can guess what she was calling him, mum was only half dressed, but a few steps behind her, was the sailor, when he saw me, he asked if the man in the room had caused all the damage to my face, I just nodded, the sailor was so huge he picked the man up by the scruff of his neck with one hand, with the other hand, he lifting him off his feet, the sailor then throw the man straight through the closed, sash window, the sound of all that smashing glass and old wood, sounded so loud, I guess I must have been in shock, I didn't know what to do, mum sent me to my sister's room and told me to stay there."

"it was then we saw the sailors car pulling up around the back of the house, I could from where I was, just see as he hurriedly lifted the man's body, and dumped it in the boot, now at that point I didn't know if he was dead or alive, it wasn't till the next week, mum showed me an article in the evening paper, that they had found a body on the railway tracks, it was believed the man had committed suicide.

"Now mum told one of the neighbors who had heard all the glass smashing that the man was only slightly hurt, so they had driven him to the hospital for treatment, and I was told if anybody asked, that is the story I should tell them.

"Now Michael this isn't another one of your silly stories," "no Aveling no I am only telling you this now because the sailor, is now called captain he's your dad Aveling, now I am only telling you this, because my dad's home he's been released, I overheard him talking to mum that he was meeting up with your dad, but I can only guess it's about you Aveling," "Michael did your dad do that to your face," "yes."

"Michael listen to me, something is off-with what you are thinking, I know what you are saying makes sense on one hand, but I think there is more to it, so I need you to go back home, to keep listening and watching, because I know your mum had her own plans for me, and I don't think for one minuet my dad would share the money from the diamond dealer, even if they did manage to get me out of the country.

so I believe your mum and dad, are going to set my dad up for some sort of fall, to get him out of the picture once and for all. But you know dad is smart, so if he gets wind, of what they are planning, whatever they have in mind, you know he will kill them both, if he finds out, they are planning to betray him", Michael shook his head, he knew what I was saying had made since.

later that night dad arrived home in a new car, we had never had a new car in the family so everyone was excited, come to think about it doctor, apart from the bread man's van if you saw any vehicle turn onto our road, it would be something ever body wanted to get a look at, so the curtains would twitch, so we knew all the neighbors would be exchanging gossip the next few days about dads new car.

the boys all rushed out to have a go at pretending to drive, later when the boys had all gone to bed, I asked dad if I could have the keys to have a look round the car,' 'don't be silly girl, only boys drive, 'my god doctor it was the swinging sixties, mum then said it was my bed time, it had always been strange, one rule for the boys, and another for the girls. Well when I said girls I meant me, my two older sisters did whatever they wanted to by then.

We all had different bed times according to our age, but mine had often been the same as the younger boys, but I guess that's what some of the older ones, were counting on, because the younger boys always pestered me to tell them a bed time story, basically it was just the normal the three bears was a favorite, as I played the part of a grizzly bear, till someone would shout upstairs what's all that noise.

That was always my que, to tuck them in, then turning in for the night, or that's what everyone believed, but little did they know, when all the house had gone to bed, I would creep back down the stairs to watch t v, I never had been a good sleeper. I always remembered to turn off the sound, by then I was getting good at reading lips. If the actors were facing me.

The following day was a Friday, and I didn't know why I had never thought about it before, but it was amazing how many times dad arrived home often at the end of a month, and often on a Friday. Then in the evenings he would disappear and not come home till late. But there was something I needed to talk to him about.

I did try doctor, but every time I waited for someone to leave the room, someone else entered. The house was so full of family, friends of my siblings, it was an endlessness of people coming and going. But I felt dad needed to know what Michael had told me about the kidnapping, it wasn't going to be an easy conversation, so I most get him alone, just how much do I tell him, if I let on about what uncle Terry had told me.

but I knew I couldn't mention uncle Terrys name, because that would get a backlash, causing more problems in the family, so I must keep uncle Terrys name out of it, but I did need to tell dad, what I had learned from Michael.

But when I got up the following day dad had already left, so hopeful I would get more time. Or I felt until, Michael had more information for me, Mr., Mrs. Willkie were up to something, but it hadn't escaped my mind that they too could be still controlling Michaels every move.

CLICK…TAPE OFF…

CHAPTER 35

SUNDAY SCHOOL...

CLICK... TAPE ON...

Now doctor I am still having problems, with the schizoid in my cell, she is relentless, with her nasty ness, ever chance she gets, she spits on me if I turn my back on her she jumps on me, last night for no reason, I woke up as she was standing over me urinating, my bed was soaked.

So I ended sleeping on the floor, now I am trying so very hard not to punch her lights out permanently, has you know me well enough by now doctor, I am a good girl, but even I am losing my patients with her, now the real reason, if I am asked to tell the truth, is I don't want the warden to take any disciplinary actions against me.

if I make another complaint about her, in case they stop my visits with you, but I tell you now doctor if she persist I can see myself getting locked up for life, but doctor, I do have my suspicions, the shrink, doctor Milton, is winding her up, so I suspect she has made a deal of her own, with that monster, so I am trying so hard to be good.

Now for as long as I could remember doctor, I had always enjoyed going to Sunday sermons, and after the service the priest would hold a class for the younger children in bible studies. The people were nice no one ever said a bad thing about anybody, we would have bible readings, but best of all we had a choir, now I think if I am right doctor, I told you earlier, the music teacher was my favorite teacher at school, now I knew, I wasn't the best singer, but I was often given solos to sing, when the other soloist were away.so music had been for me somewhere in my mind, a place to escape to when things were so bad, at home.

Now If I helped with the younger children in bible reading studies, I would be rewarded with the most beautiful book marks. With pictures of religious thymes and flowers.

now on the following Sunday when I arrived at Sunday class, we had a new priest, now at first he seemed so nice, but as the weeks drew on, he just seemed strange, it was when the rest of the children had left, as always I helped to clean up, and put the books away, but when I was stacking the books on a shelf in the stock room, he came in I turned to look in his direction, when I heard the noise of the key in the lock being turned. Till that moment I had never been afraid of a priest, after all isn't it the church we are supposed to turn to when we are afraid, or need help.

Now the priest came up close to me, to close so I backed away till my back was touching the wall, but he just kept getting closer, it was then he said, 'now young lady I have been getting some comments from the boys,'

I was still thinking somethings wrong, it was then the hairs on the back of my neck and hands were on end, he went on, 'now young lady it's my job to get to the bottom of this, at that point he had his hands on my waist, he began to lift my blouse, as I tried to push him away he pinned me to the wall, pushing his hands hastily to my breast, and under my bra, he had a tit in each of his grubby hands has he squeezed my breasts hard, has he said, 'it's my job young lady to check these out, because if they get to big too soon, it could cause you damage,'

I don't know about you doctor, but I was thinking what kind of idiot did he take me for, that comment may have fooled some of the younger girls, but really.

As I tried to push him back, but he was too big, and too strong, I repeatedly told him to get off, it wasn't till I said, I had heard a noise in the church did he finally back away.it was then he went on to say

'Now young lady, when you come back next week, we will try to stop the hairs growing to quickly on your fanny, that's another sign you are getting to forward with the young boys in the group.

so I will need you to take off your knickers, so I can get to the bottom of your problems, now you are getting older miss Aveling it is my job to show you, how to have safe sex, so next week I will teach you how to do

216

it correctly.. ' I knew then, that day was going to be the last day, I would be attending that Sunday school, their was no way in hell, I would be returning back to that church, I know doctor what a thing to say,(no way in hell) but I was lost for words. But when I think back, to when I had told Penny she would be helped by attending church. How bloody wrong was I?

It was the following week at work, I saw him entering the store, the floor manager called us all together, and told us they were going to be having a fund raiser for the church, and they wanted volunteers to help, I was thinking they have got to be bloody joking, I didn't want that man anywhere near me, as I began walking away I felt a hand on my shoulder, as I turned around their he was, asking me, "why I had missed the previous week at church, as he needed my help with the younger children". now as I felt I owed him nothing not even an answer, I again turned to walk away, but as I turned away, it was then we were joined by my floor manager. 'Now Miss Aveling I heard the good father ask you a question,'

So looking directly at him, I said I would not be attending Sunday school again. Just as I was about to walk away again, it was the floor manager who said "Well Miss Aveling if you cannot help the good father, with the young children, I don't want you working on my floor". Now doctor I think that felt like one of the biggest slaps I had ever received, for a long while, has I loved my job, and I had worked so hard, it felt like my very own escape from all the bad in my life. Then as he, and the floor manager walked away chatting as they did so, it was like they were the very best of friends.

Later that day at lunch time I found the floor manager checking receipts finally when she looked up, 'yes miss Aveling, and what can I do for you,'. It's the father miss, 'yes Aveling what about him, 'well miss he did some think the other week that scared me, 'well Aveling you had better explain", as I did so she began to look at me with that look of doubt on her face, I knew then, she did not believe me, but after I had finished she said I needed to accompany her to the owner of the stores office.

So there we went, but I knew there and then, no one was going to believe me, but I started from the beginning telling the owner the whole, and ever dirty detail that came to my mind, I was then told to go and stand in the hall outside while they discussed things, I must have been there for the rest of the dinner break, as the other workers returned to their floors, I was receiving all the usual snide remarks, from some of the other workers, it seemed to be taking a life time, it was then I noticed, police officer Sam coming down the corridor.

Well maybe, now someone will believe me. pc Sam took one look at me, 'not you again,'but at least he smiled, he knew I would tell him the truth, because of, all I did know about the Willkie house.

He entered the owner's office, again it seemed like ages, before I was called in, when I entered, the owner and floor manager left.

So there I was with pc Sam, 'well Aveling you know I don't doubt you, I really do believe you, but I am afraid not ever body does, the floor manager is unsure, but the owner believes you are lying.so has this is a serious complaint, they decided to call the station.

so I will now explain to you what action we are going to take, first of all I would like you not to discuss this with anyone else, you will if you wish, be allowed to resume your position on the shop floor., now I have taken a written statement from the owner and floor manager. They have also been asked to take no further action.

and not to discuss it with anyone else.,' it was then I interrupted, 'please tell me you won't let him get away with it will you, he will just go on and do the same to other younger girls,' 'no Aveling I promise you, I will be reporting back to the chief, but I don't know if you understand, because he is a priest, if he is to be judged, it will be by the church, and not the police, so you keep well out of his way, and the matter will be taken care of.'

Now doctor the day I made a note in pc Sam s note book, all I had written was, ask Penny Willkie, you see doctor pc Sam also visited the Willkie house never in his uniform, but he knew there and then, that is where the girl, I had told him about, would have gotten an abortion. so all he would need to do is talk to Penny's mum, and she would confirm my story, about Gemma's abortion so after that I hoped when I told him something he would always believe me.

…CLICK…TAPE OFF …

CHAPTER 36

DADS HOME...

CLICK. TAPE ON...

Well doctor It was late on the Saturday night when dad reappeared from his last trip, so when I looked out of the window the following morning, there it was another new car, now uncle Terry had promised me, if he received any news about dad coming home he would warn me.so my mind went into overdrive, how could dad afford another new car, had he taken a down payment on me, why hadn't uncle Terry warned me.so many questions were running throw my head.

I dressed quickly, if I could get mum alone in the kitchen she may have some answers for me, when I no sooner started to ask questions dad appeared in the door way, 'get your things together you are going to stay with your grandma for a few days,' I looked over at mum for anything she could say to put my mind at rest, it was then she told me grandma had sent for dad, because Kim was about to have her baby.

Kim had been acting strangely, but she was demanding I went to stay with her, I asked mum where did dad get the new car from mum, 'oh that's not your dads Aveling he hired it at the airport, well mum don't you think it strange, when grandma sends for him he comes straight home, but when you needed him last time you had to go into hospital he didn't return for two weeks.'

'don't ask so many question Aveling get your things ',as mum had seen dad already getting into the car, from the kitchen window, I barely had time to grab my comb, I didn't need much because, if I did need a change of clothes, Kim had been the same size as me before her pregnancy. so it wouldn't be a problem, growing up we often shared cloths when I stayed over. so not wanting to keep dad waiting I dashed out of the house, but I still felt uneasy around him, as we traveled, I at least would have him all alone at last.

So it was now or never, as I started to talk, 'dad I have got something to ask you,' 'well girl get on with it,' I went on to tell him it had been Michael who wanted to protect me, because his mother was going to arranged to get me kidnapped, because Mrs. Willkie had been listening in to the conversation, when you were trying to arrange some more new papers, from the forger, Mrs. Willkie after you had left that day, convinced the forger to tell her all the details, and you know Mrs. Willkie well enough dad, to understand her so called punters never said no to her, due to all the tapes she has. so arranging my kidnaping would be so easy for her, it had been Michael, who told me all about you taking me to Africa, to be sold to someone, I only know as the diamond dealer.

I knew that wasn't the full truth, but for now it had to do, I just needed to get his attention, It was then dad screeching the brakes, hastily pulling over the car, finally at last I had his attention,

He seemed, has we would say in Yorkshire, gob smacked, about just how much I knew, it took him a while till he said, 'what tapes,'.It was then I was a little taken back, surly dad would have known all about the tapes, he went on to ask me, if I had ever told mum about the Willke house, I assured him, I would under no circumstances do anything to hurt mum. But I thought he was a bastard for going there, I wasn't sure why I said it, I was thinking about it, when the words just seemed to fall out of my mouth.

But as always his response was not what I was expecting, as he just laughed,

'look Aveling going to Africa would have been perfect for you, you would never have wanted for anything, now Aveling you were never intended for the diamond dealer, but his son Edward, a very nice young man, Edward was so rich he would have given you the world on a plate, 'dad then took a little pause before saying, 'you can wipe the name Willkie from your memories, because when I have finished with them, they will no longer exist, nobody crosses me.'

It was then I told him about the tapes in the room above the garage, also what Penny had told me. Why that room was kept for special clients, now yes, dad was a racist, but the only other thing that made him angrier was the mention of homosexuality, on simply mentioning it, I could see him tightening his face, and gritting his teeth.

I thought you should also know dad, that Mrs. Willke's has also got some very bad tapes, on the chief of police.so you cannot trust him, also two other police officers that I know about, do you remember the two officers that came to the house that day to question Luke, well they to use the Willkie house.so if you were thinking of asking any of them for help, please don't.

"Look Aveling I have never asked for help, and never the police, since, well, do you remember when the gossip that was going around the estate about my last arrest, I can't tell you the details," but Aveling I know too many of the officers are as bent, as most of the crooks I have worked with". it was then I could feel dads brain going into over drive, I think he was trying to decide what to tell me, it was then he told me he knew the chief at the local station was on the take, it was then he told me, he himself had used that information, to get out of his last predicament.

I guess dad hadn't got a clue about just how much I knew. "Dad if they have those tape on everyone, do you think they have any incriminating tapes on you, because I also know all about the coat hanger man, everyone calls Doctor Hanger, and why they needed a wet nurse," I couldn't bring myself to use the words, but I was thinking to myself, what I believed had happened to new born babies. Just thinking about what I knew, about Pennies eldest brother's prized roses, but at that time I had only suspected, I had no proof, it wasn't as if I could get a shovel and just go digging up roses.

'Aveling tell me what you know about the tape on the police chief, you see Aveling that tape can work two ways, you do understand now don't you." "Well dad I can only repeat what Penny Willkie told me, but I did give her my word I wouldn't tell anyone," "it's ok Aveling on this occasion you need to tell me everything, it could make all the difference to the outcome."

"now how do you know Penny, and exactly, what has she told you about what was on that tape", I explained we walked home together, as we were both going home in the same direction, and trust me doctor when I say walking home together was better for both of us, back in those street, in the sixties a number of crimes had been reported about a copycat killer and rapist, who had also been given the name of a notorious killer Jack the ripper, now I know I don't have to tell you what Jack the ripper was famous for, but I didn't Know as much about, the first killer back in the Victorian era, but according to the news the copycat also picked out the prostitutes who were walking the streets alone.

But looking back now it did make sense why Penny always wanted to walk home with me, as she herself was exactly that a prostitute, weather she worked from a street corner or nice house, a prostitute is what she was.

so I hadn't understood back then just how much danger, she could have been putting me in, it was then I was thinking, the scheming little bitch, I was her safety card nothing else, she just felt safer having me with her, we would pass her house first, then I had another few streets to walk alone, the more I was now thinking about it doctor, the angrier I was getting, sorry doctor you would think after all this time I had learned how to control my thoughts, and temper, but it wasn't until just a few moments ago, the penny had dropped if you can forgive the pun, but once again I have let my thoughts drift what I was talking about, so back to dad.

But I just believed Penny would have told you about the tapes dad. But clearly not.as he seemed so shocked, he gave me such a look, before asking me again to repeat, and confirm that Penny, and I walked in the same direction, I explained how she tried to trick me to be auctioned on the Friday night, but don't worry dad I would never have gone into that house, because I made mum a promise a long time ago."

I then went on to give him all the details of those repulsive tapes, everything all the dirty little, nasty secrets on the tapes, and why they kept them, it was when I told him, what Penny had told me about the chief of police asking for not just girls but also boys, so I knew the chief was also homosexual.

I told dad everything I could remember.it was then he took me by surprise, as he gently took me by the hand, something I wasn't expecting, has he lifted it to his lips he kissed the back of my hand. it was the only kiss, I could ever remember him giving me, 'now Aveling I know we have never seen eye to eye, but something we do in our life's, is above all else we protect our own.

222

that is why, and I know you never did understand but, that's why I would never have let G.G.be adopted, so I could always check on him and ensure he never comes to any harm, he's now doing very well at school, and is mum is happily married, and I know for a fact his stepdad, is a good dad to the kids. If he had been taken into care I would never have seen him again.

I know why you were so cross with me about your twin sister, But Aveling I truly made a mistake that night. but again I can assure you she is safe, and doing very well, but it did take some time convincing your mum, but it was only when I said if the truth came out, how could I tell Amy, that her daughter had died the same day she was born, it was only when I said that, did your mother agreed we should keep those details to ourselves, and no one else should ever know the truth.

but I know now when it came to you, I just didn't know how to handle you, you had your mothers nature a soft heart, but with my?, well you know what I mean don't you, Aveling out of all my children you are the only one, none of your brothers would ever understand, but you do, that sometimes in our life's we must do whatever it takes to protect our own.

But I can safely say now no one, will ever harm my family," "Does that mean Michael to," "Aveling who told you,"

I had only been guessing, but there was just something about Michaels looks, I had on one occasion drawn a quick sketch of Michael, when I had finished, I left it on the kitchen table, when mum walked in, and on seeing the picture, she said that's a good likeness of Luke, it had been then I studied the sketch, mum unknowingly had told me the truth, it was then, and only then did it make any since, why I had been drawn to Michaels soul, I believed in time he could be saved.

"no one told me dad, but Michael told me the story, of a sailor who had thrown a man who had beaten him, throw a closed window, for breaking his nose, only for the man to turn up dead the following week, and I believed a man who just visited a whore house, would never have done something like that, but the boys farther would have, it was all true wasn't it dad,"

Dad seemed to, for the first time in my life, he was listening to my every word, "look Aveling I cannot tell you the outcome of my actions, but it's time to sort out that evil, vile family once and for all, I swear to you

Aveling, I had no idea they were taking about hurting, and kidnapping you, so it has now become urgent for me to make my move,

But Aveling I had no idea you knew Penny, but if I fail Aveling, you know what you need to do," 'just as long as when you say family that includes Michael," "Aveling I have done some vile thing in my life, some-things I didn't want to do, but being in the navy I had no choice in the matter, but as I have said, family is, and always will be family, and that includes Michael, so if I fail, you do fully understand what I mean, now don't you Aveling,"

I simply nodded my head.

CLICK...TAPE OFF....

CHAPTER 37

KIMS TIME...

"Hi doctor is it ok for me to go through," 'yes Aveling, but just before you go through, what did your father mean, when he told you, that you would need to take care of things if his plans didn't go well.'

Doctor you know me well enough to understand, I am just a good girl. so what the hell would I know what he meant,"

I hadn't believed Aveling that day, I believed she knew only too well what her father had meant, I could tell with the look in her eyes, it was like the day she had got angry with me, she truly did seem like two different girls, the one who try's so hard to convince herself that has she says, she is a good girl, but when I see that look in her eyes I believe she is capable of anything, the more I thought about it maybe that is the real Aveling, and the true reason she was sent to see me.

I know the poor girl was in her own words, still suffering in that god forsaken prison, as she calls it, but I now know if she as to constantly keep looking over her shoulder for Doctor Milton, or her cell mate, not knowing when she would be attacked again, it's enough to give me a cold chill down my back, so I think Aveling must be at her wits end, but I believe we had to get her out of there, and as quickly as possible, because I am afraid if they press the wrong buttons, I can see Aveling killing one, or both of them, and I believe in my heart that is something Aveling could never come back from. But I was convinced by then she could, and would kill if pushed, and that other girl the one she calls her good girl, we would never see again.

On my last meeting with the social worker and my husband, we discussed about how we need to make a formal complaint about Doctor

Minton, but Aveling must not know it was coming from us, so we persuaded the social worker to help. But it would take time. We first needed to get Aveling transferred to another prison, till her case comes up in court. But never having done anything like this before it was proving difficult.it was then for the first time, after all these weeks I realized just how difficult it must be, to be living like that. I know it's a prison, but how is she keeping from not taking action on her prison abusers, she must be using all her will power it's no wonder the girl is only too happy to come here once a week.

but then again how could some of the things she said be real, there I go again, I have started to cross examine myself, oh this was getting me know where, but why would she lie to me, some days she leaves me so confused, was Aveling just using me to get out of that cell for a day, yes of cause she was, but that is something to be expected, but after all the time she has been here, never once have I been as sure as I am now, that this girl could kill, and would kill if pushed.

So it became my mission, to get her out of there, if only getting her moved to another prison, then if the courts found her guilty of her crimes, at least she wouldn't have to be so afraid of going to sleep each night.

CLICK…TAPE ON…

Now, Doctor, were was I oh I remember grandma's house., I still had my knife, I strapped it on under my skirt, before I even went down stair s if dad was home, I didn't know what to expect.

Now It wouldn't be long before Kim gives birth, now Kim was starting to panic, she didn't want the baby at home, but grandma said the hospital was three bus rides away.so it was not an option, they thought I could talk some sense into her, and Kim would settle down if I went to stay until the baby had been born.

When I arrived Kim looked huge, my mum would put on weight whenever she was pregnant, but Kim was so much bigger, I hadn't expected her to be so big, I asked her when the baby was due she told me any time soon, but she needed to go to the hospital first, she was adamant it had to be born in the hospital,

It wasn't until later that night when we went to bed, I asked her why she was in such a panic. girls had babies all the time, and she was in good hands, her mother had been their when my mum had given birth to some of my baby brothers,' 'yes but they say the first baby is the worst one to deliver, and because of my age, the doctor said I needed to go to the hospital.

I don't want this baby at home, 'Kim had a strange look on her face, I knew there had to be more to all this.

it was then she put her finger to her lips to shush me, then after a silence as though she was listening to see if anyone was listening outside the door, then in a very quiet voice, she whispered,' 'you don't understand they are going to kill the baby,' 'I gasped what on earth do you mean, I thought grandma was going to hand the baby over to the social services for adoption,' 'yes that's what I believed till this last week.

It was Adam who told me,' 'oh please don't listen to him Kim, it's his fault you are pregnant in the first place, does grandma know what happened that night,' 'no and you mustn't tell her promise me", Kim knew if I made a promise I would keep it. now, I know it's strange because I had been sent around to grandma's house to keep Kim calm but I couldn't help but panic myself when I heard Adams name.' 'when did you hear from Adam is he here,' Kim fell silent then after a long pause she answered me,' 'yes he's hear.

We hadn't expected him home yet, he's been with the gypsy all summer.' 'But you know what he's like when the money runs out, he comes home and spongers of mum.' 'But why do you believe him surly grandma wouldn't hurt you or your baby,'

Adam told me he overheard them talking in the kitchen, it's your dad he's the baby killer, I had heard rumors but I never believed them, and I didn't believe Adam at first but the other night, when your dad came over to visit, I crept down the stairs because if there was any truth in what Adam was saying I needed to know,' 'so what did you overhear to cause such panic.'

'It was grandma, and your dad in the kitchen, grandma asked if he could get rid of it in the usual place, or was he going to have to take it back with him and dump it at sea.' 'oh Kim they could have been talking about anything,' 'don't be so dim Aveling, your dad didn't get his reputation for nothing he's often called in for things like this, getting rid of body's is one of his specialties, and I know for a fact about some of the others,'

'but what are you talking about Kim,' 'when I was younger I overheard your dad talking to someone arranging to kill someone, and then there's the Wilkes house,' 'what do you mean the Willke's house,' 'well what do you think happens when the girls get pregnant,' well if I am honest doctor Valerie, I had never given the rumors too much thought, and I had never believed all of Penny s stories, not after her story about the private punters house. and even now I just feel so discussed by her.

the truth was too painful for me, but I knew somewhere in the back of my mind it had to be true., it was difficult to believe anyone could bring a baby into this world, just for the sake of money then dispose of the baby as if it was just an inconvenience for them, someone anyone who could do that had no sole.

I did try so hard to not think about it, and if I am being honest at the time I just thought Penny was telling me horror stories, as she did seem to get some perverse satisfaction out of scaring me. But now Kim was saying it out loud and clear. The pregnancies that went full time, it was only now I realize just how naive I have been, and if only I had been brave enough to get that shovel, and did up those rose bushes 'go on tell me everything you know Kim I need to know,'

'well after the girls have the babies just to restart their breast milk someone has to get rid of unwanted babies bodies,' 'you mean kill them, and dispose of the bodies,' 'yes and if your dad was away, after babies are born, Penny's mother would just, wrap them in a sheet, then put them in a shed outside, until Michaels older brother, would pick one of the nights, when the house was closed, then bury them under his roses. But I overheard your grandma, and dad saying to keep the number of bodies down, your dad would dispose of some of them, out at sea. Depending on his assignments.

Now I know back in the fifties they didn't have the contraceptive pill, but surly doctor Valerie, they could have done something, anything but that, Kim told me not to be so dim, I must admit the more I listened the more I felt sick.

They had to have the babies just to restart the milk, the more I heard the more stupid I felt. I had remembered Penny telling me the more money they made, if they had a sister who was producing breast milk.

Kim then went on to tell me they used to, if and when necessary they had an unwanted pregnancy, they would send for the man the one referred to as the coat hanger man. but if he wasn't around then they would try all the old wife's tales, even getting the girls drunk in the bath, with a bottle of gin, if that wouldn't do the job, it was often someone using brute force. but one way or another they, the babies had to be gotten rid of. The last thing they wanted in the house, was a crying baby.

Now I knew in Penny's house there was Penny plus two older sisters, and the mother, four females in total, four women plus all those working girls working for just a few shillings. It was bound to be as they say an occupation certainty, that these things would happen, thinking back I also remembered apart from Michael he had an older brother, who was always boasting about how good his roses were at the bottom of the garden.

'So you see Aveling, you know it was too late when grandma found out about me being pregnant, so she couldn't get the coat hanger man. And when she took me to see a doctor, it wasn't the family doctor because there would have been too many question,

so she never intended to call the social services, because they could have taken me away from home, and grandma relies on the government money to make up the rent money, 'so there I was at grandma's house, normally believing everything was sort of ok, fine, but now I knew there was a whole other world going on all around me, after Kim had calmed down,

I was lost for words I didn't know what to do, what to say, and if I am honest, I just wanted dad to take me home, it was then I heard his car engine, dad had left without saying another word to me.

After many tears Kim, and I settled down to sleep, then it was about one am when Kim stared, at first just couldn't seem to get comfortable, after a while it became clear she had started in labor, I went to wake grandma, but she hadn't been to sleep she was still up, and down stairs talking with Adam, when I entered the room they went silent,' 'so she's started has she,' yes grandma you need to come,' by the time we got upstairs Kim was crying with the pain, grandma who I thought would be saying kind words to her, just told her it had only just got started, and it was going to get a lot worse.

Adam had followed us upstairs and was standing in the door way watching over every think, I was hoping grandma would send him away but she didn't, after about an hour Kim's cry's had turned into screaming, it was then grandma started to look worried.

she said it looked like a breached birth, it was then Adam still standing in the door way said, 'oh for god's sake just stick a fucking knife in it and cut it out, just stop that little bitch from screaming, she's hurting my ears, 'now at the side of the bed, there had been a very heavy glass lead ash tray, and before I knew what I was doing, I had picked it up, and sent it hurling in his direction, it first hit the door frame, shattered into bits, some of the pieces cut his face he was livid,' 'you little bitch,' it was then grandma seemed to start panicking 'she shouted at Adam to go to the phone box and call for an ambulance, it was a good walk to the phone box, Adam just turned round And said,'

'she can get her own fucking ambulance,' grandma looked dreadful there was blood everywhere,'I had been wearing a long white nighty and it was also getting covered in blood, 'don't worry grandma I will go, it will be quicker,' I pushed past Adam still standing in the door way, just for a second he grabbed my arm, 'don't you think for one minute you are getting away with this, has he was still holding something to his face that was still bleeding, 'go to hell Adam, 'I didn't wait for his reply. by now I believed It would be life or death to get Kim to the hospital as quickly as possible.

I ran as fast as I could, the streets were empty, the moon was shining, but the clouds would often kept it hidden, so it was quite dark as I ran as fast as I could, but it seemed to take ages till I reached the phone box, after calling for an ambulance. I knew it would be important to get back as quickly as possible, I didn't want to leave Kim any longer than necessary with Adam in the house. I started back toward the house, I had an eerie feeling that someone was watching me, it must have been about two thirty in the morning, I then saw a strange car following me, it had turned off the head lights, has I turned to look to see if I knew the driver.

I felt a cold shiver down my back, and in what seemed just a second I felt something pulled over my head, I wasn't sure what was happening I felt a cold panic inside, I needed to get back to help grandma, I hadn't expected someone to grab me from behind, not there not then, but as my feet left the ground, everything had gone black someone had pulled a sack over my head, uncle Terry had warned me it would happen quickly, my thoughts turned to sheer panic. I was wearing only my panties and blood soaked nighty, it was then I wished I at least had the knife with me, but with everything happening in that room, I just took off when grandma yelled for an ambulance.

It was then I could hear voices it was Adams, 'I told you she was a little screamer didn't I, and watch those feet, 'I was kicking desperately trying to get free, but it was no good as they slammed me into the boot of a car, once in their I pulled the hood off over my head, but the boot was locked tight as I tried to kick myself out.

We had traveled for some time, and the road seemed to be getting bumpier, I knew that meant we were leaving the main highways, my mind was in over drive, I didn't know how many men were in the car, but I believed I knew what they had in mind, feeling around the car boot to see if I could find anything to defend myself when they opened the boot,

I thought I had found the car iron, used for changing tyres, if I had been lucky enough to find a gun, right there and then I would have had no hesitation in pulling the trigger, but one tyer iron was better than nothing, the drive seemed to go on forever, when we finally stopped, I could hear voices, more than three, I was terrified but I was not going to make it easy for them. then the boot opened, as I waited to be pulled out of the boot but a group of men just stood there, as I looked up at them, then one of them shone a torch into my eyes,' 'well well just look at this, they really are green, and yes she is surly one of the prettiest ones I have ever seen,'

It was one of the other guys who asked,' 'are you sure no one will come looking for her.' 'quite sure, I will just say she panicked when she saw all the blood back at the house, and yet again run away from home, she's run away so many times, I don't think anyone will bother looking for her, so how much, 'they seemed to be talking among them self's about prices as I laid there, still holding the tyre iron close to my chest.

it was then I heard a women's voice, she was holding out a hand towards me, 'you come with me little lady, 'I hadn't heard an accent like hers before, it seemed a little Irish but I wasn't at all sure,

still holding the tyre iron as I turned round I saw Adams smug face, I lurched forward raising the iron,' 'you bastard,' 'well I told you she was feisty didn't I,' I had just caught him on the arm, it wiped that silly grin of his face, but were the hell was I.

Well doctor I will save what happened next for another day, looking at the clock it's time for me to go.

CLICK...TAPE OFF...

CHAPTER 38

ESCAPE...

...well doc hear I am again, sorry if we are a little late Tom and Jerry were late picking me up. Something about a robbery on the high street. I think Tom and Jerry were a little put out, that they had to baby sit me, when all they wanted to do is help with the robbery.

Private note to doc

If at that time If I was honest, I was thinking to myself if, they could have planned their robbery the same day as my escape. Now that could have been most helpful. But never mind that's something for now I need to keep to myself.

End of note

CLICK...TAPE ON...

Now doctor there I was standing in a field, surrounded by gypsies there were only a few caravans with their lights on, the old woman dragged me over to the lead caravan. pushed me inside, then into a room with a bed the full size of the tiny room. I was desperately looking for a way out, there was a dividing door between that room and the rest of the van. And just one small window.

I tried the door but I had been locked in, it was then I heard engines starting, I could hear shouting from outside as, I looked out the window it was like the whole field had suddenly lit up by cars, vans, and lorrys headlights, I could see some think that looked like fairground equipment loaded on to the lorries, so I wasn't sure if it was gypsies, or the traveling fair ground, but. as we all pulled out of the field, once on to the road, it was the early morning, I was growing sleepy but at the same time desperately trying to stay awake, so I could find some way to escape.

But as we pulled into the road, very close behind us was another gypsy van so there would be no point in trying to get out through the window. it was then I must have fallen asleep. The convoy must have been traveling for some time because when I finally woke, the sun was high in the sky.

We had pulled over into what I could only describe as a farmers field, as I looked out of the window all I could see were fields, and forest a little while later the old gipsy woman pushed some tea and a sandwich through the door, I could hear voicers talking,

The old gipsy was explaining to some of the others she needed to know for sure I was a virgin, because where she intended to sell me they always checked.

I didn't have a clue what she was intending to do. shortly after the door opened, and in came a group of women they grabbed me pushing me firmly back onto the bed, they then began to pull off my knickers, then pushing my legs hard apart, it was then the old gipsy woman came in, there was barely room to breathe let alone move.

'now now girls gently let's not damage the goods ',she then examined me, 'well well a real little virgin, she's going to fetch a good price with those looks, 'After they had all left the room, it was like they were speaking with each other, but it felt like I was invisible has they were making their plans. But has I was still sitting on the edge of the bed with the door open, the old woman then looked directly at me, her face was dark, it was badly scared, she didn't seem to have any teeth, but when she looked at me, she knew I was listening to every word, she then began to speak to the others with a different language, I could still understand a little when I realized it was German.

One of the older women had expressed concerns that her teenage son had been looking me over, and was showing a deep interest in me, so she wanted to make an offer, to buy me for her son. Has he needed a wife?

After some debate it had been decided the best price would be fetched at the auction, has it was my green eyes that made my price higher than normal. So auction it was. But they had promised the gipsy boy's mother he could have the next girl. Later that day as the caravans and gypsies had settled down for the night, I knew I had to escape but it was like, ever little move I made the old woman would be checking on me,

And whenever I looked outside the only window, there was a young man looking in at me, I thought to myself this is not going to be easy.... Now if I am not mistaken all you want to hear, is how I got out of that bloody caravan, oh! Sorry doctor mum says bloody is a swear word.

So let me begin again, as the night drew on, the moon was just a crescent, I could hear snoring inside the caravan, the old gypsy woman had been knocking back whisky all day, but outside I could just see a shape moving about by the moon light, I believed it to be the young man who had been watching me earlier, but I had to get away that night.

Now I had overheard the women taking about crossing at dawn with the tides, from what little German I knew, it was then I remembered thinking thank god, I had been listening when dad was trying to teach the boys German, they were saying something about getting me to drink an hour before the tide to ensure I slept the whole way across, and just how they had intended me to be tied, and hidden under the bed in a secret compartment, it was then I knew this wasn't the first time they had held someone a prisoner, so I waited and waited, it was just as the moon had fallen and the sun was about to rise.

I pushed open the window slowly, it was a very small window but if I could just get my head throw, then I hoped the rest of my body would follow I knew being the daughter of a sea captain the ferries left with the tides, and that meant very early, I could no longer see any one, moving about outside, so it was now or never. I pushed the window till I knew I could just squeeze out stepping softly, now the day before the gypsies had removed my shoes, I had heard them saying it was to stop me from running away.

I guess they didn't know me at all, but I couldn't chance opening the door to find them, the old gypsy had been snoring, but it was too much of a gamble, because this would be my only attempt at getting away, if I was found, I wouldn't get another chance, the gypsies would make sure of that, I had no doubt.

So I would have to leave now, so slipping quietly out of the window just praying no one was awake. I pushed the window gently closed behind me, not wanting to draw any body's attention to it.

but I had only gone a few steps, when I almost fell over something, as I looked down, I was just one step away from standing on him, there he was the infatuated gypsy boy, I paused to see if my eyes were deceiving me, but no he must have been, well it wasn't easy to see him clearly, but he couldn't have been more than sixteen or maybe seventeen, himself, I guess the gypsies, married the children early, but what was I thinking.

I needed to get the hell away from the camp, I stepped so close to him but he didn't stir, then it was over the hedge row, but, left right witch way should I go., it was just then I remembered as a little girl, my late grandma Nora would say, if you ever lose your way or get lost, just follow your nose, and then someday, you would find your way back from anywhere in the world safely home, as love was like a shining light, and the heart knew the best direction to go.   `

so I started to run towards the tree line, now I know this sounds a little strange doctor, but it wasn't like I remembered what grandma had said when I was a little girl, it was more like she was there talking to me, but don't worry doc I knew that wasn't real.

I had no idea where I was, only that it couldn't be too far from the ferries, as I reached the tree line, I looked back it was all still quiet at the camp site so I continued, desperately thinking the sun was now busting over the horizon, then I could hear dogs barking.

it was just a matter of time before they would find me gone. then the chase would be on, but I knew there was no way I could out run the dogs, but I had seen has a girl an old, black and white movie, were if dogs were chasing you they could lose the trail, if I could just reach a stream or river, as I was looking back toward the camp site, just praying please god help me, just as I was turning back around, I found myself slipping the ground below my feet had turned into I slippery slide as I slipped down, splash,

The water was freezing but I didn't care, all I needed to do was swim in the opposite direction than the current to the other side, but the river seemed huge but never the less I had to swim, I knew that the direction of the water was going out to sea. Now the nighty that I had left grandma's house in, was billowing up and floating on the waters top.

Now if my chasers saw that it would have been like a flag drawing attention to me. I could hear the dogs barking getting closer, I had to act quickly pulling the nightie over my head. but I lost hold of it, as I watched, panicking as it started to float downstream, I had just reached the opposite side but it was so thick with reeds and tree growth, so I just hung on to catch my breath.

It was then I saw two men on the other bank, the dogs were barking as the nighty flowed past them, I saw them clearly has they watched the nightly floating out of sight, they then turned around, and I could see them turn, and disappear back in the direction of the caravan site.

I hung there for what seemed like agers too afraid to move but then the cold became an issue, and very quickly. I had to get the hell out of that water. I pulled with all my strength, but the mud was making it very slow going but finally, gripping tight to some reeds, or roots I wasn't too sure what, then finally I was out.

Looking down at my body I could see blood seeping out of serval wounds, I must have picked up as I ran, it was then as I tried to stand I felt the pain in my feet, as I looked down seeing that they too had blood oozing, but the greatest pain wasn't the wounds, once again it was the cold, it was like my whole body started to shut down.

Not having anything to use to cover any of the wounds, I looked around in the hopes of finding something to wrap over them, but only leaves, so as I stood there in just a tiny pair of knickers with open wounds, I looked around for something, anything but nothing, no buildings just more trees.

As I tried again to take my first step, the pain was too much, and I fell to my knees, as I started to crawl I knew I had got to find shelter, something anything to cover myself, with each movement it got harder, and harder.it was then I realized just how cold I really was, I didn't want to, but it was like I couldn't stop it, as warm urine ran down my leg. I felt so ashamed god knows why, it wasn't like anybody had seen me, but just the thought of wetting myself at my age felt so wrong, I had barely had time to get my thoughts together.

It was then I heard the sound of dogs barking again, I needed to hide, but I knew if they had picked up my sent again all was lost.so as I just laid there in the long grass with my heart pounding, and my mind racing.

CLICK …TAPE OFF…

CHAPTER 39

BARKING DOGS...

'Well doctor hear I am again, it was a longer ride than usual, due to some sort of demonstration in town, I think I heard someone say it's something about voting, is it all right for me to go through,'

'Well Aveling I was hoping to talk to you, the prison has asked me to do some blood samples, and a medical on you this week.' 'No I don't think so doctor, you can have the blood samples, but nobody is touching my body end of. so do you want to take the blood samples now, or when I have finished,'

'Now if you don't mind Aveling, but you must understand we are all just trying to help you, a full medical will just help me in getting you the right treatment.' 'and you have had my reply doctor no one is touching my body, what the hell is wrong with you doctor, after hearing all my tapes, at least I thought you of all people would understand, no one touches my body its mine.

when I am dead you can do what the bloody hell you want to with it, but for now it's mine and I will fight, no I will kill you if you, if you try forcing me with restraints,' 'ok ok Aveling I was just trying to help you. 'I at that time felt, no I knew, Aveling was more than capable of killing someone, it was hard to say but there was just something in her voice, that day it sent a cold chill down my spine, as I remembered the day when she told me her father told her she knew what to do if anything happened to him, so I now knew what he had meant, that her brothers and sisters didn't have it in them to kill, but regardless of Aveling having her mothers, as she tried to convince me good nature, it wasn't something, anyone would expect

Aveling to do, she looked so innocent so young, but I began to feel afraid of her. but I convinced myself I could handle her believing it wouldn't take many more visits to get to the bottom of all her stories,

At least this time at last I would get some blood samples, I was choosing my words carefully so not to upset her, as I knew if she were to get upset, she would just waste time in the back room drawing pictures, and not talking on the tape. but the prison service were adamant that they needed her to have a full medical.so I asked again, if she would just show me her scares,

So after taking her bloods, she looked very coldly at me, has she said in that deep angry voice I had heard before, "So doctor you want to see my scares do you, well here take a look, "has she lifted her top clean over her head, I gasped, I hadn't seen so many burn marks like it before, there was also some old scaring that looked more like whipping marks, but Aveling had never mentioned anybody ever whipping her, so this left me stood there staring at the poor girls back, as I leaned forward to touch them, it was then she pulled the top back on.

then as Aveling started to walk passed me into the other office, I believed I had just again been talking with the other girl, the girl I believe Aveling try s so hard to keep under control, the girl my husband had warned me of, all those months ago. But I did feel a little confused why had she never spoken of the whipping marks, there were so many of them, I then realized I had just done the very thing Aveling tried to avoid, she didn't need my sympathy, she needed help.

But now I had seen them, I had to know who did it to her, but not this visit she was already in one of her angry moods, so I decided, it was something that would keep till next time.

CLICK…TAPE ON…

Well now where was I, oh I remember,

It was then, two tiny yapping poodles found me, and not too far behind a face I didn't recognize, she almost fell over me trying to pull her dogs back. 'oh my god, oh my god, who are you how did you get here", she took her coat off, wrapping it tightly around me, I can't tell you doctor how that coat felt it was still warm from her body heat, but as she tried to help me to stand, but it was no good I had used all my bodies strength, just to get there, she promised she would be back but had to go for help.

as I lay there looking skywards, thinking, why me, I had always tried to be a good girl, my mind was going to placers remembering when I was so very young, thinking how could so many men, get away with hurting so many girls, I was hoping Kim and her baby were ok, I remembered asking god to keep them safe, at that moment every minuet seemed like a life time, then voicers, things started to go in, and out of focus. When I finally woke up I was in the hospital. Only to find out a whole week had vanished.

well doc the sessions seems to feel shorter I think, well I hope by now you have something to report back to the social services with. but I dreed to think how you would put anything, I have said to you, that wouldn't look so bad, so crazy writing down, but I guess that's your problem, I did try to warn you all those weeks ago, just how bad things were just to say, let alone put on paper, well don't get me wrong doctor, I know you just have a job to do, but I am never too sure just how explicit you need me to be. But it doesn't, and never does make any sense to me, so hell knows what you make of it all.

Well when I finally woke up I was in hospital, I could hear voices, they just didn't have a clue who I was, or were I had come from, and that right there and then, it seemed so perfect, I didn't have to worry about dad selling me, I didn't have to worry about Adam, grabbing me, I didn't have to worry about the gypsies, and that's the way I intended to keep it, I knew we had traveled at least a day away from when Adam first snatched me,

So I told them my first name, I wasn't sure if I did it with any fore-thought at first but, telling them just how I had ended up there and how, knowing what I did about people, I believed they wouldn't find my story viable, so I intended to keep it to myself, along with my age, full name everything,

I think at first, that is why they sent me to you, they had guessed by then I was holding out on them so here I am.

But back to my hospital bed, so from then on, I had no idea, who I was, or where I had come from. Only that my name was Aveling, and that's the way I intended to keep it. I had been in hospital about a week, it was time for them to move me on, as my wounds had healed,

If they believed I was under twenty one, it would be the children home, if they thought I was older I would be placed elsewhere. But as they hadn't had any reports about a missing girl, no one seemed to know what to do with me.

But after what seemed an age, it had been decided the only option would be a children's home, as no one else had room for me, now I had overheard the matron talking to a lady in a blue suit, well I said overheard, but it was more like lip reading their lips, and at best I was only getting about seven word in ten, then filling in the gaps it was never a perfect way to find any information but sometimes a little information was all I needed.

.but the matron told her they believed I was boarder line case, because they could only guess my age, and at that time they believed my age was mid-teens, due to my height, and I was doing my best to act all shy, just like Penny had once shown me, I wasn't sure why but it just at that time seemed the best thing to do. so the choice was a children's care home, I foolishly thought, that had to be better than where I had come from.

But I thought at that time, I had read the lips incorrectly why call it a care home something didn't make sense.

Now when I arrived at what they were calling a children's care home, it seemed more like, well how could I explain, as we entered the huge gates, looking intently at the building in front of me, it was more like a building directly from a Charles Dickens story, old and stuffy part house, but another part of the building had that look of an old hospital, maybe they had used it in the war to take the over spills from the main hospitals.

On entering, there was a smell that just filled the air, it reminded me of grandads house with the smell of bleach, and old boiled cabbage not to pleasant, but hoping for the best. I was greeted by a woman dressed in a matrons uniform but without any of the insignias, along with a young girl, who seemed about nine/ten, "now Aveling this is Mrs. Stornoway, and she will be looking after you now, so be a good girl",Mrs. Stornoway, then signed papers and my escort then left.it was then Mrs. Stornoway, instructed the young girl to show me where I would be sleeping, I was taken to a large bedroom, with seven other beds.

the young girl I learned was Ellie, Ellie told me she was just ten years old, as I began to ask her questions, I learned there were all girls in the dorm as it was called, and another eight girls across the landing. Plus another two rooms further down the corridor with just as many girls in. to me that seemed a lot for a children's home, but never having been in one before I assumed that was normal. Ellie explained the older girls over eighteen were on the top floor, and the lower floors were for the younger girls like herself.

My first question, "no boys," "not here but they have another building across the field,' she paused 'we are not allowed over there and they are not allowed over hear, 'I was just thinking perfect, when there was a loud noise, it was has Ellie explained the dinner gong, it seemed as young girls came from all directions, jostling to be first in line, as we were all seated in the dining room, I knew this was one of those times to keep my gob firmly shut, the less they knew about me the better.

I thought the best thing to do was, just do what the other girls did, we then were led in prayer to count our blessing, we were then to line up and pick up a plate, and follow the line of other girls, we were each given spoonful of potatoes then peas and then a ladle of something that looked like chicken stew, on returning to the seats the girls all never spoke a word, when I tried to ask a question I was shushed. After all plates were cleaned, we lined up again to hand in our plates and drinking beakers, it was then a lady who introduced herself as Mrs. Swan, who had been serving, she asked me if I was the new girl, 'yes'.

I was then escorted into the kitchen for washing up detail, as she looked me up and down,'

'You seem a little old to be here, girls your age are normally placed into services,' 'what's service", but she didn't answer. After kitchen duties I was again teamed up with Ellie, who continued to show me around. we met up with Mary, she had the nick name of bossy boots, as she was older than most of the girls, Ellie told me, Mary did seem a little strange, as she would often just disappear, but when asked by the other girls, Mary refused to answer, she refused to say anything about where she had been, but as if like magic she would reappear, but to me this all sounded like a secret I would need to know, because if she had a way of getting out of here, then I needed to know where to.

But who was I to criticize someone else's behavior, on my first day there, but Mary gave out the orders, and Mary must always be obeyed as she was the dorm prefect, but then if I needed to get information about the house then Mary would be a good source of information. "Gosh doc is it that time already" has there was a loud knock at the door.

CLICK...TAPE OFF...

CHAPTER 40

YOUNG GIRLS...

Private note just my thoughts today doctor,

Tom and Jerry didn't seem to please to be picking me up, I could tell from their attitude, so the return journey back to the cell, was interesting it was as though I had become invisible, as they snapped at each other about the detail of being assigned to me, yet again they believed by now the trips would be over.

Tom understood why the Sargent always insisted it took two of them, I could only remember on one other occasion Tom turned up alone, but as I understand it was due to there being a shortage of staff, but as he didn't mention it to Jerry, I just thought Tom didn't want him to know anything about that day, when I had tried to escape from the car. I was just guessing that Tom hadn't told him, but as they drove back to the cell, I had started to call colditz, after an old black and white movie I had seen a few years ago, I remembered the film because of all the idea's the men came up with to escape regardless of how long it took them, by then I had become obsessed with escaping, so if the toilet visits didn't work I needed a plan b.

that day the journey seemed to take so long, as they passed the stop for me to use the toilet without a word but, I decided to just keep quite on that trip, it wouldn't be a good idea to stress them out over one loo stop, but I needed them to use the same loo stop, and if they were reassigned I could end up with officers that were not so understanding.

End of note

CLICK...TAPE ON...

'Well doc I'm back again, 'but without even looking up, doctor Valerie told me the tape was ready for me,'

I knew I must by now be getting to use to my days away from my cell, but I just needed to keep the visits up for just a little while longer,

Well doc that's how I landed in the home, thinking finally only girls at least for a while I could feel safe. But has the first days there drew to a close, I learned all was not what it seemed, as the girls all gathered for bed, the lights went out, with only the light of the moon shining through the window, I had been given the bed closest to the window, so as I looked over at Mary she and her friend Clair, they very quietly tip toed over to my bed,

As we chatted away they were telling me the rules of the house, some seemed quite Victorian, but I had lived in worse places, it wasn't till they told me not to ever make a fuss about anything, or they would take me to the exam room, 'what's the exam room, 'it was Clair who explained, if girls were caught out of bounds or anything that seemed to be breaking the rules.

they would be taken by force to the room down a white corridor to what they called the hospital wing, where they would be strapped down, and were they would have electrodes strapped to their heads and an electric charge would shock them over and over again, my god doctor Valerie, I thought treatments like that went out with the Victorians.

I asked if they had ever been taken Mary said no, but you could see in her eyes how afraid just talking about it made her, then I asked Clair but her face answered my question for me. All she would say was I should just stick to all the rules, and maybe they wouldn't take me. I guess that said it all, as she explained most of the girls at one time or another had been taken, Clair did tell me one girl had only used one swear word, but it had been enough to be taken to the shock room.

But that wasn't the worse of it. Has they both explained that one of the so called doctors, Doctor Clark had his own form of punishment. Late at night mostly at the weekends, he would come into the dorm, he would choose one of the girls for what he insisted was naughty girls punishment, he would take them to exam room.

He would then offer them a choice, did they want to be wired up to the shock treatment machine, or his own private form of treatment, I didn't for one minute, believe he actually wanted an answer to that question.

at first Mary told me she once went after one of the girls he had taken, late at night although she had, been afraid, but she wanted to know what happened in that room, and the other girls in the dorm, would just not talk about it, so she believed it must be really bad, so she had followed him keeping a distance, but after what she saw, Mary always managed to hide at night, after what she had witnessed him do to one of the other girls, she told me of how, for the first time when she had only been at the home a few weeks, she watched as Doctor Clark ordered a poor girl to strip bare. then he strapped her down on the table, were the electric shock treatments took place.

That's where she watched him, as he started to torture the girl, all the time telling her if she said anything, he would take her back to the treatment room the next day, and do the same to her as he did to poor Sally, Sally was one of the girls, I hadn't spoken to, I had tried the morning I arrived, but she just gave me a cold stare, and I remember thinking to myself, it was like she had been through her own battles with abuse, as they always said it take one, to know one.

but Sally s face was blank her eyes just looked dead inside, Mary went on to explain poor Sally, has they say, has had to many shock treatments, and now simply does not respond to any one any more, after Mary told me what she had seen that night, when she had followed that so called doctor, he started with pushing strange things inside the girls fanny.

Now Mary didn't know the names of those torture implements, after watching him for just a few minutes Mary told me she had started to feel sick, when she saw him pushing what she could only explain, as something that looked like half a tennis ball, I think Mary must have meant a contraceptive cap, I think that's what it's called I saw my sister, Pam showing one to my sister Rennie, but I guess it had been something Pam herself had only just heard about, now after they both left the bedroom that day, I did pick it up, but in my mind I simply could not understand how anything so big could fit inside the vagina. so how the hell it stopped unwanted pregnancies I hadn't got a clue.

So with his victim strapped down, Doctor Clark could do just about anything he wanted to, but when the girl started to scream, it was, then climbed on top of her, pushing his erect cock as deep as he could.

he then started to slap the girl across the face, yelling at her if she didn't shut up there would be far worse to come, it was then Mary wanted to stop him but how, she knew if she just barged into the room, she had nothing to stop him with, so with tears in her eyes she went on to explain as she began to walk away she could still her the poor victims cry's all the way back to the stairs. "Oh Aveling I felt so guilty, I didn't do anything to help her, but I, I just walked away",

I asked Mary if Doctor Clark had ever tried to take her, it was then she told me she had only been at the home a few months, so that's why she followed them that night, and up to now before he comes into the dorm room, some of the other girls had helped to keep her hidden from him, now Mary was eighteen but she was so tiny she could hide in some of the smallest places.

But the other girls, wanted me to warn you, because i had seen him reading your paper work, and i overheard him saying to his friend, he was going to have a good weekend as there was a new girl. In the house who was also a virgin.

Apparently Doctor Clark always took the virgins as soon as they came in, it always seemed to excite him, Mary also told me she had been abused by her own father, and in her notes it was clearly noted that she wasn't a virgin anymore, so she believed that's why he was never too keen on taking the time looking for her.

now were ever I stayed, the first thing I would look for, is an escape route, and failing that anywhere I could to hide, but these girls had me impressed, now Mary was very little, and even I have to admit, the girls had some very strange hiding places for her.it was then I asked Mary how she ended up in the home.

Apparently Mary was caught, in the grounds of a very high end hotel having sex with young men for money, by the police, then when she was asked questions, she told the social services officer, not to worry she always used rubbers, as that is what one of the boys called condoms. Mary then went on to explain it was all perfectly normal, as most of the other girls, she hung around with, all did the same thing, to Mary it was no big deal, but Mary was carrying a bowie knife just like the one I owned, but when the police checked it they found blood, but Mary refused to say who's blood it was, then she was sent to the home, on chargers of prostitution.

Now as part of the hospital checks on Mary, she was found to have contracted a sexual transmitted disease, so she was asked to give a list of names, of the men who she had sex with, there were so many, she struggled remembering their names, but every one needed to be checked, and, by some miracle, all the men's tests came back clear.

So it was then the matron, insisted there had to be another name for that list, it was only then Mary told them the only name she hadn't given was her fathers.

But he insisted she was lying, apparently it was her father who had called the social services in the first place, complaining he couldn't control her, and she needed to be taken into care. But the matron called the police, and they insisted he had to take the test, at first he refused, it was then the police threatened to get a court order, so the police told him they would also need a list of all the women he had slept with, as that was law, so if he continued to refuse, he would be arrested,

It was only then he agreed to the take the test, when that test came back positive he had been arrested, he only pleaded guilty finally when the case was taken to court, now in court he insisted, it hadn't been rape, as Mary had asked him to show her how to have sex, and she had instigated the whole thing.so he received only a caution, I found that ridiculous, but there was then nowhere for them to send Mary, until she told them who's blood was on the knife, and poor Mary had ended up at the home, until her own court case for prostitution was to be heard, but as you know Doctor, things back then took so long for the bureaucrats to complete the paper work.so she was prescribed some medication to take care of the std.

It was then i believed, the so called house doctor, doctor Clark decided to leave Mary alone, but Mary went on to tell me all about him.

Mary said, he had over thirty five, sometimes more, girls to pick, and choose from off the top floor, Mary went on to explain that different girls were coming, and going all the time, but she was also told by the other girls there in the dorm, that, three girls had just disappeared, over the last year but no one knew why, or were they had gone, it was assumed by the authorities that they had simply ran away, but it was always after they had been taken late at night by the Doctor.

The following day passed quietly, we all had school lessons, but it was strange taking a class with girls of all different ages, the dorms were split up into agers, the older girls were on the top floor with me, the younger girls were on the second floor. and on the ground floor were the officers, lesson rooms, and the canteen then down the long white corridor were the treatment rooms, well that is what everyone else called them, but to me well I would find out all about them later, but for now doctor it's time for me to leave.

CLICK...TAPE OFF...

CHAPTER 41

LOSE KNIFES...

Private note

Another week passed and there I was again, it had been a while since the good doctor Valerie, had tried to get me to make a complaint in writing, about the abusers, I didn't see any point they always got away with it. over the years I had heard most of the excusers, it was the girls fault for wearing such a short dress, the girls were flirts, it was the girls fault she made me do it, etc. etc. it was always the girls fault, and what ever happened to the abusers nothing. End of note.

CLICK...TAPE ON...

Well doctor I had always believed I was one of the lucky ones, yes life wasn't a bed of roses, but somehow, there by the grace of god, I was surviving, the weekend seemed to come around very quickly that first week, then out of nowhere Mary came running up to me, trying to hide behind me, 'it's him he's hear iv just seen him, in his white coat going down to the hospital wing, 'she held on tight begging me not to let him take her, now I knew Mary was having some sort of panic attack, over the time she had been in the home, she had heard all sorts of horror stories from the girls, but the fear in her eyes was genuine.

now regardless of everyone calling her bossy boots, if you had seen her face that day doctor, you would have understood, I knew many girls from school that always came over as bullies, but when as they say the chips were down, they would rather run away than fight, but I hope by now doctor you know there was no way I would run from a bully.

It's alright Mary I promise you he won't be taking any more girls out of the dorm at night, she looked up at me with her sorrowful big brown eyes.

Just for a moment her eyes reminded me of G.G.

After dinner I was working in the kitchen, when I hadn't got a clue what I was going to do, but I knew I had to stand up to him, I had promised Mary, and I never broke a promise, I knew in the dorm there was no escape for me.

but what I was most worried about is that, I was told the so called doctor had been talking to a friend, he was overheard by one of the girls mention he was going to have fun that weekend did this also mean, there were two of them to fight off.

now the dorm room was three stories up, it was one of the first things I had looked at when I had arrived, I always looked for a escape route, but I had found none, the main door of the house was locked at eight pm, and only the matron kept the keys on her belt, apparently Mrs. Stornoway liked to go to the cinema on the Friday or Saturdays, so she handed the keys over to the doctor. now I was still on kitchen duties, but I knew I needed something anything to fight with, I desperately looked around the kitchen, it was then I saw the knife left out on the table it was only a small paring knife but it was better than nothing.

This was one abuser that was going to get more than he bargained for. later that night he walked into the dorm as though the girls were there for him to pick and choose from, he was wearing his badge of office, or as I would put it a white coat, but he was so full of himself, 'are there you are miss Aveling, you need to come with me to have your medical.'

it must have been late I looked around at all the girls faces, one of them was crying all of them looked afraid, even little Mary climbed out of her hiding place running over to me clinging on to my night dress, he swiped her away, 'not tonight my little one I am saving you till later, after you have finished all you treatments, 'by that I was only guessing that they had put Ellie on a course of antibiotics for the s.t.d.

the sound of his grating deep old voice ran a cold shudder down my back, he had that old man smell, stale tobacco, old cloths smelling of moth balls, just the smell of him turned my stomach, all I was wearing was a pair of knickers 'under my nighty that I had been given when I had arrived at the home, I had pushed the knife precariously down the front of the knickers, just praying it wouldn't slip out as I tied to stay calm,'

walking down the long corridor till we reached a cold sterile room it did look like, and smelled like a hospital room, so I was glad I had been told, what to expect, so I thought I was prepared, we had no sooner arrived, when I sensed he was about to pounce, he told me to remove my cloths and lay down on the couch, I looked over at what he was calling a couch, but seeing all the leather straps I was no way going to make this easy for him.

'I don't think so doctor,' 'don't you dare tell me no young lady, now remove your cloths, 'by now I had retrieved the knife, holding it clinched tight in my hand he looked over at me, 'you silly little girl if you think that's going to stop me,' his whole body language had suddenly changed,

Just like I had seen from the other abusers, he lurched over at me pushing me into a small steel table with two shelfs, now has he was so hell bent on getting the knife from me, he had knocked it out of my hand, it shot clean across the floor, as it did so, he went to retrieve it, he didn't see on the lower shelf of that table what I saw, and so I took my chance, it was a steel kidney shaped tray with a few used steel scalpels,

I hastily grabbed them he hadn't seen me, as he returned with the kitchen knife, he then held it close to my neck pushing just enough to make it painful, but being careful not to break the skin, I had no doubt about what his intentions were, so has he pushed his face close to mine telling me all the things he had planned for me that night, his breath was so bad, it smelled like he had eaten a dead frog, he was now telling me exactly what he did to his little virgins who kicked up a fight.

I took my chance, and has his face was so close to mine his sick smile showing, misshapen, discolored yellowing teeth, his breath now so close, just made me want to vomit. I lowered my hand containing the scalpels gripping them tightly together, before he could react, I plunged them deep into his inner thigh pushing them as hard as I could into his leg, I knew that was my only chance, he staggered backwards, looking down all I could see was the scalpels still in him, now it was my turn to lurch forward, my dad had always said if you get sent to prison, it may as well be for a sheep never the lamb, and if I am being honest I never did understand what he was referring to till then.

Thinking of all the other girls upstairs, this was one man who would never hurt any of them again, I pulled out the scalpels even though he was begging me not to, but how many girls had begged him not to hurt them,

But as I pulled the scalpels out I ripped the wound even wider, he slumped to the floor repeating himself, "you've killed me you've killed me", I felt at that moment he had to die.

but as I lifted the blade to slit his throat, he fell backwards, the blood flow was now plain to see it just ran over his leg like a full running tap, 'he screamed at me, telling me, I had cut his femoral artery", whatever that was, his last words to me were, 'go and get help, you stupid, silly, little bitch'.

well this was one stupid, silly little bitch, that really didn't care, so I just stood there, looking directly at him has he bleed to death, his face slowly distorted has the last of the blood ran across the floor. as I walked out of that room, I looked back the blood was still running towards a floor drain hole in the middle of the floor, I remembered thinking such a lot of blood, for such a shriveled up old man, but with such a lot of blood I didn't believe anyone could survive that, but to be honest, doctor Valerie if you were to ask me there and then, how I felt well your answer would have been, summed up in one word. Satisfied.

CLICK...TAPE OFF...

CHAPTER 42

BACK TO THE DORM...

CLICK...TAPE ON...

Well doctor you wanted to know why I had two escorts, I guess you think you now know, but you don't not yet.

as I returned to the dorm, Mary bless her little heart was stood there looking for me, through the landing bannister, I could see clearly she had been crying, I wrapped my arms around her. Don't you worry any more, he can never hurt you again.it was at that moment I just prayed the devil to take him. I felt strange thinking of my father, thinking it really did run in families. the apples as they say, never fall far from the tree. I had finally let my poor mum down, and all I ever wanted to be was a good girl.

Now doctor, you do see I had no choice, sorry, I am struggling for the right words...after I had killed him, not something I ever thought I would say, I calmly returned to the dorm with all the other girls, most of them were so afraid I could feel there pain, there was a cold chill in the room that night, but there was something else, a feeling I couldn't put my finger on, but it was a feeling of confusion.

Most of the girls, had no idea of what had just happened, in that so called punishment room, with its Victorian tools of torture, they were just curled up in their beds some clearly shaking, traumatized by what the bastard had done to all of them over the years, so I guess most of them were expecting me to return in tears, shaking, but I just reassured them, they didn't need to worry any more.

He was dead, and if anybody asked them anything the following morning just tell them the truth. Now as I settled some of the girls who were still clearly shaken, back to sleep, when the room was again silent, I sat on my bed just staring out of the window, the moon was shining brightly I remembered thinking what a beautiful night to die..

Now there was a silence in the dorm that felt eerily calm, the girls were so quite most of them, I guess not too sure what to say to me.

I felt how I could have turned out so bad. all I had ever wanted was to be a good girl, it was then Sally came over she struggled with her first words, as it had been, months since she had spoken to any one, she wanted to tell me her story, as I sat there numb, she began to explain to me her story, of how she had been placed there, in that so called children's home, I felt like laughing, just thinking of the word, home this building was so very far from being a home. And that man who called himself Doctor Clark, was as far from being a caring doctor, as Jack the Ripper.

So now you think you know Doctor Valerie, it was the death of Doctor Clark that put me in prison the first time, now you think you know why I have two chaperones, but you still don't know, the whole truth,

So I felt regardless of how I was feeling, I needed to pay attention to Sally, she needed to know someone anyone would just let her talk, and believe her. So When Sally had been sent to the home, it wasn't long before doctor Clark, had her in his sights, now if you could have met her doctor Valerie you would understand, because, she was just one of the girls who was so naive, yes she was old enough to be on the top floor of the home with the rest of us, but her looks were those of a much younger girl, and she was so skinny, so very, very skinny, it looked like she hadn't eaten food for a very long time, now do you remember doctor, all those weeks ago when I first came to see you, I can remember you saying to me, to start with my earliest memory, it reminded me of were Sally had begun her story.

now the years when you are, regularly being abused, Doctor Valerie often seem so long, it feels like the torture would never end, her so called father had always abused her, calling her stupid, incompetent, lazy, men like that always had a way of shouting out orders they would make you feel so afraid, well I think you get the picture doctor, abuse is abuse no matter how its delivered, if you try to explain it, well as I see it as something that make your life unbearable, over the years I lost track how many times I just wanted to curl up into a tight ball and die, so even when you hear someone raise their voice, your whole body tenses up ready for what was coming next.

So when you know nothing different, that just becomes the norm, no matter how bad things get, while you are living that way you know no difference. You just believe every girl is going through the same thing. so even when your head is so full of the horrors of the day, just trying to sleep, knowing that your dreams would fill your very sole, with the recurring nightmare of fear.

it was like you could hear the voices, yelling at you clean my shoes, fetch the coal in, the orders were endless in my life, but I obeyed, so others would not have to suffer., so I knew it was hard trying to endlessly push those thought to one side, so desperately wanting to think of good things, even little things like looking through the window watching a sun set, now someone once said, surly when the abuser left the house to go to work, or whatever, surly you could relax.

But it was then when everything was quiet, and still, you didn't even dare to put the radio on, because, if he/she came home early from work, and heard the music, it didn't matter what music was playing, the abuser would accuse you of listening to the devil, now I knew to my cost if I pushed the wrong buttons, the abuser would end up beating me, now you may think this is crazy Doctor, so let me explain.

Once the beating was over, they would be exhausted, then hopefully they would leave you alone, but if you did nothing, then all evening your nerves would be on end, just waiting for the next explosion of anger, and when you live like that, it destroys your very sole, so the men who had caused so much pain for Sally, calling them men in my mind was to respectful they were not men but monsters. The torment Sally had experienced was all too much for her innocent mind to processes, so she just disappeared into her own world.

The shear fear, of what comes next. Just eats away at you, Sally told me in details what that so called abusive doctor, had done to her. She had received so many electric shocks, that even when she had been taken back to that cold hospital room, for just a regular check up by one of the nurses, as soon as Sally laid down on that table, her body would lose all control, and begin to jump, and twitch, often ending in her urinating herself, as if she was going through the electric shock treatment. Regardless of the fact, that there were no wires, or pads connected on her body,

Just as she was made to lay down, it was only then when the nurse complained, did Sally no longer, receive such treatments again. But also her story of how she came to be there herself. But before I get to Sally's story, let me tell you what happened next at the so called children's home.

I had not one regret of what I did, that night everything just felt so surreal, the next morning I found it so difficult to wake up, now for me it had never been a problem getting out of bed, if the sun was shining and the birds were singing I was awake, but that morning I woke up exhausted, the girls had all dressed, and making such a clatter,

But what I was expecting to hear were sirens from a police car, but thinking about it I guess no one had found him yet, but just as I was thinking about it, I heard the commotion down stairs and then the sirens,

I looked through the window, it was quite a sight, we were then hastily rushed into the dining room for breakfast, having always being told to remain quiet when eating, this morning the room was full of questions, as the girls from my dorm sent massagers around the room to inform the other girls, I really did not know what I expected to see, it was just like any other day, except the girls were happy some were even singing, it took a while then, one of the girls, made up her own words to an old song. "Ding dong the doc is dead, we can all sleep safely in our beds. ding dong the doc is dead…"

It took only seconds for all the girls to fill the room with the chanting, the matron, and the other staff tried in vain to hush them, as the police were now in the room, desperately trying to hush the girls, after they succeeded, that was when one plain clothed officer stood forward, to address us.

Now young ladies, does anyone here know anything about last night, the room fell deadly silent, I stood up, calmly stating, 'I think it's me you are looking for, but I need to know is he dead,' 'yes,' the girls all cheered all together, has I walked slowly out of the room with two police officers one on each side of me, I was pushed into the back of the police car, as I looked through the window the girls had flowered us out side, I could hear little Ellie shouting three cheers for Aveling, I think the police and the staff thought the girls had all gone mad, they clearly didn't have a clue what that man had done to those young minds and sprits.

That so called doctor, called, himself a man, I called him a monster, so answer me this question doctor, why do so many monsters live among us.

CLICK…TAPE OFF…

CHAPTER 43

THREE MEALS A DAY...

When Aveling first arrived at my surgery, I knew things were bad, the sight of her guards, as she nick named them later Tom and Jerry, were two of the biggest men I had ever seen, although I had doubted the need for them, things were now becoming very clear.as a doctor I could not condone any one taking another's life, but to simply have no remorse, just how cold was this child, I say child as that in truth, is what I believed she is, but to have seen so much, known so much heart ache, I in my heart I still believed I could help her.

But how. Now I have asked for help from the social services, and even my husband, had heard those tapes, there was no way I could help her burry the facts, she had killed, without I hint of remorse.

I tried to understand the girl, I knew she was in my belief two different soles, one minuet she would be taking to me like an adult, then in middle of a sentence start to talk like a little girl, but it wasn't just the talking, when she behaved like a little girl her whole body language changed even down to swinging her leg under her chair, I had always struggled with Avelings reports, trying to stay as close as possible to keep it in her own words, but sometimes it was impossible.

CLICK...TAPE ON...

Well now doc you think you have finally found out why I am here, with you now, but let me enlighten you.

Now let me see, what did happen next, but first doctor let me tell you about, the story of Sally Scot, yes doc that was her full name, and I know you have been listening to some bazar things, but this is one part of the puzzle I think you should know, now with statements from the girls, and other evidence. I was taken to another building.

.but the truth was it is a prison, the inmates just seemed a little more damaged, and dangerous.

but because the others had all learned out why I was being held, they kept well away from me. and it seemed they had been holding me in there forever, but it didn't bother me, if they just left me alone.

I could think of so many worse placers to be staying, it was to me more like a holiday camp than a prison during the day time, but the nights when we were locked in, that was a living hell.

Now I am sure I told you earlier, that I had been put in a cell with another woman I referred to as a schizoid, you may consider my remark as un lady like, but let me assure you when I said schizoid that was an understatement, but according to the staff that was the only available cell, now she would in my opinion needed to be locked up in an asylum for the criminal insane, for example.

As you know my monster brother Luke tried to suffocate me some time ago, well my new cell mate did the same, during my first few days there, it was in the middle of the night when I felt the pillow being pushed over my face, just getting her off me was a struggle, but even when I complained to the jailers they took no notice, they said that they would make a note of the incident, on my file, it was like according to them I was already guilty, of the crime I had been charged with.at that time I remembered one of the guards, spitting at me as I passed her, she mumbled something about I was the worst of killers because I had killed a good man a Doctor.

so once again I was sleeping in the curled up corner of the bunk too afraid to sleep, as I starred at the walls, feeling sorry for myself, I had no one, I missed my mum so much, but I remembered feeling so very very lonely. I knew I could never go home again, I made myself a promise, they wouldn't hold me for so much longer.

but we did have three meals, yes doctor three meals a day. I was even allowed pens and paper, so I could draw, and as you know I loved to make pictures, but my sharpest imagers, pictures were those of the people who had made my life a living hell, their faces would be something that were seared into my memory, people who I desperately wanted to forget, but never could, that was as I saw it my punishment, trapping my mind in with those monsters, the mind could be such a cruel prison.

The wardens thought I was such a twisted girl, because I didn't want to mix with the other girls, but I knew if I mixed with them, most would want to tell me there stories, I understood there need to talk to someone, anyone who would listen, it was like I had become some sort of magnetic heart, they could simply talk to. But at that time, my mind was so full of anger.

I needed to make sense of my own night mares, before I heard anyone else's. if only the guards would listened to me but, they thought I was already guilty, before the court decided my sentence, in my mind I was guilty, and I expected to be going to prison for a very long time, after all I did kill him. But only god, and I knew the truth, the whole truth.so as time dragged on, my only prayer to god, was a very selfish one, I would pray for freedom, I would wrap my thoughts into a tight ball, and think of my childish den in the old hedge, were I could remember my friend the fox, I know so many years had passed, but I imagined he would still be there.

Now as i said earlier when it comes to the paper work, the bureaucrats would only move at their own pace.

So I guess the courts, must have, at some time got the facts through from the home, you know what I mean Doctor, the statements etc.., and after the statement I had made, I guess someone had belived me after all it was only Dr Clarks finger prints on the knife, but I just wanted my day in court, and get it all over and done with,

Anyway after they came to their decision, they decided it had been self-defense, it was there impression, that has I hadn't intended him any harm, after all I had only used the scalpel that I had found in the room, and it was only then, after he had attacked me in the middle of the night, in the operations room, some where the doctor should never have been at that time of night.

So now I know how crazy this sounds Doctor, but I was planning in my head all the things I intended to say in court, so by then when they said there would be no court case, you would think how happy I should have felt, but I wanted to take the stand in court, and tell, no yell at the world all about that evil place, I was then given a release date, I cannot tell you doctor the relief, and surprised I felt. but as they believed I would be a bad influence to the other girls, if they returned me back to the same care home.

They decided then my age was about late-teens, it was time for me to get a job.it did seem to take so long after they had made the ruling to when they did release me. at that time I made myself a promise, they would never send me back in there again, after all I was the good girl.

But again I have strayed from Sally Scots story, that night after the doctor was dead, Sally sat on my bed, silent tears running down her cheeks, so I cradled her face in the palm of my hands, as she took a deep breath, I knew it was only because she believed the homes doctor was dead,

She told me that as long as she could remember, she had lived alone with her father, she had never known grandparents or any other family, and she shared a home with her farther, in a quite coldesac in a semidetached private house. Some of The neighbors always said hello, but generally speaking, ever body kept themselves to them self's.

Sally had never known what her father did for a living, he always told her she was a special daughter.so she could never play out with other children, because they would give her germs, and that would make her very sick.

it was the next door neighbor, who worked as a teacher's assistant, who had asked her father, why Sally wasn't at school, it was only then he finally enrolled her, but it was there when talking with some of the other girls Sally realized what was happening at home was not normal not normal at all.

But when she started school, she had been instructed not to say any-thing about what happened at home, because if she spoke out, they would take her away, and lock her up for being a naughty girl. For telling stories, he had often hurt her, as she explained the beatings came all too often, if her cloths were not in perfect lines in the wardrobe, or she left her shoes in the wrong place, she was beaten all too often. she started to tremble as she told me how she remember screaming, after on one occasion, she left some dirty clothes in the washing machine, and forgot to start the machine, the beating was relentless, afterwards she could barely stand.

But he would never let her bring any friends home, it was always just him and her, she had grown to know nothing else.

she then went on to tell me, just how strange he was, but wishing and hoping things would get better, as she grow older, but the older she got the stranger he became, even if she did everything perfect, he would shout at her almost every night, as she grow older, accusing her, all the time, that he knew she had been sneaking boys into the house when he was at work, it wasn't true but he became obsessed with her ever move.

but it was just a few days after her eighteenth birthday, she had wanted to get a job, but he would demand she stay at home, as someone had to keep everything clean, and she needed nothing, he wasn't providing for them both. she remembered him coming home saying he had a gift for her, as she had opened it she found sex toys, Sally told me how he said, if she was going to be going around with boys she needed to know how to use them properly, she told him she had never been with any boys but he just kept calling her a whore.

It was later that night after she had gone to bed. Sally told me she was half asleep, when she felt someone climb in bed with her, as she tried to turn around to see who it was, then a pillow case was pulled over her head, it was then quickly tied, tightly around her neck, as she struggled, but being so tiny she had no chance of getting him off her, she knew then it was her own father, as he started to rip her panties off, as he continued to call her a whore, Sally went on to tell me in detail how he had raped her so violently that she had started bleeding, and continued to bleed well into the next day.

Now that was just the start of that poor girls hell, as she continued to tell me he would just come home from work and demand she serviced him, as that was her duty now she was a woman, it would take place anywhere in the house, she could be just washing up dishes, when he would come up behind he, telling her not to move as he would raise her skirt then pulling of her panties, demanded she continued to wash the dishes, as she was a dirty little whore who needed to keep clean.

Sally was just praying, someone, anyone would come and stop him, but looking back, he always chose the days he knew the, has he called them the buzzy body neighbors were out, to inflict the things, that he knew would cause the most pain. It was after one complaint from the next door neighbor, about the noise coming from the upstairs bedrooms, her father dismissed it by saying, and it was the radio. He then changed the bedrooms around, so now sleeping in the room flirtiest away from the adjoining wall.

Sally at that time, didn't know why he did anything, she just knew she needed help, but when Sally did try to speak about what was happening to her. Sally's father always had the perfect answers, even when a neighbor asked Sally, where had she received so many bruisers from, Sally was too afraid to answer at first, but on that occasion, Sally decided to ask for help.

later that day the neighbor called around to see her father, her father explained it away, by saying Sally was just clumsy, and saying those disgusting things, about him to get attention, so it was then Sally, knew at that time things were never going to change. But the neighbor did tell him if she saw anymore bruising on Sally she would call the police.

Later that very night, Sally took a beating that made my blood boil, when she explained he didn't just hurt her on the outside, but the inside, and how he had used the sex toys, forcibly pushing them inside her, and with them still inside, he then rolled her over, and raped her in her arse, he told her if she said one more word outside the house, about anything that went on inside, he would kill her.

CLICK...TAPE OFF...

CHAPTER 44

GETTING HELP...

Just my private notes doctor for you to find later...

Now doctor it was a few weeks ago, I noticed when I was being transferred from... my cell to you, I thought I saw the same vehicle following us, now I didn't tell Tom and Jerry, because at first I thought it was just my imagination. but no it was defiantly following us, I hadn't just seen it behind us, but on my last visit it was parked just a little way down the road from the surgery the car was all black, now I know you have been sending out my details to schools, I even heard you had placed an advertisements in the newspaper.

Now if you said it was a girl with green eyes, it would have been like sending up a signal flair, to those who did know me. so I guess that is when someone had tracked me down.so now my mind went into overdrive trying to work out who.

After all this time, now if it is my father, with or without John, but surly not, and after all it was dad's best talent, talking with people in authority. So I knew him well enough, if he had been the follower checking to see if it was me. He would then after confirming it was me, he would have gone directly to the police, to convince them to drop all chargers.

mum always said it was is best talent, she used to say he had the gift of the gab, it was just the way he was, he would have convinced, the world with his word skills, I was innocent of everything. Even if I had already owned up admitting my guilt.

but no why would he wait, and then follow me at a discreet distance, that just didn't make any sense, but thinking about it I was still worth a lot of money to him. but no, so in my mind I ruled him out, then there was Michael from the Willkie house, always telling me he loved me, and no one else would have me, but no, he I believed would have lost interest in me a long time ago.

but thinking about it someone must have told him by now, that he was my half-brother, I am sure, surly dad would have told him the truth by then, but then there were the gypsies, Adam had sold me to, and they are not the kind of people who would give up on an asset, but then there was the silent gypsies boy who never took his eyes of me, so you do see my Delmer don't you doctor, I could go on, there were a few others who I haven't even mentioned in my tapes, who would like to get their hands on me, for one reason or another.

Now it was on one of those toilet stops, I had all those weeks ago requested. as per normal Tom had checked the toilet was empty before letting me in, then waiting outside to prevent anyone else going in, so you can believe me, when I say just how shocked I was to find a message waiting inside for me. now of all places it was written on the loo paper, so who ever had left it must have been the last person in there, I tried desperately trying to remember the woman who had just passed me on her way out of the toilets.

but how did they know witch stall I would use, so I dashed from one stall to another, and sure enough the same massage was also copied in the same place, it told me they had left a pencil inside the cardboard inner, so I could leave a reply, I hastily read and flushed the message.

Now I know you would love to know from who, and why, but I am sorry doctor, that is one piece of information I will not be offering, for you and all your so called experts to track down. let's just say you would need a very long arm to find me, but let's get back to the message, it had read, did I need help, now knowing who was offering, I was only too glad to ask for help, I told them about the screws, but I was finding it hard going.

So I asked them to unscrew them but make it look like they hadn't been touched, then the following week I would escape through the window, so if they could have transport waiting for me. I would be all there's. now I would never have gone with just anybody, so trust me doctor when I tell you now, I will be so well looked after, it really was my knight in shining amour, well maybe not amour, but he did have wheels. but you need to know doctor, I did believed if you could, you would have helped me in the beginning, so I am sorry, as I have just been using our visits, after I found out you were betraying me, so it was then escape seemed my only option.

End of thoughts, I really hope you do find my notes, but any way, you did say if I could wright it down, I will someday feel so much better.

End of note.

CHAPTER 45

SILENT TEARS.

CLICK...TAPE ON...

Well doc her I am again, but I still think you need to know the whole story,

You see when I was placed in the children's home, that is honestly what I believed that is what it was, just a home for children, but I was wrong.

the truth was it was the only place they could find for me, when I was released from the hospital, as I had insisted I had no memory of my past just that my name was Aveling.in fact it was a home for mentally ill, and troubled girls, some of the girls on the first floor were too young to even know why they were there, who needed to be given special care not just locked up, I wasn't there long, and no one had ever told me, the truth. I know, I know, Doctor Valerie just me being so bloody naive again, will I ever learn.

But let's get back to Sally, now Sally was constantly being abused, but by then her father had insisted she move into his bedroom and bed, she was just so frightened by him, she just did as she was ordered, it had been going on for months, but like me Sally was still naive about these things, so it wasn't long before, she could feel something moving inside her body, at first she thought it could have been an object that her father had left behind, on one of his sick sex nights, but she just thought it would come out on its own,

now one night after he had finished fucking her, after she cleaned up and tried to get to sleep, Sally had started to feel pains in her back, as the pain began to grow, she woke him up, but he just rolled over, refusing

269

to acknowledge her pain, she started to shake him hard wake up, 'please dad the pain it's so bad, help me, 'it was then she felt a whoosh of fluid in the bed.

After that he must have felt the bed wet to, so he throw the bed cloths back and saw blood and fluid, shouting at her you stupid girl, how could you let this happen,

As she lay there in agony she begged him to get a doctor, "shut up girl you don't need a doctor, now do as I say, put your legs up and hold them back, while I take a look", she felt like she needed to push, has she did so, she could feel him pulling, and hurting her more, and more, it seemed to go on and on, after what seemed like most of the night, it was then she saw the baby on the bed it seemed so big, Sally had no idea how it had got there, only that it must have grown inside her. now Sally s collage never thought it necessary in the fifties/sixties to teach biology, and having no mother, left poor Sally with absolutely no knowledge about sex.

She was still crying with the pain, but it was then I believed her instincts kicked in, she asked him to pass her baby, she needed to see, the baby, now crying loudly, as he started to shake the baby, yelling at it to shut the fuck up over and over again.

she begged him to let her old it, she told him the baby would be quiet if he let her old it, it was then he passed the baby to her, she explained the baby stopped crying, just as soon as he passed it over to her.

she hadn't seen what he was doing because, she was just hushing the baby she told me, it looked just like a big doll, that comment reminded me of my dolly, but now being so much older, I knew there was no comparison. he then went over to the dresser, and opened the top draw she thought it strange, but he then left the room, when he came back in, he was holding a plastic bin liner, and a towel he laid them out on the top of the chest of draws.it was then he snatched the baby from her, placing it on top of the unit, it all happened so quickly, she saw him reaching into the top draw, it was then he pulled out a large old pocket knife.at that second Sally believed he was just going to cut the umbilical cord.

He then opened the old knife, and before she could say another word, he cut the babies throat. there was blood ever were, he started to shout at her, 'get up girl, and start getting this bloody mess cleaned up,'Sally did her best to do as he told her, but by then she was just so exhausted, he then disappeared down the stairs taking the baby with him, and out the back door. When he returned, she screamed at him were was her baby.

Don't be stupid girl you can't keep a baby here, anyway its dead, and buried, so help me turn the mattress, and get some clean sheets, Sally must have still been in so much pain, shock, I hopeful will never experience that kind of pain, to lose a child to me just seems unbearable, how Sally must have felt, I tried to speak to her, but it was then with such a lump in my throat I found, I could not speak

On hearing her story my heart just bleed for her, I always remembered after mum had given birth, she would be in bed for days,

Shortly after Sally had returned to bed still with tears in her eyes, Her father, then started to rub his hands all over her, his attitude had changed, 'there there, you poor little thing, 'he then within minutes went on to rape her again.

The next day he acted like nothing had happened, he told her for being a good girl, she could have the day off from cleaning the house, as he got ready, and left for work, as if nothing had happened.

She watched as he walked away from the house. When he was totally out of sight, still dressed in her dressing gown, she found herself thinking what if the baby wasn't dead, maybe she could give it the kiss of live she had heard about, I know that sounds mad, doctor Valerie, so still dressed in her nighty and dressing gown, she fetched a shovel from the shed, found a new patch of dirt that looked like it had been freshly dug. again my mind flashed back thinking again as to how I had felt, but my baby hadn't been real it had just been a doll.

After she found the body Sally gently unwrapped the towel her farther had used to take the baby out of the bedroom with. She saw the little babies face, as she continued to cry silent tears, I think at that point something inside her soul died, she didn't know what she was doing, it wasn't until her time in court, that the neighbor, who had seen her digging in the garden in her bed cloths that morning, looked over the fence to see if Sally was all right.

But what the neighbor had seen, is Sally sitting there, rocking a dead baby in her arms. The neighbor had called the police, now when the services showed up, they sent for her father, Sally thought to herself it's all over now they will lock him up for killing her baby. But that's not what happened, he told the police he had no idea Sally was pregnant, she must have been messing around with the boys in the park,

He convinced them she must have given birth after he had left to go to work, then she must have panicked, and killed the baby, after all it was her who had been sitting rocking a dead baby in the garden, next to a newly dug hole to bury the poor little thing, they believed him, and because of Sally's age she had been sent to the secure, children's care home, only then for the mad old doctor Clark to continued were her father had left off. But coupled with the electric shock treatment it had just been all too much.

Now as Sally told me her story I sat in silence, I knew what it was like not to be believed, as I continued to cradle her in my arms, it was then I asked her, 'would you like me to kill him for you, 'now yes doctor Valerie I knew how crazy that sounded, but by then I believed Doctor Clark was well and truly dead, so regardless of the who or why, I had killed that monster, in my own heart I knew then, and there, I could if necessary kill, I had crossed that invisible line drawn in the sand that once crossed you could never go back.

It was then Sally looked at me, she didn't have to say a word, I knew exactly what she was thinking, 'no he's still my father,' 'no Sally, he not fit to be called a father he's a monster,' 'would you like me to make his life miserable if I ever get out of here,' 'can you,'she replied shaking, just until I get out of here myself ", 'I promised her I will do my best, as I sat just holding her for what seemed like a lifetime, her bones were showing through her skin she was just wasting away 'just until you get released from hear, But I in my heart I knew, Sally was never going home again. I couldn't explain back then doctor it was just a feeling.

but you know me by now doctor Valerie, I never break a promise,

CLICK TAPE OFF...

CHAPTER 46

TRUST IN ME ...

Now there had been a few new problems in the cell were I was being held, that crazy cell mate of mine, had tried to kill herself, at first she told the matron, it was me that I had tried to kill her, but luckily for me I had been sent out of the prison early that morning, I had been sent over to the courts for processing, so it was another two weeks before I was allowed to visit doctor Valerie again.

'Well doc hear I am again shall I go through,'doctor Valerie looked up said hello, and I walked past into the back office. but I was starting to think the visits wouldn't, and couldn't go on for very much longer.

CLICK...TAPE ON...

Well doc the police finally did a good job, after all the paper work was all sorted out, I had a new surname Aveling Smith so original, they found me a job at a nearby hotel cleaning, but it came with a small bed room tiny but plenty of room for me, it's not like I had a lot of cloths or anything, but it was lovely the first day I put on my uniform, everything was new, and it smelled to me like a dream.

So for a few months I worked hard following my orders, now I did want to write to my new friends, and Sally at the home but I believed everything would be read, so I chose my words very carefully. Over the coming weeks I managed to get Sally to tell me her last address. Has I did still have a promise to keep.

On my days off work, I traveled by train to see the house were Sally had lived, but can you imagine what I found there doctor, he did still live there, he was living with a woman, and two young girls, I couldn't believe my eyes, I thought he would at least be living alone, it became routine for me on my days off to visit the house, so I could check on those two little girls, because I knew he was a monster, and sooner or later he would show his real self to those little girls, and I would make sure he would get his punishment one day.

but one of the things that never made sense to me, now, yes I had met Sally, held her head in my hands, but I hadn't had a good look at Mr. Scott, I had only seen him from a distance, but he looked nothing like Sally, so I at first guessed she must look like her mother, but she never knew her mother. but after I got a closer look at Mr. Scott, if I had painted a picture, you could have seen for yourself, I did then doubt if I had the correct man, but after more checking I confirmed without doubt, he was the man, the right man, Sally s monster of a father.

It wasn't long before the girls I believed to be about six and eight, came outside, and went for a walk down the street alone, I followed them as they turned a corner, then they entered a playing field, and park.

Now doctor the last thing I wanted to do is scare them, so I just sat down on a swing, it wasn't long before they came over to me, we just chattered about general thing, for two small girls, everything had seemed normal, then one of them told me they were both at the same school Sally had been, so just making small talk, I learned they were called Carol, and of all names Sally, yes doctor Valerie you heard me correctly Sally.

I wanted them to trust me, it was so important for me to get them to trust me however long it takes. I believed if they trusted me fully, if he did anything to them, if they couldn't tell their mum, maybe they would tell me.

so when it got time for me to leave, I asked will you be back next week, the younger one said they often went to that park, it was the closest to home, so the following weeks on my days off. it became routine for me, I would push them on the swings play ball with them, I was hoping they would say something I could work with, but It wasn't long before,

I found the younger girl there by herself, I asked were her sister was, she told me her mum had got to go, to stay with their grandma for a few weeks, because there grandad was ill, but there mother didn't want them to lose any school days.

So There stepfather was going to be looking after them, he had told the youngest girl, she was big enough to go to the park on her own, as her sister needed to take care of some chores, she explained it did feel strange because her mother had always insisted they went to the park together.

But he told the younger girl to go alone, this all seemed too familiar to me, I asked the younger girl Sally to take me directly back to her house, not wanting to scare her, I told her I needed to use the toilet, so we returned to the house as I had the younger one with me, I believed we would just be able to walk straight inside but as, she tried to open the front door it was locked, so I asked her to take me round the back, I asked her to be very quiet so we could surprise her sister.

Now she had barely opened the door when I heard muffled screams from upstairs. I never believed my body could move so fast, I charged up the stairs and started to push the doors open one by one. it was behind the second door I found him beating Carol, Mr. Scott was yelling at her, the cloths in the wardrobe were not in line, the shoes were not paired up correctly.

now I had been punished in my life time for things that at the time never seemed to make any sense, but this was ridicules, and I am sorry doctor, but I tried always to be a good girl, but as he hit her so hard, I swear I felt that pain myself, then I guess the blue mist arrived, so by then I was so out of my mind I picked up the biggest, the heaviest, thing I could find, and on that occasion that was a bedside table lamp, so, with all my bodily strength I picked up the lamp, then smashing it down onto is head,

Now the younger girl had followed me up the stairs, and was by now consoling her sister, who was still crying sitting on the bed, she was clearly shocked she looked so scared. I asked Sally had he ever beaten her, her reply "no but he beats mummy all the time, he says he has to because she is so stupid",

has he laid there out cold, blood pouring off the back of his head, I opened the front window, and it was still the middle of the day so plenty of people were walking about, I screamed for help and told a passerby to get an ambulance,

I yelled at her the front door was locked, so she needed to come round the back, as I turned away from the window I saw the monster getting back up to his feet, and it was then doctor.

I truly lost control, and that is the real reason I am here today, so you see they did need to lock me up again.

Because when I hit him again, I had used every ounce of strength in my body, he was one animal who would, if I had my way that day, I would send him straight to hell, for what he did to my Sally, to join Doctor Clark, and if that meant I would also go to hell, well if I stopped him from ever doing to those little girls, the same thing he did to my Sally then so be it.

Oh its ok doc don't panic, sadly I didn't kill him that day, but I wanted to, but the police said it was excessive force, he needed thirty two stiches. so It was me they arrested that day, and after he got out of the hospital, he told the police he had only been helping the young girl, as she had slipped in her room as she was getting changed into her play cloths, and that is why she had the bruisers, so after she had her play cloths on, she could then join her sister at the park, it was then when he claimed to have had heard a noise coming from the next bedroom,

The girls were too afraid to say anything bad about him. But knowing monsters like I do, I knew he would have something to use, to push them into submission. I am only guessing he probably threatened to beat their mum. And no one else had seen him smacking the girl, it was my word against his.so let's face it doctor, I had met men like him before, he had a way with words.

he had told the police that I had made everything up, and that he had found me steeling from the house according to him I was just a common house burglar, he was one of the men, who my mum would say, he had the gift of the gab. But I was the one who had only recently been realized from a secured cell.so it was me who had no right, to be in his house, so back to lock up I went.

Now I had only been locked up for a few days, when I had a visitor.it was the new Mrs. Scott, she wanted to hear my side of the story, she explained to me that he told her, he had just caught me steeling, it was then she had to know the true facts, about that day, but when she tried to talk to her girls, they just seemed so quiet, and withdrawn.

But it was what her daughter Carol said, that I was there friend, nothing seemed to make any sense to her, so it was then she asked a neighbor if she knew anything, now the neighbor had lived there a long time, she was the one who had found my sally sitting in the garden that day, rocking her dead baby in her arms, so she asked Mrs. Scott how Sally was doing, now at first Mrs. Scott thought the neighbor was enquiring about her daughter Sally.

so Mrs. Scott replied, Sally was fine, so the neighbor then asked if she could have the address of the home, so she could send Sally a letter, up to then Mrs. Scott had no idea her husband had a daughter in a special care home, it was only then, Mrs. Scott had even more questions, so that was when she was told all about my Sally, but when she asked her husband later that day, he said it was nonsense, he told her he had never been married before, and he had no children, so he then went on to beat his wife again just for asking questions.

but on that occasion his wife who had for so long accepted it, trying hard to convince herself, that she and her daughters had a roof over their heads, they had food to eat, but when it came to her girls, then that was when he had crossed the line, if he had been beating Carol that day, Mrs. Scott needed to know the truth, but poor Carol was too afraid to say anything,

It had never accrued to me, that Mrs. Scott would believe my story all about my Sally, not for one minute, or she would even trust me doctor, I was as baffled as her. About his story. Why would he deny ever having had a daughter, just for a second, I thought had I got the wrong man, but no my eyes did not deceive me that day, I caught him red handed beating Carol, but sometimes when you are so angry, then think about things later, you begin to doubt yourself.

Now I knew when the blue missed has you surrounded, the whole world is shut out, and your body, and brain just seem to act all on its own, But how could he get away with what he had done to my Sally, then simply claim that Sally had never existed. well maybe he could try to forget her, but I will insure, the new Mrs. Scott never does.

I asked her why she wanted to ask me all those questions, surly it would be better coming from his daughter Sally, it was then Mrs. Scott, told me, she had visited the special care home, where they had been holding Sally, it hadn't been easy to get any details, as no one wanted to talk about what had happened that day, she had only got brief detail, from the library newspapers archives, about what had happened that day, but it did say were Sally had been sent for her own good, but when Mrs. Scott arrived at the care home that day, so she could get the answers to all her questions, only to be told Sally had killed herself, a few days earlier. After being told, that I had been arrested again, by one of the other girls.

it was only then Sally felt she could go on no longer, it felt like I had been slapped, with the biggest hand ever, you know doctor when you meet someone with a sole like an angel, who's life had been destroyed by a man, no monster, like Mr. Scott, you begin to question gods motives for putting us here, after pulling myself together,

I told the new Mrs. Scott everything Sally had told me, I always found if I watched someone's face closely, it would tell me if she had believed me or not, this woman who I had never seen before that day, when she had entered the room she just seemed confused.

But now when I looked at her face it was my belief, she seemed genuinely shaken, I asked her not to take my word for anything but Sally told me she had made a statement to the police about what had happened that day. The new Mrs. Scott explained she had asked to see Sally's statement but was told, it was a sealed case. And as she wasn't Sally's real mum they could give her no more details. But hopefully after listening to me, maybe she would take her girls and get the hell away from that monster.

it was only after my Sally had seen a psychiatrist, her words had been twisted, and when I had first met her, she seemed so lost, over the time she had spent in that house, she had told many people what had happened, but no one believed her, and after her abuse at the hands by someone who called himself a doctor, Sally had fully withdrawn form life,

It was like when she told me her story, Sally had only done so, because of what I had done to one of her abusers. now when I look back it was like she had already given up all hope for herself, I still remember the day I first looked into Sally s eyes, it was like she had already died, but simply living day by day, till she could meet someone, anyone who would believe her, has I know myself what it feels like, when the whole world seems to be pushing, hard to fit you into that invisible pigeon hole, you do understand what I mean now Doctor don't you, that imaginary place the bureaucrats, believe we should all live in, it's just so much easier for them to make sense of something they really had no idea of, or understanding of.

So I had this time to try harder, for someone just any one to believe me, whenever I told them the story of a pretty young girl by the name of Sally Scott, and I do have another nasty feeling scurrying around in my brain, what if it hadn't just been the babies body, Mr. Scott had buried out in that back garden, after all were was Sally's real mum?

so I won't let them just push me away to keep me quite, Looking back I ask myself, why did they really put me into that home, was it just because they had nowhere else to put me, if that was true, for me then it must also be true for about fifty percent of the other girls, that were living there, girls who shouldn't have been placed thire.in the first place.

now I do know if someone is not a believer in god, they wouldn't understand, my next statement, but maybe I had been placed there, because inside that home worked a devil, that maybe god needed me to get rid of, and trust me doctor, that man was pure evil, I never knew his age but looking at him he most have been in his late fifties, so just how many young girls had he destroyed over all the years he had worked there, and where were the missing girls, had they really just ran away, I know I hadn't been in the home long, but I had looked hard for any escape routes but found none, so where did they go to.?

I never got to know the girls very well, but it was no wonder why some of them acted up, as the teachers would say, but maybe one day you, yes you, Doctor Valerie, and all those visitors you have with you today, that are also listening to these tapes, sitting around your table, oh yes doctor I know you are not alone, I have known for a long time, so maybe one of you can help, to get those poor girls some real help.

Now doctor over the last few week I decided there was just one person I would not let simply slip through the net, now I do admit it took me a long time, thinking of how to go about it,

Do you remember P C Sam, well he always believed in me, so I decided, in a roundabout way to get my two chaperones, Tom and Jerry to call him, has I needed them to get a message to him, Tom and Jerry having been told how violent I could be, I felt they would never believe me about anything, but it had become imperative for them to trust me, so over the past few weeks after P.C Sam had spoken with them, they saw me in a different light, and were then only too glad to help me.so it was then I decided to put my plan into play.

Now when I was in the prison the first time after stabbing doctor Clark, Sobby who was I guess about three years older than me, but still so naive, she begged me for help, I told her, has I saw it, she only had two options, first let doctor Milton continue to rape her, knowing that could be for another four years, or do what I would do, after all he drugged her the first time he raped her, I guess in the hopes to confuse the poor girls mind, so if she reported him, all he had to say was the girls mind was confused due to the effect of the drugs, for someone as sharp as he was, and with all his so called qualifications, people would have believed him.

so now it was time to show him, he wasn't the only one willing to cross the line, but as I have said before rape is rape, and if he has no morals then, we would reluctantly have to sink to his level, not something I would suggest, but as they say needs must,

So my advice was to Sobby, when he gives you the contraceptive pills, don't take them find some way off hiding them until he left her cell after sex, then flush them down the loo, has he was the only male who was allowed on that side of the prison, he could no longer call her an hysterical woman, when she was pregnant by him, but I told her she would have to abort the baby, as it was my belief if Sobby kept it, she would never put that episode of her life to rest, she had agreed with me, not something to take to lightly, but I hope I got her to see keeping the baby of a rapist was not an option.

So when I was returned to prison after smashing a lamp over Mr. Scott head. The first day on my return I heard from one of the girls that Sobby had just had a test that very morning, it was positive, now I needed to talk to her as soon as possible.so I sent my message via the prison jungle drums, so Sobby, and i met up in my cell later that day, Sobby told me she and one of the other girls got jobs in the medical wing, so they could get ahold of the test kits, until she was sure, the result was positive.

So I asked Sobby to wait just a little while, till I could get my plan in play, looking back if it hadn't been for me making these tapes no one would give a dam, so as you, yes all of you there listening today, go home tonight back to your lives, maybe some of you, could get through to some of the girls in prison, to reassure them if they made new statements, as they needed to tell the truth, about what has happened in the prison, with the shrink Mr. Milton, that they wouldn't get any repercussions, so I implore you just visit them, and hear their stories, just as you are listening to mine,

Now I knew, the last place Mr. Scott wanted to be, is in a court room, but I hadn't counted on him telling his solicitor, that he had felt sorry for me, as I must have misinterpreted what I had seen, and has nothing had been stolen,! so he requested if they just offered a light sentence, for bashing him over the head with a lamp, so they offered me seven years, if I took responsibility and owned up and admitted my guilt,?

CLICK...TAPE OFF...

CHAPTER 47

REMEMBEING
THE DAISY...

'Now doc I don't know about you, anymore, but there was no way I would accept any deal, as in my heart and soul, what I did was right. Because I am a good girl. But if I could have done things differently I would have, so is it ok for me to go through, Aveling your actions, yes are understandable but you know it's not for you to decide who needs to be punished, you should have told someone, oh trust me Doctor I tried, and I tried, but as always no one was listening.

The last tape …

The nights were drawing in, and it seemed quite dark outside, it was then I remembered back, to when I first met Aveling, trying hard to believe how such a little girl, could turn into such a cold hearted killer. when Aveling had arrived that day after her short conversation with me, she quickly passed me by, and once again went into the back office, I was listening intently for the tape recorder to start, but Aveling seemed to take longer than normal I felt something was wrong, just a feeling of foreboding, the more I tried to tune into the noises from that back office, then there it was, for a moment I suspected Aveling had somehow guessed this was going to be her last visit.

CLICK…TAPE ON…

Now I know you have been looking at me more and more strangely over the last few visits doctor, trying to work out if any of my tapes were true, so as this is the last tape, you will ever hear from me. the little picture of a bunch of daisy's, on top of this tape are for you, because I have always drawn a daisy on my cloths ever since I watched as my eldest sister, rolled up my pretty new daisy dress, and burn it on the fire, I decided by drawing the daisy s everywhere, my mind would not let me ever forget what happened that day, in that old coal cellar smelling of damp. Even just talking about it now, I can still smell that smell, of coal dust, and old mold.

Regardless of what everybody says the sooner you forget the better you will feel, not true abuse is something a girl never forgets, so has I remembered in the cold damp coal smelling cellar, where one after another tooth, by tooth that was pulled out, it became a memory that is burned into my very sole.

now I know this sounds crazy, but I needed to be vigilant, around all men, and let's face it, even men in gods uniforms of black smocks, and dog collars, had no regards for the children they were asked to take care of, as I knew only too well, so if you couldn't trust men of god, who do you trust, so the daisy s, well I believed it was the daisy s that focused me on the fact, if they could grow, in some of the most hostile placers, well maybe I could do the same.

So now in there wisdom, the powers of the courts decided, or should I say the bureaucrats, decided I needed to see a shrink, sorry doctor psychiatrist, and that is why I am hear. Now I know doctor what you have been up to, thanks to Tom and Jerry, so let me just say hello again, to all your guests now sitting around your table, all listening to my thoughts, my tapes, there because it's up to them to decide whether to let me free, or to be held indefinitely, till I admit guilt, giving up seven years of my life, now that is something I have no intentions of doing. Now having grown up among monsters.

One of the first lessons you learn is trust no one, I did think on that second visit with you. you were telling me the truth about wanting to help me, telling me everything I said would be confidential, as you did indeed promise, you were after all a doctor, but then it was a so called doctor,

Doctor Clark who abused for so many years, all those innocent young girls who couldn't help them self's, men like that have an answer for everything, I think the one I heard most was, the girls were just hysterical teenagers, so he was there to help them, but that monster, doctor Clark was killing there very souls, with that Victorian electric shock treatment, and before you tell me again Doctor, how wrong it is to cause harm, or even think about it, oh how I would have loved to have plugged that evil monster into that machine. Looking back remembering how he died, well just let me say it was too quick for a monster like him. Sorry doc but you always said, I should tell the truth.

Now some of the things I have mentioned but thank fully, you didn't pick up on, so let me explain, whenever I was waiting for Tom and Jerry to pick me up, I would be waiting in an area with a large window looking down the corridor, as they walked towards me I would read their lips, so I have known for a long time, you were consulting with other people, and you were also playing the tapes for them, I don't know how many people will be there today listening. But I'm thinking if I am correct you won't be alone.

So there today with you, Maybe your husband, another social worker or two maybe, an officer from the courts and you, but now let's not forget the newcomer, has I had requested the prisons very own, psychiatrist doctor Milton, with the help of Tom and Jerry, who I would like to thank for arranging that for me, now I believed doctor Milton only took a back step with me, after he learned I was getting outside treatment, so I think he was worried what I would be saying, well he knows now.

He often asked me what I was telling you doctor Valerie, I dare say he has already been pleading his innocents on hearing what Sobby, and I have been up to. anyway After Tom, and Jerry had spoken with, PC. Sam and been assured if I told them I was innocent then innocent I was, so he asked them if they could help me they should do so, so this will now be for Milton the last day of being a so called psychiatrist.

Now if you are there Doctor Milton, I have a message for you from Sobby, she is pregnant, now I know the first thing you will try to do is protest your innocents, then you may even be tempted to get up to leave, but may I advise you to stay in the seat, because just outside the office door I have arranged with, now my very good friends Tom and Jerry, two of their very best officers they know, to arrest you, and it gives me the greatest of pleasure to inform you, you will be charged with at least twelve accounts of rape, you will also be charged with supplying drugs, now has I believe it, you are not even a qualified medical doctor.

So you will be charged with twelve accounts of endangering the girls life's, and my favorite, the charge of torturing them when they were defenseless in strait jackets, I have also requested all the other girls who you have abused by you, to make new statements to the prison warden. so I am dam sure you will be going to prison, for a very long time, and trust me doctor Milton if you do ever get released, remember to look over your shoulders, as one day we may meet again. If you have any doubts just ask doctor Valerie, when I make a promise, I will one way or another I will keep it, now when you are behind bars, it will be well known by then, to all the other male prisoners, you like to rape defenseless girls, so I know you will be getting nothing less than you deserve.

Now Doctor Valerie It was all those weeks ago, I decided not to trust you. But I guess you did need to hear the truth. What I have told you is all true, but for two little things.

But the first wasn't really my lie, that first day I had been sent to see you, my file said I was, in my late teens.

But it was wrong I was in fact twenty, but I knew if they knew my real age, they would have sent me directly to prison, for what I did to Doctor Clark, and it would have taken so much longer before I received any help, but I am now just twenty one, it just happens to be my birthday today,

but the fact I am only five feet, and one inch tall, it always made me look so much younger, I hated Penny Willkie for telling me so many lies, but then again it was Penny who showed me how to act, oh so innocent, by little things like braiding my hair, I got the impression that lately you had guessed my chidish personer was just a good act, but it never cesed to amaze me how many I did fool with my looks, and I had, had to grow up so fast living in the environment back then, so I didn't see any point in correcting them, if they said I was in my late teens then that's what I will be. not that I think age as anything to do with the way, most people have treated me.

I do know, I still don't believe Mr. Scott was the real father of my Sally, I have no idea how you can prove it, but please hear my last request, and try to get to the bottom of that story because if I am right, Mr. Scott needs locking up before he can harm any more little girls, and maybe take a closer look at that garden of his. if not for me, I beg you do it for my Sally, now as you know I am not bad at reading lips, so has I have been waiting for pick up, it became habit for me to read Tom and Jerrys lips, has they were discussing, All about those months when you have been checking around all the districts, for a girl who had been reported missing.

But they were looking in all the wrong placers. But when my uncle Adam had said to the gypsies, no one would come looking for me he was wrong. I have been told I must be heartless to say, I have no remorse or any feeling for any of the monsters/ men I have attacked, as there have been to many to mention.in the tapes I made for you.

it would have taken me a lifetime to mention them all, I believed there must have been at least six other men who have scars for touching me, uncle Terry was right, the knife came in very handy most men would back off, when they saw the knife, but the ones who now have scars well they did attack me first, so I did need that knife. so when very early in the tapes, If I said I was sorry for anything, I had done. I was not sorry, I feel no remorse, if I am being truthful, my only regret is that I didn't kill them all, because looking back I now realize, they would only have gone on to attack other girls.

Now for my other little lie. but just before I give you that fact. I did want to thank you for all those toilet stops. And you will find some private little notes that will help you to fill in any details you may need, I have left for you in your second office, in an envelope taped to the bottom of the second draw. Another little trick I saw in an old black and white war movie.

Now I think you will have guessed by now, that the truth is, at the toilets, I have been preparing my escape, so when I was leaving your surgery door just a little open, it had nothing to do with volume of sound, I really didn't care if you had overheard, it was simply the wall clock above your desk, I would be working out how long, it would take me to make this last tape for you, how much time it would take for you to play it.

because by the time you will be listening to my last tape, I have decided not to trust my future, in your hands, because like I have said you cannot be trusted any more, you betrayed me, I can remember telling you, when I give my word, my promise my bond I keep it, has for all those people you call experts, there with you, listening with you, judging me. without really knowing me at all,.

I guess by now they have already made their minds up, but I have no confidence that they will make the right decision. Has for Doctor Milton, your presence is now required at the other side of the door, where if everything had gone according to my plan, you will find your escorts, so don't keep them waiting, so doctor Milton, you can go to hell, and send my regards, to auntie Alice, and Doctor Clark.

So running the risk of being locked up for seven years, or indefinitely for doing, in my mind the right thing. is something I will not allow you all their today, to decide …

So good buy, oh! My other little secret.

My very own little lie, is ……..

MY NAME IS NOT.

AVELING.

CLICK…………………..

Printed in Great Britain
by Amazon

71071301R00177